THE
KILLER
QUESTION

Also by Janice Hallett

The Examiner

The Christmas Appeal

The Mysterious Case of the Alperton Angels

The Twyford Code

The Appeal

THE KILLER QUESTION

Janice Hallett

ATRIA BOOKS

NEW YORK   AMSTERDAM/ANTWERP   LONDON
TORONTO   SYDNEY/MELBOURNE   NEW DELHI

ATRIA
BOOKS

An Imprint of Simon & Schuster, LLC
1230 Avenue of the Americas
New York, NY 10020

First Atria Books hardcover edition September 2025

ATRIA BOOKS and colophon are trademarks of Simon & Schuster, LLC

Simon & Schuster strongly believes in freedom of expression and stands against censorship in all its forms. For more information, visit BooksBelong.com.

For information about special discounts for bulk purchases, please contact Simon & Schuster Special Sales at 1-866-506-1949 or business@simonandschuster.com.

The Simon & Schuster Speakers Bureau can bring authors to your live event. For more information or to book an event, contact the Simon & Schuster Speakers Bureau at 1-866-248-3049 or visit our website at www.simonspeakers.com.

Manufactured in the United States of America

1 3 5 7 9 10 8 6 4 2

Library of Congress Control Number: 2025937712

ISBN 978-1-6680-8353-6
ISBN 978-1-6680-8355-0 (ebook)

For quizzers and quizmasters everywhere

Judge a man by his questions, rather than his answers.
—Voltaire

French writer, satirist, historian, and wit.

Born November 21, 1694.
Died May 30, 1778.

Key figure in the Enlightenment.

Real name
François-Marie Arouet.

Imprisoned in the Bastille twice: 1717 and 1726.

Wrote more than 20,000 letters and 2,000 books.

On his deathbed, a priest asked him to renounce Satan.

He replied, "This is no time to make new enemies."

Heart and brain embalmed separately from his body.

Buried in the Panthéon, Paris.

To: Info@Netflix.com
From: Dominic Eastwood
Date: October 16, 2024
Subject: Documentary idea

Dear Netflix,

My name is Dominic Eastwood and I'm a big fan of your true-crime shows. My family and I have been captivated by *American Nightmare*, *The Puppet Master*, and *The Family Next Door*, among many others. Well, as you're based in the US, you may not have heard the story of my aunt and uncle, Sue and Mal Eastwood.

It's a complex and shocking case that unfolds over many years and with multiple layers, some of which are not yet in the public domain. This story has everything: love, passion, intrigue, tension, betrayal, deception, and . . . murder. Like *Bad Vegan*, *Bad Surgeon*, or *Three Identical Strangers*, it has that bit extra, that final twist you simply can't believe is true, and yet it happened.

Television production is a mystery to me, but the more I think about my aunt and uncle, the more their story feels like it would make a fantastic documentary.

I have all the evidence you'll need and can help with contacting police and civilian witnesses, as I've been in touch with them all to piece together what happened for myself.

So if you're interested, please let me know.

Yours sincerely,
Dominic Eastwood

To: Dominic Eastwood
From: Info@Netflix.com
Date: October 16, 2024
Subject: [Automatic Response] Documentary idea

This response is from an unmanned inbox.

DO NOT REPLY.

<u>Pitching an idea to Netflix</u>
If you have an idea you'd like to pitch to Netflix, you must work through a licensed agent, producer, attorney, manager, or industry executive, as appropriate, who already has a relationship with us. Otherwise, Netflix is unable to accept your unsolicited submissions.

To: Info@reellifeprods.com
From: Dominic Eastwood
Date: October 18, 2024
Subject: Documentary idea

Dear Reel Life Productions Ltd.,

My name is Dominic Eastwood and I'm a big fan of your true-crime shows on Channel 5 and the Crime & Investigation Channel. I recently noticed your company name on a brilliant Netflix documentary called *Why They Did It* and hope you don't mind me contacting you out of the blue like this.

You might have heard of my aunt and uncle, Sue and Mal Eastwood, who were involved in a high-profile case a few years ago. I've been conducting research for myself and discovered even more twists and turns to the story. The more I think about it, the more I feel it would make the most compelling true-crime documentary, docudrama, or both!

I have lots of information, some of it not in the public domain, so if you'd like me to send a few things through, I'd be more than happy. Alternatively, if you'd like to meet, I can travel to your offices in London.

I look forward to hearing from you in due course.

Yours sincerely,
Dominic Eastwood

To: Dominic Eastwood
From: Polly Baker
Date: October 25, 2024
Subject: Re: Documentary idea

Dear Dominic,

Thank you for getting in touch with us here at Reel Life. I'm delighted you enjoyed *Why They Did It*, our first coproduction to be screened on Netflix. The Eastwood case has a familiar ring, but I was quite young at the time, so I'm afraid I don't remember the details. I'll look it up online.

Please be aware that for a multipart documentary we need more than just an intriguing case. We need access to a wide range of people who were involved—police, friends, witnesses—to bring the story to life and animate key events for the viewer.

The best true-crime documentaries deliver that first-person testimony, but it's not easy to convince the most relevant people to speak on camera. Do you have a good relationship with the police and civilians in this case? Are they confident, articulate, and willing to tell their stories?

Please feel free to send across any background info you have. If it sounds like something she'll be interested in, I can pass it to my boss when she gets back from LA.

Best,
Polly Baker
Production Assistant
Reel Life Productions Ltd.

To: Polly Baker
From: Dominic Eastwood
Date: October 25, 2024
Subject: Re: Documentary idea

Dear Polly,

Your reply arrived in the middle of my visit to the site where so much action took place. That has to be a positive omen! I'm thrilled you want to hear more about it.

Please, may I request that you *don't* look up the case yet? You see, what was reported isn't the whole story and I'd love it if you could witness events as they unfold, so to speak, rather like the viewer would. I'll send through everything I have—in bite-sized chunks—and if, at any time, you don't wish to read any more, just say.

So, I am sitting writing this in what looks like a typical English pub called The Case is Altered. It's situated in the county of Hertfordshire, to the northwest of London. Photos attached. You'll see it's nestled down a narrow lane that leads to a disused boatyard and tumbledown pier on the River Colne. But no one who gets that far down the lane lingers for long, including me. Some places have an aura about them.

Tall trees loom on either side, making the area rather gloomy, even on sunny days, but perfect for a montage of atmospheric opening scenes! That said, The Case is Altered itself has all the ingredients of a picture-perfect, chocolate-box country pub: thatched roof, leaded windows, and creeping plants snaking around a wooden trellis over the door. But if that conjures up expectations of a cozy bar, deep red carpets, oak panels, and a roaring fire, you'd be wrong. Now, anyway.

My aunt and uncle, Sue and Mal Eastwood, were landlords here from December 2017 to October 2019. Since then it's been frozen in time—first by the pandemic, then by red tape, and finally, malaise—as a result, its doors remain closed. They only opened today when I applied my shoulder to them.

At one time this place thrived, thanks to constant river traffic on one side and, on the other, the regular footfall of thirsty workers walking home along the main road. But that was long before Sue and Mal arrived, full of plans to revive a failing business—their first pub and the start of a whole new career.

They had no other family and, after a disagreement, sadly fell out with my parents, and by default me, many years ago. But they were not lonely here. During their short tenure, my aunt and uncle were close to a core of regular customers and other publicans in the county, in particular those attached to the same brewery, many of whom are exactly the sort of engaging and articulate "characters" who would bring a documentary to life!

After many months and several requests from me and my solicitor, the police finally forwarded the case file, and that, along with other information not made available at the time, is what I'll send through for you to read. It paints a picture of Sue and Mal as community-minded people determined to make their new venture a success. From the refreshed decor inside and out to the weekly quiz nights, they were entirely focused on reviving the fortunes of The Case—and this hard work paid off.

So where did it all go wrong? That's what television viewers will want to know. Yet, as you read the following, you'll see that what you know can be fatal.

Best wishes,
Dominic

How much do <u>you</u> know?

Monday Quiz

8 p.m.
at

The Case is Altered

just off the A416, after St. Luke's Church and before the
Morrisons turnoff

Teams of up to six
£1 per person

All welcome

The Case is Altered
Quiz Rules

1. £1 per person. Cash only.

2. Teams of up to six adults—you may have fewer than six, but not more.

3. Cell phones must be switched off or turned to silent and PUT AWAY!

4. Keep the noise down. You won't hear the next question if you're talking.

5. Music rounds will be played ONCE only.

6. Your answer sheet will be marked by another team. Disputes should be referred to the quizmaster.

7. The winning team will take home the pot, minus £10.

8. The quizmaster's decision is final. It is always final, even if he is subsequently proven to be wrong.

Text received by Sue & Mal, The Case is Altered, September 1, 2019:

Unknown number
What time does it start?

Text messages between Mal and Sue Eastwood, September 1, 2019:

Mal
Text from an unknown number asking what time "it" starts.

Sue
They mean the quiz. I put a photo of the poster on Facebook.

Mal
Looks dodgy to me. I'll forward it to Arthur.

Sue
DO NOT send that text to the police. Reply "7:30 p.m. for 8 p.m."

Mal
This could be anyone.

Sue
Yes, anyone interested in quizzing. The leaflet is on the internet. Remember our little chat: we need more teams to give our regulars some healthy competition. The Plucky Losers always win. It looks bad.

Mal
Complete strangers? We didn't discuss that.

Sue
REPLY WITH "8 P.M."

Text messages between Unknown Number and Sue & Mal, The Case is Altered, September 1, 2019:

Unknown number
What time does it start?

Sue & Mal, The Case is Altered
It's off. Canceled. We're closed.

Unknown number
[BLOCKED]

Ye Olde Goat Brewery Ltd.
"Pubs with panache"

Hertfordshire Region

The Rainbow

The world-famous Rainbow puts the heart in Hertfordshire. The county's leading LGBTQ+ bar is open to all with its weekly themed events, live music, and drag and comedy nights. Sean and Adrian invite you to stay awhile, meet new friends, enjoy a range of craft and commercial beers, and browse the Gin Library—before throwing shapes on the dance floor.

Tom's Bar

Our renowned gastropub is run by two award-winning chefs, sisters Flo and Mimi, who bring their own quirky take on pub grub to Hertford Town Centre. Relax with a pint and a platter of mini jellyfish burgers or nibble on crispy salt-roasted mealworms with your prosecco. And if you're wondering who Tom is, look no further than the portrait above the electronic log fire: celebrated Victorian novelist and poet Thomas Hardy, who we think once enjoyed an overnight stay nearby.

The Lusty Lass

There's been a pub on the site of The Lusty Lass—offering food and accommodation to weary travelers—since the fifteenth century, although Peter has been resident landlord since just 1989. Situated along the motorway north from London, The Lusty Lass is a portal to the past, with what is thought to be an original ceiling beam now preserved in glass and used as a table. The Lusty Lass can be seen in an episode of *Most Haunted* from March 2004, when a team of psychic investigators attempted to contact its many ghosts!

The Brace of Pheasants

Put the craic in St. Albans with a nostalgic journey back to the auld country at The Brace. A dynamic Irish bar, this charming venue offers a packed weekly program of live music, pub games, regional dancing, and social events. You're never lonely with landlords Diddy and Con in charge of your diary. And if you fancy a pint of the black stuff, why not soak it up with some delicious homemade soda bread and a packet of Taytos?

The Case is Altered

At this friendly and welcoming thatched country pub by the river, landlords Sue and Mal are proud of the changes they've made in the two years since taking over. A row of bicycle racks in the avant garde, and a weekly quiz night, means The Case is a sporting and social hub for the local community.

Text messages between Mal and Sue Eastwood, September 2, 2019:

Mal
Sean and Adrian are world-famous. Flo and Mimi are award-winning. Diddy and Con are charming, and Peter is haunted. We have a bike rack and a quiz!

Sue
If I'd realized it was going to be printed on the regional flyer I'd have written something better.

Mal
How can a bike rack be avant-garde anyway?

Sue
Autocorrect. It was all glitchy on my phone. I thought they were asking what we'd done to improve the pub in the last year, so I typed "bicycle racks in the alehouse garden."

Mal
Where did you type that?

Sue
The brewery's questionnaire for the Fam.

Mal
Fam?

Sue
Annual General Meeting! Autocorrect again! I typed AGM and it changed to Fam.

Mal
At least none of the others mention their quizzes. We should promote it more. It'll be the making of The Case.

Sue
Oh yes, it's our USP. Look at the new people we've met since starting it. All thanks to you and your questions! Where are you, and do you have the pub phone?

Mal

I'm in the avant garde digging out old cans from the flower beds, and yes, I have the pub phone. In fact I can hear WhatsApp dinging now—I'll bring it in.

Tom's Bar

Terry L
wrote a review today
Bedford, United Kingdom
324 contributions, 108 helpful votes

Date visited	**August 29, 2019**
Visit type	**On a culinary tour of Hertfordshire**

Nothing like it looked on TV

I brought my 88-year-old father to this so-called "gastro" pub with high expectations. We'd seen Ross Kemp and Paul Whitehouse eat here on *The Trip*. The food had looked delicious and the view stunning. Unfortunately, we are not famous enough to get the same treatment!

Dad's starter was stone-cold and covered in a layer of yellow horse fat so tough it could beat Jason Statham in a fight. There was a very fine green hair in my soup that I think may have come from a parrot. Everything was underdone—the leeks were hard, the green beans were dry, and a good vet could have got my steak mooing again.

The waitress had a nose ring. She took a photo of us but when I looked at it the next day, I was horrified. Dad and I have our glasses raised over our desserts—it would've been the best picture of us ever taken, one to treasure, but we're OUT OF FOCUS! The focus is on a couple of total strangers kissing across their table in the background! I felt like calling up Tom's Bar and asking for their names, so in fifty years' time when my kids look at the picture, they at least know who the stars of it are.

On the top of the menu it says: "A meal you will remember for the rest of your life." Well, Dad's already forgotten it.

Response from Tom's Bar
Responded on September 2, 2019

Dear Terry,
Thank you so much for choosing Tom's Bar to enjoy a special meal

with your father. We're so sorry to hear you were disappointed. It is our mission that everyone who visits us embarks on a thrilling culinary adventure, guided by our menus and our expert table attendants. On this occasion it seems we fell short and we apologize unreservedly. The trust our customers place in us is not something we ever take lightly.

However, we should point out that we have never been featured on television and I wonder if you've confused us with Txoko? This is where Rob Brydon and Steve Coogan ate on *The Trip*. It's a harborside seafood restaurant in Getaria, Spain. I'm afraid we are in the center of Hertford and could never compete with those views!

Just to clarify, your father would have ordered huîtres en pot. This dish is sealed with a layer of seasoned and melted butter, most certainly not horse fat. It is refrigerated so the buerre sets into a crisp "lid" that is "cracked" open to reveal the treasure inside. It is always served cold. We are happy to assure you the "green hair" in your soup was shredded samphire, not from a parrot. It sounds as if you ordered your steak "rare." Perhaps in future a medium or well-done order would be more to your taste.

Your father has already forgotten the meal? But it was only three days ago. We don't wish you to worry unduly, but I wonder if, given his age, you might consider seeking medical advice?

I do apologize for the disappointing photograph. If you would like to return to Tom's Bar with your father, and make yourself known to us as the author of this review, there will be a free drink and starter waiting for you. Our maître d' will personally ensure you have some wonderful photographs for your family to enjoy in future.

Ye Olde Goat Ltd. WhatsApp group, Hertfordshire, September 2, 2019:

Mimi & Flo, Tom's Bar
Happy One-Star Monday!

Sean & Adrian, The Rainbow
What a corker! Thanks for sharing.

Diddy & Con, The Brace of Pheasants
Offered them a freebie too! You're a pair of saints.

Mimi & Flo, Tom's Bar
Always upsetting when someone doesn't enjoy what they eat. We've done our best to put it right and now we're moving on. So, which quizzes are we all doing this week? We're second edition, number nine.

Diddy & Con, The Brace of Pheasants
Question set 89 from the second edition.

Peter Bond, The Lusty Lass
1st edn, 21.

Sean & Adrian, The Rainbow
First time using the third edition (has anyone dipped in yet?), quiz number 1. Did *The Cheats* show up anywhere last week?

Sue & Mal, The Case is Altered
Not with us. They never have. Perhaps they don't know we're here.

Sean & Adrian, The Rainbow
Still setting your own quiz, Sue? Going OK?

Sue & Mal, The Case is Altered
Mal enjoys putting the rounds and questions together, bless him.

Peter Bond, The Lusty Lass
More trouble than it's worth.

Diddy & Con, The Brace of Pheasants
Came to ours again Friday. Keep your eyes out, Sue: one chap looks like the council burned his sleeping bag, another looks like the police have his hard drive. There's a girl my age with hair like a banshee. Her man's the loud one, a thin piece in a big orange jacket, he's the ringleader. Beware the orange puffy coat.

Sean & Adrian, The Rainbow
Like a giant satsuma on two skinny stick-legs. What happened, Diddy?

Diddy & Con, The Brace of Pheasants
Con told them they could drink, fine, but not quiz. Satsuma looked ready for a row and she was muttering under her breath, but we had a lot in, they were outnumbered, so they sloped off.

Mimi & Flo, Tom's Bar
Orange puffy jacket? They were here Wednesday, all loud and obnoxious! Called themselves The Goon Squad. Didn't realize it was The Cheats. THEY WON!

Diddy & Con, The Brace of Pheasants
Oh no, Flo, how much did they get?

Mimi & Flo, Tom's Bar
It's Mimi. They got top marks in almost every round and won £14.

Peter Bond, The Lusty Lass
First rule. Keep eyes on any team scoring consistent 8+ rounds.

Mimi & Flo, Tom's Bar
Feel so STUPID. Can't believe we didn't put two and two together.

Sean & Adrian, The Rainbow
Feel a *bit* sorry for them. They've got to be desperate to cheat for £14.

Diddy & Con, The Brace of Pheasants
You're too kind, Sean.

Sean & Adrian, The Rainbow
I remember when they came to our karaoke night. Satsuma picked up the mic and everyone groaned, thinking we were in for a drunken piss-take. He sang "Sweet Gingerbread Man" and it was *beautiful.* Everyone fell silent to listen.

Sean & Adrian, The Rainbow
That song is about being happy, but he made it sound so sad and full of regret. Heartbreaking.

Sean & Adrian, The Rainbow
Seeing someone down on their luck singing about being on top of the world.

Sue & Mal, The Case is Altered
There'll be no sympathy for cheats if they ever show up at The Case.

Text messages between Unknown Number and Sue & Mal, The Case is Altered, September 2, 2019:

Unknown number
The quiz tonight.

Sue & Mal, The Case is Altered
Of course, my dear. What would you like to know? I'm Sue. Mal and I are landlords at The Case. That's *The Case is Altered* pub on a road off the A416, just after St. Luke's Church and before the Morrisons turnoff. If our little parking lot is full, drive up to Turrington's Wood Yard and park in their driveway, they don't mind (our customers have been parking there for the two years we've been here and no one's complained). The quiz starts at 8 p.m., but I recommend you get here half an hour before to bag a table. Teams of up to six people—you can have fewer, but no more. It's a pound each to enter, and the winning table gets the pot minus £10. Bring your own pens and scrap paper. No phones allowed. The quizmaster's decision is final. It is ALWAYS final—even if subsequent evidence proves him to be wrong. If there's anything else, reply to this number. We look forward to welcoming you.

Unknown number
Where are you, again?

Sue & Mal, The Case is Altered
A little lane off the A416, left after St. Luke's Church and before the Morrisons turnoff.

Unknown number
Does the road have a name?

Sue & Mal, The Case is Altered
If you put "The Case is Altered, Fernley" in the satnav, it'll take you straight to us.

Unknown number
But what's the *name* of the road?

Sue & Mal, The Case is Altered
You won't need the name.

Unknown number
It's a simple question. What's the name of the road your pub is on?

Sue & Mal, The Case is Altered
Bell End.

Unknown number
THERE'S NO NEED TO BE RUDE I ONLY ASKED HA HA HA HA

Text messages between Sue and Mal Eastwood, September 2, 2019:

Sue
Just had another one.

Mal
Make a note of the number, I'll forward it to Arthur.

Sue
It's "unknown" again. The police don't want to hear about kids playing pranks. It's simply irritating. I typed out the whole spiel too.

Mal
It's harassment.

Sue
Have you finished tonight's questions, and do I need to set up the overhead projector?

Mal
A. Yes. All ready for printing. 2. No. There are no picture questions this week.

Sue
Mind the pub phone while I'm opening up—but don't forward ANYTHING to Arthur.

THE CASE IS ALTERED PUB QUIZ

September 2, 2019

Rounds	Max points
1. Today's News	10
2. On this day in 1949	10
3. Sport	10
4. Art & Literature	10
5. Film & TV: soap operas	10
6. Music: name the artist and song title (Clue: answers include references to Shakespeare's plays)	20
7. History & Geography	10
8. General Knowledge: bits and bobs (Clue: answers include "bit" or "bob")	10

Marathon round: Political anagrams

Find the names of twentieth-century UK prime ministers   20

Quiz teams and where they sat

Linda & Joe & Friends
Linda & Joe

The Plucky Losers
Chris & Lorraine
Jim
Rita & Bailey
Keith

Spokespersons
Erik, Jemma
Ajay, Tam
Dilip

"The Cheats"
Disqualified

Let's Get Quizzical
Margaret & Ted Dawson
Sid & Nancy Topliss
Bunny & George Tyme

Ami's Manic Carrots
Jojo, Evie
Harrison
Rosie, Fliss

Final scores out of 110

The Plucky Losers	89
Spokespersons	87
Let's Get Quizzical	64
Ami's Manic Carrots	58
Linda & Joe & Friends	44
"The Cheats"	Disqualified

Text messages between Mal and Sue Eastwood, September 2, 2019:

Mal

You never should've put the quiz up on Facebook. That's where they saw it.

Sue

Don't blame me! None of this is my fault.

Sue

Have they all gone?

Mal

Sorted.

Sue

Arthur's on his way.

Mal

No! Call him back and say it's all fine—he's not needed.

Sue

There were four of them and one of you. Where are you now?

Mal

Out by the shed, getting my breath back.

Sue

Come back and do the quiz. I've handed out the marathon round, but everyone's waiting for it to begin.

Mal

Give me a minute.

Sue

You OK?

Sue

I'm keeping your question folder safe from prying eyes.

Sue

Come in now before it looks strange.

Mal

In a sec. Just calming down.

**Text messages between Mal Eastwood and PCSO Arthur McCoy,
September 2, 2019:**

Mal
Cheers, Arthur.

Arthur
Pleasure, Mal. Happy to have been nearby when we got the call. Lucky
they'd all gone.

Mal
I sorted it pronto. Sue needn't have called you.

Arthur
Best to call BEFORE things get out of hand, not after. If it happens again,
you do the same.

Mal
They won't show up again.

**Text messages between Thor's Hammer and Sue & Mal, The Case is
Altered, September 3, 2019:**

Thor's Hammer
Top marks, Mal! We thoroughly enjoyed last night's quiz. As ever, it was
a well-balanced mix of topics. Meaty questions and a challenging but
doable marathon round.

Sue & Mal, The Case is Altered
Congratulations on the win, Chris. Apologies for that upset and delay at
the start. There's a local team notorious for cheating at pub quizzes in the
area. I had to act quickly and make sure they didn't come back.

Thor's Hammer
You leaped into action like a superhero!

Sue & Mal, The Case is Altered
Soon as I saw him, I knew. It was the orange puffy jacket. Only hope it
didn't spoil the night for everyone.

Thor's Hammer

Not our night, Mal! I speak for all The Plucky Losers when I say your Monday quiz is the highlight of the week.

Sue & Mal, The Case is Altered

I'm not surprised, Chris. You've won six of the last seven quizzes.

Thor's Hammer

Now and again the Spokespersons beat us to the top spot, but that's par for the course. Keep up the good work!

Ami's Manic Carrots WhatsApp group, September 3, 2019:

Bianca

Gutted couldn't make last night's quiz 🤐 how'd it go? Did we come last? 😬

Fliss

No.

Bianca

Awesome!

Fliss

We came second-to-last.

Bianca

Oh.

Fliss

Linda & Joe beat us to the bottom.

Harrison

You missed a fight, Bee 🥴 a bunch of sketchies turned up—got salty when Mal told them no.

Fliss

Oh yeah, you missed some vagues who tried to get in.

Jojo

V tense for a hot minute.

Bianca

And I missed it all. Classic me. 🫣

Evie

It was horrible, Bee. 😱 It could've got nasty.

Jojo

Then that Fed we sometimes see on his bike showed up.

Harrison

If it turned really bad, someone would've stepped in to break it up.

Jojo

Who, though? Let's Get Quizzical are all 70 at least. Linda and Joe walk with sticks.

Fliss

The cyclists, or Chris and Lorraine's table?

Rosie

Lucky they'd gone by the time we left. That lane is creepy enough at night—we don't need sketchies lurking in the woods.

Ye Olde Goat Ltd. WhatsApp group, Hertfordshire, September 3, 2019:

Sean & Adrian, The Rainbow

Heard there was trouble at The Case last night. You both OK?

Sue & Mal, The Case is Altered

One of The Cheats will be sporting a shiner this morning, after Mal "had a word" outside.

Diddy & Con, The Brace of Pheasants

Good for you, Mal! Give them a warning they'll remember in the mirror the next day!

Peter Bond, The Lusty Lass

Beware the vengeful customer.

Diddy & Con, The Brace of Pheasants

That's the trouble with The Case. It's all thatch and roses during the day, but at night . . . 😱

Mimi & Flo, Tom's Bar
At least we can rely on the door team from Flappers. They've got us out of trouble before now, but The Case . . . I hate thinking of you two stuck out there.

Sue & Mal, The Case is Altered
Don't know what you mean.

Diddy & Con, The Brace of Pheasants
We looked at taking on The Case when it was up for grabs, years ago now. But stuck down that dark lane, no lights, no pavements, no thanks!

Mimi & Flo, Tom's Bar
If trouble breaks out, you're on your own.

Sean & Adrian, The Rainbow
There's always customers who'll get you out of a corner. If you've got a good crowd, you can handle a few dopes.

Diddy & Con, The Brace of Pheasants
We couldn't see how to make a pub so isolated into a viable business, let alone a safe one.

Sue & Mal, The Case is Altered
Well, it takes time, but we're getting there.

Mimi & Flo, Tom's Bar
What tenancy are you on, Sue?

Sue & Mal, The Case is Altered
Twenty years.

Sean & Adrian, The Rainbow

Mimi & Flo, Tom's Bar
I'd have negotiated a shorter term until I could be sure the business was there.

Peter Bond, The Lusty Lass
Time is experience.

Sue & Mal, The Case is Altered
We're in this for the long term. And The Case isn't as isolated as it looks. We've got the wood yard next door, Morrisons is only a mile away, and the local PCSO is on our side. I think we're safer for being *off* the pub-crawl circuit.

Sue & Mal, The Case is Altered
Mal here. You all think The Case is isolated?

Mimi & Flo, Tom's Bar
Are you OK, Mal? Heard there was trouble last night.

Sue & Mal, The Case is Altered
Spotted Satsuma Man the second he arrived. Turned him and his mates back around the way they came and, like the cowards they are, they ran off, leaving him to deal with me on his own. Bruised knuckles are a small price to pay for the integrity of our quiz.

Diddy & Con, The Brace of Pheasants
Good for you, Mal.

Peter Bond, The Lusty Lass
Trouble begets trouble.

Text messages between Warwick Roper, General Manager of Ye Olde Goat Brewery Ltd., and Sue & Mal, The Case is Altered, September 5, 2019:

Warwick Roper, GM
The bike racks. An update?

Sue & Mal, The Case is Altered
Hello, Mr. Roper, thank you for your message. Sue and I hope you're in good health and enjoying the weather. You've read the AGM flyer, and yes, we're happy to confirm the bike racks are complete, which is excellent news.

Warwick Roper, GM
How little did they cost?

Sue & Mal, The Case is Altered

Practically nothing. We recycled something from the shed. Each rack is completely different. Here's a pic.

Warwick Roper, GM

Mother of God. What the hell is that?

Sue & Mal, The Case is Altered

Some old farm machinery? Not sure, but it was rusting in the shed and now it's been polished up and reclaimed, so our customers can cycle here and save the planet. Everyone loves the modern design. We have a whole cycling team who drink here all the time. They suggested installing bike racks in the first place, so a large group of satisfied and regular customers there!

Warwick Roper, GM

Bottom line is how much you spent.

Sue & Mal, The Case is Altered

Nothing.

Warwick Roper, GM

Good man.

Text messages between Sue and Mal Eastwood, September 5, 2019:

Sue

We saved money when you laid the concrete base yourself, but I paid Manny and Mark to dig out the foundations, plus we bought all those new rivets. Why did you tell Roper we spent nothing?

Mal

We don't want The Case to attract his attention with repeated claims for money.

Sue

But the brewery are responsible for "substantial building work." I thought you'd run it past him at least.

Mal

He's never ventured out here, and I'd like to keep it that way for as long as poss.

Sue

Agreed. But he knows we do all the cleaning and bartending. We can claim SOME expenses!

Mal

We'll swallow this cost, to keep him at arm's length. That way, when we need something more expensive done, he can't accuse us of draining brewery resources.

Sue

You're always kowtowing.

Mal

Am not!

Sue

You've never got over having to admit you couldn't open the till.

Mal

It was our first day! Anyway, wasn't me who shook a negroni AND poured an old-fashioned into a pint glass for the same customer.

Sue

That was our second day! I'll speak to him next time.

Text messages between Unknown Number and Sue & Mal, The Case is Altered, September 9, 2019:

Unknown number

Hello. I'd like some info about tonight.

Sue & Mal, The Case is Altered

Think you're funny?

Unknown number

Oh. Is it a comedy night? It says a quiz on Facebook.

Sue & Mal, The Case is Altered

We're on Bell End, BELL END.

Unknown number

I know. I've looked you up. My quiz team and I are without a Monday fixture and we'd like to come along tonight. We're six friends who enjoy exercising the little gray cells.

Sue & Mal, The Case is Altered

It starts at eight.

Unknown number

Thank you. The street name Bell End could indicate a bell pit was once situated in the area, although we're so far south of traditional mining areas it's not probable. Alternatively, it could be a truncate of Bellows End. A family by the name of Bellows owned most of this land in the sixteenth century, hence Bellows Lane, Upper Bellows, etc. The simplest explanation is that it was originally called Belle End, meaning a pretty lane with no through road (a nice way to say "dead end"), but over time the last "e" has been dropped.

Sue & Mal, The Case is Altered

Get here by seven thirty or you'll have to sit on a stool.

THE CASE IS ALTERED PUB QUIZ

September 9, 2019

Rounds	Max points
1. Today's News	10
2. On this day in 1953	10
3. Sport	10
4. Art & Literature: theater special	10
5. Film & TV: police on-screen	10
6. Music: name the artist and song title	
(Clue: answers include names of the seasons)	20
7. History & Geography	10
8. General Knowledge: hamming it up!	
(Clue: answers include the letters "ham")	10

Marathon round: Country outlines

Spot the country from its outline   20

Quiz teams and where they sat

The Plucky Losers
Chris & Lorraine
Jim
Rita & Bailey
Keith

The Shadow Knights
Six quizzers

Spokespersons
Erik, Jemma
Ajay, Tam
Dilip

Linda & Joe & Friends
Linda & Joe

Let's Get Quizzical
Margaret & Ted Dawson
Sid & Nancy Topliss
Bunny & George Tyme

Ami's Manic Carrots
Jojo, Evie
Harrison, Bianca
Rosie, Fliss

Final scores out of 110

The Shadow Knights	101
The Plucky Losers	91
Spokespersons	83
Let's Get Quizzical	58
Ami's Manic Carrots	56
Linda & Joe & Friends	41

Text messages between Mal and Sue Eastwood, September 9, 2019:

Mal
All OK? Locked up?

Sue
Nearly. Well done. All seemed to go smoothly from the bar!

Mal
New team scored 101. Bit too high for my liking.

Sue
Now you're not going to be awake all night, are you?

Mal
Chris walked out at the end without a word. He'll complain. I know.

Text messages between Thor's Hammer and Sue & Mal, The Case is Altered, September 10, 2019:

Thor's Hammer
Is this Sue or Mal? Never know which of you it is on this number.

Sue & Mal, The Case is Altered
Sue. It's the pub phone, so we share it. How can I help you, Chris?

Thor's Hammer
Bit pissed off about last night, TBH.

Sue & Mal, The Case is Altered
Why's that, love?

Thor's Hammer
First, they sat on our table. Second, I asked where they were from and the tall one who seemed in charge said "Magrathea." Third, they won.

Sue & Mal, The Case is Altered
Tables can't be reserved—they arrived before you. The Case welcomes patrons from anywhere, and they wrote down more correct answers than any other team. Can't say fairer than that.

Thor's Hammer

We always sit by the speaker, because Keith is hard of hearing. They are NOT from Magrathea—it's a fictional planet from a Douglas Adams book—and they got 101 out of 110. It's not fair, Sue.

Sue & Mal, The Case is Altered

This is Mal now. I am the quizmaster, my decision is final, and I have no ax to grind with The Shadow Knights.

Thor's Hammer

101 out of 110? Are you kidding me? They have to be cheating.

Sue & Mal, The Case is Altered

Not at all. They're clearly a committed team who quiz regularly.

Thor's Hammer

Then they're pros and it's REALLY not fair.

Sue & Mal, The Case is Altered

You could tell by watching them how seriously they take it.

Thor's Hammer

We support your quiz every week. Now they've swooped in and flown off with our prize!

Sue & Mal, The Case is Altered

That collective air of calm concentration. Perfect poker faces. No more than one drink each. No time or energy wasted in idle chitchat, with each other or anyone else. I respect any team that takes the quiz that seriously.

Thor's Hammer

They're bandits.

Sue & Mal, The Case is Altered

They won £19. I doubt we'll see them again.

Text messages between Unknown Number and Sue & Mal, The Case is Altered, September 10, 2019:

Unknown number
We enjoyed the quiz last night, thank you, Mal. Sue was very welcoming, and winning made our visit to The Case is Altered extra-special.

Sue & Mal, The Case is Altered
This is Sue, and you're welcome. Thank you for coming. There's a quiz here every Monday if you want to defend your title.

Unknown number
We may do that.

Sue & Mal, The Case is Altered
What's your name, so I can file your number in our database? We don't send spam, because neither of us knows how.

Unknown number
They call me General Knowledge. I know a bit about everything, and not a lot about anything.

Sue & Mal, The Case is Altered
But your name? What do people call you? It's for the phone address book.

Unknown number
The General.

Text messages between Jojo and Sue & Mal, The Case is Altered, September 11, 2019:

Jojo
Looking for the contacts of a guy on The Shadow Knights' table on Monday? On the bench seat beside the radiator. Swept-back hair, slim waist, muscly arms.

Sue & Mal, The Case is Altered
Hello, Jojo, it's Sue. Can I ask why you want the lad's number?

Jojo

It's for Rosie. You know she had a really bad breakup last year? Well, she hasn't looked twice at anyone since then—until The Shadow Knights walked in. He's gorgeous, right?

Sue & Mal, The Case is Altered

Oh. Well, I don't know what data-protection laws have to say about that.

Jojo

But he's GORGEOUS, Sue.

Sue & Mal, The Case is Altered

I know the young fellow you mean. He was with his dad, wasn't he?

Jojo

Exactly! How can I make a move when he's there with fam? Just his number, or his full name, so I can find him on socials . . . please, Sue, please please please.

Sue & Mal, The Case is Altered

This is for Rosie?

Jojo

Yes. It's to help a friend who really should get back in the race after a traumatic breakup.

Sue & Mal, The Case is Altered

I'm sorry, Jojo, love. I've looked up the data-protection rules and instances in which I can divulge a customer's number don't include matchmaking.

Jojo

Oh no! That is such a shame, Sue. You know how difficult it is for teams to mingle when there's a marathon round on the table. It means we can only chat afterward, and his team left immediately. Could "someone" pass that number to me, on the down-low? I won't say where I got it from. Promise.

Sue & Mal, The Case is Altered

I'll tell you what. If The Shadow Knights come to the quiz again next Monday, I'll have a word with the young man's dad and say Rosie thinks his son is a bit of all right, and would the young man like a chat with her? How about that?

Jojo

NOOOOO! If you do that on Monday, my funeral will be on Tuesday.

Sue & Mal, The Case is Altered

We do funerals, if anyone asks.

Jojo

NO! Forget I mentioned it.

Text messages between Thor's Hammer and Sue & Mal, The Case is Altered, September 13, 2019:

Thor's Hammer

Which questions did The Shadow Knights get wrong?

Sue & Mal, The Case is Altered

I can't remember, Chris, love. That was Monday. It's Friday now.

Thor's Hammer

Does Mal still have the answer sheets? Could you ask him, please, Sue?

Sue & Mal, The Case is Altered

This is Mal now. Any answer sheets left in the pub go straight in the recycling bin.

Thor's Hammer

Could you do us a favor and get them out?

Sue & Mal, The Case is Altered

Bins were collected Wednesday.

Sue & Mal, The Case is Altered

And no, I'm not going to the recycling center to look for them.

Thor's Hammer

Can you remember which questions they got wrong?

Sue & Mal, The Case is Altered

I think they dropped a music question, left a couple of anagrams blank—other than that, I don't recall.

Thor's Hammer

Can you do me a favor and keep their question sheets from now on?

Sue & Mal, The Case is Altered
They won't come back. IMO prize money here is not enough for a crack team like The Shadow Knights.

Thor's Hammer
But if they do. Keep their answer sheets?

Ye Olde Goat Ltd. WhatsApp group, Hertfordshire, September 13, 2019:

Sean & Adrian, The Rainbow
Word of warning. Two of The Cheats showed up last night—without Satsuma Man. We didn't realize it was them until we spotted their phones out during the first round.

Diddy & Con, The Brace of Pheasants
Oh no! What did you do?

Sean & Adrian, The Rainbow
Adrian took them aside for a chat. You know what he's like—civility itself. He said if they wanted to quiz, they'd have to put their phones away, sit with him at the bar, and not leave their seats the whole time. If either of them "popped to the loo" or outside for a vape, their entry to the quiz would be invalidated immediately, with no refund.

Diddy & Con, The Brace of Pheasants
That's generous of you. We just boot them the F out. Once bittern.

Mimi & Flo, Tom's Bar
Same. When we recognize them. I don't think I would, without the one in the orange jacket.

Sean & Adrian, The Rainbow
Adrian says it's only fair to give folk another chance.

Peter Bond, The Lusty Lass
Lucky is the landlord with time and patience to babysit vagabonds.

Sue & Mal, The Case is Altered
Adrian sat with them all evening? Did they say anything?

Sean & Adrian, The Rainbow

No, no. He would have, but didn't have to. They sloped off immediately.

Sue & Mal, The Case is Altered

Has anyone had a team in called The Shadow Knights? Scored an unprecedented 101/110, to the chagrin of our regulars.

Mimi & Flo, Tom's Bar

Who's the chagrin?

Sue & Mal, The Case is Altered

It means annoyance or irritation.

Mimi & Flo, Tom's Bar

They haven't been here.

Diddy & Con, The Brace of Pheasants

Nor here.

Peter Bond, The Lusty Lass

Physical descriptions?

Sue & Mal, The Case is Altered

Three men, three women. Various ages. All a bit nerdy. More focused and serious than your average pub quizzer.

Diddy & Con, The Brace of Pheasants

Were they ducking into the toilets every chance they got? Nipping out to take urgent phone calls or smoke? That's when Dr. Google is on the team.

Sue & Mal, The Case is Altered

Stayed in their seats all night. No phones out during the quiz. Bought one alcoholic and then one soft drink each, plus chips in the intermission, and put all their change in the staff tip can. Applauded the quizmaster at the end and sent a thank-you text the morning after.

Mimi & Flo, Tom's Bar

If they won fair and square, then what's the problem, Mal?

Sue & Mal, The Case is Altered

Our most regular regular says they must be cheating to score so well across the board. Maybe he's envious and The Shadow Knights are simply a very good team. Or perhaps they've found a new way to cheat.

Peter Bond, The Lusty Lass

Or—and don't take this as a criticism, Mal—perhaps your quiz is too easy.

Diddy & Con, The Brace of Pheasants

That's why we don't set the questions ourselves. I'm thick as, and Con's no better.

Sue & Mal, The Case is Altered

I assure you I take great care while compiling our questions. I make sure they are clear and simple, not ambiguous or disputable, and that they appeal to a broad range of quizzing abilities. The Pub Quiz Network questions are boring and anything topical is out of date the second it's published.

Sean & Adrian, The Rainbow

I'm sure Mal's quiz is fine and the regular winners have simply been blindsided by a serious quizzing team. Some people have all the smarts and like to flaunt it. Isn't that why they go from quiz to quiz? The regulars will have to up their game, that's all.

Sue & Mal, The Case is Altered

True. Chris's team dominated before—now they have something to aspire to.

Sue & Mal, The Case is Altered

But still, The Shadow Knights are intriguing.

Sean & Adrian, The Rainbow

If they show up here, we'll keep an eye on them and report back. 🧐

Peter Bond, The Lusty Lass

A message for Diddy/Con: it's "bitten" not "bittern." Bittern is a sea bird.

Sue & Mal, The Case is Altered

I knew that.

Text messages between Mal and Sue Eastwood, September 16, 2019:

Mal

Have we heard from The Shadow Knights? Are they coming to tonight's quiz?

Sue
No word from The General. I put his number in the pub phone—I can text him and ask?

Mal
No, no, no. Let sleeping dogs lie and all that.

Text message between Mal Eastwood and The General, September 16, 2019:

Mal
Hello. You don't know this number because you messaged the pub phone before, which is where I got your number from. But this is Mal, quizmaster from The Case. Wondered if your team fancies coming to our quiz again tonight? Good to have fresh faces and new blood in the place last week. You'd be very welcome if you decided to pop by again. 7:30 p.m. for 8 p.m.

The Plucky Losers WhatsApp group, September 16, 2019:

Thor's Hammer added Lorraine, Keith, Rita & Bailey, and Jim to this group

Thor's Hammer
Starting this group so we can coordinate things re the quiz. That new team got our table last week. We don't want that happening again. It put us off our stroke and that's why we lost for the first time in ages.

Rita & Bailey
Bailey and I can get to The Case for 5 p.m. tonight, Chris. I'll save the table.

Thor's Hammer
You'll do that, Rita? Thank you, that's the commitment we need, team!

Lorraine
You'll sit there for three hours, Rita?

Rita & Bailey
If we get our table back, we'll get our quiz mojo back. We're leaving now.

THE CASE IS ALTERED PUB QUIZ

September 16, 2019

Rounds	Max points
1. Today's News	10
2. On this day in 1963	10
3. Sporting films, plays & TV	10
4. Shakespeare: life and works	10
5. Film & TV: law & order	10
6. Music: stage musical special	20
7. History: serial killer special	10
8. General Knowledge	
(The answer to each question is a person.	
For a bonus point, say whether they are dead or alive.)	20

Marathon round: Political anagrams

Find the names of twentieth-century US presidents   20

Quiz teams and where they sat

The Shadow Knights
General Knowledge + 5

The Plucky Losers
Chris & Lorraine
Jim
Rita & Bailey
Keith

Spokespersons
Erik, Jemma
Ajay, Tam
Dilip

Linda & Joe & Friends
Linda & Joe

Let's Get Quizzical
Sid & Nancy Topliss
Bunny & George Tyme
Margaret & Ted Dawson

Ami's Manic Carrots
Jojo, Evie
Harrison, Bianca
Rosie, Fliss

Final scores out of 120

The Shadow Knights	120
The Plucky Losers	99
Spokespersons	90
Ami's Manic Carrots	74
Let's Get Quizzical	66
Linda & Joe & Friends	27

Text messages between Mal and Sue Eastwood, September 17, 2019:

Mal
120 out of 120. It's incredible. How did they do it?

Sue
Go to sleep. Why are you texting in the middle of the night?

Mal
I deliberately included some marginal questions, just to test them. All correct. What's their secret? Saw you speaking to him afterward. Get any info?

Sue
I had a chat with The General. He's perfectly nice and polite.

Mal
Must revamp our questions. Might resort to a quiz from the network's "advanced" book, to see where the holes in their knowledge lie.

Sue
NO! Then our regular teams will score even less. Poor Linda and Joe will get nil points and won't come again. There's NOTHING odd or creepy about The Shadow Knights. I've been trying to sleep for the last hour and this is not helping. Switching my phone OFF now. NO MORE TEXTING.

Mal
Been awake an hour, have you, Sue? Seems The Shadow Knights are on your mind too.

Mal
Odd and creepy. I never said that.

Text messages between The General and Sue & Mal, The Case is Altered, September 17, 2019:

The General
Thank you for an excellent quiz.

Sue & Mal, The Case is Altered
You're welcome, General. Congratulations on your win. Again.

The General

Thank you. We were especially pleased to get some of those trickier questions correct.

Sue & Mal, The Case is Altered

Your team is so clever. Our questions are too easy for you.

The General

Not at all.

Sue & Mal, The Case is Altered

It wouldn't surprise me if you ditched The Case is Altered and found a more challenging quiz. All the pubs in this area of the brewery's Hertfordshire network run weekly quizzes. I can recommend them.

The General

We're here to stay, Sue.

Sue & Mal, The Case is Altered

What do you do? I imagine you're all professors or scientists. People who know things other people don't.

The General

Far from it.

Sue & Mal, The Case is Altered

I see a lot from the bar. How a team reacts when they all know an answer, or when no one does. How they sort it out when they disagree. Your team seems to communicate without saying much at all.

The General

Did you know "The Case is Altered" was first used as a proverbial phrase in the sixteenth century? Coined, anecdotally, by legal scholar Edmund Plowden. It describes a situation where evidence emerges during court proceedings that means an entire legal case is turned on its head. It's not uncommon for pubs to be in legal dispute, and instances of the pub name may be because they were retitled following legal victories. Usually so long ago that no one remembers what or when.

The General

Ben Jonson used it as the title for a play, interestingly—one he later ejected from his canon. Do you know how your establishment came by its name?

Sue & Mal, The Case is Altered
I don't.

The General
Another thing about Jonson's play: it's unfinished. Or the final pages are lost. Either way, no one knows how it ends, whether there was a final twist—or not.

Sue & Mal, The Case is Altered
Everyone loves a mystery, eh? If you want to know where else you can quiz, just ask.

The General
See you next Monday.

Text messages between Thor's Hammer and Sue & Mal, The Case is Altered, September 17, 2019:

Thor's Hammer
Thanks for passing me The Shadow Knights' answer sheets, Mal. Much appreciated.

Sue & Mal, The Case is Altered
Mal did WHAT?

Thor's Hammer
Hi, Sue. Could you give the phone to Mal, there's a good girl.

Sue & Mal, The Case is Altered
This is Mal. What now?

Thor's Hammer
No crossing out. No notes. No misspellings. No mistakes.

Sue & Mal, The Case is Altered
So?

Thor's Hammer
The Shadow Knights not only get every answer correct, they write it down perfectly. 120 answers and all exactly as if they'd copied them out of a book.

Sue & Mal, The Case is Altered

Probably do all their scribbling and working out on separate sheets of scrap paper.

Thor's Hammer

Or they know the pub-quiz books inside out. Memorized each set of questions.

Sue & Mal, The Case is Altered

I set the questions myself, Chris. Have done from the start. The Shadow Knights are VERY good quizzers and if what The General told Sue is right, then they're here to stay.

Thor's Hammer

Not good news. Not good at all.

Sue & Mal, The Case is Altered

If The Plucky Losers want to reclaim their place at the top, then turning up three hours early and getting hammered before the quiz starts is probably not the best strategy.

Thor's Hammer

Ah, yes. Rita and Bailey were kind enough to reserve our table. Didn't pace the alcohol intake very well, and the result was a period of intrusive chanting, followed by eerie singing and finally loud snoring. It won't happen again.

Text messages between Sue and Mal Eastwood, September 17, 2019:

Sue

Do NOT pass one team's answer sheets to another!

Mal

Why not?

Sue

It's wrong. Data protection for starters.

Mal

Don't be so sanctimonious.

Sue

If The Shadow Knights found out and confronted us, we've got no good reason except apparently favoring The Plucky Losers, and how bad would that look?

Mal

They won't find out, will they?

Sue

I mean it. Answer sheets, once handed in, belong to the pub and are not available to view. It could cause trouble we don't need and it's not up for discussion.

Text messages between Me [Rita] and Sue & Mal, The Case is Altered, September 19, 2019:

Me

What's going on, Sue?

Sue & Mal, The Case is Altered

I don't know, Rita, what's going on where?

Me

Chris and Lorraine say the quiz isn't on anymore.

Sue & Mal, The Case is Altered

Don't know why they'd say that. The quiz was on Monday as usual, although I wouldn't be surprised if you didn't remember much about it.

Me

Chris called in a huff this morning and said the quiz is over. Done. Finished.

Sue & Mal, The Case is Altered

Oh. Well, if The Plucky Losers decide not to quiz anymore simply because a better team beat them, it's a shame. If you want to join another team, I know Linda & Joe are always looking for teammates.

Me

Linda and Joe? That's a good idea. I know Linda a bit from the school. See you Monday.

* * *

Me
MAL! Mal? Is this Mal?

Sue & Mal, The Case is Altered
It's Mal now. Hello, Rita.

Me
Just remembered! Saw a fella looked exactly like you on the telly last night.

Sue & Mal, The Case is Altered
That'll be Ryan Reynolds. We're often mistaken for each other.

Me
Was he in The Bill?

Sue & Mal, The Case is Altered
Are you sure, Rita? The Bill was screened from 1984 to 2010. Unless you've got yourself a time machine, I doubt you were watching it last night.

Me
It was one of those old channels you end up watching by accident. Bailey was hogging the remote, so I couldn't switch over. He looked exactly like you.

Sue & Mal, The Case is Altered
Well, I've never been in The Bill. Then again, nor has Ryan Reynolds, which is another thing we have in common.

Me
I can picture you in a police uniform—hat and everything.

Sue & Mal, The Case is Altered
That'll be the air of authority Sue tells me I have.

Me
There you go! See you Monday.

Text messages between Lorraine and Andrew, September 19, 2019:

Lorraine

Morning, Andy! It's been YEARS since the canal litter cleanup. Do you remember, you were doing a placement for your university degree? Chris and me, we've never forgotten your enthusiasm or your wicked sense of humor! We hope, firstly, that this is still your number, secondly that you still live near here, and thirdly that you're having a whale of a time in whatever high-flying job you're doing now.

Andrew

Sat at work. Staring at the keyboard. Hands shaking so much I can see the keys clearly, but not my own fingers.

Lorraine

Bless! You free next Monday night?

Andrew

Why?

Lorraine

Chris and I have a team in the local pub quiz. We're looking for new members who *know* things. I remember you were doing a science degree and we heard you went to work in politics.

Andrew

I studied political science and work in social housing for the council. I shove young people in and out of temporary accommodation. It's soul destroying.

Lorraine

Political science! That's what we're after. Current affairs! Still at the same flat? Chris will pick you up at seven on Monday.

Spokespersons Cycling Team WhatsApp group, September 19, 2019:

Ajay

Anyone else had a call from Chris?

Dilip

Chris at Spinning Wheels or Chrissy from Dykes on Bikes?

Ajay
Neither. He's on the quiz team that sits across the bar from us. Has he called any of you?

Jemma
Nope.

Tam
Not me.

Dilip
He doesn't have my number.

Ajay
He didn't have mine. Don't know where he got it.

Jemma
What did he want?

Ajay
Not sure. Just a cryptic message. I'll call him back later.

Tam
Shout if the quiz is canceled. Don't want to trek over to The Case if it's not on.

Text messages between Thor's Hammer and Lorraine, September 20, 2019:

Thor's Hammer
The Shadow Knights had a youngster. Looked twenty, tops.

Lorraine
Yes, he was with the fair-haired man. He won't want to move teams, not if he's . . . you know.

Thor's Hammer
What?

Lorraine
With his family.

Thor's Hammer
I know THAT. But he could be their secret weapon.

Lorraine
I doubt it, Chris. Ami's Manic Carrots are young and they never do well.

Thor's Hammer
Because they're ALL young. Let's Get Quizzical are all old and they don't rise to the top, either. Diversity, Lorraine, that's the key to winning quizzes. We need a young person to cover questions about R&B music, reality television, and computer games. It's not enough to replace one team of codgers with another. Have you spoken to Jim?

Lorraine
Putting it off.

Thor's Hammer
He has to know. Go on—I told Rita.

Lorraine
You're not texting at work, are you? Be careful.

Thor's Hammer
Early break. They're cleaning the burners after a leak.

Text messages between Lorraine and Jim, September 20, 2019:

Lorraine
Hi, Jim. How are you?

Jim
Everything OK, Lor?

Lorraine
Jim, Chris and I have been talking about the quiz and *he* wants to revamp our team. Chip out dead wood and fish for fresh new blood. Educated people who remember what they've read, who love facts and figures, who know about culture and can spell.

Jim
I'll have a think, see who comes to mind.

Lorraine

No! Of course *you* don't know anyone like that, Jim! But Chris and I, we've met some clever people over the years and we're mining our address books.

Jim

Is this because that bunch of nerds keeps blowing us out of the water?

Lorraine

No!

Lorraine

Well, in a way.

Jim

The quiz is just a bit of fun. Passes the time while drinking, eh?

Lorraine

See, that's the attitude we want to stamp out. Chris says it's time to move up. Attain the next level.

Jim

We always win, Lor!

Lorraine

Until The Shadow Knights arrived. You were there! A wake-up call if ever there was one. We've only come this far thanks to Chris and me. He has an encyclopedic knowledge of pop music and I read a lot. But that's not how quizzes are won. Diversity is key.

Jim

So, I'm not diverse enough now?

Lorraine

There are holes in our knowledge bucket, and you're one of them. I'm sorry, Jim, but The Plucky Losers no longer require your services. Which reminds me, we need to change the name. It was supposed to be ironic. Now it sounds as if we're embracing failure.

Jim

Well, that's just made my day. My sister and brother-in-law are throwing me off their drinking table!

Lorraine

QUIZ TABLE. That proves my point, Jim. See you at Kylie's 21st on Sunday. You can talk to Chris there, it's all his idea.

Text messages between Tam and Sue & Mal, The Case is Altered, September 20, 2019:

Tam

Hi, this is Tam from the Spokespersons quiz team. Thanks for the bike racks.

Sue & Mal, The Case is Altered

No problem, Tam, love. You'll be delighted to hear they're 100% recycled. Mal salvaged an old farm machine the last landlord left behind in the shed and set bits of it in concrete. He's quite handy like that. We paid two chaps from an employment scheme to help. Nice to support the local community.

Tam

It means we can cycle to the quiz and back. Keep up our night-riding experience.

Sue & Mal, The Case is Altered

You're fitter and braver than me! We're pleased you asked, because we'd never have thought to install bike racks if you hadn't.

Tam

Can I ask something else? I hope it's not too cheeky.

Sue & Mal, The Case is Altered

Of course you can. Fire away.

Tam

Could you stock a range of vegan protein drinks or organic electrolyte replacement brands for us?

Sue & Mal, The Case is Altered

That's a bit tricky. Our stock is controlled by the brewery.

Tam

We don't drink alcohol or caffeine. Sweet carbonated drinks are full of additives. Water is neutral hydration and not adequate when you're training as hard as we do.

Sue & Mal, The Case is Altered

You'd best ask Ye Olde Goat yourself. If the cry goes up, "We are the customers and we demand vegan protein," they'll have to listen.

Tam

The trouble is, that'll take time. We'd bring our own drinks, but you have a sign up saying that only food and drink purchased on the premises may be consumed.

Sue & Mal, The Case is Altered

Perhaps we could waive that rule for you? I'll ask Mal and see what he says. We don't want valued customers to go without the sustenance they need to get here and home again!

Text messages between Mal and Sue Eastwood, September 20, 2019:

Mal

Valued customers? They drink water all night and certainly don't trouble our stocks of chips and nuts. I've never seen men so skinny.

Sue

They're serious cyclists and good quizzers too.

Mal

They always score well in the sports rounds, I'll give them that. They were one of the few serious challengers to The Plucky Losers before The Shadow Knights appeared.

Sue

Go on—we don't want to lose a team. Even if the brewery finds out we're selling vegan drinks, it's not the crime of the century, is it, love?

The Brace of Pheasants

Dwayne B.
wrote a review on September 19, 2019
Boston, Massachusetts
9 contributions, 0 helpful votes

Date visited   **September 14, 2019**
Visit type   **as a couple**

Too much soccer

My wife and I are on a tour of Great Britain and, being Irish-American, decided to spend the evening cozying up to the crack at an authentic Irish bar. Unfortunately, the whole place was in uproar over a soccer game. We never found a table to sit at because we couldn't get through the crowd of men in soccer shirts who kept bursting into songs we didn't know. Everyone in the place was glued to the big screen. If I wanted that sort of thing I'd go to a sports bar. When we eventually ordered I asked for a small white wine but, apparently, that was the moment Kerry scored. I don't know who Kerry is, but he's a popular player. When the cheering had died down I was handed a pint of Guinness and was too scared of the barman to argue.

We hoped to soak up a genuine Irish atmosphere but all we got was singing in a foreign language, curse words, and finally a fistfight in the middle of the floor. The men rolling around punching each other, to cheers from the crowd, weren't even thrown out.

Response from The Brace of Pheasants
Responded on September 19, 2019

You're touring Great Britain looking for an authentic Irish bar, you say? If you looked under a rock, would you expect to find an elephant? For the love of the saints, go to IRELAND to find your Irish roots, not the home counties of England. You visited us on the day of the All Ireland Football Final replay. I'd say that was a pretty damn authentic experience of an Irish night in an Irish pub, and the very essence of the craic, but what the feck do I know?

The fight you saw? I'll tell you who that was: me. Heard there was a gobshite in the bar. A fecking eejit who gave us a one-star review and dragged our online average down with their fecking poxy opinions. I battered the head off him—now feck off, yer langer.

Ye Olde Goat Ltd. WhatsApp group, Hertfordshire, September 23, 2019:

Diddy & Con, The Brace of Pheasants
Rise and shine, everyone! It's One-Star Monday.

Sean & Adrian, The Rainbow
Priceless! 😂

Sue & Mal, The Case is Altered
Hope Mr. Roper doesn't read it.

Diddy & Con, The Brace of Pheasants
It's an authentic, on-brand response. He'll love it.

Sean & Adrian, The Rainbow
You've never shared a one-star review from The Case, Mal. Don't tell us you never get them.

Sue & Mal, The Case is Altered
We get them all right. I might find them funny—if we weren't scarred by the ones we got in our first week.

Mimi & Flo, Tom's Bar
Did rival pubs bomb you with bad reviews? Happened to us.

Sue & Mal, The Case is Altered
We'd had a full refit and every system developed teething problems. That and the fact we'd never run a pub on our own meant a perfect storm of one-star reviews.

Sean & Adrian, The Rainbow
You learn on the job. No shame there. Which quizzes are you guys doing this week?

Diddy & Con, The Brace of Pheasants
Question set 90 from the second edition.

Peter Bond, The Lusty Lass
1st edn, 22.

Mimi & Flo, Tom's Bar
Second edition, number fourteen.

Sean & Adrian, The Rainbow
Third edition is going down well, so we're sticking with it: quiz number two.

Sue & Mal, The Case is Altered
Did The Shadow Knights come to any of your quizzes last week?

Peter Bond, The Lusty Lass
Negative.

Sean & Adrian, The Rainbow
Beginning to wonder if The Shadow Knights exist, Mal.

Sue & Mal, The Case is Altered
They exist all right.

Sean & Adrian, The Rainbow
I'm joking. 😄

Diddy & Con, The Brace of Pheasants
What's wrong with them, Mal?

Mimi & Flo, Tom's Bar
What should we look out for? Cheating?

Sue & Mal, The Case is Altered
I don't know. Maybe. Just interested in what you think of them, that's all.

Spokespersons Cycling Team WhatsApp group, September 23, 2019:

Erik
Ajay, are you seriously joining another quiz team?

Ajay
Good news travels fast. Thanks, Jemma.

Jemma
Well, someone had to break it to the team.

Tam
That's 💩. Something we said?

Jemma

Why you? Do they think you know more than we do?

Dilip

You're joining another team, AJ? Bet it's the old boomers.

Tam

Or the new super-nerds. 🤓

Ajay

Neither. The Plucky Losers.

Tam

Why? We do OK. We've even won a couple of times when The Plucky Losers were on vacation. I love our little team. 😕

Erik

I thought we had something.

Ajay

Guys, it's not like I cheated on you. It's a quiz. It's no big deal.

Erik

So, let's get this clear: you'll cycle with us to The Case. Then sit with another team for the evening. Then cycle home with us. 😳

Ajay

Is there a problem with that? Chris and Lorraine invited me—how could I say no? None of you would have refused either, if they'd asked you. It is what it is. OK?

THE CASE IS ALTERED PUB QUIZ

September 23, 2019

Rounds	Max points
1. Today's News	10
2. On this day in 1985	10
3. Sport: break a leg (sports injuries special)	10
4. Literature: crime fiction	10
5. Name the film these lines came from (Bonus point: guess the actor who spoke them)	20
6. Music: guess the song from the intro	20
7. History & Geography of the British Isles	10
8. General Knowledge: link round (The last letter of each answer will be the first letter of the answer to the next question)	10

Marathon round: National flags
Identify the countries these flags belong to   40

Quiz teams and where they sat

The Plucky Losers
Chris & Lorraine
Ajay
Keith
Andy

The Shadow Knights
General Knowledge + 5

Spokespersons
Erik, Jemma
Tam, Dilip

Linda & Joe & Friends
Linda & Joe
Rita & Bailey

Let's Get Quizzical
Sid & Nancy Topliss
Bunny & George Tyme
Margaret & Ted Dawson

Ami's Manic Carrots
Jojo, Evie
Harrison, Rosie
Fliss

Final scores out of 140

The Shadow Knights	139
The Plucky Losers	129
Let's Get Quizzical	93
Spokespersons	83
Ami's Manic Carrots	69
Linda & Joe & Friends	64

Ye Olde Goat Ltd. WhatsApp group, Hertfordshire, September 24, 2019:

Sue & Mal, The Case is Altered
Listen to this! The Shadow Knights showed up again last night and got 139 out of 140. I planted some tough questions too. Niche subjects. Oblique formats. The only question they got wrong was in the music round and everyone got that one wrong.

Sean & Adrian, The Rainbow
What were the tough questions?

Mimi & Flo, Tom's Bar
Go on, Mal, see if we know them! What's an oblique format?

Peter Bond, The Lusty Lass
Willing to flex the old gray matter.

Sue & Mal, The Case is Altered
Name the freezing point of oxygen?

Sue & Mal, The Case is Altered
Which star sign was singer Meat Loaf born under?

Sue & Mal, The Case is Altered
What was Carrie Fisher's middle name?

Sue & Mal, The Case is Altered
What is Sally Lightfoot?

Sue & Mal, The Case is Altered
Any takers?

Mimi & Flo, Tom's Bar
Is Sally Lightfoot the Speaker of the House of Commons?

Diddy & Con, The Brace of Pheasants
No, Flo, she was in that big musical. Con is racking his brains for the title.

Sean & Adrian, The Rainbow
We've had Sally Lightfoot here. She's a drag queen from Market Harborough.

Sue & Mal, The Case is Altered
"What" is Sally Lightfoot, not "who."

Peter Bond, The Lusty Lass
Ms. Lightfoot is a crab. A red-and-blue crustacean from the isles known as the Galapagos.

Mimi & Flo, Tom's Bar
Is that an oblique format?

Sue & Mal, The Case is Altered
An oblique format is simply when a question isn't straightforward. For example: which of these films was Amy Adams NOT in: The Hug, Big Eyes, or Junebug?

Sue & Mal, The Case is Altered
In this instance you have to deduce a negative, not just remember a fact. It's where teamwork comes in. If quizzers have memorized facts and are relying on their recall, then I want them to work a bit harder. With an oblique format, the memory gang has less of an advantage.

Diddy & Con, The Brace of Pheasants
We haven't seen any of those. Are they on Netflix?

Mimi & Flo, Tom's Bar
We sympathize, Mal. If this team keeps winning, the others will get bored and go elsewhere. Have the other teams said anything?

Sue & Mal, The Case is Altered
Afraid so. Chris and Lorraine have been coming to The Case since before our tenure. Nice couple who've had a lot to contend with. He's not best pleased. I can see they're trying to up their game by poaching members from other teams, but so far it hasn't got them a win.

Mimi & Flo, Tom's Bar
Bless.

Sean & Adrian, The Rainbow
Yeah, that's rough. Sending love.

Peter Bond, The Lusty Lass
The Hug.

Sean & Adrian, The Rainbow
What was the music question everyone got wrong?

Sue & Mal, The Case is Altered

They had to name the song and the artist from the intro. Let's see if I can post it.

Sue & Mal, The Case is Altered

[music clip]

Sean & Adrian, The Rainbow

Hello, 1988!

Mimi & Flo, Tom's Bar

Don't know it.

Diddy & Con, The Brace of Pheasants

You've stumped everyone. Who is it?

Sue & Mal, The Case is Altered

The Swindle Sheets with their only track "You're Wrong."

Mimi & Flo, Tom's Bar

Super-obscure!

Sue & Mal, The Case is Altered

Exactly. If anyone got it right, I'd know they were cheating.

Sean & Adrian, The Rainbow

Careful, Mal. Some people know their music inside out. Unreleased tracks, albums, chart positions, recording studios, labels, the lot.

Sue & Mal, The Case is Altered

Ha, this is the twist! The Swindle Sheets don't exist. There's a thing on the internet called Choon. If you sign up, it lets you make little instrumental bits of music and upload them. I played with it all day yesterday and put an original track on one of those streaming places an hour before the quiz began.

Sean & Adrian, The Rainbow

Get you, Mal! You might have an accidental hit on your hands.

Sue & Mal, The Case is Altered

If anyone put the right answer, they would HAVE to be using an audio-scan app while the quiz tracks were being played.

Mimi & Flo, Tom's Bar

That is clever.

Sean & Adrian, The Rainbow

So now you know The Shadow Knights aren't cheating.

Peter Bond, The Lusty Lass

Unless they realized your little game. Swindle Sheets. "You're Wrong."

Mimi & Flo, Tom's Bar

I doubt it, Peter! If it flashed up on Shazam, I'd think it was real.

Diddy & Con, The Brace of Pheasants

If you're anything like us, they only get sixty seconds to write their answer before we're on to the next question.

Mimi & Flo, Tom's Bar

But they'd have the rest of that round to think about it.

Sue & Mal, The Case is Altered

It was the last question. They had sixty seconds max before the paper had to be handed in. I don't play music tracks twice.

Sean & Adrian, The Rainbow

What did they put for that track?

Sue & Mal, The Case is Altered

Mal's rummaging through the bin looking for last night's answer sheets.

Mimi & Flo, Tom's Bar

It sounds like a track from the late 80s. Like Sean said. So their guess is probably something that was a hit then.

Sean & Adrian, The Rainbow

Hazell Dean. Rick Astley. Anything Stock Aitken Waterman.

Sue & Mal, The Case is Altered

Mal's back.

Diddy & Con, The Brace of Pheasants

Kylie, Sonia, Mel & Kim.

Sue & Mal, The Case is Altered

You won't believe this.

Sean & Adrian, The Rainbow
What?

Mimi & Flo, Tom's Bar
To be fair, any 80s synth music would be a decent guess.

Sue & Mal, The Case is Altered
They wrote down a track from a recent album. Out this year. A REGGAE album.

Diddy & Con, The Brace of Pheasants
Put us out of our misery!

Sue & Mal, The Case is Altered
"Got to Do Better Than That" by The Dualers. Not only did they realize the track was a deliberate test of their honesty, but they came back with a fitting riposte in the space of sixty seconds.

Sue & Mal, The Case is Altered
It's a message. To me. More than that—it's a challenge.

Peter Bond, The Lusty Lass
Time for sneaky-beaky.

Text messages between Lorraine and Andrew, September 24, 2019:

Lorraine
Thanks for coming last night, Andy. We'd never have scored 129 without you. Keith, Chris, and I all think Mal has made the questions tougher.

Andrew
It's a change to be somewhere other than work or bed.

Lorraine
What do you think of Ajay? We lured him over from the Spokespersons. He got that question about Lady Jane Grey right and was pretty good on world flags.

Andrew
Didn't really speak to him.

Lorraine

That's agreed then. He stays. Keith is our 80s and 90s music man (plus he's a solid-gold car mechanic if you need one). Ajay cycles, so he covers sport, plus history. Chris is 60s and 70s music, and I pick up the literature and general-knowledge questions. You're politics, current affairs, and science.

Andrew

You want me to come next week?

Lorraine

Of course! If The Plucky Losers are going to challenge The Shadow Knights we need to assemble a full team with members who play to each other's strengths. There are two spaces left and we need to fill them with bright young quizzers.

Andrew

I'm only 34.

Lorraine

We're thinking 18–25. Ideally, gamers who watch reality TV, listen to Kiss FM, go clubbing, and have their eyes on the pulse of popular culture. Anyone at your work?

Andrew

At the council? No.

Lorraine

Be alert is all I'm saying, and if you come across someone—anyone—invite them for next Monday's quiz.

Andrew

Won't meet a soul who isn't a client between now and then.

Lorraine

And be thinking of a new name. The Plucky Losers isn't right for us anymore.

Andrew

Not good at creative things.

Lorraine

Lovely! Well, 7:30 p.m. next Monday at The Case. See you there!

Text messages between Thor's Hammer and Sue & Mal, The Case is Altered, September 24, 2019:

Thor's Hammer
Any chance of moving a bigger table to our spot by the speaker?

Sue & Mal, The Case is Altered
Why?

Thor's Hammer
We're expanding the team. It's a bit tight in that corner.

Sue & Mal, The Case is Altered
I'll see what Mal can do.

Thor's Hammer
And we're changing our team name from next Monday.

Sue & Mal, The Case is Altered
Just write the new one on the top of each answer sheet.

Thor's Hammer
The Plucky Losers isn't right for us anymore. Shakespeare said it best: "You have lost no reputation at all, unless you repute yourself such a loser." That's Othello.

Sue & Mal, The Case is Altered
I'll let Mal know you're called That's Othello now.

Thor's Hammer
No! Henceforth we are to be called The Sturdy Challengers.

Spokespersons Cycling Team WhatsApp group, September 24, 2019:

Ajay
Entries to the St. Albans 50 are open. March 21 next year. Are we signing up?

Ajay
A nice short ride out, to kick the season off?

Ajay
I can book us in today if we all confirm? Team discount 5%.

Dilip
Maybe.

Tam
Not sure.

Jemma
Might be busy that day.

Ajay
Let me know. It'll sell out fast. Ditto the cycling show on December 7. Anyone up for cycling there and back?

Ajay
It was fun last year. Anyone?

Dilip
Ajay, are you joining Chris and Lorraine's team permanently?

Ajay
You mean the pub quiz? Well, they are kind of assuming I'm on their team now. They're dead serious about beating The Shadow Knights. Asked if I knew any good quizzers we could lure to our table!

Ajay
Feel sorry for them.

Tam
So you were asked to find good quizzers and you didn't think of us?

Jemma
Cheers, mate.

Ajay
We can't all join them. We'd have eight in the team, and six is the maximum.

Dilip
Why did they ask YOU and not any of us? I'm curious.

Ajay

I asked Chris the same thing. He said you lot always looked to me for the answer after every question. He said that means you see me as the most knowledgeable member of the team.

Ajay

I'd never thought about it before, but he's right. You ALL expect me to have an answer for every question. Even when it's a subject you're well aware I know literally NOTHING about.

Ajay

It's a lot of pressure and I feel obliged to come up with an answer. Then when I get it totally wrong—because I know nothing about equestrianism, or baking, or whatever—it's ME who got it wrong. Not a criticism, but you know what I mean.

Ajay has been removed from this group

To: Let's Get Quizzical [group]
From: Sid Topliss
Date: September 24, 2019
Subject: Triumph at last

Congratulations, Team!

This is the sort of good-news email you only get to send once in a blue moon: third place in the quiz, behind Chris & Lorraine and The Shadow Knights, and with a whopping 93 points, our best score ever. Proof that if you wait long enough, greatness will find you. Thank you for your hard work against the odds too, because those were Mal's hardest questions to date. Happily, what we lacked in general knowledge, we made up for with the marathon round. We should celebrate with a meal or something.

Remember the old days, when Dave and Wendy were in charge at The Case? Jukebox, cigarette machine, peanuts trodden into the carpet, funny little fellow who'd collect the glasses all night for a free pint before closing time. Fights every week. Nancy'll tell you about the time Dave dragged Wendy through the saloon. Said she'd better go now, cos if she looked at another customer like she just looked at some chap in the bar, then she wouldn't have legs to leave. Next day at opening time she was back behind the bar as normal. All forgotten! Those were the days, eh?

I was thinking last night: it's only us six left now, from back then. Shame the boathouse and pier burned down. Then the new road was built and all but very local traffic was diverted. I wonder how much longer Mal and Sue can keep it going, I really do.

When you consider all the changes around you over the years, you can't help but think about your own life, can you? When I first drank at The Case, it was before I met Nancy. One of our early dates was in the beer garden, August bank-holiday Monday, 1983. We had our whole lives ahead of us. We could've gone anywhere, done anything. So why didn't we? Life's funny like that. You live from day to day, "in the moment" as they say now, but it's only when you look back that you realize you should've been thinking further ahead: to now, when you'd be looking back and regretting what you didn't do—when it's too late. There's no getting that time back. It's gone. Tragic. Enough to make you cry your eyes out.

Sid

To: Let's Get Quizzical [group]
From: Bunny Tyme
Date: September 26, 2019
Subject: Re: Triumph at last

George has a confession. I'm sending this email so he can't chicken out.

To: Let's Get Quizzical [group]
From: George Tyme
Date: September 26, 2019
Subject: Re: Triumph at last

When no one was looking, I glanced at my phone and got the African flags. That's why we did so well in the marathon round, not because I know all the flags. Sorry.

To: Let's Get Quizzical [group]
From: Margaret Dawson
Date: September 26, 2019
Subject: Re: Triumph at last

We never thought you knew all the flags, George, only that you had a run of lucky guesses. You "glanced" at your phone and "got" the African flags? You make it sound as if the African flags are always on your phone and you accidentally saw them! You must've googled them deliberately. Although as my Ted says, if you'd cheated properly we'd have won. Still, better not play that trick again or Mal will ban us from the quiz.
    Maggie

To: Mal Eastwood
From: Sid Topliss
Date: September 26, 2019
Subject: We cheated

Dear Mal,
I'm ashamed to tell you this, but our team cheated on Monday. It's only just come to light or I'd have let you know sooner. One of our members checked some of the flags on his phone. We hereby disqualify ourselves and assure you it won't happen again.
    Yours sincerely, Sid

Text messages between Mal and Sue Eastwood, September 26, 2019:

Mal
Sid just sent an email confessing that Let's Get Quizzical cheated on Monday. Looked at a phone for the marathon round. They came a distant third.

Sue
Oh dear! To cheat and still not win, what a shame.

Mal

A comprehensive failure! Made me chuckle anyway. What shall I say?

Sue

"Don't let it happen again"?

To: Sid Topliss
From: Mal Eastwood
Date: September 26, 2019
Subject: Re: We cheated

You came a distant third with 93 out of 140, Sid. That's not the score of a committed cheat. I won't condone it, because a single glance at your phone for one question is cheating, but the quiz is over and done with, the answer sheets have been recycled (and the recycling collected). Don't let it happen again.

Mal

To: Let's Get Quizzical [group]
From: Sid Topliss
Date: September 26, 2019
Subject: Re: Triumph at last

Safe to say that news is a blow, George. I didn't expect to hear of such behavior from you. I've told Mal and formally withdrawn our team from Monday's results. Mal was rightly shocked and disappointed, but after some lobbying from me, he agreed not to ban our team outright.

He and Sue will be watching us from now on, and rightly so. He recommends the guilty party foots the entire team's drinks bill for the next quiz night. He says this works well as a deterrent at future quizzes.

Sid

To: Let's Get Quizzical [group]
From: George Tyme
Date: September 26, 2019
Subject: Re: Triumph at last

Sorry. Drinks on me next Monday.

Text messages between Andrew and Fiona, September 27, 2019:

Andrew
This is Andrew from the housing office about the pub quiz I do on
Monday nights. I mentioned it.

Fiona
k

Andrew
The Case is Altered in Fernley at 8 p.m. this Monday.

Fiona
k

Andrew
Want to go?

Fiona
k

Andrew
Does that mean yes?

Fiona
ok

Text messages between Andrew and Lorraine, September 27, 2019:

Andrew
I've found a young person. She's in temporary accommodation. At her
"needs and expectations" interview she mentioned she'd been to a club
the night before.

Lorraine
Good! How old is she?

Andrew
19. I have to be careful, it's not the done thing to invite a client out for the night. Especially not one who's so young. It'll look really bad.

Lorraine
It's hardly a date!

Andrew
She probably won't turn up anyway.

The Sturdy Challengers Quiz Team WhatsApp group, September 27, 2019:

Thor's Hammer added Lorraine, Keith, Andrew, Ajay, and Fiona to this group

Thor's Hammer
Be we Plucky Losers? Nay! We be Sturdy Challengers to yonder Shadow Knights! Unsheath your swords and gird your groins for victory!

Fiona
who tf is this?

Fiona
Thor's Hammer? wtf?

Andrew
Sorry, Fiona, that's Chris. Why does your phone think your name is "Thor's Hammer," Chris?

Ajay
It's a great name for a phone! So this is the new quiz WhatsApp? Thanks for including me.

Thor's Hammer
Henceforth our team is The Sturdy Challengers.

Ajay
Brilliant! Cheers, Chris. See you Monday.

Thor's Hammer

Everyone please take this weekend to study: Kings & Queens of Britain, changes in postwar European geography, modern pop music, the Highway Code and Ordnance Survey symbols.

Ajay

Mal loves to throw in rounds about musicals and plays. He thinks it makes him look clever. I'll look up some Shakespeare facts!

Lorraine

Good idea, Ajay! Round one is always Today's News, so read the newspapers! Mal and Sue get the Daily Mail, so any topical stories they set come from there.

Keith

Got chatting with Mal last week. Found out he listens to Radio 2. It's where he gets inspiration for the classic tracks in the music round. I've retuned the garage radio accordingly.

Thor's Hammer

Well done, Keith! Very useful intel. Everyone, listen to Radio 2 and pay attention to the artist and title of every track played.

Andrew

Even Fiona?

Thor's Hammer

Fiona has permission to listen to her modern pop, dance, and R&B music, but the same applies: pay attention to the artist and title of each track.

Fiona

k

Andrew

She means "OK."

Lorraine

Team, you haven't met Fiona yet, but she's a young girl Andrew befriended. To our great delight, he's used his charm and charisma to talk her into bed with us. Thanks, Andy!

Andrew

I didn't "befriend" her. Just met her through work. Isn't that right, Fiona?

Fiona

k

Andrew

She's been moved into temp-acc in Fernley and I mentioned she might feel more at home in the area by joining things. That's all.

Andrew

She probably won't even show.

The Rainbow

Sam97869564
wrote a review September 28, 2019
London, United Kingdom
97 contributions, 13 helpful votes

Date visited	September 27, 2019
Visit type	on my downward journey to bankruptcy and destitution

How much??????

How can they justify £12 for a cocktail? My friend was over from Brazil and he wanted to see what a LGBT+ bar was like over here. He could've flown back to Sao Paulo and gone to one on his doorstep for what we paid. The only reason for these prices is that The Rainbow is the only decent gay bar for miles. It's here or go into London and pay West End prices as well as a taxi home. It's financial prejudice.

Response from Adrian at The Rainbow
Responded on September 28, 2019

Dear Sam97869564,
Thank you for your valuable feedback. I'm delighted you chose our establishment to treat your Brazilian friend to a night out. It's so good to know that we're the best gay bar around and that you compare it to the West End of London! The £12 cocktail you enjoyed is The Rainbow Kiss. It's our signature drink and we are exceptionally proud to offer it: a blend of exclusive mystery ingredients (available on request) over an artisanal gin base. Its premium price point reflects the quality and originality of the mix. Once tried, never forgotten, and Monday–Wednesday available at a £2 discount between the hours of 5 p.m. and 6 p.m.

Ye Olde Goat Ltd. WhatsApp group, Hertfordshire, September 30, 2019:

Sean & Adrian, The Rainbow
Welcome to a new week, my friends . . .

Mimi & Flo, Tom's Bar
Nice one!

Sue & Mal, The Case is Altered
How to turn a one-star review into a free ad.

Sean & Adrian, The Rainbow
That's my Adrian! Now, this week we're sticking with book three and doing quiz number three.

Diddy & Con, The Brace of Pheasants
Still working through the second. Quiz 91.

Peter Bond, The Lusty Lass
1st edn, 23.

Mimi & Flo, Tom's Bar
First edition, quiz one (but we're updating some of the questions).

Sean & Adrian, The Rainbow
You'll have to, Flo, that edition is years old now.

Sue & Mal, The Case is Altered
I've got a marathon round that'll test The Shadow Knights.

Diddy & Con, The Brace of Pheasants
What is it? Give us a shot!

Sue & Mal, The Case is Altered
Ah, walls have ears, Diddy, walls have ears.

THE CASE IS ALTERED PUB QUIZ

September 30, 2019

Rounds	Max points
1. Today's News	10
2. On this day in 1991	10
3. Sporting mishaps: accidents, controversies, and cheating	10
4. Literature: famous monologues	10
5. Film & TV: award-winning films and shows	10
6. Music: name the artist and song title	
(Clue: each artist is also an actor)	20
7. History & Geography of the USA	10
8. General Knowledge: ant and dec	
(The words "ant" or "dec" will appear in each answer)	10

Marathon round: Elements

Fill in all 118 elements on the periodic table　　　　118

Quiz teams and where they sat

The Sturdy Challengers
Chris & Lorraine
Ajay, Keith
Andrew, Fiona

The Shadow Knights
General Knowledge + 5

Spokespersons
Erik, Jemma
Tam, Dilip

Linda & Joe & Friends
Linda & Joe
Rita & Bailey

Let's Get Quizzical
Sid & Nancy Topliss
Bunny & George Tyme
Margaret & Ted Dawson

Ami's Manic Carrots
Jojo, Evie
Harrison, Rosie
Fliss, Bianca

Text messages between Thor's Hammer and Sue & Mal, The Case is Altered, September 30, 2019:

Thor's Hammer
Are you having a laugh, Mal?

Sue & Mal, The Case is Altered
Chris, love, you can't text while Mal's doing the quiz.

Thor's Hammer
Look around you, Sue! Who among the great unwashed clientele at The Case is Altered will know the entire periodic table BY HEART?

Sue & Mal, The Case is Altered
We'll see.

Thor's Hammer
But it's not fair!

Sue & Mal, The Case is Altered
You know as well as I do, Chris, that for the duration of the quiz, the quizmaster is God. He is all-seeing and all-knowing and, if you question him, you won't get an answer.

Thor's Hammer
I'm having a word, though, Sue. I really am this time.

Final scores out of 208

The Shadow Knights	206
The Sturdy Challengers	84
Spokespersons	70
Let's Get Quizzical	69
Ami's Manic Carrots	68
Linda & Joe & Friends	38

Text messages between Sue and Mal Eastwood, September 30, 2019:

Sue
You have to stop testing The Shadow Knights. It's spoiling the quiz for everyone else. Chris is seething.

Mal
I know. I can see his ears steaming from here. Well, it's not my fault he didn't concentrate in chemistry class.

Text messages between Thor's Hammer and Sue & Mal, The Case is Altered, September 30, 2019:

Thor's Hammer
Who has the phone? Sue or Mal?

Sue & Mal, The Case is Altered
Sue's given it to me, Chris. How can I help?

Thor's Hammer
The entire periodic table? What kind of marathon round is that?

Sue & Mal, The Case is Altered
A challenging one.

Thor's Hammer
We only got as many as we did because Andy has a mug with the noble gases on it.

Sue & Mal, The Case is Altered
There you go. The answers are all around us.

Thor's Hammer
You've never asked a single question about the periodic table in all the months you've been running the Monday quiz. You could at least have tipped me the wink.

Sue & Mal, The Case is Altered
That would give your team an unfair advantage.

Thor's Hammer
Just one question in a previous quiz and we'd have glanced at it, at least.

Sue & Mal, The Case is Altered

I can't be dishing out clues to some teams and not others, can I?

Thor's Hammer

The Shadow Knights knew what the marathon round would be. How else would they have got every element right?

Sue & Mal, The Case is Altered

The Shadow Knights clearly have the entire periodic table in the knowledge base of the team.

Thor's Hammer

Pissocks! They're either sourcing the answers at their table or seeing the questions in advance.

Sue & Mal, The Case is Altered

Neither. To my knowledge. And I watch them VERY closely.

Thor's Hammer

No offense, but how advanced is your knowledge, Mal? Perhaps they've hacked your computer. You'd be none the wiser.

Sue & Mal, The Case is Altered

I don't always use the computer. Drew the periodic-table grid with a pencil and ruler. There was no way they could've known that would be the marathon round, even if they hacked the laptop, which I'm sure they haven't, because it's wireless.

Thor's Hammer

Perhaps someone close to the quizmaster is passing information to The Shadow Knights. Someone you'd never suspect of wrongdoing . . .

Sue & Mal, The Case is Altered

If you mean my good wife, Sue, then I'll pretend I didn't read that, Chris.

Thor's Hammer

I'm not the only one who's noticed how pally she is with The General.

Sue & Mal, The Case is Altered

Sue is a first-class landlady who knows how to make customers feel welcome.

Thor's Hammer

Is that what they call it now?

Sue & Mal, The Case is Altered
The Shadow Knights give everyone something to aspire to, and that's a good thing.

Thor's Hammer
From now on, The Plucky Losers will focus on what's important: getting things right!

Sue & Mal, The Case is Altered
Thought you'd changed your name?

Thor's Hammer
I mean The Sturdy Challengers.

Text messages between Andrew and Fiona, October 1, 2019:

Andrew
Thanks for coming. You got that Love Island question straightaway, and the rest of us were clueless.

Fiona
k

Andrew
And we came second, so not a bad start for the new team. Even though we were 122 points behind The Shadow Knights.

Fiona
k

Andrew
You disappeared before I could offer you a lift. Did you get home safely?

Andrew
You got back all right?

Text messages between PCSO Arthur McCoy and Mal Eastwood, October 1, 2019:

Arthur
You awake?

Mal
Still in bed. Was that a blue light down our lane just now?

Arthur
Houseboat tried to moor up next to the old pier early this morning. Charred remains crumbled and trapped their bow.

Mal
Silly buggers! That's what you get for mooring illegally. Thanks for letting us know.

Arthur
I'd get out of bed if I were you, Mal. When the pier collapsed a whole lot of rubbish trapped under it was suddenly dislodged. A few things have come up.

Mal
Like what?

Arthur
A shopping cart, a motorbike, and a dead body. That's in the order they appeared, not in importance, according to my notes.

Mal
Sue's making tea and coffee for the forensic team. Pastries are in the oven and bacon rolls are coming down to you on a tray. You're welcome to use the toilets at The Case, and we can open up if you need a warm space to work.

Mal
Anything else at all, Arthur, and we're here for you.

Arthur
Thank you, Mal, very kind and much appreciated. Some of the team are on their way up now. I'm standing over the body, keeping an eye on it. Making sure nobody contaminates the crime scene. Very important job.

Mal
Rather you than me, Arthur. Any idea who it is?

Arthur
He doesn't look his best at the moment, Mal. Senior Investigating Officer says he's likely been underwater for a week at least. If it weren't for his puffy orange anorak filling with air, he might have stayed under—barge or no barge.

Arthur
Ask Sue to save a bacon roll for me, there's a lad.

Text messages between Lorraine and Thor's Hammer, October 1, 2019:

Lorraine
Can you talk?

Thor's Hammer
No. It's a tricky moment.

Lorraine
Sorry to interrupt you at work, but this is important. They've found a body in the river by The Case.

Lorraine
Sue says it's one of the louts who tried to join the quiz a few weeks ago.

Thor's Hammer
How does Sue know that?

Lorraine
From what she says, they've turned The Case into a police hub.

Thor's Hammer
They won't know so soon who it is. Can't text any more. Sticky situation here.

Ami's Manic Carrots WhatsApp group, October 1, 2019:

Evie
It says on the HertsNews app they've found a body in the river right by the quiz pub. 😨

Bianca
Gross!

Harrison
Have any of you been down that lane? Past the pub, right to the end? It's crazy.

Fliss
No way.

Harrison
You're walking along and suddenly there's the water. Like NO fence or signs—nothing.

Jojo
How do you know, H? Who would even go down there?

Harrison
A few weeks ago I fancied a smoke after the quiz. It was the night Mal threw those sketchies out. You'd all gone and I didn't want to stand in the bar on my own, so wandered down the lane to see what was there. It was mega-dark, creepy trees rustle all around you, like a giant monster shivering and, as the traffic fades, a gentle rhythmic lapping of the water takes over, along with the deathly creaking of old wooden beams as they're slowly consumed by the river.

Rosie
Shut UP! You DID NOT go down that lane on your own!

Evie
Argh!! You're such a horror writer, H!

Bianca
Turned the car around down there once. There's an old boathouse and jetty.

Fliss
It used to be a marina.

Evie
I don't want to go there at night anymore. Anyone know another quiz we could go to instead?

Jojo
I like The Case is Altered.

Fliss
Because it's cheap or because of The Shadow Knights?

Jojo
The Shadow Knights have made the quiz interesting, don't you think?

Harrison
They're just a quiz team.

Jojo
I know, but the room comes alive when they walk in.

Rosie
Tom's Bar runs a quiz, but that place is so expensive, we'd have to share a drink.

Bianca
The Rainbow does too, but I've never been there. Have you, Harrison?

Harrison
Yeah, but it's always rammed and like Tom's Bar: one pint, six straws. There's nothing wrong with The Case and it's the cheapest pub around.

Evie
I don't want to socialize somewhere people are murdered.

Harrison
They weren't necessarily murdered where the body was found. That lane is the perfect place to dump a body.

Fliss
How do you know it's murder? From what Harry says, they could've fallen in the water. Especially if they were wasted or high.

Harrison

Right. Or they could've washed downriver from anywhere.

Evie

Bianca, can I get a ride with you Monday?

Bianca

OK.

Rosie

Can I?

Bianca

Yep. Fliss?

Fliss

Yes please.

Text messages between Warwick Roper, General Manager of Ye Olde Goat Brewery Ltd., and Sue & Mal, The Case is Altered, October 1, 2019:

Warwick Roper, GM

Extensive coverage of The Case is Altered on HertsNews, Hertsmere Radio, and BBC Hertfordshire.

Sue & Mal, The Case is Altered

Aw, thank you, Mr. Roper. Mal and I are thrilled!

Warwick Roper, GM

"The man's decomposing body was pulled from the River Colne at Bell End, less than 100 meters from The Case is Altered pub."

Sue & Mal, The Case is Altered

Our address too! You can't buy that publicity.

Warwick Roper, GM

A dead body will drive footfall to The Case, how?

Sue & Mal, The Case is Altered

Because we're famous?

Warwick Roper, GM

"The body of a male in his forties had been pinned underwater by a large, sharp implement. Police are considering the possibility he'd been drinking in The Case is Altered immediately prior to his death."

Sue & Mal, The Case is Altered

It sounds horrible when you say it like that, but the fellow was a regular troublemaker. He terrorized the pubs around here—ask them at The Rainbow and The Brace. They've even caused a ruckus at Tom's Bar. There's a group of them. It's my guess one of his mates has done him in. Well, Mal and I, we've read the Olde Goat management manual from cover to cover and we see challenges as opportunities. This one will help us build our client base, you'll see.

Warwick Roper, GM

There's a fine line between famous and notorious. Be the former. Not the latter.

Sue & Mal, The Case is Altered

This is Mal, Mr. Roper. Sue is right. People are morbid. They want to solve crimes. Why else would there be so many crime series and documentaries on TV? If you look at our takings in the next few weeks, I guarantee there'll be an improvement.

Warwick Roper, GM

We'll see.

Text messages between Sue and Mal Eastwood, October 1, 2019:

Sue

What's happening? How close have you got?

Mal

I'm hanging around by the white tent, but no one seems up for a chat at the moment.

Sue

Where's Arthur?

Mal

Vaping by the river with someone he used to work with. I'm trying to peer in whenever I can.

Sue

Don't hamper the investigation. Be careful.

Mal

Most of the old pier has gone. Washed downriver. If that barge hadn't tried to moor up, the body would've stayed put.

Sue

Where's the barge now? Do the owners want a bacon roll?

Mal

Moored up by the old boathouse. I doubt they want a bacon roll.

Sue

Have you asked them?

Mal

No.

Sue

How do you know unless you ask?

Mal

Because their boat is called The Whittling Vegan. He makes woodcrafts, she sells crystals and "hemp products" and does tarot readings.

Sue

I'll find something vegan for them.

Sue

Where are you? Did you meet the vegans? Are they nice?

Mal

Just been looking around their houseboat. It's a floating boho palace! You've got to see it.

Sue

Bit busy. Six police need cinnamon buns warmed up and their shift is changing, so more are turning up. Remember to invite the boat people in. They're welcome to join Linda and Joe's quiz team.

Mal
Eating a sandwich made of toasted spelt bread, with scrambled tofu instead of egg.

Sue
What have they said about the body?

Mal
That the spirit of the dead man guided them to it—no one would've found him otherwise.

Sue
Did the spirit say anything else?

Mal
Apparently not. The vegans had no intention of stopping here, but ran out of logs for the burner and he thought he could nip to Morrisons.

Sue
It's a bit of a walk, especially if he has to carry logs back. Does he need a lift?

Text messages between Me [Rita] and Linda, October 1, 2019:

Me
That's always been a dodgy lane, even as a working boatyard. Remember when Pam and Eddie ran The Case? They never liked their regulars going down there, not even to park.

Linda
There was always colorful talk about what exactly those boat people did. Joe won't go down there for a smoke, even now.

Me
Bailey's the same. Not that he smokes.

Linda
How are Pam and Eddie?

Me

They live near the Iron Bridge in Shropshire now. My Olivia bumped into them a few months ago. They asked how the new landlords were getting on and it sounded as if they thought the place was a hopeless case.

Linda

A hopeless CASE!

Me

I told her, they'd never run a pub before—and it showed at first—but they learned and now they're slowly getting it back to what it was in the old days us codgers talk about.

Me

Where else would we go of an evening?

Linda

Isn't it funny that Sue and Mal came *down* here from up north, while Pam and Eddie moved *up* north when they retired. It's like they swapped places. They're such a lovely couple, Sue and Mal, I hope they can keep it going.

Me

They do their best, but we're the last of the old regulars and I doubt any of the young folk who turn up for the quiz will be as loyal as we are.

Extract from a witness statement made by Malcolm Eastwood, October 1, 2019:

My name is Malcolm Eastwood and I am landlord at The Case is Altered, where I share tenancy with my wife, Suzanne.

On the evening of September 2, 2019, I was about to start our weekly pub quiz, when a group of customers came in. I realized immediately that they were notorious local troublemakers, known for rowdy behavior and cheating. While I'd never seen them before, we swap information with other publicans in the area and I recognized them from their descriptions.

I knew that if I allowed them to stay they would spoil the night for everyone, so I asked them to leave. The woman and two of the men duly retreated outside. However the man in the orange puffy anorak stood his ground, so I bundled him out quickly. Then, in the small space between our two sets of entrance doors, he and I were alone. We exchanged insults and several light punches. After some awkward grappling we both stumbled outside and the man lurched off. By then he was clearly resigned to being barred. He had not, to my knowledge, sustained any blows to the head or other serious injury, and was not disorientated or really any the worse for our little scuffle. His friends had already slunk away.

I was winded and didn't want to return to the bar before I was back to my usual self, so I sat for a minute or two on a bench in the ale-house garden to get my breath back. I also rinsed my hands under the outdoor tap. I'm not sure how long I was there. It could have been ten minutes or more. The troublemakers hadn't returned by the time I went back inside so I assumed they'd gone back up Bell End toward the main road. However, as I was reentering the pub and glanced back over my shoulder, I thought I caught a glimpse of the orange jacket through the trees, which made me wonder for a moment if they'd gone off into the woods rather than up the lane. I made a mental note to call the police immediately rather than deal with it myself if any of them tried to come back, though that didn't happen. My wife had called our local PCSO in my absence and he arrived shortly after. The quiz night continued without further incident.

I am very disturbed to hear the body pulled from the river this morning was wearing an orange anorak and could be the man I threw out of the pub that night. If indeed it is, I have no idea how he ended up there. The last I saw of him, he seemed perfectly healthy and nowhere near the water.

Text messages between Thor's Hammer and Sue & Mal, The Case is Altered, October 2, 2019:

Thor's Hammer
What's this about a body at The Case?

Sue & Mal, The Case is Altered

It was in the river. The police have taken him away now, but they've still got their tape up and you can't go down there. We're open as usual, though.

Thor's Hammer

It's the fellow Mal chucked out of the quiz—that's what Lor heard.

Sue & Mal, The Case is Altered

Well, that man wore an orange anorak, and the body was wearing an orange anorak, but that's more circumstantial than forensic, so Mal says.

Thor's Hammer

Ho-ho-ho! I bet he does.

Sue & Mal, The Case is Altered

This is Mal. What do you mean, Chris?

Thor's Hammer

If the boys in blue hear that you and an orange thug had a scuffle, you'll be in the frame, mate. Better not book a foreign vacation till you've cleared your name.

Sue & Mal, The Case is Altered

I've already given my statement to the boys in blue and told them all about the scuffle. In any case, they can look at my bank balance and decide whether I can afford to bump off potential customers.

Sue & Mal, The Case is Altered

Arthur's requested details of who was quizzing here that night, so you could be asked to make a witness statement. It might take them a while to get around to you, mind.

Thor's Hammer

Did you see the body?

Sue & Mal, The Case is Altered

No, but the lady vegan from the barge did, and she said it had been run through with a big rusty spike. Someone wanted to make sure he stayed under.

Thor's Hammer

No one with any sense. It's popped up within weeks! Where would you even get a piece of kit like that?

Sue & Mal, The Case is Altered

No idea, Chris, but IF it's the same fellow, at least our quiz should be undisturbed from now on.

Thor's Hammer

Speaking of which, anything you want to say about next week's marathon round?

Sue & Mal, The Case is Altered

No.

Thor's Hammer

Every Olympic gold-medal winner of the modern age? American states and their capitals, in reverse alphabetical order? Every bone in the human body from the big toe up?

Sue & Mal, The Case is Altered

Good ideas, but no.

Thor's Hammer

Remember that first week you and Sue opened The Case? I do. I remember a pair of blue-arsed flies with all the gear and no idea. If it wasn't for me, showing you how to change your barrels and check your beer lines, The Case would be a soft drink shop to this day.

Sue & Mal, The Case is Altered

You can count on a taxing marathon round, Chris. That is all.

Extract from a witness statement made by Christopher Thorogood from The Sturdy Challengers, October 3, 2019:

I was quizzing at The Case with my team the night a chap waltzed in with his mates and had a row with Mal. I'd not seen any of them before and certainly didn't know them. It held things up by at least twenty minutes but we won the quiz by two points, so no big deal in the end.

I was concentrating on giving my team a pep talk, so first I knew of it was when Mal thundered out from behind the bar. I barely caught sight of the orange anorak everyone's talking about. It was a month ago and since then we've had a lot on our plate. The Shadow Knights started coming to the quiz, stole our table, and have been running away with the win every week. It's not fair and Mal knows how I feel about them. We're upping our game, but if they're cheating then what chance do we have? Sorry, yep. We left at the usual time, about half ten, something like that. Didn't see anyone, hear anything, nothing. The lane was as dark and quiet as it always is.

The Sturdy Challengers Quiz Team WhatsApp group, October 4, 2019:

Thor's Hammer
I've given my statement to an officer of Her Majesty's police force. Mal said they'll be in touch about September 2nd so get your stories straight!

Thor's Hammer
That's a joke.

Andrew
They won't want my statement. It happened before I joined the team.

Thor's Hammer
Mal said something else: You can COUNT on a taxing marathon round. Just a thought, but everyone brush up on your math.

Lorraine
Times tables. Prime numbers. What else is there?

Andrew
The clue might not be in "count," it might be in "tax." Name all the current tax codes.

Ajay
Don't even know my own tax code. The tax clue might be vaguer, like: "Name every chancellor of the exchequer since World War II."

Thor's Hammer

That's an easy one to study. Everyone get googling and give the list a glance before tonight.

Lorraine

An anagram of "marathon" is "ha matron." Name all the Carry On films in order!

Thor's Hammer

I've put "You can count on a taxing marathon round" into an anagram solver and it says: "Hoax contumacity on an orangutan."

Lorraine

"Contumacity" means "deliberate disobedience to authority."

Thor's Hammer

Hoax contumacity. Fake disobedience to authority. Where does the orangutan come in? Think, everyone, think!

Andrew

We don't know it's an anagram—or do we?

Ajay

"Orangutan" means "old man of the forest." I trekked through Malaysia in 2007.

Thor's Hammer

Thank you, Ajay! "Old man of the forest, your disobedience to authority is fake."

Thor's Hammer

I'm not getting any clues out of that. Anyone?

Fiona

time

Thor's Hammer

A marathon round about time?

Andrew

She means "tears in my eyes."

Lorraine

Oh dear. What have we said to upset her?

Andrew

Tears of laughter.

Thor's Hammer

Everyone, study what you can, ready for Monday night. If you're driving, remember the lane might still be cordoned off, so park out on the main road and walk down.

THE CASE IS ALTERED PUB QUIZ

October 7, 2019

Rounds	Max points
1. Today's News	10
2. On this day in 2002	10
3. Sporting accolades: who won what?	10
4. Literature: five-word plots—guess the play	10
5. Film & TV: for a bonus 5 points, guess the connection	15
6. Music, 90s special: name the artist and song title	20
7. Where in the world? (Each answer starts with the next letter of the alphabet to the answer before, so try to get the first answer correct!)	10
8. Famous liars, cheats, and deceptions	10

Marathon round: Counties

Name all 48 ceremonial counties of England   48

Quiz teams and where they sat

The Sturdy Challengers
Chris & Lorraine
Ajay, Keith
Andrew, Fiona

The Shadow Knights
General Knowledge + 5

Spokespersons
Erik, Jemma
Tam, Dilip

Linda & Joe & Friends
Linda & Joe
Rita & Bailey
Cloud & Wind

Let's Get Quizzical
Sid & Nancy Topliss
Bunny & George Tyme
Margaret & Ted Dawson

Ami's Manic Carrots
Jojo, Evie
Harrison, Rosie
Fliss, Bianca

Final scores out of 143
The Shadow Knights   141
The Sturdy Challengers   130
Let's Get Quizzical   104
Spokespersons   98
Ami's Manic Carrots   87
Linda & Joe & Friends   66

Text messages between Thor's Hammer and Sue & Mal, The Case is Altered, October 7, 2019:

Thor's Hammer
You could have put "count" between asterisks or something. Just so we knew "count" was the clue.

Sue & Mal, The Case is Altered
This is Sue. What do you mean, Chris?

Thor's Hammer
Mal said: You can count on a taxing marathon round. We focused on math, tax, and orangutans.

Sue & Mal, The Case is Altered
Never mind the marathon round. That poor young girl on your team is HOMELESS! We got chatting during the intermission. Her mom's in hospital, her dad's nonexistent, and she lives in a bed-and-breakfast hostel.

Thor's Hammer
I know. Andy met her through his work.

Sue & Mal, The Case is Altered
You knew and didn't offer her somewhere to live?

Thor's Hammer
She's not our responsibility. Andy's looking for a studio flat for her—I heard them talking.

Sue & Mal, The Case is Altered
Well, he can stop looking. As of now, she's staying at The Case in our spare bedroom. Mal will give her a lift to college.

Text messages between Mal and Sue Eastwood, October 7, 2019:

Mal
Is this wise?

Sue
YES!

Mal

We're taking in strays now?

Sue

That poor girl needs a proper bed and a room of her own, not some filthy B&B. It's only until she's back on her feet.

Mal

If you say so.

Sue

Don't be so grumpy! She can help us out behind the bar. She's studying hospitality and this will be hands-on experience of a working pub.
Anyway, what were you doing giving Chris a clue to the marathon round?

Mal

I didn't.

Sue

He said you told him to "count" on a taxing marathon round and that was a clue to the "ceremonial counties" question.

Mal

I said that, but it wasn't a clue. How is that a clue?

Sue

I don't know, but if word gets out there'll be trouble.

Text messages between Sue Eastwood and The General, October 8, 2019:

Sue

This is Sue from The Case is Altered. Well done on another resounding victory, General!

The General

Thank you, Sue.

Sue

I meant to congratulate you last week too, only your team leaves so quickly after the final score I didn't get the chance. It would be nice to have a longer chat sometime.

The General

Thank you.

Sue

The Shadow Knights aced that quiz. You knew the entire periodic table. We weren't expecting that.

The General

No one expects the entire periodic table.

Sue

Then last night you rattled off all 48 ceremonial counties of England and we weren't expecting that either.

The General

When Dmitri Mendeleev created the periodic table in 1869, he left gaps for elements that hadn't yet been discovered. He was a genius of course and knew many things. But he was also humble, because he realized and accepted there were many things he didn't know.

Sue

That's nice. You're welcome at The Case any night. We could have a proper chat another day, if you fancy it.

The General

Sue, may I ask you something?

Sue

Of course.

The General

The Sturdy Challengers: Chris and Lorraine. Something's happened there. Am I right?

Sue

How do you mean?

Sue

Yes, love. It has.

Text messages between Sue and Mal Eastwood, October 8, 2019:

Sue

Then he said, "Something's happened there. Am I right?" So I said yes. I was thinking of what happened to them, but now I wonder if he meant Chris's work—you know how top secret it is.

Sue

Hope I haven't put my foot in it with The General. I like our chats when he orders drinks for the table.

Sue

Wouldn't you think if he had a question about anything, it would be about the body? It's all anyone else is talking about.

Mal

You texted The General. On your phone, not the pub phone.

Sue

So?

Mal

Why?

Sue

Why not? Just passing the time of day.

Mal

You don't "pass the time of day" with any of our other customers.

Sue

I want The Shadow Knights to feel welcome, so they keep coming to the quiz.

Mal

The Shadow Knights are upsetting our valuable regulars, and therefore me.

Sue

Chris shouldn't be so childish, and neither should you! It's only a quiz.

Mal

I'll pretend I didn't read that last bit.

Sue

The General is very, very nice and I enjoy his banter when he comes to the bar. If I want to chat with him on my personal phone, I will.

Mal

I see.

Sue

What do you mean?

Mal

The General is tall, he's good-looking. A bit of a twinkle in the eye. If I was that way inclined, I might fancy him myself.

Sue

I do NOT "fancy" The General!

Mal

Fancy him all you like—then remember how happily married you are.

Sue

What's it looking like down there in the shed?

Mal

Manny and Mark moved things around in here when they worked on the bike racks. They'll remember the rusty spike that used to stick out of the machine like a flagpole.

Sue

We should tell Arthur it came from our shed.

Mal

No point. Anyone could've taken it out at any time—the lock's always been dodgy. Anyway we've given our statements to the police and never mentioned it.

Mal

No one would be any the wiser if those whittling vegans hadn't literally barged their way into our lives.

Sue

Very nice they are too, and lovely of them to join the quiz last night.

Text messages between Linda and Sue & Mal, The Case is Altered, October 8, 2019:

Linda
That couple from the barge?

Sue & Mal, The Case is Altered
They live on a houseboat and sell hemp, if you want some.

Linda
Are they really called Cloud and Wind, Sue?

Sue & Mal, The Case is Altered
This is Mal. I had a very interesting chat with them when they arrived, followed by a tasty spelt bread and tofu brunch. When they met, he felt he'd finally found someone to give him energy and direction. So instead of a wedding, they had a renaming ceremony—she's the Wind, he's the Cloud.

Linda
In that case, from now on Joe is the Cart and I'm the Horse, because I've been dragging that man around like a dead weight for years.

Sue & Mal, The Case is Altered
Linda, you and Joe are the most devoted couple we know! I'm only sorry the boat people didn't improve your quiz score.

Linda
We go to The Case for the company and the chat, not the quiz. Heard any more about the dead man, Mal?

Sue & Mal, The Case is Altered
It's Sue now. No, we haven't. I doubt they'll tell us much more.

Linda
Wind said there's negative energy trapped down the lane, and when she walked through it on her way up to The Case, she had a strong sense that medieval atrocities were carried out there. She said perhaps there was a ducking stool where the old boatyard and pier used to be.

Sue & Mal, The Case is Altered
Well, you and Joe won't be coming to The Case for the chat again, if that's what Wind was talking about!

Linda
I wonder if she's right, though, Sue?

Sue & Mal, The Case is Altered
It's Mal again. Now don't you go spreading rumors about ducking stools at The Case, Linda. We want female customers to feel welcome here.

Story from HertsNews, October 11, 2019:

Murdered man named as former actor

The man whose body was discovered beneath a disused wooden pier on the River Colne has been named as Luke Goode (43), a former actor who lived in Nimrod Close, Hertford, and had been missing since the night of September 2. His partner, Stephanie Young, paid tribute to him by saying that he was a caring man with no enemies in the world. "We are devastated at his loss and ask that anyone with information about what happened to him come forward to solve this terrible crime."

The police say that information can be passed anonymously to the investigating team via the usual Crimestoppers number.

Ye Olde Goat Ltd. WhatsApp group, Hertfordshire, October 11, 2019:

Sean & Adrian, The Rainbow
"No enemies in the world"? They should speak to our door team!

Diddy & Con, The Brace of Pheasants
Is it definitely the fella from The Cheats?

Sue & Mal, The Case is Altered
It's definitely him.

Sean & Adrian, The Rainbow
Explains why he slayed at karaoke. Trained actor.

Peter Bond, The Lusty Lass
Your sins will find you.

Mimi & Flo, Tom's Bar
If the last you saw of them was when you booted them all out, and that's the night he went missing, then the other Cheats might know what happened.

Sue & Mal, The Case is Altered
He was with two men and a woman, all of them drunk and loud. It's possible they went down the lane to the river, got in a fight, then tried to hide the body. Whatever happened, I'm sure it'll all be forgotten soon.

Mimi & Flo, Tom's Bar
How did your audit go, Diddy?

Diddy & Con, The Brace of Pheasants
Mr. Roper grilled us all day, then left with not a hint as to whether we'd passed muster or not. That man has the management skills of a rhino.

Sean & Adrian, The Rainbow
Aw, sorry, guys. If it's any consolation, he's the same with us and we've grown our net profits more consistently than any pub I've ever worked in.

Mimi & Flo, Tom's Bar
This is the silly thing. We know we've had a good year, but he still makes you feel like you're doing CPR on a gasping business.

Diddy & Con, The Brace of Pheasants
Our year's been OK. Not much better than last, but no worse. Don't know whether I should say, but he hinted that Ye Olde Goat is looking to open a new theme bar. Asked how we'd feel if they wanted to rebrand the Brace.

Mimi & Flo, Tom's Bar
What sort of theme bar?

Sean & Adrian, The Rainbow

Not LGBTQ+. The Rainbow is THE destination pub for Hertfordshire's LGBTQ+ community. There's no room for another in the county.

Mimi & Flo, Tom's Bar

And we're THE gastropub. We're less than two miles away from The Brace—the market for fine, edgy dining isn't that big.

Peter Bond, The Lusty Lass

Competition is the thief of joy.

Sean & Adrian, The Rainbow

What exactly did he say?

Diddy & Con, The Brace of Pheasants

He only said it in passing and didn't mention a theme.

Sean & Adrian, The Rainbow

The Brace is already a theme bar. It's The Lusty Lass and The Case that might be in for a revamp.

Sue & Mal, The Case is Altered

Oh no, love. I hope not. All that disruption, and it might not make any difference to our takings.

Sean & Adrian, The Rainbow

There's no sports bar in their chain, as far as I know. No American-style diner either.

Sue & Mal, The Case is Altered

Neither of those would work here.

Mimi & Flo, Tom's Bar

Or maybe one of those family pubs with a ball pit and jungle gym.

Peter Bond, The Lusty Lass

Fun and games.

Diddy & Con, The Brace of Pheasants

That'll be a scare tactic to keep us working hard at the grind.

Sue & Mal, The Case is Altered

I really hope so, Diddy. It might not look like much to outsiders, but we're rooted here now. We love The Case as it is. We're turning it around too. Gradually.

Text messages between Andrew and Fiona, October 11, 2019:

Andrew
I've been calling all day. Please pick up.

Andrew
If you don't pick up, I'll have to go to the B&B to look for you, and The Arches is right over on the other side of the borough.

Andrew
I'm at The Arches. Can you hear me and the duty manager knocking on your door? Please answer or pick up. If not, I'll track you down at college. You don't want that.

Andrew
I'm at the college, but classes have finished. No one here knows anything about anything. Literally there's no record of whether you attended classes today or not. You could've been abducted by aliens. Unbelievable.

Andrew
I'm back at The Arches and will make them open your room. Sorry, but I can't think what else to do. Please, Fiona, PLEASE respond.

Andrew
Your room is empty and the man I thought was the duty manager is a resident with delusions of grandeur. The real duty manager is super pissed off.

Andrew
Posted a "missing person" alert on the Hertsmere intranet.

Andrew
Contacted social services, who have started their search process. Is your social worker Seema, Sheena, or Aseema—I obviously didn't catch the name, and when I called back and asked for her again, no one had *any idea whatsoever* who I wanted to speak to. WTF?

Andrew

You've obviously moved out of The Arches so I'm driving around all the stations, bus garages, hospitals, and hangouts asking for you.

Andrew

If you're OK, Fiona, please send me a text. Just a "k" to let me know you're all right.

Andrew

Posted your pic on Facebook, Instagram, and Twitter, asking anyone who's seen you to get in touch.

Andrew

Your police "missing" picture has gone viral in Hertfordshire and Bedfordshire. Please contact anyone you know and tell them to call the police, to say you're OK.

Andrew

It's my final line of inquiry: I'm ringing the pub to see if they saw you leave with anyone after the quiz.

Andrew

I don't appreciate the phone being put down on me. Not after the day I've had.

Andrew

How can you answer the pub phone but not your own?

Andrew

So I've finally stood down all the emergency services and am back at my desk, with all today's work still here waiting for me. So firstly, your housing application.

Andrew

If you'd mentioned you were thinking of moving into the pub, I'd have advised you to NOT do that. I can change your status to "living with friends or family," but it knocks you back down the priority list.

Andrew

I've let social services know you've moved. No one has any idea who those publicans are. They could be serial killers running an international organ-trafficking operation, for all we know. But there you are, moved in and living with them.

Andrew
Now my line manager has sent a curt email highlighting a paragraph in my contract that says I should pass missing clients to her, not pursue them myself. But she works from home on the Isle of Man, 500 miles and a ferry ride away! There's literally no one else here who CARES.

Fiona
time 😂

Text messages between Andrew and Sue & Mal, The Case is Altered, October 11, 2019:

Andrew
I just wish someone had mentioned it to me.

Sue & Mal, The Case is Altered
I'm sorry, love. I didn't think we'd need to let anyone know. She told us she's nineteen.

Andrew
She IS nineteen.

Sue & Mal, The Case is Altered
I was married at nineteen.

Andrew
With no family and a background in care, she's a vulnerable person and will be for years yet.

Sue & Mal, The Case is Altered
Oh, I see. Yes, we're very sorry. I hated the thought of her alone in a grubby B&B. What should we do? Don't tell me we have to kick her out.

Andrew
There's another tenant moving into her room at The Arches. I can shuffle her paperwork, but still, it'll delay the process. Something else for today's workload.

Sue & Mal, The Case is Altered

Thank you, love. She's settled in the spare room and helps Mal with the bottling up.

Andrew

Are you paying her for that work? Sorry to sound harsh, but I have to tick a box about exploitation on the form.

Sue & Mal, The Case is Altered

Oh, Andy, bless you. Fiona isn't exploiting us! She's happy to pitch in for bed and board, and Mal will give her a lift to college and back. No one wants to feel like a charity case, do they?

Andrew

That's not what I meant, but OK. Well, I can check on her every Monday at the quiz.

Sue & Mal, The Case is Altered

You're a big part of Chris and Lorraine's team now. I know they appreciate it.

Andrew

Happened by accident. Not sure if I go every week because I enjoy it or because I don't want to let them down.

Sue & Mal, The Case is Altered

Fine by us, either way! How do you know them?

Andrew

A community litter pickup nine years ago. Sorry, the casework's looming over me. Then I have to study backyard birds and international time zones. I'll see you on Monday, and if Fiona gives you any trouble, let me know.

Extract from a witness statement made by Dilip Ghosh from The Spokespersons, October 11, 2019:

I cycle to the Monday quiz with my friends: Erik, Jemma, and Tamsin. Ajay used to quiz with us, but he switched to Chris and Lorraine's team a few weeks ago. I don't know why because we've all cycled together for years but . . . He still rides with us, there and back. I don't remember much about the quiz on September 2, only the incident with the vagrants. Probably because it's unusual so it sticks in my mind. I've not seen any of those people before or since.

It all happened just before the quiz began so everything was late starting—and finishing—that night. There was a twenty-minute delay at least, so while we'd usually get back out on the road at 10:30 p.m. we were closer to 11 p.m., which was annoying because it's Monday and if you're out late it makes you tired for the rest of the week. I'm a surveyor and we've got a lot on at the moment.

Afterward I felt guilty. Like we should've got up and helped Mal deal with the troublemakers, but it all happened so quickly. Literally, as soon as they came through the door he shooed them out. When he came back in he was shaken up and it crossed my mind things had got nasty outside. I saw he had grazed knuckles but he looked victorious, if you know what I mean. Proud of himself that he got rid of them.

There's only one other thing I remember that might be relevant. Don't know whether I should say because it might be nothing, but later, when we were getting our bikes off the rack, I saw the guy from the Manic Carrots come out of the pub. He didn't turn left to walk up the lane, but right toward the river. He seemed in a hurry too. I barely clocked it at the time, but why was he going the wrong way, and at nearly 11 p.m.? I don't know him, so I've never asked.

Spokespersons Cycling Team WhatsApp group, October 11, 2019:

Erik
Has everyone given their statements to the police now?

Dilip
Yep. Told them I didn't see anything that night.

Jemma
Same and same.

Tam
Thought it would be scary or exciting, but it was really mundane.

Erik

Life goes on, right? The pub is still open, the quiz went ahead Monday.

Dilip

We'd definitely have got more counties if Ajay was still in the team. He used to drive for DHL.

Tam

We're WAY down the table without him. Even Let's Get Quizzical beat us.

Jemma

It's like he's been with The Plucky Losers forever.

Dilip

The Sturdy Challengers. They changed their name, remember.

Erik

You can call a horse a duck, but you can't make it quack.

Tam

Why did he switch teams anyway? None of them cycle.

Dilip

They don't even look like runners.

Erik

Good news about the protein drinks. Thanks, Tam.

Tam

Extract from a witness statement made by Harrison Walker from Ami's Manic Carrots, October 11, 2019:

I remember when four sketchies tried to crash the quiz. Sketchies? Rough and disheveled, rowdy with drink or drugs. The type you're wary of because they're unpredictable. I didn't know them and they weren't quiz regulars. Heard them before they even got through the door. Shouting something like, "Oy, oy, oy! The goon squad are here!" One of them had a really booming voice, quite threatening. He was first in and he wore a bright orange puffer jacket, the color you get in

TK Maxx because it doesn't sell at full price, and a pair of Converse so ancient the uppers had come away. Strange what you notice, isn't it? He had sores on his face and knuckles, and his teeth were . . . The sort of person you should feel sorry for, but they're trouble, so you don't. I feel bad about that, especially now . . .

Anyway, Sue was about to hand out the marathon round. She was like me and the girls, she froze, but Mal stormed over, face like thunder. "Oh no you're not!" he said, or something like that. You could tell he's used to dealing with drunk people, because he didn't hesitate or seem fazed. Bundled them all out and that was that.

He was gone for a while, so the quiz was late, but the sketchies never came back. The rest of the night was pretty usual as far as I remember.

Text messages between Sue and Mal Eastwood, October 12, 2019:

Sue
Why did you cut me off just then? I only asked what Arthur wanted on a Saturday.

Mal
Fiona was there. We don't want her to worry. Arthur was just giving me an update. He's in the middle of taking witness statements from our customers.

Sue
Been thinking. That night was the last quiz BTSK. Before The Shadow Knights.

Sue
Or put another way: Luke Goode was killed and at the very next quiz The Shadow Knights appeared.

Mal
Stop it! No connection. No connection at all.

Text messages between Sue and Mal Eastwood, October 14, 2019:

Sue

The Shadow Knights are here. All six. Not one has missed a quiz yet and they've been coming for weeks.

Sue

The General is always polite and friendly. All of them nod and smile. Nice people.

Mal

We don't know any of their names.

Sue

The General—General Knowledge. Everyone calls him that. You're right, we don't know the others' names. He buys all the drinks, and when I go up to the table to collect the papers or ask them anything, he's the one that answers.

Mal

You've been chatting up The General every week; ask their names.

Sue

I have NOT been chatting anyone up! Anyway I'd have to check the data-protection laws.

Mal

Say it's for a prize draw or something. In fact you don't have to say it's for anything. Just ask them their names. If they refuse to tell you, that's downright suspicious.

THE CASE IS ALTERED PUB QUIZ

October 14, 2019

Rounds	Max points
1. Today's News	10
2. On this day in 2012	10
3. Sport	10
4. Who wrote it? (Name the author or playwright and, for a bonus point, whether they are dead or alive)	20
5. TV sitcoms of the 1970s	10
6. Music: name the artist and song title	20
7. Which year? Name the year this happened	10
8. Who said it? 10 famous quotes	10

Marathon round: Landmarks

Identify 50 pictures of famous international landmarks	50

Quiz teams and where they sat

The Sturdy Challengers
Chris & Lorraine
Ajay, Keith
Andrew, Fiona

Spokespersons
Erik, Jemma
Tam, Dilip

Let's Get Quizzical
Sid & Nancy Topliss
Bunny & George Tyme
Margaret & Ted Dawson

The Shadow Knights
General Knowledge, Brigitte
Pamela, Lynette
Edward, Wilfred

Linda & Joe & Friends
Linda & Joe
Rita & Bailey
Cloud & Wind

Ami's Manic Carrots
Jojo, Evie
Harrison, Rosie
Fliss, Bianca

Final scores out of 150

The Shadow Knights	149
The Sturdy Challengers	133
Let's Get Quizzical	130
Spokespersons	118
Linda & Joe & Friends	91
Ami's Manic Carrots	89

The Sturdy Challengers Quiz Team WhatsApp group, October 15, 2019:

Thor's Hammer
Well done, team, we're starting to close the gap between us and The Shadow Knights. Only sixteen points difference. We may not have had the exact questions and topics we'd studied, but there's been an effect: your minds have started to absorb more detail and retrieve it faster. Give us a few more weeks and we'll be right up there with the SKs.

Lorraine
We ALL played a role in last night's score. There was a question for each of us, that only we knew and no one else in the team did. Isn't that right, Chris?

Thor's Hammer
Yep. More or less.

Ajay
Cheers, Chris and Lorraine. I'm setting the box to record all the quizzes this week: The Chase, Tipping Point, Countdown, Pointless, and House of Games. It's a good way to get in quiz mode.

Thor's Hammer
Agreed. Thanks, Ajay.

Andrew
When are they on? I'm working late all week.

Lorraine
You don't have to watch them live. You can stream them or watch old episodes, they're screened all the time on the repeat channels.

Keith
You're aiming at the waist, mate. University Challenge, Only Connect, Mastermind. Then try Counterpoint or Brain of Britain on Radio 4. Get old eps on BBC Sounds. That's my secret.

Thor's Hammer
Good point, Keith. Any episode of any quiz you watch will be useful. Not just for the questions and answers but for the sheer act of quizzing. Get in the groove. Train your brain. Nudge those neurons. Hype your hippocampus.

Lorraine
That's the part of your brain that helps you learn and remember things.

Thor's Hammer
Right: everyone get to The Case, next Monday, 7 p.m., to secure our table and continue our streak TO THE TOP!

Extract from a witness statement made by Evelyn Cavanagh from Ami's Manic Carrots, October 15, 2019:

I used to go by bus and walk down the lane from the main road, but ever since the body, Bianca has picked me up. She picks Rosie and Fliss up too now. Jojo drives straight from her work and if Bianca can't make the quiz she'll pick us up, but Harrison comes from the other direction so he gets there and back by bus. I won't go to that pub on foot now, not even in summer.

That night was horrible. I remember texting Bianca about it afterward because she wasn't there. A gang I'd never seen before burst in. Everyone froze, except Mal. He marched over and threw them out, but there was four of them so if they'd got nasty he might have been really hurt. He was lucky that night.

He came back after about fifteen minutes, then a police officer arrived, but it'd all calmed down by then. The quiz finished later than usual so Fliss, Rosie, and I had to run up the lane to catch our bus. Harrison must've known he'd missed his, because he stayed behind. I don't remember him running up the lane with us, anyway.

I'm really shocked to hear about the body. If it wasn't for the quiz team I'd never go there ever again. I'm saving up for driving lessons, because it's too dangerous at night.

Ami's Manic Carrots WhatsApp group, October 15, 2019:

Jojo
Last again. Sigh.

Fliss
It's not about winning.

Rosie
We were never going to get all those landmarks.

Harrison
Those new vanilla protein shakes are nice.

Evie
I was creeped out all evening. Knowing that body was found just along
the lane gives me the creeps. The police officer who took our statements
was super-reassuring, but still.

Jojo
It's really bwwwergh being "the team that's always bottom." Like we're
thickoes.

Rosie
Linda & Joe only beat us by a couple of points.

Jojo
Exactly. Everyone looks down on them and us. We're the teams that make
up the numbers.

Bianca
It's a boomer quiz. Set by boomers for boomers. No one expects us to
know shit from the last century.

Fliss
No one expects Linda & Joe to REMEMBER shit from the last century.

Evie
I like not feeling any pressure. I can simply enjoy a night out with my
friends. Or I did before the murder.

Harrison
Aw, love you, Evie.

Fliss
We don't go to the quiz to show off.

Harrison

If we started getting great scores we'd feel more pressure, and pressure creates anxiety.

Fliss

This 👆

Jojo

It would be nice not to be LAST all the time. I'm just saying, that's all.

Harrison

You'll have to impress The Shadow Knights some other way, Jojo.

Text messages between Sue and Mal Eastwood, October 15, 2019:

Sue

Brigitte, Lynette, Pamela, Edward, and Wilfred. Plus The General, of course.

Mal

The Shadow Knights?

Sue

I expected them to have mysterious medieval monikers, like in Lord of the Rings.

Mal

Notice The General didn't reveal his.

Sue

They all call him "General." I hear them from the bar.

Mal

149 out of 150. The only one they got wrong was a landmark pic that I put in to fool them.

Sue

What? Don't do that! It's not fair on the rest of the quizzers. Especially when it's the marathon. They waste time on the trick question and have less left for the real ones.

Sue

Which question was it?

Mal

Number eleven.

Sue

I'm looking at it now. No idea. What is it?

Mal

It's a deceiving angle on that rusty farm machine in the shed. I cropped it from a pic I took when I first thought about making bike racks out of it. With that spike against the sky, it looks much bigger than it is.

Sue

But that's THE spike! What are you playing at?

Mal

No one knows that but us! Most put tall buildings. The Burj Khalifa, the Empire State, The Shard. I can see why. A lot of those big fellas have spiky antennae on top.

Sue

What did The Shadow Knights put?

Mal

Nothing. They left it blank. As if they knew it was a trick question.

Sue

What did you say it was, when you read out the answers? I don't remember you admitting it was fake.

Mal

I said it was the top of an unfinished tower on the Sagrada Familia in Barcelona.

Sue

Be careful!

Mal

How else do I level the playing field? If The Shadow Knights win all the time, sooner or later the other teams will get fed up and go elsewhere.

Sue

I have an idea. A round that doesn't test knowledge, education, math, or memory.

Mal

What does it test?

Sue

We'll talk about it in the morning.

Extract from a police interview with Stephanie Young, October 16, 2019:

Interviewing officer: PCSO Arthur McCoy

AM: Sorry to meet you under such tragic circumstances, Stephanie. Thank you for chatting with me.

SY: Why's it taking so long? It's been two weeks since Lukey was found and this is the first time you've asked me to come in. Not even called me.

AM: I've been calling the number we have for you but I'm afraid today's the first time you've picked up.

SY: Oh, yeah. The charger I borrowed was faulty. Been too upset to answer anyway.

AM: How are you?

SY: Still in shock. Can't believe Lukey's not here anymore. Keep meaning to go where he was found, put some flowers down, and light a candle in his memory. Can't seem to get my act together.

AM: I know, it's hard. I won't keep you long, but we do need to hear your account of what happened on the night of September 2.

SY: I can't remember, that was ages ago . . .

AM: The night Luke disappeared. The last time you saw him.

SY: Oh, right. Last time I saw him's a bit hazy. We were barred from the pub, which wasn't fair. How can they bar us when we've never even been there before? The quiz was busy too so would've been a good pot to win. Maybe twenty pounds even.

AM: Who was that? Who's the "we" you're talking about there?

SY: Me and Luke, Micky and Fezza. They're both on house arrest and didn't want trouble. When we were chucked out Fezza said "Fuck it, I'm walking back," because he thought his dealer owed him a fiver. Micky said he'd go with him. It's miles away and if we weren't gonna pick up quiz winnings . . . I didn't wanna miss curfew at the hostel for no reason.

AM: And Luke? What did he do after you'd been ejected from the pub?

SY: Luke had a scrap with the barman, so he was last up the lane. He kept looking back at the pub, sort of puzzled. Said he'd seen some man he knew and was gonna wait and speak to them later. I asked how much they owed him, and he laughed.

AM: He laughed?

SY: Yeah, so I said, "Well, you watch out for that barman, because he's landed one on you already. Keep out his way."

AM: The barman?

SY: Bloke who chased us out the pub. I could see him then, through the trees, rinsing his knuckles under the outside tap. Lukey said, "Yeah yeah, I'll see you later." I said, "Aw, come with us, babe," but he lost it and said, "Away, you filthy bung, away!"

AM: What's that?

SY: He meant "Fuck off," but not nastily. Sometimes he spoke in his posh voice and it made people laugh.

AM: Whoever it was he'd seen, he wanted to speak to them on his own?

SY: S'pose so. He told me to go, so I did. Feel terrible now, because if I'd stayed he wouldn't have been murdered.

AM: You don't know that. Here, take a tissue. I won't keep you much longer.

SY: But now I've thought about it some more.

AM: Go on . . .

SY: I thought, was Lukey in trouble with the bloke he'd seen in the pub? Did he know they'd want to hurt him? If he did, then when he got rid of me, he saved my life. He did, didn't he? Whoever killed him might've killed me too.

AM: You could be right, Steph. Your Luke would be proud to do that, wouldn't he? Can I just check, did Luke definitely say it was a man he'd recognized?

SY: You think he was cheating on me?

AM: I don't know, but unless he definitely said it was a man we can't be sure it wasn't a woman, that's all.

Ye Olde Goat Ltd. WhatsApp group, Hertfordshire, October 18, 2019:

Diddy & Con, The Brace of Pheasants
Everyone going to the AGM?

Mimi & Flo, Tom's Bar
We'll be there.

Sean & Adrian, The Rainbow
We'll go in the morning, but the afternoon was a waste of time last year.

Diddy & Con, The Brace of Pheasants
They want us to wear "a costume that represents your pub." 😑

Peter Bond, The Lusty Lass
Hereby claiming the greatest dilemma.

Mimi & Flo, Tom's Bar
We can wear our chef's hats for the keynote, but that'll be it.

Sean & Adrian, The Rainbow
We could don full Pride regalia, but I know what'll happen. Everyone else will have a tasteful T-shirt with their signboard printed on it, and we'll be the pair of feather-bedecked multicolored fools. Like last year.

Diddy & Con, The Brace of Pheasants
There's all the St. Patrick's Day clutter we could dig out, but truth be told, we hate the shamrock-and-leprechaun thing. Con would dress as a pint of Guinness, but it'll clash with Olde Goat branding.

Sue & Mal, The Case is Altered
Can we get away with last year's costume, do you think?

Diddy & Con, The Brace of Pheasants

You're the luckiest, you two! Those judge's wigs and gowns cover a multitude of sins!

Sue & Mal, The Case is Altered

They do, but T-shirts with our signboard on would be much better advertising. Thanks, Sean.

Sean & Adrian, The Rainbow

What will you do, Sue? Close the pub for the day?

Diddy & Con, The Brace of Pheasants

How do you get by with no support behind the bar? You two must be chained to the place.

Sue & Mal, The Case is Altered

Not anymore—we've taken on a member of staff. Well, when I say "taken on," she's a young homeless girl we're putting up until she's back on her feet.

Diddy & Con, The Brace of Pheasants

Did you get references, Sue? Can you trust her? There are some funny people about.

Sue & Mal, The Case is Altered

Oh, she's a dear! We're showing her the ropes. Our fingers are crossed she takes to it well enough to cover for us while we're at the AGM.

Sean & Adrian, The Rainbow

Our bar team is tipping twenty now. We're SO busy.

Mimi & Flo, Tom's Bar

We hire from a private catering college.

Peter Bond, The Lusty Lass

A pub thrives or dives according to its staff.

Sean & Adrian, The Rainbow

You're a trouper, Peter. However big your team, you're still managing the Lass on your own.

Peter Bond, The Lusty Lass

You're never alone with a furry crocodile.

Sue & Mal, The Case is Altered
Whatever you meant, Peter, autocorrect has changed it to furry crocodile.

Peter Bond, The Lusty Lass
What we called our four-legged comrades during my days in the service of Her Majesty. My furry croc is a Labrador called Sarge.

Mimi & Flo, Tom's Bar
Aw, that's sweet.

Sue & Mal, The Case is Altered
Anyway, we'll be taking on even more staff soon. Our quiz brings in customers from further afield and gets coverage on local "What's on" sites that wouldn't mention us otherwise. That's how we got our team of young people and a group of cyclists that come every week.

Sue & Mal, The Case is Altered
Not to mention the murder—now that really HAS put The Case is Altered on the map!

Text messages between Mal and Sue Eastwood, October 18, 2019:

Mal
I've just called the pub phone. No answer. It's not good for business. Where are you?

Sue
Out front. Must've left it in the bar.

Mal
I'm parked outside college, waiting for Fiona. One kid walked by in a B&Q polo shirt. Another has a Deliveroo bag on his bike. Fiona is a good worker. We should make her an official member of staff.

Sue
Maybe. We need to speak to Arthur.

Mal
What've our staffing issues got to do with Arthur?

Sue

I popped out to take a picture of our hanging sign for the T-shirt printer. Hadn't looked at it in ages. Well, you don't, do you?

Mal

They said it would last ten years and it's only two years old. It should look as good as new.

Sue

Something's wrong.

Mal

What?

Sue

You need to see for yourself.

To: Dominic Eastwood
From: Polly Baker
Date: October 25, 2024
Subject: Re: Documentary idea

Hi Dominic,

Thank you for sending me the "first episode"! I'm totally feeling the community spirit your aunt and uncle created, as well as the unfolding mystery.

An isolated pub, a body in the river, a mysterious quiz team, and whatever Sue means about the pub sign has got me on the edge of my seat! Of course any good story will deliver *lots* of hooks *all* the way through and I can't wait for the next one. Do send through more just as soon as you can!

Best,
Polly

To: Polly Baker
From: Dominic Eastwood
Date: October 25, 2024
Subject: Re: Documentary idea

Dear Polly,

Thank you for getting back to me so quickly. I love the idea that what I've sent so far could be the first episode! You're right, what you've read sets the scene, but it's not the story. Do rest assured there are plenty of hooks along the way!

I should tell you now, my aunt and uncle were keeping a secret of their own. You see, Suzanne and Malcolm Eastwood had another career entirely before they arrived at The Case.

The following documents could make a fantastic episode two . . . however, it's Friday and of course you'll want to be getting home. We can chat again next week when you've had a chance to read the following.

Have a good weekend and best wishes, Dominic

Hulme Police
Operation Honeyguide

In association with the National Crime Agency
Anti-Kidnap and Extortion Unit (AKEU)
Senior Investigating Officer: Detective Chief Inspector Lewis Parry

Confidential Briefing Notes, May 6, 2014:

Good morning, everyone. This is to formally welcome three new officers on board Operation Honeyguide. Sergeant Melody Obasi—whom we all know as Dee—Sergeant Suzanne Eastwood, and Constable Malcolm Eastwood. You'll all appreciate that, with recent events, we'll need more officers on this operation and these three are among our best and most experienced professionals in Hulme Police.

For the benefit of those newbies, I will recap. Operation Honeyguide is our confidential investigation into the kidnap of Beata Novak and now, sadly, another victim, Chloe Cunningham.

On Friday May 3, nail technician Beata Novak, a twenty-nine-year-old Polish national, disappeared from her rented room in a house of multiple occupancy (HMO). Subsequently her employer received a note that read, "Don't call the police. Call Darren Chester on . . ." followed by his last-known number. "Tell him: show your face or she dies."

The note refers to Darren Chester, local drug dealer for the Maddox Brothers, responsible for at least 70 percent of drugs trafficked to the North of England. Beata was in a relationship with Darren Chester, who also started a relationship with Chloe earlier this year, when he met her at a local tennis club. We believe neither woman knew about the other.

Beata's employers called the police and Operation Honeyguide was established. In the days since, we've been trying to find Beata and trace Mr. Chester. Intelligence from our CIs is that he's fled, following an altercation with Jerry Maddox. Now the brothers want his head. It's our guess they took Beata to try and smoke him out, realized he was seeing Chloe too and now they've kidnapped her as well, in a further effort to get their hands on him.

Miss Cunningham is twenty-two years old, lives with her parents on Moorcroft Lane outside Pinfield Village, and works for the family property business. On May 5, yesterday afternoon, she had an appointment to show a potential new client some land the company intends to develop. Unfortunately that turned out to be a ruse and Miss Cunningham's car was found parked near the grade crossing in Axeford. She hasn't been seen or heard from since. Like Ms. Novak, her phone was switched off immediately and is now missing.

A typed note arrived through the letterbox of Chloe's parents' house the same evening, at which point they contacted the police. A copy is being passed around now, if the new officers could look at it, thank you. You'll see it reads: "We have Chloe. If you call the police she will die. Call Darren Chester, tell him: show up or they both die."

I cannot stress enough how sensitive this is. The Maddox Brothers DO NOT know the Cunninghams have gone to the police. If they do, there is every chance they will kill both women. They've got history here, folks. Remember Jordan Carlyle? No one who saw that body will forget it in a hurry. So bear that in mind, and no discussing Operation Honeyguide with anyone outside this room.

Those visiting the Cunninghams must do so in plain clothes and unmarked cars. Park on Ashtree Drive—behind the house—walk up the lane, and ring the bell at the tradesman's entrance.

NB: There is an information restriction in place. Officers must neither discuss this case with anyone who does not have clearance nor acknowledge the existence of this case. This restriction is in the interests of victim safety and operational integrity. It applies both inside and outside Hulme Police.

Conversation between Sergeant Suzanne Eastwood and DCI Lewis Parry, recorded by Sergeant Suzanne Eastwood's body-worn camera, May 6, 2014:

SE: Thank you, guv!

LP: What for, Sue?

SE: For saying all that about us. Best and most experienced—

LP: Had to say something—

SE: And including us in this operation. Mal and I—

LP: I need officers to sit with Chloe's parents when the family liaison officer can't be there. That's what you two'll be doing.

SE: We're not normally—

LP: I know. But you're competent enough, and staffing is at breaking point. There's literally no one else available for pastoral care of the victims.

SE: Aw, guv. That's lovely of you. I'll tell Mal—

LP: Tell him what? I said you're *competent*. It's not a compliment. It means the job gets done and no one dies.

SE: Oh. Dee too?

LP: Not Dee! Dee is a brilliant officer—she's already made a key contact in the Maddox firm—but she's new to the area and, for one reason and another, I don't want to put undue pressure on her, so . . . look, Rhys is due a break over in Pinfield . . .

Conversation between Sergeants Dee Obasi and Suzanne Eastwood and Constable Malcolm Eastwood, recorded in Unmarked Car 1, May 6, 2014:

ME: Did you hear that? The best and most experienced officers in Hulme Police!

SE: Congratulations, Dee.

DO: Thanks, Sue. What for?

SE: Honeyguide. Lewis said it was *you* he was talking about, not me and certainly not Mal!

ME: Eh!

SE: Our first time on a secret operation. That's a career high! I felt like James Bond being briefed by Q.

ME: Q doesn't brief the double-O operatives. Q stands for quartermaster. He dishes out the gadgets. Bond is briefed by M.

SE: Well, what does M stand for, then?

ME: I don't know, do I! It's just an initial of their name.

SE: M stands for Judi Dench?

ME: Judi Dench was killed in *Skyfall*. It's Ralph Fiennes now.

SE: I can't get an M out of Ralph Fiennes, either!

DO: Never a dull moment with you two!

SE: Oh, there's plenty of dull moments when you live with a quizzer. [*Pause*] Wish this rain would stop. That's a lovely view when you can see it.

DO: Two innocent young women kidnapped by a gang, all for their drug-dealing two-timer of a boyfriend.

SE: Wherever they are, I hope those two girls are shit-talking him into little bloody pieces.

ME: Sue! Inappropriate.

SE: Sorry.

DO: Let's hope, eh.

ME: Don't like keeping things quiet. Why have they brought *us* on, *now*?

DO: Parry told me more boots needed on the ground since the second girl went missing. A blue-eyed, blond property developer from Pinfield this time, not *just* a Polish beautician with no family.

ME: Speaking of family, I heard the guv say he wants you two to give Rhys a break and keep the girl's parents busy?

DO: Yeah, reassure them we're doing all we can and check they haven't told friends or family. What a job. We best get going, eh, Sue . . .

SE: The guv thinks we're still changing into our civvies—we can get away with another cuppa.
      [*Silence as they drink tea*]

ME: Rather you two than me. I never know what to say to emotional people.

SE: Putting it off, to be honest. Oooh! This tea is still hot, Mal. That new flask is dead good. See that, Dee. We got it in a picnic hamper. Fortnum & Mason. Treated ourselves for when we go on summer drives.

ME: Weren't cheap, but we'll get use out of it.

DO: The girl's parents live on a private road. Moorcroft Lane. Don't think I've ever been there. The house doesn't have a number either, only a name. Downview.

ME: Well, that's my cup empty! See you later. Don't forget the quiz tonight. I'll put supper on when I'm in, so we can get away quickly. [*Constable Malcolm Eastwood exits the car*]

SE: Thanks. Aw, bless him. There are two things he cooks: scrambled egg on toast and a scrambled-egg toasted sandwich. It's no wonder we eat out so often.

DO: Is this the Police Association quiz?

SE: I'd invite you, but we can't have more than six in a team, and The Beat Goes On are full at the moment. Credit where it's due, we're climbing up the regional table. If we keep up this winning streak, we could get a place in the national league.

DO: Then you don't want me on your team! I'd be rubbish. I could google the answers for you.

SE: And get us disqualified for cheating? Mal's pride'd never recover.

DO: You're lucky, Sue. Mal's a gem. [*Pause*] I had to have my last boyfriend arrested.

SE: You did *not*! That's hilarious! [*Pause*] Sorry, Dee. Was he violent?

DO: No. The whole time we were together he was near to perfect. Didn't have a job, but was never short of money and told me he was an orphan with a trust fund. I thought, ah, that's why he's so nice: adversity is character building, and all that. Turned out he'd been fired from every job he'd ever had and his family disowned him because he was a compulsive petty thief. I caught him in MAC knocking my favorite shades of lipstick into his man-bag. He was living with a copper and had a serious case of kleptomania.

SE: *You* turned him in!

DO: What sort of officer would I be if I didn't? Worst of it was that I had to hand over every gift he'd ever given me, even the lacy underwear! All of it nicked from M&S, TK Maxx, and John Lewis. How embarrassing was that? Luckily, it were my friend Nat who . . . [*Pause, whispers*] you know, she headed up the case. Kept it discreet.

SE: Aw, was that your friend who passed away?

DO: Yeah. It were just before she went off on maternity leave, when she were . . . diagnosed. She got so ill so quickly, and I were running around helping her and Callum with the kids—meant I could put Mr. Lightfingers to the back of my mind. After Nat passed I had a proper turn; counselor said it were grief for Natalie *and* the relationship—because I hadn't processed either.

SE: Don't blame you . . .

DO: They transferred me to Hulme for a fresh start.

SE: Ah, that's why you arrived out of the blue. Well, Parry said he won't put pressure on you, so play your cards right and you can have an easy ride for a while yet!

DO: Did he? That's nice of him. But I'm fine now, honest. [*Pause*] Most of the time.

[*Silence*]

SE: Must seem dull here after a big city center.

DO: Things are a bit slower. More time to think, and I'm not sure if that's good or not.

SE: Now, Dee, you're a great girl, your luck's gonna turn, you're gonna get that promotion to inspector, I know it, and—in time—you'll find someone you deserve and who deserves you.

DO: Maybe. But you know, single isn't so bad.

SE: But being in a couple is . . . well, two's better than one.

DO: That depends.

SE: Don't know what I'd do without Mal, even when he's at his most irritating.

DO: Right! We can't put this off any longer. Turn on the satnav, I'll need it for this place in Pinfield.

Downview visit 1, May 6, 2014:

*Subjects: Caroline Cunningham, 47, and Piers Cunningham, 49,
Downview, Moorcroft Lane, Pinfield Village
Interviewing officers: Sergeant Dee Obasi and Sergeant Suzanne
Eastwood
Present initially: Family Liaison Officer, Sergeant Rhys Davies*

SE: [*Whispers*] I've not seen anything like it before. It's breath-taking . . . Never knew these houses were here and we've worked this county for twenty years.

DO: Says here they were only built two years ago. The Cunninghams' company was one of the developers. It's a proper millionaires' row. But I bet they'd swap it all for their daughter. Hi, Rhys.

RD: Hi, Dee, Sue. The parents' names are Caroline and Piers. They're in the conservatory. Shell-shocked. We've got their phones. [*Whispers*] But do us a favor, if you see them with an iPad or laptop, get it off them. They say they haven't got them, but . . .

SE: Where should we . . . ?

RD: Sorry, yeah, down the corridor, turn right before the kitchen, past the pool and gym—yes, really—and left at the big gold urn.

SE: [*Whispers*] I could see myself living here, Dee, how about you? [*Footsteps echo as they walk through the house*]

DO: You bet . . . Hello, Caroline, Piers. I'm Sergeant Dee Obasi and this is Sergeant Sue Eastwood. There's no news; we're here to say hello because we've been assigned to Chloe's case. Now, it's a silly thing to ask, I know, but how are you both?

CC: Devastated. Numb.

PC: They've taken our phones.

SE: I know. Did Rhys explain? An abduction like this is a very sensitive crime. The people responsible . . . can be ruthless when they want to be.

DO: It's crucial the gang believes the police aren't involved. The taskforce will communicate with the kidnappers using your phones. It's protocol.

SE: That's why we're in plain clothes, parked three streets away, and walked up the lane to the side entrance.

PC: Rhys said. But aren't you out looking for her?

CC: We can't sit here and do nothing. That won't find her.

DO: It's not so much a case of "finding" Chloe . . .

SE: She's not been taken at random.

DO: Chloe's boyfriend, Darren Chester, is a business associate of a local gang. He's crossed them in some way and has gone AWOL. I'm afraid they're using your daughter to force him out of hiding. Did Rhys explain they took his other girlfriend first, Beata Novak?

PC: He did.

CC: She didn't tell us about this Darren. We thought she was playing tennis or with her girlfriends. We were glad she was getting out and about, she works so hard—

PC: Have you heard from him? No. Didn't think so.

DO: We're looking for Darren because he's a fast track to getting both women back.

SE: These gangs have a certain code of honor. If they say they'll let Beata and Chloe go when he shows his face, then likely as not they will.

CC: He won't show his face!

PC: A drug dealer? Seeing two women? Lying to both? Hopping off the face of the earth when he could just turn up and get them freed . . . The gang may have a code of honor, but he obviously doesn't!

CC: You should be out there with search teams. Looking in sheds, flats, drug dens. With pictures of Chloe's face everywhere, those men'll know how much she's loved and . . . and she'll be too risky to keep and they'll let her go.

DO: Shhh, Caroline, I know it's difficult—

PC: Difficult! Hah!

CC: She's all we've got . . .

SE: I know. It's the worst thing that's ever happened to you, but we see these crimes all the time and we know how to get the best outcome for the victim. Now, I can see from her photo that your Chloe is a strong, smart, and sensible girl—

PC: Too trusting by half . . .
     [*Silence*]

CC: She's our world. All this, the business, the house, everything—all for her.

DO: She's one in a million . . . we can tell.

CC: Which is why everyone should have this picture of her. Get everyone looking.

PC: Shush, we have to let them do their job.

SE: We can see how close you all were.

CC: Close—it's like someone's come along and torn my heart out.

PC: Come on . . . chin up.

CC: We couldn't wish for a better daughter. She's why we get up in the morning.

PC: First sixty minutes after someone disappears, that's crucial. The golden hour. Then it's the first twenty-four, forty-eight hours; after that, chances of finding them a . . . alive . . . get less and less. I've seen documentaries.

CC: When can we tell people?

DO: That'll be decided by our bosses.

SE: They're trained in hostage negotiation. It's all in hand by the very best officers for the job.

CC: Will there be search parties?

PC: I want to take part in any search. I want to be there.

CC: Will we have to go on the news?

PC: We'll do that too, if we have to.

DO: Let's hope we get her back—get them *both* back—before any of that's needed. Not all cases end up in the spotlight. It depends on the circumstances.

CC: We want our girl back safely.

SE: So do we. And, believe me, we're working around the clock to make sure that happens.

PC: We'll do anything you need us to do.

DO: For the moment, we need you to sit tight. Try to keep yourselves busy and—

SE: Hey, Caroline, why don't you take me around your beautiful garden . . . I'd *love* to see it. We've only got a little patch of lawn that's a mud bath in winter and the surface of Mars in summer. Come on.

DO: And I can see your wine collection from here, Piers. Let's have a tour. I can't drink on duty, so it's all safe with me!

[*Later, a whispered conversation by the door*]

RD: Thanks, you two. You've given me a break, and them.

DO: Yeah, we gave 'em a break from each other too. When he was talking about his 2013 Petrus Pomerol, I think Piers forgot about Chloe for a millisecond. How was Caroline, Sue?

SE: Without Piers around, she wanted to talk. She's focused on the worst-case scenario, got visions of Chloe dying.

DO: Oh no . . .

RD: Thanks for the brief. I'd best get back.

SE: Thanks, Rhys.

RD: Waiting game.

DO: Yeah.

Conversation between Sergeants Dee Obasi and Suzanne Eastwood, recorded in Unmarked Car 1, May 6, 2014:

SE: Our garden is Mal's pride and joy. He's got it looking perfect. I only said that to get a closer look at the enormous "outdoor room" with the firepit and fountain.

DO: Ah! And what was it like?

SE: Oh, Dee, it was beautiful, but no wonder: they've got two gardeners! I said, "What you need here, Caroline, is a hot tub—we've got one and it's a treat to sit out there in the bubbling water when it's minus five outside," and you know what she said? "Oh, hot tubs are so tacky. We've got a built-in spa beside the indoor pool."

DO: Cheeky!

SE: I daren't mention our steam room after that!

DO: You've got a *steam room*, Sue? Aye-aye! How the other half lives, eh! And there you were pretending you live in a one-bed flat.

SE: We *do*—ever since we put a steam room in the second sodding bedroom! Long story. Doctor recommended it for Mal's arthritis.

He priced up the cost of joining a posh gym, for the steam room there, or putting one in ourselves and that won. It's ever so good, Dee, you're welcome to give it a go any time. Of course I dare not mention it to Caroline, it's bound to be a cheap version of the one they've got!

[*Silence*]

DO: You two had a long chat out there.

SE: Yeah, she could talk without Piers hearing her, so opened up a bit, you know. She got it all off her chest.

DO: Puts your own probbies into perspective, don't it.

SE: Yeah. [*Pause*] Hark at me: "All in hand by the very best officers for the job." I've no idea if they are or not, I've never met anyone from AKEU.

DO: I'll feel rotten for the rest of the day now. Mostly we see folk *after* the worst is over, when the crime itself is done and dusted. Cases like this, where we're still in the middle of it, no one knowing how it's going to pan out . . . [*She shudders*]

SE: Reminds me of those accidents you go to where the victim is fatally injured but still alive.

DO: Oh, don't, Sue, I've never had that, that would be . . .

SE: There was this one time—

DO: Don't! I don't want to know!

SE: OK, then. I must've learned to put it aside after all these years. Compartmentalize it, as they say. [*Pause*] Her mom and dad reckon Chloe is all they've got, yet they've got a lot more than most. That house is beautiful. Kitchen bigger than our entire flat! We're talking three million at least and it's practically brand-new. For only the three of them.

DO: Look at this. Piers Cunningham has been director of four, five, six . . . *nine* different companies over the years. Most recently Wrenstone Property Ltd. He resigned from all posts last year and was replaced by Chloe, few months after that house was purchased for—and here's where you score a Brownie point, Sue—3.2 million.

SE: How do you know all that?

DO: Companies House. You can find out all sorts. Here's the page.

SE: Aw, that's technical googling, that. Does it need a password?

DO: No. It's public info!

SE: Anything that needs log-in details, I'm out. Mal's the same.

DO: I thought Mal was a memory man!

SE: Oh, he can tell you which king married which queen and when, but practical stuff just doesn't stick. He has to write everything down: birthdays, anniversaries, every bloody password, customer number, and "special phrase" for all our accounts.

DO: Look, at the end of the last financial year, Wrenstone Property Ltd. had cash reserves of nine hundred thousand pounds.

SE: Nearly a million. We're in the wrong job, Dee.

DO: Means nothing, does it, when their only child is missing?

SE: You're right. And her being twenty-two means nothing either. She's still their little girl. Lost, alone, and in danger.

      [*Silence*]

To: Dominic Eastwood
From: Polly Baker
Date: October 25, 2024
Subject: Re: Documentary idea

Hi Dom,

You're right: it's Friday, but it's quiet in the office. My boss is away and we're not in production at the moment, so I've devoured everything from "episode two." The fact your aunt and uncle were former police officers is really intriguing. If you've time to send through any more, or perhaps some of your own memories of your aunt and uncle, then do. I'm happy to read on.

Best,
Polly

To: Polly Baker
From: Dominic Eastwood
Date: October 25, 2024
Subject: Re: Documentary idea

Hi Polly,

No problem! Yes, my aunt and uncle met at police training college. Mal was a year ahead of Sue and she joined him at the same station—I clearly remember them, very smart and proud in their uniforms. Neither seemed particularly ambitious and only my aunt made it to sergeant. However, they were both very personable. I can well imagine them getting the most reluctant suspect to talk.

They were in their late forties, so retired from frontline police work not long after Operation Honeyguide ended. Lots of former police go on to run pubs and bars, especially if dealing with the public was something they enjoyed about the job. Handling drunks doesn't faze coppers, especially after as many years as Sue and Mal put in.

But this is the thing: a criminal grudge can follow someone out of the force and into civilian life. If they're behind the bar of a "public house" every day—with people from all walks of life coming and going—they're a sitting target. Unfortunately, when things like that happen, innocent people get caught in the crossfire—just like Chloe Cunningham. Perhaps the next set of documents could be "episode three" . . . I probably don't need to tell you that in 2014 Operation Honeyguide went catastrophically wrong. And that it had equally devastating repercussions in 2019.

Best wishes,
Dom

THE CASE IS ALTERED PUB QUIZ

October 21, 2019

Rounds	Max points
1. Today's News	10
2. On this day in 1977	10
3. Sport: commentators special	10
4. Art & Literature	10
5. Plays within plays: onstage and in film	10
6. Music: name the artist and song title	20
7. Name the country this city is the capital of	20
8. Playing tag! Ten advertising taglines: name the brand	10

Marathon round: Say what you see!

Identify 100 famous people by these cryptic pictures   100

Quiz teams and where they sat

The Sturdy Challengers
Chris & Lorraine
Ajay, Keith
Andrew, Fiona

Spokespersons
Erik, Jemma
Tam, Dilip

Let's Get Quizzical
Sid & Nancy Topliss
Bunny & George Tyme
Margaret & Ted Dawson

The Shadow Knights
General Knowledge, Brigitte
Pamela, Lynette
Edward, Wilfred

Linda & Joe & Friends
Linda & Joe
Rita & Bailey
Cloud & Wind

Ami's Manic Carrots
Jojo, Evie
Harrison, Rosie
Fliss, Bianca

Final scores out of 200
The Shadow Knights   197
Ami's Manic Carrots   157
The Sturdy Challengers   148
Let's Get Quizzical   143
Spokespersons   139
Linda & Joe & Friends   99

Ami's Manic Carrots WhatsApp group, October 21, 2019:

Jojo
OMG! What happened?

Bianca
We smashed it!

Fliss
We were 40 points behind the winners, tho.

Bianca
Fliss! 🫥

Harrison
Help! I've got a nosebleed from being so high on the winners' table.

Rosie
How good was that? Quizzes are fun when you're at the top.

Evie
I even forgot the dead body for a bit.

Harrison
Perhaps his ghost came back and sat on our table, psychically transmitting the answers. 👻

Evie
Harry! Don't say that.

Fliss
We'd be disqualified for having an extra team member. It was the marathon round that did it. For once it wasn't "Name these boomer icons."

Jojo
The other teams aren't used to doing cryptic visuals. Even on The Shadow Knights team, I bet the younger guy, Ed, did most of them.

Evie
Remember Boodie's Picture Time!

Harrison
Everyone our age does. That's why we scored so highly.

Fliss

We smashed it. But we're still a long way behind the Knights.

Bianca

We should enjoy the moment. Next week it'll be "Name these dead white people" and we'll be back with Linda & Joe.

Evie

OMG, I need to sleep but still buzzing! Night-night, everyone.

The Sturdy Challengers Quiz Team WhatsApp group, October 22, 2019:

Thor's Hammer

Just nine more points and we'd have been second.

Lorraine

Ami's Manic Carrots did very well.

Keith

They only beat us on the marathon, but Mal is handing out marathon rounds so huge they can swing the scores either way. Theoretically a team can win the quiz proper but end up mid-table because they flunked the marathon.

Lorraine

Young people seem to like those Catchphrase pictures.

Andrew

There was a cartoon and a series of books. I used to buy them for my nephews.

Thor's Hammer

Unfortunately our young person wasn't a fan, or she'd have scored more highly for us.

Fiona

q

Andrew

What Fiona means is, she wasn't given books as a child, so she was at a disadvantage.

Ajay

But Lorraine said it. Even us "old" folk should remember the TV show Catchphrase—that was exactly this sort of picture riddle.

Keith

Onward and upward, team. We can see Mal is looking to make the marathon more significant. We should study visual quizzes and IQ puzzles. Will forward a list of books, once I've researched them.

Text messages between Thor's Hammer and Sue & Mal, The Case is Altered, October 22, 2019:

Thor's Hammer

A key, a man with the head of a bird, a chess piece, and a photograph of Dracula?

Sue & Mal, The Case is Altered

Hello, Chris, love. What do you mean? Did you leave them in the bar? We didn't find anything when we locked up last night.

Thor's Hammer

Marathon question 44. The round is called "Say what you see," yet apparently the correct answer is Keira Knightley.

Sue & Mal, The Case is Altered

I'll hand you over to Mal, love.

Sue & Mal, The Case is Altered

Key = self-explanatory. Ra = Egyptian sun god. Knight = the chess piece. Lee = Christopher Lee, in his Dracula costume.

Thor's Hammer

The marathon rounds are getting too long. Our team spent ages looking at those pictures and we failed miserably. We're a team of good quizzers. If you want to keep us as regulars—not to mention your other loyal teams—then the marathon round will have to be within the realm of possibility.

Sue & Mal, The Case is Altered

Two out of six teams got question 44 correct. That's a successful ratio.

Thor's Hammer
I want to register our disapproval. That's all.

Sue & Mal, The Case is Altered
May I remind you of our quiz rules. The quizmaster's decision is final. It is always final, even if he is subsequently proven to be wrong.

Thor's Hammer
I'm just saying, that's all. The quiz means a lot to some in our team, and when it's weighted against us, they don't like it.

Sue & Mal, The Case is Altered
I need to make the quiz fair to all. The Shadow Knights got three questions wrong last night. I'm starting to break them.

Thor's Hammer
Can we lodge a polite request for fewer marathon questions next week? That way at least we can concentrate on a realistic number of answers.

Text messages between Mal and Sue Eastwood, October 22, 2019:

Mal
He only wanted to complain about the marathon round.

Sue
No one noticed the hanging sign. There are still enough leaves on the trees to hide it from view.

Sue
It could've been like that for months.

Mal
I'll speak to Arthur.

Sue
DON'T! He's a PCSO on a rusty old bicycle.

Mal
Exactly. He's not going to dig deeper, is he?

Sue
WHATEVER YOU DO, DON'T DRAG ARTHUR INTO IT.

Text messages between Mal Eastwood and PCSO Arthur McCoy, October 22, 2019:

Mal

Like to report an act of vandalism.

Arthur

You must be psychic, Mal! Just this minute writing my own statement for September 2. Been working my way through your esteemed clientele.

Mal

First encounter with the law for most of them, as far as I know. Certainly their first murder.

Arthur

Go on, what's happened?

Mal

Our hanging sign is a painting of two barristers arguing across a courtroom. Close up, it's pretty amateurish, but not our design—the brewery gets them made. It's been defaced with paint.

Arthur

Surely it's twenty feet up a pole! Must be an Olympic shot-putter to have thrown paint all the way up there!

Mal

They didn't throw paint at it. They painted over it. It's dry too—could've happened weeks ago.

Arthur

Has anyone my side requested your security camera footage for September 2?

Mal

Not yet, but when they do I'll have to come clean. Our system hasn't worked since we arrived two years ago. I've had so much on my plate it slipped my mind.

Arthur

Shame. The footage might have shown where Luke Goode went and could've caught the vandals too. I'll swing past yours later, take pictures and help you lodge a complaint. You're a local business and shouldn't have to put up with this sort of hate crime.

Mal

Not sure it's a hate crime as such. But you should know something else. One of the barristers—in the picture—has been stabbed and the other has a noose around their neck. They've both been murdered.

Spokespersons Cycling Team WhatsApp group, October 22, 2019:

Erik

Second to last.

Dilip

Hate those picture things. Couldn't believe it when Mal handed them out. The marathon round was like a book. What's going on?

Tam

The Sturdy Challengers were beaten by Ami's Manic Carrots. It was a freak result.

Jemma

So having Ajay on their team didn't make any difference. 😂 He deserted us for nothing!

Dilip

He was poached. 🔍

Erik

You can't say no to Chris and Lorraine.

Tam

That's a FRIED egg.

Jemma

I'd have said no. You don't just switch teams. You don't even socialize with other teams. There's a quiz at stake.

Dilip

We can chat, though? There's an *a priori* assumption that everyone doing the quiz will observe the basic rules of not cheating, sure.

Jemma

How's the law course going, Dilip?

Tam

Not that well if he uses the emoji of a FRIED egg in a FRYING pan to illustrate the word "poached."

Dilip

Just pointing out that it's easy to SAY we won't socialize with people we're in competition with, but sometimes you need to do exactly that to get the measure of your opponents.

Jemma

You can chat and be civil, while being loyal to the team. Ajay jumped teams and that is way, way off the scale.

Dilip

Extract from a witness statement made by PCSO Arthur McCoy, October 22, 2019:

On the evening of September 2, 2019, at 20:00 I received a phone call from Sue Eastwood, landlady at The Case is Altered. I've got to know Sue and her husband, Mal, very well because I like to maintain close contact with local businesses and community figures. I find them down-to-earth, honest people, and recently learned that they are former police officers.

On the call, Sue said a group of troublemakers notorious for cheating at local quizzes had turned up at The Case and that Mal had thrown them out. He was arguing with them outside and she was concerned he was outnumbered and not as young as he used to be.

I was a mile or so away, on the other side of the big Morrisons checking a faulty streetlight I'd reported last week had been repaired, so I jumped on my bike and arrived at 20:22. I recall seeing two men and one woman walking along the main road as I turned down Bell End, but at the time had no reason to suspect they were involved in the altercation. I now know them to be Stephanie Young, Michael Conaty, and Farhad "Fezza" Darya, all of whom are known to the police and who returned to town after being ejected from The Case.

When I arrived the trouble was over and Malcolm was starting the quiz. I didn't see anyone hanging around outside. Without wishing to disturb the event, I spoke briefly to Sue behind the bar, who assured me all was well, and I left by about 20:25. I checked the lane but it seemed deserted, so I cycled back to the main road.

The body of Luke Goode was discovered concealed in the nearby river on October 1, 2019. I understand he had arrived at around 20:00 with Young, Conaty, and Darya, but had remained behind to speak to someone he knew and was not seen again by friends or associates. While he had been dressed in brightly colored clothing, it is quite possible he hid from my view when I arrived and left that night.

In the weeks since, I have been conducting witness interviews. None of the customers in The Case is Altered that night admit to having known Mr. Goode, nor to having recognized him in the short time he was there. It makes me wonder who among them is not being entirely honest.

Text messages between Me [Rita] and Linda, October 22, 2019:

Me
Who are that couple, Linda?

Linda
Remember the houseboat that found the body? They're still moored up at the end of the lane.

Me
They've been on our team for weeks now. Is there something funny about them?

Linda
What do you mean?

Me
Only she talks to someone called "Lizzie." The chap's name is Claude, I'm Rita, you're Linda, Joe is Joe, and Bailey is Bailey. Who's Lizzie?

Linda
Her spirit guide. She was a servant girl in Victorian times. But don't tell Mal—we aren't allowed more than six on a team. And it's Cloud, not Claude.

Me
I thought they were Claude and Wendy!

Linda
Wind. Cloud and Wind.

Me
Are those their real names?

Linda
No, Rita. They're hippies. But it's what they call themselves, and that's self-identification, according to my Olivia. It's all the rage.

Me
I wonder what their actual names are?

Linda
For goodness' sake, don't ask. Anyway, you've got a pseudonym yourself.

Me
I have not!

Linda
On my phone you come up as "Me."

Me
Oh, that! I put that in when I first got it, because it's MY phone. Everyone knows it's me.

**Text messages between PCSO Arthur McCoy and Mal Eastwood,
October 22, 2019:**

Arthur

I see what you mean. Lucky the sign is so high up in the branches and the lane so dark, no one's noticed it and got offended. I'll log the complaint, so you've got all the paperwork for the brewery.

Mal

Oh, they won't need to know.

Arthur

What about their insurance? They'll need to take the sign down to clean it and, if it's beyond repair, order another one.

Mal

I'll clean the sign myself.

Arthur

How will you get all the way up there? And when you do, how nifty are you with a paintbrush?

Mal

I don't want to bother the brewery, especially when our AGM is coming up.

Arthur

You shouldn't have to put up with your property being defaced.

Mal

I was more concerned with what the graffiti "says." Say what you see, Arthur. Two lawyers being hanged and stabbed.

Arthur

You and Sue aren't lawyers, though, are you!

Mal

What it says is: "The law means nothing to us."

Mal

As you say, it's not clearly visible, and regulars don't look up anyway. Perhaps it's best to leave it where it is.

Arthur

Up to you, Mal.

Text messages between Sue and Mal Eastwood, October 22, 2019:

Sue

Do you listen to anything I say? I told you not to mention it, FFS!

Mal

He needs to see it. In case anything worse happens.

Sue

If I hadn't gone to take a picture for our AGM T-shirts, we'd not have noticed. It could've been there for months. When was the last time you even looked at it?

Mal

When it was installed.

Sue

Exactly. If it was someone with a bigger grudge, they wouldn't have stopped there, would they? Probably just locals.

Sue

The Cheats could've come back and done it that night. We don't know where they went after you came back inside.

Sue

Now you've told Arthur, we have to tell the brewery.

Mal

I'm not telling Mr. Roper! He sees our books—he has enough to worry about.

Mal

We'll leave the sign where it is for now. We can wear last year's lawyers' robes and wigs to the AGM. No one has spotted the graffiti and, if they do, we'll deal with it in the moment.

Sue

You dealing with things "in the moment" is what got us here.

Mal

Let me remind you that if anyone comes after us, we're ready—thanks to me. You know what I mean.

Mal
Which is more than The Shadow Knights are for Monday's quiz.

Extract from a witness statement made by Michael Conaty, October 23, 2019:

My name is Michael Conaty. I am thirty-one years old and of no fixed abode. I'm making this statement voluntarily via my lawyer after hearing from an acquaintance that the police want to speak to me about the murder of my friend Luke Goode.

I last saw Mr. Goode on the night of September 2, 2019, when I went with him, Stephanie Young, and a man I call Fezza to The Case is Altered public house in Fernley. We wanted to take part in the quiz and win some money that we intended to share. It was the first time we'd ever been to that pub.

I was not enthusiastic because it's a long walk out of town, but Mr. Goode and Ms. Young insisted and put pressure on me to agree. I think they wanted the money and needed a team. Also, I weren't sure if it was within my house arrest conditions, but Mr. Goode said it would be fine.

The minute we got there, we were thrown out. The landlord said we were cheats, but we'd never been there before. Steph, Fezza, and me nipped back out quick, but Luke was stuck in the double doors with the landlord. You know when there's a set of double doors, then another set? To keep the cold out? They had a rumble in there. It didn't occur to me to get involved because I knew Mr. Goode could handle himself in a fight. It wasn't worth it—I'd just end up back inside. I was pissed off we'd gone all that way for nothing.

Us other three started walking back up the lane. Fezza said a bloke owed him money so he'd go back to town and get it. Mr. Goode caught us up, but he looked serious and said he'd seen an old friend in the pub and would wait till closing time to talk to them. I thought, and pardon my French, "Fuck that." It was only just gone eight! Steph wanted to stay with him, but Luke told her to go with us. I didn't think that was strange because Mr. Goode would probably tap his old mate for cash and she was best out of it. The three of us left. I didn't look back or see where Mr. Goode went. I didn't see him again until someone showed me his picture in the paper after he'd died.

I knew Mr. Goode for a few months and found him entertaining company and a good friend. As soon as I met him, I felt I'd known him for years. He had his demons, but he was one of the good guys. I'm sad and sorry to hear what happened to him, but I had nothing to do with it. I don't know of anyone who would have a grudge against him or want him dead.

The Case is Altered

MissB1988
wrote a review today
Hertford, United Kingdom
125 contributions, 77 helpful votes

Date visited   **October 24, 2019**
Visit type   **Number Two**

FREE Toilets

Was BUSTING after a big shop in Morrisons but FFS their toilets were out of order. Cue a desperate google search and found this place. Left my hazards on in the lane while I dashed in, did the business and was back in the car before the hand dryer cut out. Didn't even need to buy anything. Five stars for the toilets being near the door. Otherwise, it's one star cos I didn't have anything to drink or eat. Won't visit again unless Morrisons toilets are still out of order. SORT IT MORRISONS!

Response from Sue at The Case is Altered
Responded on October 24, 2019

Dear Miss B,
Thank you for your review. I'm very pleased you enjoyed our toilets. We pride ourselves on the highest standards of cleanliness and decoration, so your five stars are much appreciated. However, I can't help but notice that, officially, your review gives us just one star. Could you perhaps change that official rating to the five stars for the loos and not the one star for the services you didn't use? We'd be grateful if you could. Thank you.

Ye Olde Goat Ltd. WhatsApp group, Hertfordshire, October 28, 2019:

Sue & Mal, The Case is Altered
Here you go. Happy one-star Monday from The Case. Sue is rightly proud of her polite reply.

Diddy & Con, The Brace of Pheasants
The cheek of them!

Sean & Adrian, The Rainbow
😂 Thanks Mal, that's cheered us up.

Mimi & Flo, Tom's Bar
What are people like? Have they changed it to five stars?

Sue & Mal, The Case is Altered
Doubt it. We've sworn off the bloody site. I'm polishing tonight's quiz questions and trying to forget it.

Diddy & Con, The Brace of Pheasants
We're doing the quiz on page 90, second edition.

Mimi & Flo, Tom's Bar
Second edition, number eighteen.

Sean & Adrian, The Rainbow
Third edition, quiz number six.

Peter Bond, The Lusty Lass
1st edn, 26.

Sue & Mal, The Case is Altered
Does anyone know where someone might get a pub sign made? Not the pole, just the hanging-picture bit.

Diddy & Con, The Brace of Pheasants
Is there a problem with your sign, Mal?

Sue & Mal, The Case is Altered
It's Sue. Mal's out "doing research" for the quiz. Our sign is fine. Asking for a friend in a drama group up north. They're putting on a play set in a pub and are looking into how much a real sign would cost.

Mimi & Flo, Tom's Bar

They're pricey, Sue. Ye Olde Goat supplied ours. They're hand-painted.

Sean & Adrian, The Rainbow

Oh yes, they're designed and made individually. We HATE ours. It looks like a multicolored tunnel drawn by a three-year-old.

Peter Bond, The Lusty Lass

Nothing sophisticated about a rainbow.

Diddy & Con, The Brace of Pheasants

Which play are they doing?

Peter Bond, The Lusty Lass

My lusty lass sells fruit and veg.

Sean & Adrian, The Rainbow

I've seen her, Peter! She has a well-stocked stall.

Peter Bond, The Lusty Lass

I was clear to Ye Olde Goat: nothing tacky or we won't attract women slash families. The result, a woman standing behind a huge pair of watermelons.

Diddy & Con, The Brace of Pheasants

Which play is your friend's drama group doing, Sue?

Sue & Mal, The Case is Altered

The Iceman Cometh by Eugene O'Neill.

Diddy & Con, The Brace of Pheasants

You can't beat Mamma Mia.

Mimi & Flo, Tom's Bar

Don't talk to us about pub signs.

Sue & Mal, The Case is Altered

Why are you rolling your eyes?

Mimi & Flo, Tom's Bar

Ye Olde Goat briefed the artist that it should be a portrait of Thomas Hardy. He googled "Tom" Hardy.

Sean & Adrian, The Rainbow

No! Tell me that's a joke!

Mimi & Flo, Tom's Bar
No joke. Luckily the portrait looks nothing like Tom Hardy either—so our sign is officially a portrait of Thomas Hardy "when he was young."

Sue & Mal, The Case is Altered
Oh no! Ours is two lawyers arguing across a courtroom, but it was put up in winter and when summer comes it's mostly covered by the leaves of a big tree.

Sean & Adrian, The Rainbow
Have fabulous weeks, all. 🌚

Sue & Mal, The Case is Altered
Happy quizzing! (Mal is holed up in the office writing questions for the rest of the day now.)

Diddy & Con, The Brace of Pheasants
You too, Sean. 🖤 Good luck, Mal!

Mimi & Flo, Tom's Bar
Love you all!

Text messages between Mal and Sue Eastwood, October 28, 2019:

Mal
The Iceman Cometh?

Sue
It's the first play I thought of that's set in a pub. I think Lee Marvin was in the film.

Mal
It's set in an American bar. Do American bars even have signs like ours?

Sue
I don't know—and nor would a local amateur drama group.

Mal
Don't disturb me. I'm working on tonight's quiz. Let's see The Shadow Knights storm this one!

Sue
And if Chris has some ripe words for us afterward, you can deal with him.

THE CASE IS ALTERED PUB QUIZ

October 28, 2019

Special 100th Birthday Quiz

Rounds	Max points
1. Today's News	10
2. On this day in 1955	10
3. Sport	10
4. Literature	10
5. Film stars 1920–1980	10
6. Music from the 1950s: name the artist and song title	20
7. Caribbean food, music, history, and culture	10
8. General Knowledge	10

Marathon round: Sitcoms

Name these 20 TV sitcom characters	20

Quiz teams and where they sat

The Sturdy Challengers
Chris & Lorraine
Ajay, Keith
Andrew, Fiona

Spokespersons
Erik, Jemma
Tam, Dilip

Let's Get Quizzical
Sid & Nancy Topliss
Bunny & George Tyme
Margaret & Ted Dawson

The Shadow Knights
General Knowledge, Brigitte
Pamela, Lynette
Edward, Wilfred

Linda & Joe & Friends
Linda & Joe
Rita & Bailey
Cloud & Wind

Ami's Manic Carrots
Jojo, Evie
Harrison, Rosie
Fliss, Bianca

Text messages between Thor's Hammer and Sue & Mal, The Case is Altered, October 28, 2019:

Thor's Hammer
What in the name of Almighty Bob is going on, Mal?

Sue & Mal, The Case is Altered
Stop texting, Chris! If Mal sees you, he'll assume you're googling and you'll be disqualified.

Thor's Hammer
Fat lot of good googling would do tonight!

Sue & Mal, The Case is Altered
I think that's the idea, love. Remember: the quizmaster is God. Take it up with Almighty Mal tomorrow.

Thor's Hammer
That I will. That I will.

Final scores out of 110

Ami's Manic Carrots	72
Linda & Joe & Friends	68
Let's Get Quizzical	54
The Sturdy Challengers	53
Spokespersons	53
The Shadow Knights	49

Ami's Manic Carrots WhatsApp group, October 28, 2019:

Harrison
Best night of my LIFE!

Evie
Can't sleep! £23!!!

Fliss
£3.83 each.

Evie

OMG, a latte at Starbs. 🥤

Rosie

One mini bao bun at Juju Island 🥤 (less 17p).

Harrison

Parking at the Atrium Retail Hub for up to three hours off-peak 🥤
(with 3p change, but theoretical because you don't get change at those
machines).

Bianca

I'll be driving, but you guys could share a shot of Jager at next week's
quiz.

Fliss

I suggest putting the £23 into a kitty so we pay for our quiz entries for
three weeks, with enough left over for chips (on the third week).

Harrison

How to spot a financial advisor in a crowd. 👆

Fliss

We should enjoy the victory. Unless Mal pulls a stunt like that every week
we won't beat the top teams again.

Harrison

Do you think he wanted to give us a better chance?

Bianca

Us and the oldies' team—they came second.

Rosie

It's like the whole world order has shifted and it's a new dawn.

Jojo

Mal changed the quiz to stop The Shadow Knights winning. They didn't
look happy.

Evie

They win all the other weeks. They'll be fine.

Text messages between Thor's Hammer and Sue & Mal, The Case is Altered, October 29, 2019:

Thor's Hammer
Mal.

Sue & Mal, The Case is Altered
This is Mal. What can I do for you, Chris?

Thor's Hammer
That quiz was an abomination. An insult. It spat in the face of everything serious quizzers stand for. The serious quizzers who frequent your run-down establishment every Monday, providing much-needed cash through your till. All our hard work preparing for YOUR quiz, reading, memorizing, practicing: all for nothing. You made baboons of your loyal regulars.

Sue & Mal, The Case is Altered
I leveled the playing field, Chris. It meant that age, experience, education, memory function, and knowledge—all qualities usually tested in a pub quiz—counted for nothing. Tonight's quiz tested imagination, empathy, humanity, and humor. I have to say, the rankings were quite surprising. What wasn't surprising, though, was how close the results were. Only 23 points separated the entire table.

Thor's Hammer
That's what's important to you? Making sure the losers are happy?

Sue & Mal, The Case is Altered
Making sure the quiz is watertight. Last night proved to everyone that if The Shadow Knights are cheating, then the "leak" does not come from our side. Sue knew what I was doing. Fiona knew what I was doing. I put everything on my hard drive, in my emails, on my phone and my laptop. If The Shadow Knights had access to any of them, it would have shown up in their answers. I watched them leave last night and they were every bit as disgruntled as you.

Thor's Hammer
"Tonight's quiz is a little different." That's what you said at the start. Yes! A fallacy!

Found in my Uncle Mal's notes:

Tonight's quiz is a little different. The answers are not to be found in quiz books, encyclopedias, or Google. This afternoon I visited Bayview Care Home and spoke to a lovely lady, Shirley Thompson, who celebrated her 100th birthday last week. Now, Shirley was born in Canaan, a very small village in Tobago, on October 22, 1919. She tells me her life began again at the age of about 30 when she journeyed with her family to London, where she trained to be a nurse. She retired in 1979 and expresses great surprise and delight that she has lived so long as to see her great-great-grandchildren. Shirley is very cheerful and likes to laugh, although her memory is not what it was, but we had a nice chat and she agreed to help me with tonight's quiz. I asked Shirley every question I'm going to ask you now. I suggested that she tell me the answer if she knows it or, if she doesn't know it, give me a guess—either serious or jokey. Because tonight I'm not asking you to answer the questions—but to tell me the answer Shirley gave me. For every answer, you must think, "What would Shirley say?"

Text messages between Sue and Mal Eastwood, October 29, 2019:

Sue
I knew Chris wouldn't like it.

Mal
His team had just as much chance of getting the questions right or wrong as anyone else. No one knows Shirley; everyone had to imagine themselves in the mind of a Windrush centenarian with Caribbean heritage and mild memory loss. I have to say the old girl knew more about sport than I'd have guessed!

Sue
It was a good idea. Maybe not for every quiz, but as a novelty, and it gave Ami's Carrots and Linda & Joe's team a boost.

Mal

What do you mean "not for every quiz"? I thought you could pop into a local primary school and get answers from a class of eight-year-olds.

Sue

You aren't serious.

Mal

Get the teacher's permission. Bright eight-year-olds, not thick ones.

Sue

Why me?

Mal

It looks bad, a man speaking to kids.

Sue

No way.

Mal

Why not?

Sue

Because we've got more to worry about than the quiz.

Ye Olde Goat Ltd. WhatsApp group, Hertfordshire, October 29, 2019:

Diddy & Con, The Brace of Pheasants

What's this we're hearing about your quiz, Mal?

Sean & Adrian, The Rainbow

What happened? Not more trouble at The Case?

Mimi & Flo, Tom's Bar

The Cheats back again?

Sean & Adrian, The Rainbow

No, Flo! The Cheats were murdered. One of them, anyway.

Diddy & Con, The Brace of Pheasants

Our barman knows someone who goes to The Case and he said it was set by a 100-year-old woman.

Mimi & Flo, Tom's Bar
What?

Peter Bond, The Lusty Lass
FUBAR.

Sean & Adrian, The Rainbow
That is WILD! Would the old lady set ours? OMG, wait till I tell Adrian!

Sue & Mal, The Case is Altered
Slight exaggeration there, Diddy. Mrs. Shirley Thompson didn't SET the questions, she answered them. Our quiz this week didn't test who knew the most, but who could guess most accurately the answer that a happy, healthy, 100-year-old lady would give to each question.

Sean & Adrian, The Rainbow
Our quizzers wouldn't like that. Some take it seriously. Did you get complaints?

Sue & Mal, The Case is Altered
Yes.

Mimi & Flo, Tom's Bar
Why did you do it, Mal? Was it something to do with The Shadow Knights?

Sue & Mal, The Case is Altered
It's good to change things every so often. Keep our quizzers on their toes. Last thing we want is for the quiz to get boring.

Mimi & Flo, Tom's Bar
Still, complaints from regulars is never good.

Sue & Mal, The Case is Altered
It's just for one week. Back to normal next week. And, Peter, I've compiled quiz rounds on acronyms before now and I know very well what FUBAR means. Last night's quiz was not effed up beyond all recognition. FFI. Far from it.

Text messages between Sue and Mal Eastwood, October 29, 2019:

Sue

You told the other olde goats that next week's quiz is back to normal. I hope that's true. We don't need this aggro.

Mal

If The Shadow Knights are cheating I want to know how and it's a process of elimination. Phase one is complete: our house is certified clean. Let phase two begin!

Spokespersons Cycling Team WhatsApp group, October 29, 2019:

Erik

Quiz a bit different this week.

Dilip

It's boring at the bottom. Why do the teams who are always last come back week after week?

Tam

The pressure's off. If you're not going to win, you can relax and enjoy the quiz.

Erik

Our strategy was to try and answer each question correctly, as usual, and it didn't work. That was The Shadow Knights' strategy as well. They came last, we came second to last. Best thing about it was scoring the same as The Sturdy Challengers.

Tam

Shall we readmit Ajay to this WhatsApp?

Dilip

Why?

Jemma

No way.

Tam

Why not? He needs to know meet times so we can all cycle together. Safety in numbers.

Erik

No. He's on a rival team. I'll text him the meet times.

Text messages between Andrew and Fiona, October 29, 2019:

Andrew

Hi, Fiona. The quiz was strange last night. Did you know Mal was going to do that?

Fiona

ys

Andrew

So he went off to a care home to interview an elderly resident?

Fiona

ys

Andrew

Well, even though Chris and Lorraine weren't amused, and Keith was silent for the entire quiz, it was at least interesting. Nice of Sue and Mal to let you off bar duties for the night.

Fiona

Sue says don't let Chris n Lorraine dwn

Andrew

Very true! No one wants to let Chris and Lorraine down. While you're texting words, can I ask how you're getting along at the pub? It's awkward at the quiz table with everyone there. Is your social worker up to speed on your living situation?

Fiona

ntg

Andrew

Not that good?

Fiona

no thank gd

Andrew

Your team has to know where you are. I'll try to speak to them. Are you still going into college? Do you get three meals a day at The Case? Are you on the payroll for your job behind the bar? What's life like with Sue and Mal?

Fiona

cool

Andrew

The thing is, I only know you from your housing applications and, given your background—not your fault, I hasten to add, you can't help where and to whom you're born—but you might not be the best judge of what's normal and what isn't. Sue and Mal could be anyone.

Fiona

time

Andrew

Why are you laughing now?

Fiona

M n S are ex feds

Andrew

Sue and Mal used to be in the police? Wow. That's news to me. Game changer. That's a HUGE relief. Phew! Thanks, Fiona, that's put my mind at rest. I can get back to my other clients in this towering pile. Have a great week and see you next Monday.

Fiona

k

Andrew

Oh, and if Mal starts behaving strangely—asking odd people to answer quiz questions—perhaps tip us the wink?

Fiona

wtf?

Andrew

Let us know if he's planning another weird quiz.

Fiona

k

To: Let's Get Quizzical [group]
From: Sid Topliss
Date: October 29, 2019
Subject: Happy day!

Congratulations, team! Crack open the bubbly, bake a cake, and light the fireworks. We've got to celebrate the first time we've placed top three—without George cheating—and in a quiz where you had to guess what a stranger might answer too. Happy days!

Obviously if a lady of 100 has *ever* known the capital of Azerbaijan, she isn't going to remember it, so our guess of "Constantinople" hit home. If you think about it, it's the capital city old folk tend to remember because it was changed to Istanbul in 1930 and that was a fact drummed into them at school. It stands out in their minds long after other knowledge has faded away. That's our answer of the night, and a big thanks to Nancy for suggesting it.

Imagining myself in the shoes of Shirley Thompson for three hours yesterday has got me thinking about my own mom and dad. If they were alive today, Dad would be 121 and Mom 119. Safe to say if they hadn't died when they did, they would definitely still have been dead by now, but it doesn't stop me wondering what they'd have made of the modern world.

Dad was a comms officer in the navy and Mom always said how interested he was in new technology. He'd have had an iPad and a laptop. I bet he'd have bought the latest cell phone as soon as it came out. What sort of Facebook profile would he have made for himself?

Then there's Mom. She learned to drive for her job, and although we didn't have a car growing up, I'm sure she'd have got one eventually. Would she have taken to an electric car, though? It's a different experience, so our Lloyd says, but you get used to it and after a while you don't have to be towed to a charging point as often. I'm sure Mom would've been keen to protect the environment because she'd have four grandchildren to think about.

She never got to meet any of them, nor did Dad. I often think about that. The unfairness of them both dying before their son and daughter grew up, let alone their grandchildren. The strange thing is, it's not something I ever thought about years ago. I was eleven when Dad died and seventeen when Mom went, and that was that. My sister and me, we were on our own and we didn't get much help or sympathy from anyone. We were never led to believe it was anything we should feel sorry for ourselves about!

Eleanor married Mike, and then Nancy and I got married and life went on. Strange as it sounds, over the years I've even felt glad I got their deaths over and done with early in life. When I saw friends struggle to care for elderly parents: watching them get less and less like the people they knew, dealing with the emotions of it all, and understanding exactly what you're about to lose for good. I'd escaped that and thought, "There's an upside to everything" more than once.

These days, whenever my mind wanders, it's not to the kids, but to Mom and Dad, the few years they had together, and with us, and how they'll always be young. I'm three times as old as either of them ever was. If we were to meet now, I'd look like the parent! I got no complaints about my life. When it happens to me, they can hammer that lid down and know that I'm ready for the final nail. It's just I can't get over my sadness for poor Mom and Dad, who never got to live even half the life I have.

Sid

To: Let's Get Quizzical [group]
From: George Tyme
Date: October 29, 2019
Subject: Re: Happy day!

Thanks, Sid, we enjoyed our night at the pub as usual, and what a laugh to see the serious teams taken down a peg or two! Their faces were like a row of smacked arses.

She didn't think to mention it last night, but Bunny knows the old girl Mal mentioned. She visits Bayview with the choir and Shirley is the oldest resident there. Says you can still chat with her, even though she's pushing 101. Marvelous.

Bunny and I were in The Case last week and the young lady on Chris and Lorraine's team was behind the bar. I said to Sue, "Who's that you've got here now?" and she said, "It's Fiona. She was living in a B&B with tramps, so we said she could move in here." Mal takes her to college and she works in the bar five nights a week. Getting along fine apparently. They're a lovely couple, Sue and Mal. We're lucky to have them at The Case.

George

To: Let's Get Quizzical [group]
From: Margaret Dawson
Date: October 29, 2019
Subject: Re: Happy day!

Bunny knows the lady who answered the questions? That's cheating. The whole idea of the quiz was that we didn't know who had answered, so all teams were equal. We should come clean to Mal and let him decide whether we broke the rules or not.

To: Let's Get Quizzical [group]
From: Bunny Tyme
Date: October 29, 2019
Subject: Re: Happy day!

I don't KNOW the lady. I saw her in the lounge at Bayview last Christmas and we had a quick chat about whether she enjoyed the sing-along. I didn't ask her where the 1980 Summer Olympics were held or who won Eurovision with "All Kinds of Everything." If I'd known what Mal was planning I still wouldn't have asked, because that would have been unfair.

You're right, George: Sue and Mal are good to take that young girl in. I'm assuming they don't know her from Adam and that's a risk when someone's in your home day and night. It may not even be her who's dodgy. She might have friends who are criminals, or a boyfriend who wants to get what he can out of a nice middle-aged couple. She might unwittingly pass information to people who use it for a burglary. Pubs can be targeted for protection money, illegal alcohol-smuggling, and plain old theft. The number of old folk killed in their homes is shocking. Sue and Mal are either very foolish or very brave.

Anyway, thanks for a great evening, team. It was nice to come second and lovely to see Ami's Carrots win for the first time. It beats me why a group of youngsters like that turn up at The Case every week—it's not exactly a jiving nightspot. If I knew which one was Ami, I'd have congratulated her by name.

To: Let's Get Quizzical [group]
From: Sid Topliss
Date: October 29, 2019
Subject: Re: Happy day!

That's put a wrench in the works, Bunny. You should've mentioned your conflict of interest to Mal last night. I'll have to let him know and he can decide whether to keep our second-place finish in the records.

To: Mal Eastwood
From: Sid Topliss
Date: October 29, 2019
Subject: We cheated again

Dear Mal,
It is with great embarrassment that I have to confess our team benefited from an unfair advantage in Monday's quiz. I had no idea at the time, but Bunny is friendly with the lady whose answers you wanted us to predict.

We hereby disqualify ourselves and I assure you, personally, that I will do my best to ensure it doesn't happen a third time.

Yours sincerely, Sid

To: Sid Topliss
From: Mal Eastwood
Date: October 29, 2019
Subject: Re: We cheated again

I've had a look at your answer sheet, Sid. If I were to consider this issue demographically, I'd say your advantage was not in Bunny's friendship with Shirley but in the close generational proximity of Shirley to the Let's Get Quizzical team. Now, I'm not suggesting any of you are nearing your centenaries, but Shirley is one of our last remaining representatives from your parents' generation. Having been brought up by them, you're more familiar with that generation than the other teams, perhaps more even than you realize. Shirley may have grown up in a Commonwealth country rather than the UK, but she's spent sixty years in Hertfordshire, and her children, grandchildren, and great-grandchildren have kept her in touch with the modern world. Correct me if I'm wrong, but something about Shirley reminds you of your parents? If you had any advantage over the other teams last night, then that was it and, in my eyes, it's not unfair. Your second place stands.

To: Let's Get Quizzical [group]
From: Sid Topliss
Date: October 29, 2019
Subject: Re: Happy day!

So, Malcolm says we had an unfair advantage last night thanks to Bunny's relationship with Shirley. It's tough, but the quizmaster's decision is final. He says the best way for us to move on from this whole affair is for Bunny to buy the drinks at next Monday's quiz. I'm happy with that. See you then,

Sid

To: Mal Eastwood
From: Bunny Tyme
Date: October 29, 2019
Subject: A question from me

Dear Mal,
Sorry to bother you, but Sid says you told him I should buy the drinks at the quiz next Monday. Is that true?
   Love, Bunny

To: Bunny Tyme
From: Mal Eastwood
Date: October 29, 2019
Subject: Re: A question from me

I told him nothing of the sort, Bunny. That Sid is a crafty one! If I were you, I'd only trust him as far as I could wrap him up and mail him.

To: Mal Eastwood
From: Bunny Tyme
Date: October 29, 2019
Subject: Re: A question from me

Thank you, Mal. That's all I need to know. Don't mention anything, please. I'll deal with Sid in my own sweet way . . .

   While I'm here emailing you, can I tell you something? It's about that young girl who's staying with you. Now, she seems very nice, if a little bit quiet, but you and Sue are so trusting and bighearted, I'd hate for you to be taken advantage of.

   There was this friend of a friend I had—happened years ago. She and her husband took a youngster in, just like Fiona. Nineteen, twenty, that sort of age, but had no family and it seemed like the decent thing to do, especially as a young person might get in with a bad crowd if they're not supported. This couple, their own children had grown up and moved away, but they ran a small plant nursery and could always use some extra hands, so they made up a bedroom, gave the girl her own space and three meals a day. In return she helped out at the nursery, so she didn't feel like a burden. The weeks went by and the couple thought the arrangement was working. Then they began to feel unwell. Tired all the time and off their food. They took a week off to rest, but it made no difference. Had their gas appliances checked—nothing wrong there. Changed their diets, bought some vitamins, but still they'd feel sleepy at all times of the day. At night they'd be out like two lights and would wake up at ten, feeling like they hadn't slept a wink.

Meanwhile the girl stepped up. Did their shopping, booked doctor's appointments, looked after their business, and was soon running it single-handed. The doctor recommended a vacation, so the couple went off on a cruise. Within twenty-four hours of boarding the ship they both felt a whole lot better and, six weeks later, they arrived home.

Stood on the doorstep with their cases and duty-free, they were puzzled to discover their keys wouldn't open the front door. They texted the girl, who'd messaged them just a couple of hours earlier to say how she was looking forward to seeing them again . . . only she didn't reply. The couple looked through their lounge window to see an empty room. All the furniture—everything inside had GONE. Then the front door opened.

"Can I help you?" It was a lady they'd never seen before, mop in hand.

"Are you a cleaner?" the couple asked.

"This is my new house!" she said with a laugh. "You should've seen the state the last people left it in."

It wasn't their home anymore.

To cut a long story short, Mal, the girl had been planning it for months. While the couple were unwell she transferred ownership of the house and business into her name. They'd given her access to their credit and debit cards and to their company accounts so that she could buy things and run the business on their behalf. She SOLD both house and company right under their noses. She'd cleared every bank account they had, sold anything and everything of value. And why did they feel so much better on that first day of their cruise? Because they were no longer taking the drugs she'd been secretly feeding them for months.

It was the perfect crime, so the police said, because who recommended they go on the cruise? Yes, a private doctor she'd booked for them. Her BROTHER. He'd posed as the consultant who assured them they were merely tired and needed a long break. Of course, police eventually caught up with them, but by then the poor couple had lost EVERYTHING.

I'm sure that's not what's going on with that young lady, Mal, but I don't want to see you and Sue destitute on the streets or murdered in your beds.

Lots of love, Bunny

To: Bunny Tyme
From: Mal Eastwood
Date: October 29, 2019
Subject: Re: A question from me

Thanks for that, Bunny. Good to know you're looking out for us, but I can assure you the most Fiona would get out of our bank accounts is a good laugh. I can't see anyone wanting to take over tenancy at The Case, by fair means or foul, and neither Sue nor I are keen on the idea of cruising. But I understand your concern and appreciate the sentiment. Now, you make sure Sid gets his comeuppance for trying to make you pay for his booze.

Mal

Text messages between Mal and Sue Eastwood, October 29, 2019:

Mal
Fiona hasn't shown an interest in the accounts or admin for the pub, has she?

Sue
She doesn't show an interest in anything except her wages. Hardly surprising. Now the novelty has worn off, she can see she's stuck in this place with us two fuddy-duddies. She comes alive for the quiz, though, doesn't she—bless. It's the effect of the other young people, I'm sure. Pity we can't attract them the rest of the week.

Mal

Something Bunny said made me wonder if we should be careful what she does and doesn't see.

Sue

We don't have anything suspicious hanging around, do we?

Mal

It's in the safe.

Extract from a witness statement made by Farhad Darya, November 1, 2019:

My name is Farhad Darya. I am forty-four and last lived at Halfway House, although I haven't been back there in a while. I'm making this statement via my lawyer. I appreciate it's taken the police a while to find me and apologize. I have been a user of drugs but am now clean.

I met Mr. Luke Goode on a rehab program in a community clinic. I can't remember exactly when. He was a great bloke and could make you laugh just by saying something in a funny way. He'd sing for us in the evenings because someone else on the program could play the piano in the clinic. Very happy memories. I heard rumors he was an actor and had been onstage with some famous people but I don't know how true that is.

I met Mr. Goode and his friend Steph on September 2, 2019. They would ask me to go with them around the pub quizzes because I've got the smallest phone and can google answers under the table.

The pubs were getting wise to us, so Mr. Goode said we should try one farther out. He'd seen an ad on Facebook for a quiz in Fernley. We got there and I don't know how they knew us, but they threw us out before we could sit down. The bloke said we were cheats!

Micky, who was with us, him and me, we knew it was a lost cause and started walking home straightaway. I wanted to get a debt back from someone who owed me, anyway. Luke was in the pub longer than we were and when he came out he was holding his nose like he'd been decked. He said he was all right but that someone he used to work with was in the pub and there was something about them. He didn't say what, but there was a look in his eye. Like he had a plan or something. I assumed it was about money, maybe that person owed him. He told Steph to go back to town with us.

When I looked back, Luke was walking through the trees—you could see him a mile away in that orange coat he'd lifted from a charity shop. I assumed he would hang around outside until his old friend left the pub.

I didn't think anything of it, even when I didn't see Mr. Goode in the following days and weeks. I'd got a place at Halfway and was making a go of it. I was shocked to hear about Mr. Goode's body in the river. I have no idea how he ended up losing his life and had nothing to do with it.

Text messages between PCSO Arthur McCoy and Mal Eastwood, November 1, 2019:

Arthur
Want to know the latest?

Mal
You can never know too much, Arthur. Fire away.

Arthur
Murdered male pulled deceased from water down by yours most likely died by single blunt-force trauma to head.

Mal
Thanks for keeping us in the loop.

Arthur
Trained as an actor up north.

Mal
Heard he was an actor, yep.

Arthur
Couldn't find work. Moved down here. Still couldn't find work, but found drugs and alcohol instead. Got in with a rowdy lot.

Mal

Shame.

Arthur

Seen or heard anything from the others he was with?

Mal

Thankfully not.

Arthur

We've spoken to them now. All profess their innocence and seem quite plausible.

Mal

Plausible? That's the sign of a good criminal, Arthur! They look you in the eye and lie without a flicker. Such commitment to the facade of innocence they believe it themselves.

Arthur

You're right there! But saw them myself, walking away from the scene. They'd need to have killed him immediately on leaving the pub, or doubled back and ambushed him. Neither very likely. Then there's the question of motive.

Arthur

Hear anyone mention they recognized Luke Goode? Perhaps worked with him in the past?

Mal

No. There are no actors in our pub that I know of, but we'll keep our ears open.

Arthur

Any more acts of vandalism?

Mal

None at all, thank you, Arthur. Anything else, let us know.

Ye Olde Goat Ltd. WhatsApp group, Hertfordshire, November 2, 2019:

Diddy & Con, The Brace of Pheasants
What was the name of that crack quiz team, Mal?

Sue & Mal, The Case is Altered
This is Sue, love. They're The Shadow Knights.

Diddy & Con, The Brace of Pheasants
We had them here yesterday! They won with a twenty-three-point lead.
Only dropped three points the whole quiz.

Sue & Mal, The Case is Altered
This is Mal now. What did they say, Diddy? Are they coming back to The
Case?

Diddy & Con, The Brace of Pheasants
They didn't say, but a few of our regular teams would be happy if they
never showed up again.

Peter Bond, The Lusty Lass
New blood runs cold.

Sue & Mal, The Case is Altered
I didn't intend for the special quiz to scare them away. I should've been
clear it was a one-off.

Mimi & Flo, Tom's Bar
What do they look like? We'll keep an eye out for them.

Diddy & Con, The Brace of Pheasants
Their top fellow is called The General and he has a military air about him.
A blond fellow and his son in his twenties. The women, we didn't get their
names, but all look like they work in university libraries.

Sue & Mal, The Case is Altered
That's them. Elite quizzers all. Did you notice anything odd about them?

Diddy & Con, The Brace of Pheasants
Well, Con takes great pride in our mailing list, so we collar new teams for
their contacts. But when I asked The General for his number or email, he
declined to give any details. Very politely, I might add.

Sue & Mal, The Case is Altered

They're a mystery. And they want to remain one.

Sean & Adrian, The Rainbow

We'll look out for them too. Although you have to book a table in advance for our quiz, so if they show up they'll HAVE to leave full contact details.

Sue & Mal, The Case is Altered

That's interesting to know, Sean. If they never show up at The Rainbow, that could be the reason why.

Text messages between Sue & Mal, The Case is Altered, and The General, November 2, 2019:

Sue & Mal, The Case is Altered

Hello there, General! Will we be seeing you at our quiz on Monday? It's very popular now and we like to know how many tables are needed.

Sue & Mal, The Case is Altered

In case you were afraid the quiz would be an unusual one, like last week, then I can assure you that was a unique occasion in honor of Mrs. Thompson's 100th birthday and not a taste of quizzes to come.

Sue & Mal, The Case is Altered

Not that you seemed afraid. I don't want you to abandon The Case. You really liven up our quiz nights. As for last week's quiz, well, you know how good it feels to finish at the top of the table. It gave a welcome boost to our loyal teams that historically don't score very highly.

Sue & Mal, The Case is Altered

If there's anything else you need to know, just ask. I hope to see you on Monday.

Text messages between Mal and Sue Eastwood, November 2, 2019:

Mal
I might've given too much away to The General. Mentioned the unusual quiz gave the other teams a chance to shine. It now looks like I did it deliberately to stop The Shadow Knights winning.

Sue
You did do it deliberately, but giving the others a "chance to shine" is a good thing. Proves we're "inclusive," like Fiona says everything must be.

Mal
She was talking about college courses. Interesting The Shadow Knights have been coming to our quizzes, without fail, for two months, but only went to a different quiz when they lost.

Text messages between Sue Eastwood and The General, November 2, 2019:

Sue
Hello, General. Are you looking for a new home quiz now?

Sue
If you're not coming to ours anymore, my offer of a drink here on a quieter night still stands.

Text messages between Mal Eastwood and Diddy & Con, The Brace of Pheasants, November 2, 2019:

Mal
Quick question. How much did The Shadow Knights win last night?

Diddy & Con, The Brace of Pheasants
£30. It was a good turnout.

Text messages between Mal and Sue Eastwood, November 2, 2019:

Mal
I think The Shadow Knights might be quizzing for money.

Sue
No, they aren't! Divide any quiz prize by six and you're talking loose change. If they were quizzing for money they'd go to the big-bucks pubs.

Mal
For the big-bucks tournaments they need ID just to take part. These little pub quizzes are all cash-in-hand winnings. Tax-free.

Sue
Tax-free peanuts! Speaking of which, Fiona's employment code has come through. She's officially on our payroll. You need to draw up a proper contract.

Mal
Will do. Meanwhile we have to sweat it out until Monday to see if The Shadow Knights turn up again.

Sue
Whether they do or not, it's out of our hands, but there is one thing—in Fiona's contract, you should stipulate that she doesn't tell anyone we used to be police.

Mal
Why would she think that?

Sue
When we were clearing out the office she saw some papers and an old warrant card. I told her I kept it as a souvenir, that she shouldn't say anything as people are funny when they know, and she seemed fine, but best to have it in writing.

Mal
While you were both clearing out the office? That was ages ago—did you not think to mention it sooner?

Sue
Didn't think it was important.

Mal

Of course it's important. We've kept it from even our closest regulars for two years! You should've been more careful!

Sue

It's not something to be ashamed of, is it?

Mal

I disagree. The less people here know about it, the better.

Sue

I told Fiona not to say anything, and she agreed. Most things I say go in one ear and out the other, so I bet this didn't even register on her radar.

Ami's Manic Carrots WhatsApp group, November 2, 2019:

Bianca

Can't make Monday's quiz. Covering a friend's shift.

Harrison

Aw, we'll miss you. At least you were there for our winning moment.

Fliss

We could ask Fiona to make up the numbers.

Jojo

Fiona who?

Fliss

The girl on Chris and Lorraine's team. Does anyone know her?

Harrison

She's nineteen, works behind the bar during the week, but they let her have Monday nights off to do the quiz. She was in a B&B, and the new guy who works in housing got her on the team. When Sue and Mal found out she was homeless they said she could live at the pub. She's in her first year studying hospitality at the new vocational college in Fernley.

Fliss

You chatted with her maybe ONCE at the bar and you found out ALL that?

Rosie

What did you think, Harry? Is she OK?

Fliss

She might shake us out of the last-place rut we're in.

Evie

We should be careful. Could be one of THOSE situations.

Fliss

Making a new friend? Winning the quiz?

Evie

When you see someone's on their own and feel sorry for them, so you invite them into your circle. Then you realize WHY they were on their own—they're clingy, creepy, disruptive, or controlling. Your friends ghost you because they associate you with the new person, and there's nothing you can do about it, because by then they've got you. They know everything about you—your hopes, dreams, and what buttons to press to control you. You're their helpless puppet. The worst thing is, you can't get rid of them without a MASSIVE drama.

Rosie

Oh God, yes. I vote we stay as we are.

Fliss

You're overthinking again, Evie.

Harrison

And I thought I was the writer around here! That made me shiver. 👻

Bianca

I'LL BE BACK NEXT WEEK! This guy's mom is having chemo and he wants to spend the evening with her. I try to be nice to someone who's going through a hard time and my "friends" can't wait to replace me behind my back.

Harrison

No! You're irreplaceable, Bee.

Bianca

We're a team. The six of us. Another person would upset the dynamics, whether they're a creep or not.

Fliss

I just saw her on that team with all those old people and thought she might like to spend one week with us. We'd get to know her. She'd get to know us. We might do better in the quiz.

Harrison

Fliss has victory fever. One win and she's rethinking the whole team.

Fliss

I don't see the problem.

The Sturdy Challengers Quiz Team WhatsApp group, November 3, 2019:

Thor's Hammer

We checked with Mal at The Case this lunchtime and he assures me tomorrow's quiz will be normal, even though he hasn't ruled out "shaking things up" again in future. I've been refreshing my memory of films and entertainment. History of: Bond, Ealing, Hammer, and Carry On. Oscar winners. Bafta winners. Grammy winners. Tony winners.

Lorraine

I've been learning facts about US presidents, such as oldest, youngest, shortest serving, longest serving, who died in office, who was assassinated, whose faces are on Mount Rushmore.

Ajay

Continuing my Olympic and Paralympic Games fact odyssey. I'm up to the 1980s and looking at starting on Premier League facts too.

Keith

No need, Ajay—Chris and I are Premier League nuts. This week I've studied US music: Nashville, Motown, Tamla, Muscle Shoals, Stax, Disco, Hip-Hop, Grunge, EDM.

Thor's Hammer

Andy and Fiona?

Andrew

Sorry, team, I've had to work today. Still here. A while ago my colleague went long-term sick. I said I'd take her caseload while they recruit. Only they're taking so long I don't think they are.

Andrew

This is how it is now. Feel like I live at my desk and only go home temporarily. When I get home, I feel like a stranger, as if I'm not part of my own life. Time stands still in that flat, but while at work I'm in a high-octane race against it—a race I'm losing. Got this buzzing in my ears.

Thor's Hammer

Bit disappointing, Andrew. You're our UK political-history buff. Fiona?

Fiona

cartoons

Thor's Hammer

OK. Well, I can't see how watching cartoons will be useful, but you never know.

Text messages between Andrew and Fiona, November 3, 2019:

Andrew

I'm sure Chris is delighted you're studying cartoons, because last week goes to show anything can happen at The Case is Altered quiz.

Fiona

ha ha

Andrew

k

Fiona

def cartoons

Andrew

Definitely cartoons? What do you mean?

Fiona

saw Mal's notes 🙄

Andrew

Right. OK. Not sure what to do with that info. Oh my God, Fiona. I wish you hadn't mentioned it. OK. Did you *accidentally* catch a glimpse, so you know *roughly* what the marathon is, but you didn't see any *actual* questions? If you saw the *actual* questions, that would be too much of a . . . not cheat as such, but a *thing* and I'd have to tell Chris.

Fiona

n

Andrew

OK, well, that's a relief. If we can keep it between ourselves, we don't need to mention it to anyone else. Agreed?

Fiona

k

Andrew

Good. Mal shouldn't leave his notes lying around where you can see them. Really, it's on him, right?

Fiona

k

Andrew

He did leave them lying around, didn't he? Where did you *glimpse* them?

Fiona

in the safe

Andrew

But you did only *glimpse* them?

Fiona

ys under his

Andrew

Under his water pistol?

Fiona

time 🤭

Text messages between Andrew and Lorraine, November 4, 2019:

Andrew

Sorry, Lorraine. Hate to bother you with this, but something came up last night.

Lorraine

Don't tell me you can't make the quiz, Andy.

Andrew

I'll be at the quiz. The problem is Fiona. Mal should've been more careful with his quiz questions, but somehow she saw a quiz round—enough to know it's "cartoons."

Lorraine

That sounds like a marathon round. Maybe "Name these characters" or "Which cartoon is this scene from"?

Andrew

Something like that. Should we tell Mal?

Lorraine

Mal works hard on the quiz, we don't want him to abandon a whole round just because Fiona might have seen what it was about.

Andrew

You're right, but I wanted to escalate the issue. Make it a team decision. I don't know Mal very well, but as a former police officer, he'll be a stickler for honesty.

Lorraine

He used to be a copper? I never knew that.

Andrew

Fiona mentioned it. Sue too.

Lorraine

Now you've said it, I can see them in the uniform, and they were very quick to support the police when they set up shop down the lane.

Andrew

So if they find out we have an unfair advantage, I doubt they'd overlook it.

Lorraine

Thanks, Andy. You did the right thing. Keep it to yourself for now. See you tonight.

Text messages between Lorraine and Thor's Hammer, November 4, 2019:

Lorraine

Sorry to message at work, but this is important. Fiona wasn't being obnoxious when she said she'd been watching cartoons. She's only gone and seen Mal's question sheet! Andy told me.

Thor's Hammer

This would happen on the day we've got a big maneuver. Can't leave the floor, it's my turn to run the collider. I'll be fired if they see I've got a phone on me.

Lorraine

Andy says we should tell Mal we've got an advantage.

Lorraine

Mal and Sue used to be police. Did you know?

Lorraine

They're keeping that quiet, aren't they?

Thor's Hammer

In toilet. Just rung Keith. He's confident about Marvel and DC characters, so he's got CBeebies on in the garage now. Lor, you look up cartoon characters from The Beano, The Dandy, and The Eagle.

Lorraine

Does "cartoons" mean cartoon strips, moving cartoons, or both?

Thor's Hammer

Fiona will know modern Disney princesses, which is a big thing. But very RECENT and very OLD cartoons will be our Achilles' heel.

Thor's Hammer

Also manga and anime. I don't know the first thing about them, so get yourself a working knowledge of their history and characters before tonight.

Lorraine

You don't think we should mention it to Mal?

Thor's Hammer

We don't know what the questions are—only that one word: cartoons. I've left a message on Andy's phone to call Fiona and tell her not to mention anything to Mal or Sue. If she has already, he must let me know before the quiz starts.

Thor's Hammer

Don't assume you'll remember cartoon characters from your childhood, Lor. I've just googled and it's shocking how much you forget. Chucking phone in locker now and going back to the floor before someone presses the wrong button and bang! Counting on you, Lor. 🧐

Lorraine

Logan used to like Bob the Builder, Fireman Sam, and something with a friendly dinosaur. I'll know all those if they come up.

Thor's Hammer

Can't have a meltdown, love. Don't forget Pixar, DreamWorks, and Studio Ghibli.

Text messages between Andrew and Fiona, November 4, 2019:

Andrew

Tried calling you, Fiona. You didn't pick up, so you must be in class. Chris and Lorraine think it's best we don't mention that you saw the cartoon round in Mal's safe.

Fiona

k

Andrew

When you think about it, there's not much advantage. We don't even know if he means cartoon strips or films.

Fiona

k

Andrew

Was the water pistol a clue, do you think? I remember watching
something with my nephew.

Fiona

wtf?

Andrew

Might have been Anvil & Bluesy. They each have a water pistol, but only
one is loaded.

Fiona

wut water pistol?

Andrew

They stand back-to-back, take three paces, turn, and fire. 💥

Fiona

duh! Emoji fail

Andrew

But Bluesy fires at nothing, because what you don't see is that Anvil
slipped away; as soon as Bluesy realizes he fired at thin air, there's a tap
on his shoulder, he turns, and whoosh!—he gets soaked. Anvil had crept
up behind him instead. JJ watched it again and again and laughed louder
every time. It was as if knowing exactly what was going to happen next
made it even funnier.

Fiona

I meant gun, duh!

Hulme Police
Operation Honeyguide

In association with the National Crime Agency
Anti-Kidnap and Extortion Unit (AKEU)
Senior Investigating Officer: Detective Chief Inspector Lewis Parry

Intelligence interview, recorded by Sergeant Dee Obasi's body-worn camera, May 6, 2014:

Subject: Kyle Reeves, The Copper Kettle, High Street, Axeford
Interviewing officers: Sergeant Dee Obasi and Sergeant Suzanne Eastwood

DO:　Darren Chester. Works for your lot, done a vanishing act.

KR:　Don't know him.

DO:　Come on, Kyle. The firm's not that big.

KR:　He won't talk to you.

SE:　We don't wanna chat to him, do we? We want to know he's all right.

DO:　Heard he's in deep shit with the brothers.

KR:　Why do you care?

SE:　"Care" is a strong word, but we don't want his corpse showing up and ruining our day, do we?

DO:　Is that likely to happen? Have you heard that much?

KR:　Heard someone's gone. Fucked off with Frank's shipment and Jerry's money. That's a lot of assets. They're shitting it that he's starting up somewhere with his own crew.

SE:　Who's in his crew?

KR:　Not me!

DO:　Who'd have *you*, eh?

KR:　[*Whispers*] I ain't getting involved in that side of things. When you cross the brothers, they go for your family. Anyone who means anything to you. Shit gets nasty. If Chester walked through that door right now, I'd be first on the phone to 'em.

DO:　What're Frank and Jerry doing to find him? They like to get creative.

KR:　Dunno and I ain't asking either. The less you know, the better.

Conversation between Sergeants Suzanne Eastwood and Dee Obasi, recorded in Patrol Car UA889, May 6, 2014:

SE: The guv is dead impressed you've already got a contact in the firm.

DO: That's easy, Sue. Charisma. I'm *very* attractive to felons with long rap sheets.

      [*They laugh*]

SE: He seemed OK.

DO: Here's his number. Go on. Have it.

SE: But he's *your* contact.

DO: He knows *you* as well now. You never know when he might come in handy, and you'll chalk up points with the guv. Eh, when we brief Parry, *you* do the talking. Let him know you're up to the challenge.

SE: Thanks, Dee, but why?

DO: Why? Here's a tip: ask Parry some pertinent questions. Sound like you're interested and it'll go a long way.

SE: I'll work on being pertinent, but . . .

DO: I don't like him dismissing you, Sue. You're worth more than that.

DCI Lewis Parry's informal meeting with Sergeants Suzanne Eastwood and Dee Obasi, May 6, 2014:

LP: OK, shoot.

SE: We met with Chloe's parents and Dee's CI.

LP: And?

SE: He didn't mention Beata and Chloe by name, but he's heard rumors someone's pissed off the firm, stolen their drugs and money, and hinted at the Maddoxes' rep for targeting family—

LP: OK. Cheers.

SE: Guv, are there any descriptions of the potential client Chloe went to meet?

LP: Nope. No one saw him. The area of land Chloe was showing him is behind Devil's Croke Woods. Middle of nowhere. Whoever drove her car back to town went miles out of their way to avoid every traffic camera, and abandoned it in a camera blindspot. They even walked through two front yards to avoid a camera at the grade crossing.
[*A phone rings*]

SE: So they knew exactly where they wouldn't be seen.

DO: Sorry, guv, I've got to answer this.
[*Sergeant Obasi's voice moves farther away*]
OK. I can take them. Yep. Don't you worry. I will. Six is fine, I'll see you then. Bye.
[*Sergeant Obasi returns*]
Sorry, guv, the friend of mine who passed away, her husband has to work, so I'm taking the kids to their school play tonight. I couldn't say no—

LP: Don't apologize, we've all had to muck in when friends need us. Sue, you and Mal go around to the Cunninghams' tonight after Rhys clocks off. Take the unmarked Focus, no uniforms, and use the lane to the rear, just like before. Have a chat, reassure them we're doing all we can, try to distract them from taking things into their own hands. We don't want them talking to the papers. I've got no other FLO with clearance to take over.

SE: Oh. Sorry, guv, we can't. We've got a quiz tonight, an important one. We both have to clock off on time.

LP: A *quiz*? This is a kidnapping, Sergeant Eastwood. We're working with the National Crime Agency here. I'm not telling them two of my officers can't do their duty because they're reciting winners of the Ryder Cup and doing anagrams over a packet of pork rinds. There's two women held hostage!

SE: OK, guv, I'll let Mal know.

LP: Quite apart from that, those poor parents are going through hell and they can't tell anyone, even family. With no FLO, they're alone overnight. You two are going around to the Cunninghams this evening and that's final.

Conversation between Sergeants Suzanne Eastwood and Dee Obasi, recorded in Patrol Car UA889, May 6, 2014:

SE: . . . that's what he said, Mal, and I've never seen him that annoyed before. It was after I'd asked a pertinent question too!
      [Sergeant Obasi can be heard chuckling in the background]
      He's usually Mr. Zen, so I rolled over and agreed. *[Pause]* No, I didn't mention we're defending last week's win. If you wanna march in there and tell him a quiz is more important than a live kidnap case, be my guest. I don't need the aggro.
      [Silence]
      Well, Mal's not doing a happy dance, not anymore.

DO: You can see why, though, Sue. It's crucial, this one.

SE: Well, yeah, it's the first time our team has had a winning streak. None of us wants to lose it. There's a national league place at stake—

DO: I mean Parry! Operation Honeyguide!

SE: Oh.
      [Silence]

SE: He was fine about *you* clocking off on time.

DO: I got in first, didn't I? Sorry. Anyway, Parry'll want Mal to meet the Cunninghams too. So the whole team's familiar to 'em.

SE: God knows why he wants Mal within a mile of victims.

DO: Because he's a good copper! No-nonsense. Down-to-earth. He's got that reassuring manner, has Mal.

SE: Oh, don't get me wrong, I love that man from top to toe, but he can't make small talk to save his life. If he feels out of his depth he'll either tell awkward jokes or reel off facts and figures. He's happy on Traffic. Got no interest in tricky cases or climbing the career ladder. Me neither, truth be told.

DO: You made sergeant.

SE: That was a scheme ten years ago to promote women. It meant more money, so I ticked the boxes and passed the course . . . But we're not like you, Dee.

DO: What d'yer mean! We're three peas in a pod, us!

SE: You're a highflyer. You'll be an inspector one of these days. We're happy moseying around just doing our jobs, then retiring to the country. Anyway, you'd better make tracks.

DO: I better had. Sorry, Sue. But those kids have been through so much, and Nat didn't want them to miss out because of what happened to her. I'll pay you back as soon as I can, promise. Good luck with the Cunninghams.

SE: Thanks and there's one good thing—I can show Mal that house. He'll be gobsmacked!

Downview visit 2, May 6, 2014:

Subjects: Caroline Cunningham, 47, and Piers Cunningham, 49, Downview, Moorcroft Lane, Pinfield Village
Visiting officers: Sergeant Suzanne Eastwood and Constable Malcolm Eastwood

ME: We could be settling down to the marathon round now.

SE: I weren't gonna argue with Parry in that mood. [*Whispers*] Anyway, you should see this place inside. It's a mansion. The Cunninghams are *filthy* rich.
[*Faint chimes of the doorbell*]

ME: As loaded as the Dead Rummy guy?

SE: More. Tell you who they remind me of: the Tudor Lodge couple. Remember the chap?

ME: The one who advised me to put my assets in diamonds and was surprised we *didn't* go to The Bahamas every Christmas?
[*They laugh*]

SE: Yeah, and asked us how many cars we had. Not *what* car we had, but *how many*. Guess it happens when you get that wealthy—you forget how normal people live. Which is dead convenient because you feel justified in hoarding your cash instead of helping others with it.
[*Silence*]

ME: Funny. We're pretty much the same age as the Cunninghams. There's the same hours in their day as in ours. So what have they done different?

SE: Property. Dee looked 'em up online. Their company was part of the group that built this posh estate. Piers retired last year and Chloe took over. A whole property business fell into her lap at twenty-one. How about that, eh?

ME: Ah, life choices. I see.

SE: If it wasn't for her choice in men, she'd be enjoying it all now, instead of . . .

ME: Shall I ring again, or has money made them deaf to the bloody doorbell?

SE: This is the back door, isn't it? They sit in the conservatory half a mile away. I can hear someone coming. [*Whispers*] Look out for the pool and gym.

[*A door opens*]

CC: Oh, is there any—

SE: News? No, no. Did Rhys mention we were coming? This is my colleague Constable Eastwood.

CC: Uh-huh. Come in.

[*Recording picks up again inside the conservatory*]

CC: This is Chloe's dad, Piers. This is . . . did you say *Eastwood*? Same surname as . . .

SE: Yes, we're married.

PC: And you work together? Handy, I suppose.

ME: I don't know about that. Most men go to work to escape! [*Silence*] Anyway . . . very impressive mock-Palladian mansion you've got here. Palladian being the mock-Roman style popular in the eighteenth century, although first seen in England as early as the sixteenth century, thanks to the work of Inigo Jones. What's the secret of your success, eh?

[*Silence*]

SE: Mal means it's interesting where life's path leads us.

PC: This house? Business. Property development. Then we invested in a building company that had a contract with Hulme council, which was very lucrative. Chloe is finding her feet as CEO now. She has lots of plans. [*Pause*] I'm sorry, I . . .

CC: She was doing well, wasn't she?

PC: She *is* doing very well . . .

ME: Bet you know a good deal when you see one, Piers.

PC: Maybe. But at the end of the day it's people like *you* who make a difference.

SE: We like to think so. It's not an easy job these days, policing.

ME: We have to rub shoulders with the scum of the earth. Scumbags who'd rob you blind and leave you in the gutter as soon as look at you—and that's just other coppers! [*Silence*] Anyway . . .

SE: Mal, you go and make us some tea while I chat with Caroline and Piers.

ME: OK, I'll . . . is it this way?

CC: Yes, and turn right. Thank you, Officer.

SE: Aw, call us Sue and Mal.

[*Constable Malcolm Eastwood leaves the room*]

PC: Have you found Darren Chester? Can you give us *anything*?

SE: I'm sorry, no, but there's all sorts going on behind the scenes. They'll be negotiating the women's release. My colleague and I have been working on the case all day. Picking up with our contacts on the ground—the CIs—gang members who pass info to us.

PC: What did they say?

SE: I can't tell you, Piers, you understand. These things are sensitive—

PC: Of course you can tell us, we're Chloe's parents!

SE: Well, keep it to yourselves—no telling Rhys either—[*Whispers*] but we found out Darren Chester skipped off with money and a shipment of Class A drugs belonging to a couple of nasty kingpins. These sorts of people are all about the business. Darren has taken something valuable to them, so they've stolen something valuable to him. His girlfriend. Both his girlfriends.

CC: She should never have got involved with him. If only we'd known, we'd have warned her off. I blame myself for not asking questions about who she was seeing, being nosier. But you don't want to drive them away by prying, do you? We didn't want her buying her own place, moving out, leaving us on our own. We made everything as comfortable here for her as we could.

PC: We should've let her grow up, spread her wings more.

CC: I know, I know. It's our fault this happened. She's led a sheltered life—how could she possibly know the danger signs? Some bloke comes along with all the talk and she falls head over heels . . .

PC: She probably knew we wouldn't approve or she'd have mentioned him.

CC: If she . . . If anything happens to her . . .

SE: You mustn't blame yourselves. It's not your fault, or Chloe's. Drug gangs are all negotiation, exchange, and payments. It's how they operate.

[*A period of silence until Constable Eastwood returns with tea. A sudden* ding-dong *of the front doorbell.*]

ME: Are you expecting anyone?

CC: No.

PC: Not at this time of night. Must be one of your lot.

SE: No, we use the back door. You two stay there, we'll answer it.

[*A period of indeterminate noise, shouting, and radio communications before the recording ends*]

Automatic transcription of DCI Lewis Parry's morning briefing for Operation Honeyguide, May 7, 2014. Recorded by Sergeant Dee Obasi:

Good morning. To update everyone on events last night. Officers Suzanne and Malcolm Eastwood were on a victim-support visit to Chloe Cunningham's parents when there was an unexpected ring at the doorbell. On arriving at the front door, both officers saw that a note, written on the same paper and in the same hand as before, had been posted through the door. Whoever did so vaulted the gates and escaped without being seen. A copy of the note is making its way around now. It says: "Tell DC: 12 hours till one dies."

The officers opened the door to see if they could lay eyes on a person or vehicle, but wisely didn't leave the house, so they didn't give away our presence there. May I remind everyone on this case to be aware that the Maddox Brothers still do not realize we're involved. Let's keep it that way.

AKEU officers have used Piers Cunningham's phone to relay that information to the phone number we have for Darren Chester. If the gang has Chester's phone, they will see the Cunninghams are complying with their request.

We all like to think this is an empty threat, but those of us who know the Maddox gang know they are more than capable of following through on it.

Rhys is with the Cunninghams now. Needless to say, they haven't slept all night. The senior team are working overtime to try and trace Mr. Chester and the negotiators are standing by. More news when I have it. Thank you.

Conversation between Sergeants Dee Obasi and Suzanne Eastwood and Constable Malcolm Eastwood, recorded in Patrol Car UA889, May 7, 2014:

DO: You're heroes, you two!

SE: Don't feel like it, Dee. Why, what did Parry say at the morning briefing?

DO: He said you'd used your brains and not gone all out to chase whoever posted the note. I'd have been after him like a shot—not thinking for a second it'd give anything away.

ME: Sometimes it pays to be a bit out of shape, Dee.

SE: Years since I had to chase anyone. Leave that to the young officers.

ME: Truth be told, it wasn't our quick thinking . . . By the time we found our way through the house, taking a couple of wrong turns, there'd be no point chasing anyone—they were long gone.

DO: Finding that note, though. Did you show Caroline and Piers?

SE: Didn't seem right keeping it from 'em.

DO: Bet they were devastated.

SE: She got a bit tearful. He was silent most of the time.
   [*Silence*]

SE: How was the play?

DO: Aw, the boys did so well! They're only little, look. Took pictures for their dad. See that one, and here . . .

SE: That's nice. Great little costumes.

ME: D'yer know what's bugging me?

DO: What?

ME: The fact we can't talk about Honeyguide with anyone; we can't even mention it exists. It's like *Fight Club*.

DO: You what?

ME: *Fight Club*. The film. Directed by David Fincher, based on a book by Chuck Palahniuk. Stars Brad Pitt and Ed Norton. Released in 1999.

SE: I can tell he's recovered from last night—the facts and figures are back!

ME: "The first rule of Fight Club is you do not talk about Fight Club. The second rule of Fight Club is you *do not* talk about Fight Club." It's a famous film, Dee!

DO: I know the line! It's an internet meme now, Granddad.

ME: Honeyguide is a *secret* operation. I'm sure we've had other gang kidnaps that weren't.

DO: This is different, though, isn't it? You get one gang kidnapping another gang's dealers or their chemist or their accountant. This is two totally innocent victims.

SE: Mal's right. The restriction means other forces aren't briefed to look out for the girls.

ME: And if the Maddoxes don't realize we're involved, I don't get what negotiations would be going on behind the scenes, like everyone is saying . . .

DO: Trying to find Darren, aren't they? If he's arrested, the brothers'll know where he is and they'll let the women go.

SE: We hope!

DO: They know what's best. Ours is not to reason why.

SE: You know what I find strange? Caroline and Piers. Sitting in the conservatory of that palace on its snotty private road. Totally silent. Not even a clock ticking. Parents who've lost their kids are usually hysterical or angry. Why are they so quiet?

DO: They're composed, I'll give you that. Maybe they were brought up to think showing emotion is a sign of weakness. Having your daughter kidnapped isn't normal—people are going to react in all sorts of ways. At the end of the day, what *should* they be doing?

ME: Good point, Dee.

DO: Now, let's get the teas in. The usual, everyone?
[*Sergeant Obasi leaves the car. There's a period of silence.*]

SE: Reckon our Dee has designs on her best friend's hunky widower.

ME: You might be right there. And good luck to her.

SE: She was dead proud of those photos. "School play" she said! Little toddlers dressed as nursery-rhyme characters.

ME: Well, she don't seem to think anything's off about this Honeyguide business.

SE: Oh, she does. There was *something* in her eyes; she's as curious
      about the op as we are. But she's got her heart set on that
      promotion, on climbing the ladder. So ambitious is our Dee, she
      won't step on a rusty rung.

ME: I know . . .

SE: But we're not ambitious, and we will.

Text messages between Sue and Mal Eastwood, November 4, 2019:

Sue
Why is Fiona sitting with the Manic Carrots?

Mal
?

Sue
Chris and Lorraine like her being on their team.

Mal
Busy setting up. Can't text.

Sue
Hope they're not upset.

Text messages between Andrew and Fiona, November 4, 2019:

Andrew
Mal is handing out the marathon round, are you coming over?

Andrew
So, I take it from the look you just gave me you're staying with that team?

Andrew
This is awkward. Chris and Lorraine specifically asked me to find a young person to balance OUR team.

Andrew
I've said you fancied a change of scenery and that at least you gave us that "cartoons" clue for the marathon round before you jumped ship. 😁

Andrew
This marathon round isn't cartoons at all! It's pictures of rock bands.

Fiona
sry

Andrew

Lucky for us The Shadow Knights aren't here. Chris is in a better mood all of a sudden.

Fiona

k

Andrew

Put your phone away. You'll get disqualified.

THE CASE IS ALTERED PUB QUIZ

November 4, 2019

Rounds	Max points
1. Today's News	10
2. On this day in 2009	10
3. Sport: soccer special	10
4. Books that caused a stir: controversial tomes	10
5. Film & TV: futuristic TV and film	10
6. Music: name the artist and song title	
(Clue: one or the other will feature a reference to cars)	20
7. History of theater in Europe	10
8. Food and drink	10
Marathon round: Name these 30 rock bands	30

Quiz teams and where they sat

The Sturdy Challengers
Chris & Lorraine
Ajay, Keith
Andrew

Spokespersons
Erik, Jemma
Tam, Dilip

Linda & Joe & Friends
Linda & Joe
Rita & Bailey

Let's Get Quizzical
Sid & Nancy Topliss
Bunny & George Tyme
Margaret & Ted Dawson

Ami's Manic Carrots
Jojo, Evie
Harrison, Rosie
Fliss, Fiona

Text messages between Thor's Hammer and Sue & Mal, The Case is Altered, November 4, 2019:

Thor's Hammer
This is more like it!

Sue & Mal, The Case is Altered
Because The Shadow Knights haven't turned up and your team is in the lead?

Thor's Hammer
Think we'll move back onto our rightful table in the intermission.

Sue & Mal, The Case is Altered
Stop texting, Chris, or I'll have to disqualify you.

Final scores out of 120

The Sturdy Challengers	105
Spokespersons	104
Let's Get Quizzical	83
Ami's Manic Carrots	76
Linda & Joe & Friends	62

The Sturdy Challengers Quiz Team WhatsApp group, November 4, 2019:

Thor's Hammer
WE DID IT! The Sturdy Challengers are back on TOP where they belong!

Lorraine
Well done, everyone. What a night!

Keith
Decent effort all around. Found our form. Good work, team.

Lorraine
Sorry you weren't with us to share the victory, Fiona.

Fiona
k

Thor's Hammer

[gif: The Golden Girls laughing and pointing]

Ajay

Congratulations, Sturdy Challengers! TBH the cycle home was a bit strained, with Spokespersons losing by just one point. 😂

Thor's Hammer

If they spent their energy studying for the quiz they'd be celebrating now!

Thor's Hammer

[gif: The cast of *Friends* jumping up and down on the sofa at Central Perk]

Andrew

The music round. Car tunes. Songs about cars. That's what Fiona saw.

Lorraine

I'm sure Mal's handwriting isn't the clearest and Fiona mistook his scribble for "cartoons." She mustn't feel bad.

Fiona

time 😆

Lorraine

Time is a great healer.

Thor's Hammer

But Keith is our rock god—our music oracle. 🤘

Keith

Only doing my job, sir. 👈

Thor's Hammer

[gif: Beavis and Butt-Head headbanging on a sofa]

Ajay

All that knowledge about cartoons might come in handy. I don't know how. 😒

Ajay

[gif: Bart Simpson twerking]

Thor's Hammer

With any luck, we've seen the last of The Shadow Knights. 🔭

Thor's Hammer

[gif: knights from *Monty Python and the Holy Grail* shouting "run away"]

Ajay

Yeah!! If they come back, we're stuffed all over again.

Thor's Hammer

I wouldn't say that.

Ajay

I just mean, well, we didn't score anywhere near as high as they usually do.

Ajay

If they're at The Case again next week, we're back to square one.

Lorraine

I'll study food and drink.

Andrew

Eurovision: UK entries and overall winners.

Keith

Periodic table—because you can never know it too well. And modern R&B. If Fiona's gone, we'll need to know our Doha Cat from our Bay once.

Keith

Not my mistake: autocorrect. Doja and Beyoncé.

Thor's Hammer

Never complacent. I'm going back to basics. Kings and queens of England, civil-war battles, and Roman emperors. The quizzer's bread and butter.

Ajay

I'll study Wimbledon, the Tour de France, and the golf Opens.

Lorraine

You haven't left our team for good, have you, Fiona?

Fiona

n

Andrew

She means no. I think.

Spokespersons Cycling Team WhatsApp group, November 5, 2019:

Erik
ONE POINT. ONE POXY POINT.

Erik
Was still awake at 5 a.m. Kept going over the answers we nearly got.

Dilip
Same here. Billy Joel. Kazakhstan. 1923. Ear. The Siege of Leningrad. Rapa Nui.

Jemma
All stuff we should have got. Like 1605, Lyndon B. Johnson, heptathlon, and Roxy Music.

Dilip
We knew all of them, just had two answers we were deciding between and went with the wrong one. Argh!

Tam
We did really well. Only one point off the win with only four members—the winning team had six.

Erik
If we'd got TWO of those dropped points, we'd have made it. So unfair.

Dilip
It's so totally fair and that's the trouble. I've got a whole day of work to do now, followed by a gym sesh, on two hours' sleep.

Erik
I'm flying to Copenhagen for meetings. On no sleep.

Tam
Ajay would definitely have got the Wes Anderson question.

Jemma
The Plucky Challengers, or whatever they're called now, were practically dancing on the tables. I've never seen Chris so happy.

Erik
Rubbing our noses in defeat. Bloody Ajay. Why did he have to switch teams? What happened to loyalty?

Tam
He couldn't say no to Chris and Lorraine.

Erik
At the time, but he's been with them for weeks now. It's time he "couldn't say no" to coming back with his cycling mates.

Ami's Manic Carrots WhatsApp group, November 5, 2019:

Bianca
Just in after my shift. What did I miss? Did they solve the murder?

Evie
No. The killer is still at large and we're back to the bottom of the league.

Fliss
Second to bottom. Fourteen points ahead of Linda & Joe, but seven points behind the next team.

Rosie
When we first came to the quiz I remember one of us saying, "We don't play to win," and, as a team, we continue to smash that goal.

Harrison
It's true, we don't. It's simply that we enjoyed the sweet taste of victory and now we're chewing on bitter defeat. And that morsel is tough to masticate.

Rosie

Harrison
At least we know Fiona a bit better now.

Jojo
Dull night, or just me?

Harrison
Dull because we came second to last or dull because there were no Shadow Knights?

Jojo
Dull because Fiona is a 🙄. She didn't answer a single question right. In fact she insisted "Fast Car" was by Iggy Azalea when I SAID it was Tracy Chapman.

Jojo
Rosie listened to HER, not me!

Rosie
Sorry, but she insisted Iggy Azalea had recorded a version and that was it. As answer writer, I have to go with the person who's most certain.

Jojo
She was forceful, not certain!

Harrison
She's only nineteen 👦 and, to be fair, even if we'd put Tracy Chapman, we'd still have come second to last.

Jojo
You'd think living at the pub would mean she had insider info.

Fliss
Mal is more professional than that.

Bianca
So you missed me?

Jojo
Yes!! Come back next week, Bee. 🐝

Evie
Fiona is a stunner, though, don't you think? I'm twenty-three and I feel OLD.

Fliss
Hard same.

Evie
It's no wonder Ed, the young Shadow Knight, gave her his number.

Jojo

What? How do you know that?

Jojo

And when? They weren't even there last night.

Evie

After the old-lady quiz last week. She said Ed stopped her on the way out and slipped her his number on a coaster. I guess he knew they wouldn't be back.

Jojo

Has she called him?

Evie

She didn't say.

Jojo

No one mentioned it to me. Did you know that, Harry?

Harrison

I wasn't going to say anything 😑, thanks, Evie.

Jojo

It's no big deal. I like to know the tea, that's all.

To: Let's Get Quizzical [group]
From: Sid Topliss
Date: November 5, 2019
Subject: LGQ is top of the pops!

We done it, team! Third place—without George cheating or Bunny having inside information. We can all feel proud of ourselves! Thank you, Bunny, for a steady supply of beverages throughout the evening. Consider yourself fully atoned for last week's misdemeanor.

My favorite round last night was the one on futuristic films and TV. I don't know about you, but I have many happy memories of watching *Star Trek, Thunderbirds, Captain Scarlet,* and the like. There was a time I couldn't have chosen between Lieutenant Uhura and Lady Penelope, but luckily never had to.

Thinking back, it's fascinating how we imagined the future back in the past. That future is now—now. In the 60s, 70s, and 80s if you'd said "Imagine 2019" to anyone, I'd bet most ordinary folk would see a world of intergalactic exploration, advanced flying machines, and visitors from other planets. No one imagined simpler inventions that would nonetheless change the world. With man landing on the moon in 1969, pocket phones that were also cameras must have felt further away in technological development than space travel.

If you'd told me in 1976 that I could see and speak to my family in Australia any time I liked (so long as they were awake), I wouldn't have believed you.

If I said now "Imagine 2075," what do you think most people would say? Biometric technology that implants chips under our skin? Day trips to the moon? Time travel to any period in history you care to choose? Or will the world go in directions we can't possibly imagine?

What if someone finds the secret to life itself, so that no one ever dies again? Imagine that. Practically, it would be very tricky to administrate. If no one died and people carried on being born, we'd run out of resources in a flash. We'd be overcrowded. Fighting each other for vital things, like food, water, money, and living space. It would be merry chaos.

They'd have to organize a way people could voluntarily end their lives, and if that didn't work, they'd have to run a lottery to get the numbers down. Say you're 150 years old, in perfect health and enjoying your everlasting life, when a letter drops on the mat one morning telling you to report for voluntary euthanasia the following week. You'd be devastated! Your family would be inconsolable. It would be a terrible prospect looming over you—this functional, administrative ending. You'd not take it lying down, you'd be dragged screaming to meet your end, like an innocent on the journey to the scaffold. You'd wish you'd been born in a time when death was inevitable and happened when, where, and whether you wanted it to or not. You'd look back on our time and envy us.

But of course that's never going to happen. No one will be opening letters in 2075! We'll be downloading correspondence to a biological message screen on the inside of our eyelids. We couldn't claim not to have received the order to report for our legal destruction or risk being zapped in the street by a fatal Taser that boils your insides like a microwave.

Have a good week, folks! See you at the next quiz—apart from Nancy, who I'll see when she gets in from Sainsbury's.

Sid

Text messages between Sue & Mal, The Case is Altered, and The General, November 5, 2019:

Sue & Mal, The Case is Altered
Morning, General.

Sue & Mal, The Case is Altered
Wondering if you'll be at The Case is Altered for next week's quiz?

Sue & Mal, The Case is Altered
The other teams missed you last night. No Shadow Knights, no competition. You can bet the winners consider their first place a hollow victory.

Sue & Mal, The Case is Altered
The Sturdy Challengers, formerly The Plucky Losers, came first with 105, one point ahead of the Spokespersons. They nabbed your table after the intermission too. You don't want to lose it!

Sue & Mal, The Case is Altered
We've got some cracking rounds planned for next week. I can confidently say The Shadow Knights stand an excellent chance of winning.

Sue & Mal, The Case is Altered
Of course if you don't turn up, then you definitely won't.

Sue & Mal, The Case is Altered
We heard you won last week at The Brace of Pheasants. Congratulations!

The General
Thank you, Mal. Good news travels fast. A phrase first used in 1592 by Thomas Kyd in his play The Spanish Tragedy.

Sue & Mal, The Case is Altered

There's no mystery there: we're part of the same brewery chain. We coordinate our quizzes in a WhatsApp group, so those who use the quiz books don't double up on rounds, thereby giving teams who go from pub to pub an advantage.

Sue & Mal, The Case is Altered

Not that it happens at The Case. We're a shade off the circuit out here and, anyway, we write our own questions. Will we see you this Monday?

The General

We're considering our options. There's a quiz at The Rainbow, for example.

Sue & Mal, The Case is Altered

Ah yes, The Rainbow quiz. Famous for its stringent registration process that means you have to give them your life story before you even sit down.

The General

Tom's Bar looks promising.

Sue & Mal, The Case is Altered

It's a gastropub. Mimi and Flo are chefs and their focus is food rather than entertainment. What's it like to quiz at The Brace?

The General

Did you know it's only a "brace" of pheasants when there are two birds? Typically, a male and female. Any more or less and it's not a "brace." The old-English word comes from old French, meaning "two arms," and is where we get the word "embrace."

The General

Over centuries the word, and the practice of tying dead pheasants together in male–female pairs, was embedded in hunting etiquette.

The General

The term also means to strengthen something. "Brace yourself for danger" or "the fence was braced with struts." I don't believe that's a coincidence at all. There's something immensely strong about two people, whether they're a couple or not. Two is stronger than one, of course, but it's also stronger than three, because three or more people can be divided. Two people are somehow more than the sum of their parts.

Sue & Mal, The Case is Altered
I've never thought of it like that, but I'm sure you're right. You usually are, after all.

The General
It's funny, but if you have six dead pheasants, you have "three brace," but if you have one more, you simply have seven dead pheasants. There is no such thing as half a brace.

Sue & Mal, The Case is Altered
Strange, eh!

The General
There are seven dead birds tied in a row on the sign outside The Brace. That's not "a brace" of pheasants by any stretch of the linguistic origins of the word.

Sue & Mal, The Case is Altered
I wouldn't pay much attention to pub signs.

The General
I find them very interesting. They hail from ancient times. When most people were illiterate, shops, hostelries, tradesmen, and so on had to advertise their business using pictures or symbols. Else how would anyone know what was available inside? In 1393 King Richard II passed an act that required all pubs to display a pictorial sign outside by law.

Sue & Mal, The Case is Altered
Because each area had an official ale-taster who had to tell each establishment apart. I know. We learned that on an introductory course the brewery runs.

The General
The quiz at The Brace was between six teams of up to six. It started on time at 7:30 p.m. The quizmaster was clearly spoken and kept the rounds moving at a good pace. She didn't update older questions, so at one point she asked, "What is Chancellor of the Exchequer George Osborne's constituency?"

Sue & Mal, The Case is Altered

Ha! That'll be Diddy. She's strictly by the book.

The General

We found this strange, but the regulars seemed to take it in their stride. There was one thing we noticed. But I probably shouldn't share it with you, as a rival pub.

Sue & Mal, The Case is Altered

The Case and The Brace rivals? Oh no! They're a lively city-center theme bar and we're a cozy country pub. No rivalry here! What was it?

The General

One of our team members has a photographic memory. She recalled seeing the face of someone in the bar from the report of a court case years ago.

Sue & Mal, The Case is Altered

Well, it's a big pub and I'm sure it's popular with all sorts.

The General

This man was imprisoned for befriending elderly and disabled people at ATMs, then conning their cash out of them. Not sure I could think of a more shameful crime. Yet there he was, bold as brass.

Sue & Mal, The Case is Altered

I'm sure Diddy and Con wouldn't want someone like that in their bar.

The General

Have you read The Spanish Tragedy, Mal?

Sue & Mal, The Case is Altered

Can't say I have.

The General

It's an influential work on the subject of vengeance. Inspired both Shakespeare's Hamlet and Middleton's The Revenger's Tragedy. Their themes have preoccupied writers and artists down through the centuries: that is, the legal, moral, and emotional complexity of taking justice into your own hands. A dilemma we still face today.

Sue & Mal, The Case is Altered
I can see why you win every quiz you take part in, General. You know so much.

The General
Always tragedies, do you notice that? There's never been a revenge tale with a happy ending for all involved, I know that much, Mal.

Sue & Mal, The Case is Altered
You certainly know a lot, General. But not everything. This is Sue, love.

Ye Olde Goat Ltd. WhatsApp group, Hertfordshire, November 5, 2019:

Sue & Mal, The Case is Altered
Get ready, Mimi and Flo . . . news hot off the press is that The Shadow Knights might be at your quiz this week!

Mimi & Flo, Tom's Bar
Shut up! How do you know?

Sue & Mal, The Case is Altered
Sue had a text from their main man. He's the one they call The General.

Mimi & Flo, Tom's Bar
Well, they'd better know their mirepoix from their bain-marie. We always slip in a few foodie questions.

Diddy & Con, The Brace of Pheasants
With any luck, they won't come here again. We don't want them.

Sue & Mal, The Case is Altered
Why not, Diddy? They're either the best quiz team I've ever encountered or they're cheating. But if they're cheating, they're doing it so well I haven't been able to catch them at it.

Sue & Mal, The Case is Altered
What I mean is, either way, they inspire admiration.

Diddy & Con, The Brace of Pheasants
We don't like our regulars feeling put out, and when The Shadow Knights won we had complaints.

Peter Bond, The Lusty Lass

Empty vessels make the most noise.

Sean & Adrian, The Rainbow

If anyone here complained about a new team winning, I'd suggest they up their game.

Mimi & Flo, Tom's Bar

Like your style, Sean! Our regulars are all lovely. I can't imagine any of them kicking off about being beaten fair and square.

Sue & Mal, The Case is Altered

This is the bone I'm gnawing on, Flo. ARE The Shadow Knights winning fair and square?

Diddy & Con, The Brace of Pheasants

We didn't spot any cheating.

Mimi & Flo, Tom's Bar

If they show up here, like you say, then we'll let you know what we think. Hope they do!

Text messages between Sue and Mal Eastwood, November 5, 2019:

Sue

OK?

Mal

Fiona and I can look after this crowd. Have your evening off.

Sue

Crowd? Are we finally the place to be?

Mal

Eleven. That's a crowd—or would be if they huddled together.

Sue

Where's the laugh emoji?

* * *

Mal

Get down here.

Mal

Please.

Sue

A twelfth customer turned the crowd into a mob?

Mal

She's here.

Sue

Who?

Mal

Luke Goode's girlfriend, wife . . . whatever.

Sue

Coming.

* * *

Sue

I'm back in front of Bake Off.

Mal

On edge now.

Sue

I know, but Stephanie only wanted to see where Luke died. Didn't realize it'd be too dark to go down there, so she came in here to warm up and have a cry. She's gutted.

Sue

Calls herself his partner, but reading between the lines, their romance was based on drinking. "Mates" is an overstatement too. They drifted together because it's better than drifting alone.

Mal

She's a poet, is she?

Sue

I asked why they went around the quizzes and she said it's for booze money. They cheat for pennies. Sad.

Sue

She lives in a hostel, and one of those men is properly on the streets.

Sue

We keep the winnings small to avoid trouble, but money prizes of any size attract problems. A few coins are a fortune if you have nothing.

Mal

Does she have a ladder and spray can by any chance?

Sue

She didn't deface our sign, if that's what you mean. Steph has no hard feelings toward us.

Mal

I should think not!

Ye Olde Goat Ltd. WhatsApp group, Hertfordshire, November 7, 2019:

Mimi & Flo, Tom's Bar
The Shadow Knights were here last night.

Sue & Mal, The Case is Altered
Did they win?

Sean & Adrian, The Rainbow
Serious FOMO. I hope they come to us next!

Diddy & Con, The Brace of Pheasants
You don't, Sean. The Shadow Knights are nothing but trouble.

Sue & Mal, The Case is Altered
Second that, Diddy!

Peter Bond, The Lusty Lass
No one raises greater ire than a winner.

Sue & Mal, The Case is Altered
What was their score? You did quiz 20 of the second edition. Just looked it up. It has a three-star difficulty rating, with rounds on Sporting Wins and Music History. The Shadow Knights are experts on both.

Mimi & Flo, Tom's Bar
We've never had this sort of upset at Tom's Bar. Not ever. Our regular clientele are lovely. Especially our quizzers.

Sue & Mal, The Case is Altered
What happened Flo?

Mimi & Flo, Tom's Bar
It's Mimi. Flo's still in bed. The last time she was still in bed at midday was when our dad died.

Sean & Adrian, The Rainbow
What on earth happened? Are you both OK?

Mimi & Flo, Tom's Bar
Sue and Mal, what do you know about The Shadow Knights? Because they disputed almost every answer. It was as if they were there to disrupt our quiz.

Sue & Mal, The Case is Altered
They are very serious quizzers, Mimi. What do you mean by dispute?

Mimi & Flo, Tom's Bar
In the Bible, God gives Moses the Ten Commandments. On how many stone tablets are they written?

Diddy & Con, The Brace of Pheasants
Two.

Sean & Adrian, The Rainbow
Two. And my father was a vicar, so no sass.

Mimi & Flo, Tom's Bar
And that's exactly what the quiz book says. Two. The Shadow Knights put four. Because apparently Moses broke the first pair of tablets and went back for a replacement set.

Diddy & Con, The Brace of Pheasants
That's right, it's four.

Sean & Adrian, The Rainbow
I remember that now—tricky one. What did you say?

Mimi & Flo, Tom's Bar
We showed them the answer in the back of the book. They maintained it was incorrect.

Sue & Mal, The Case is Altered

Did you tell them the quizmaster's decision is final, even if they are subsequently proven to be wrong?

Mimi & Flo, Tom's Bar

We've never had to say that. Anyway, it wasn't the worst dispute of the night. We asked, "Who sang 'Walking in the Air'?"

Diddy & Con, The Brace of Pheasants

Aled Jones.

Mimi & Flo, Tom's Bar

Which is what every team put, except one. They are our loveliest regulars. Wonderful people who do so much charity work. They put "Alex Jones." The Shadow Knights were marking their answer sheet and marked it wrong.

Sue & Mal, The Case is Altered

It is wrong.

Diddy & Con, The Brace of Pheasants

It's only one letter difference. I'd have given it to them.

Sean & Adrian, The Rainbow

Why did they write "Alex"? Everyone knows it's "Aled."

Mimi & Flo, Tom's Bar

The whole team knew it was "Aled," but the person writing their answers is dyslexic and, in the stress of the moment, wrote "Alex" instead. The others didn't notice.

Sean & Adrian, The Rainbow

In that case, give them the point.

Sue & Mal, The Case is Altered

No! It's still wrong, Mimi. Aled Jones is a chorister, and Alex Jones presents The One Show. If you were making their gravestones, you'd have to get the spelling correct!

Diddy & Con, The Brace of Pheasants

Con says Alex Jones is one of those conspiracy theorists.

Sean & Adrian, The Rainbow

Really? The One Show must've changed since I last tuned in.

Mimi & Flo, Tom's Bar

We said to give them the point, but The Shadow Knights wouldn't back down.

Diddy & Con, The Brace of Pheasants

Offer the team a bag or two of peanuts to shut up. That's worked for us before now.

Mimi & Flo, Tom's Bar

It was awful! We went one way and The Shadow Knights were pissed off; we went the other way and our regulars got really upset.

Sue & Mal, The Case is Altered

It's not a case of how either team feels, Mimi. The regulars wrote down the wrong answer. They didn't earn the point.

Mimi & Flo, Tom's Bar

But they foster problem teenagers!

Sean & Adrian, The Rainbow

Tricky. I can see the issue from both sides.

Diddy & Con, The Brace of Pheasants

A gray area.

Sue & Mal, The Case is Altered

There are no perspectives in a quiz and no gray areas. Only right and wrong. The answer sheet may be paper and ink, but to a good quizmaster, it's as solid as stone. What did you decide in the end?

Mimi & Flo, Tom's Bar

We gave them the point.

Sue & Mal, The Case is Altered

Well, I wouldn't have, but when all's said and done, you are in charge of the quiz, Mimi. Don't bow to pressure or you'll find someone or other will dispute every question.

Peter Bond, The Lusty Lass

Always some Rupert who wants things by the book.

Sue & Mal, The Case is Altered

Remember the best decision is not always the most popular.

Diddy & Con, The Brace of Pheasants
How did The Shadow Knights take it?

Mimi & Flo, Tom's Bar
They were silent for the rest of the evening. They won £19 with a twelve-point lead and left without a word. We usually have such a nice atmosphere at our quiz. They killed it stone dead, and over trivial points they didn't even need.

Sean & Adrian, The Rainbow
Aw, sorry, Mimi. At least it's over now and you can be sure The Shadow Knights won't be back. Thanks for sharing what happened—if they come to us, we'll be ready.

Sue & Mal, The Case is Altered
It's all in the question! This is why I don't like the quiz books and write my own. Each question must be clear, concise, and watertight. Its answer unequivocal. There can be no room for ambiguity. The quiz questions at The Case are something I take great care over and pride in.

Peter Bond, The Lusty Lass
Be careful, Mal. It comes before a fall.

Text messages between Linda and Wind, November 8, 2019:

Linda
Hello, luvvy! We missed you and Cloud at the quiz on Monday. Are you not coming anymore?

Wind
If Lizzie says it's OK, we'll be back.

Linda
Oh. What did she say about last Monday that meant you stayed away?

Wind
She warned us—and if I ignore her, she gets angry, so I stayed home. Cloud went to bathe in the woods.

Linda

He had a bath in the woods? Does he know someone was murdered here a few weeks ago?

Wind

He immersed himself in the forest to manifest positivity and counter negative energy at the pub.

Linda

Well, it's not the most luxurious boozer around, but Sue and Mal do their best, bless them.

Wind

Lizzie says something malevolent from the past has been suppressed, but it's trying to rise to the surface. It gathers momentum as it festers, and the longer it takes to emerge, the worse the final eruption will be.

Linda

Far be it from me to correct your spirit guide, but it's already happened! That body had been "suppressed" in the water when you dislodged it, and it "erupted" to the surface.

Wind

True, Lizzie is very sensitive and she could be reading the energy that led that poor man to the water. For Cloud and me, it was truly beautiful.

Linda

Beautiful? That's not what I heard.

Wind

If we hadn't mistaken the jetty for a mooring point, he might never have been found. Now he can return to his family, they can find peace, and he can rest as he wished. No one should be buried unacknowledged.

Linda

Well, we—that's Joe, Rita, and Bailey—love having you two on our quiz team. You've given our energy a boost these last few weeks and we'll be very sad to see you leave.

Wind

Thank you, Linda! You know, Bailey saw something the night the man died.

Linda

What? What did he see?

Wind

He wasn't specific. Just said he saw "something." We weren't there, so I wonder what actually happened?

Linda

Well, there were four rough 'uns who tried to join the quiz. Mal booted them out. The main rough 'un was the one you found dead a few weeks later. Apparently they're troublemakers who go around the pubs, cheating at the quizzes.

Wind

I see.

Linda

Did you tell Lizzie? What does she think?

Wind

I told her, but if she's thinking anything, then she's keeping her own counsel.

Linda

What a contrary little madam!

Wind

Cloud has a theory, though. He says the man's death didn't cause the negative energy—it's too deeply ingrained. More likely the negative energy led to his demise. That means there's something else, something worse that happened here. THAT will be what's bubbling to the surface.

Linda

Does he have a spirit guide too?

Wind

Oh no, Linda, nothing like that. He used to be a police officer, that's all.

Ye Olde Goat Ltd. WhatsApp group, Hertfordshire, November 11, 2019:

Mimi & Flo, Tom's Bar
Second edition, number twenty.

Diddy & Con, The Brace of Pheasants
Con downloaded a quiz from the internet. TV shows of the 80s and 90s.

Peter Bond, The Lusty Lass
1st edn, 28.

Sean & Adrian, The Rainbow
Third edition, quiz number eight.

Sue & Mal, The Case is Altered
Why did you get a quiz from the internet, Diddy?

Diddy & Con, The Brace of Pheasants
After The Shadow Knights rode into the sunset with the victory last week, we promised our regulars they'd get more of a chance this week. This one is super-simple, even Con and I got full marks!

Sue & Mal, The Case is Altered
Be aware, though, the easier the quiz, the more likely you'll need a tiebreaker to decide the winner in the event of two or more teams getting the same score.

Sean & Adrian, The Rainbow
Never thought of that. I don't think we've ever had a tie for first place.

Mimi & Flo, Tom's Bar
We have and we had no idea how to call it, so we declared the team with the best marathon score as the winner. It was a spur-of-the-moment decision. Mimi said later we should have left it as joint winners.

Peter Bond, The Lusty Lass
Victory shared is victory halved.

Mimi & Flo, Tom's Bar
What do you do if it's a draw, Mal?

Sue & Mal, The Case is Altered
I've got a tiebreaker in a sealed envelope at the back of my quiz folder, ready to be deployed.

Diddy & Con, The Brace of Pheasants
How does that work—and can we steal the idea if we need to?

Sue & Mal, The Case is Altered
You can have the idea, Diddy, but each quizmaster's tiebreaker is his or her own. I call mine the sudden-death round.

Sean & Adrian, The Rainbow
It sounds quite sinister!

Sue & Mal, The Case is Altered
All the teams that tie for first place elect a representative. In one fell swoop the team's quizzing power is reduced by the power of six. Whether they win or lose depends on how well they've selected their player.

Sue & Mal, The Case is Altered
Remember a tiebreaker is as much theater as it is a test of knowledge. Your rival quizzers should face each other in the middle of the room. Ramp up the energy until you can cut the tension with a coaster.

Sue & Mal, The Case is Altered
Retrieve your sealed envelope from its hiding place. Show it to the contenders and crowd alike. You need everyone to see those questions aren't being tailored for (or against) the quizzers and, for that reason too, you don't want to be pulling the questions out of thin air, because they are the most important of the evening.

Sue & Mal, The Case is Altered
Remember the people standing in front of you each have the weight of a team on their shoulders.

Sue & Mal, The Case is Altered
Both should fear they're not up to the task and if they aren't feeling the pressure by now, then the team hasn't chosen them wisely. Insist on absolute silence in the room, bar staff included. When the TV is off, the terse fellows playing pool have stopped their game, and all eyes are on you . . . unseal the envelope.

Diddy & Con, The Brace of Pheasants
And?

Diddy & Con, The Brace of Pheasants
What happens next?

Mimi & Flo, Tom's Bar
We've got to open up soon!

Sean & Adrian, The Rainbow
Oh, Mal! Such a tease . . .

Sue & Mal, The Case is Altered
Ask the question. Each contestant answers in turn and the winner is
decided when one answers incorrectly or can't give an answer at all.

Diddy & Con, The Brace of Pheasants
So this sealed envelope has a whole round of questions in it? One wrong
move and that team loses?

Mimi & Flo, Tom's Bar
Bit harsh.

Peter Bond, The Lusty Lass
Puts the "sudden" in Sudden Death.

Sue & Mal, The Case is Altered
There's only one question.

Mimi & Flo, Tom's Bar
If you ask one question and each contestant has to answer in turn, then
if contestant one gives you the correct answer, contestant two can just
repeat it.

Diddy & Con, The Brace of Pheasants
You're right, Flo. We didn't think of that.

Sean & Adrian, The Rainbow
Have you ever had to open your sealed envelope, Mal?

Sue & Mal, The Case is Altered
Not yet. And if The Shadow Knights come back, we'll probably never have
to. But it's there, ready. Waiting.

Diddy & Con, The Brace of Pheasants
Wait. Did I miss something? What are the questions?

Mimi & Flo, Tom's Bar

Some questions have multiple answers, don't they? Like "Name an actor who has won Best Actor at the Oscars more than once." There would be an advantage in going first. Which is why Mal says they take it in turns. Presumably you toss a coin for who goes first, Mal?

Diddy & Con, The Brace of Pheasants

Is that sort of question in one of the books?

Sue & Mal, The Case is Altered

You won't find these questions in any quiz book.

Sean & Adrian, The Rainbow

Is Flo right? Can you give us an example of yours, Mal?

Sue & Mal, The Case is Altered

Impossible. Every quizmaster must formulate their own.

Mimi & Flo, Tom's Bar

Do you have a theme? General knowledge, current affairs, local history . . . Because if these questions decide who wins outright, then they're important.

Sue & Mal, The Case is Altered

They're crucially important, Flo. They should test not a person's knowledge, memory, or recall but, purely and simply: their ability to answer.

Sean & Adrian, The Rainbow

Interesting. Well, thanks, Mal, but it sounds like a lot of extra work. Think we'll cross that bridge when we come to it.

Diddy & Con, The Brace of Pheasants

Us too! No doubt we'll fall off it straight into the water . . .

Peter Bond, The Lusty Lass

Puts the "death" in Sudden Death.

Text messages between Thor's Hammer and Sue & Mal, The Case is Altered, November 11, 2019:

Thor's Hammer
Sue or Mal?

Sue & Mal, The Case is Altered
Hi, Chris. It's Mal. How can I help you?

Thor's Hammer
Just out of interest, have The Shadow Knights been in touch about tonight's quiz?

Sue & Mal, The Case is Altered
In what way?

Thor's Hammer
Are they gone for good, or are they coming back?

Sue & Mal, The Case is Altered
I hope they'll come back, but they've been quizzing at other pubs, so who knows?

Thor's Hammer
If they find a better quiz than ours, they may stick with that one.

Sue & Mal, The Case is Altered
It would depend on what they deem to be "better." They've won every time at The Case, so may prefer a quiz where there's serious competition.

Thor's Hammer
Or a quiz where they can cheat even more easily.

Sue & Mal, The Case is Altered
I've not found The Shadow Knights to be cheating, Chris. True, they drop very few points, but they're good quizzers, that's all.

Thor's Hammer
Any clues for us this week?

Sue & Mal, The Case is Altered
I haven't written the questions yet.

Thor's Hammer

Any chance we could have a round of aviation questions?

Sue & Mal, The Case is Altered

It's a marginal subject, but I'd not rule anything out.

Thor's Hammer

Good. See you tonight.

Text messages between Mal and Sue Eastwood, November 11, 2019:

Mal

Chris has requested a quiz round on aviation.

Sue

That's nice.

Mal

Tonight's rounds are already decided. Anyway, he'd have expert knowledge—wouldn't be entirely fair.

Sue

Wonder what he does?

Mal

He can't talk about it, so must be stealth technology, experimental aircraft, etc.

Sue

He lives for the quiz.

Mal

But should I add an aviation round just because he wants an advantage?

Sue

The quizmaster's decision is final, and that goes for all aspects of the quiz.

Mal

Cheers for passing the buck.

Sue

You're welcome. Is Fiona out yet?

Mal

No. I'm parked by the college gates, staring at the students coming out, looking for all the world like a dirty old man.

Sue

How to sound like an ex-copper . . .

Mal

Here she is, dawdling along, eyes down, headphones on, like I've not been waiting for her these last forty-five minutes. Back soon.

Ami's Manic Carrots WhatsApp group, November 11, 2019:

Harrison

Are we all set for the quiz tonight?

Fliss

Not sure if it'll be useful, but I looked at some trivia.

Rosie

What sort of trivia? How do you know what questions might come up?

Fliss

Most populated country in the world—India, 1.4 billion people. Least populated—Vatican City, 799 people. Largest country by land mass—Russia. Smallest—Vatican City. 54 countries in Africa. 50 states in the USA. 48 counties in England. That kind of thing.

Evie

What if someone dies in Vatican City overnight?

Jojo

Wonder if The Shadow Knights will be there.

Bianca

I'm back, so if anyone wants a lift . . .

Evie

Yes please. I drove last week and hate that horrible murder lane. Fliss and Rosie had to help me park in the pitch dark.

Jojo

At least we won't need Fiona this week.

Rosie

I can't make the quiz! It's my sister's birthday party and she's going to New Zealand next week, so we want to make it an event to remember. I totally forgot it was today.

Fliss

Enjoy.

Harrison

Happy birthday to Lauren. Hope she has a good trip.

Evie

That's a shame! We'll miss you, but eat some cake for us.

Fliss

We'll be one person short again. Is it worth asking Fiona?

Harrison

Maybe. Six heads are better than five.

Jojo

She was no use at all and stopped us scoring that Tracy Chapman point.

Fliss

She got a couple of questions right. And that could make the difference in our placing.

Jojo

We don't quiz to win, remember.

Harrison

But it's so dull coming bottom of the table all the time.

Rosie

Remember how great it was to win, Jojo? Seriously, I was happy for days.

Jojo

OK, ask her if you like. But if she joins our team again, let ME write the answer sheet. I won't be intimidated by her.

Rosie

I wasn't intimidated by Fiona. She was super-certain it was Iggy Azalea.

Harrison

It was last week. Let it go!

Text messages between Mal Eastwood and The General, November 11, 2019:

Mal

Morning, General! Can we count on your team's presence at the quiz tonight?

Mal

This is Mal from The Case is Altered. It's my personal phone number.

The General

Morning, Mal. I don't know.

Mal

Hah, finally! I've found a question you don't know the answer to.

Mal

Only joking. I heard you went to Tom's Bar for the quiz last week, so you'll appreciate now how professional we strive to be at The Case.

The General

Certain quizmasters want to be liked, so are afraid to say no. They bow under pressure, no matter what side it comes from.

Mal

You're right there, General. Dead right.

The General

You don't bow under pressure, Mal. Why do you think that is?

Mal

It's funny, but the world of pub quizzing is a small one and most of the inns in the area are linked by the same brewery, so we stay in touch. Not a quiz thing per se. It's useful when any kind of troublemaker tries to hop from pub to pub.

Mal

Not that The Shadow Knights are troublemakers.

The General

Yet the weekly quiz can bring out a fiercely competitive spirit in the calmest, mildest-mannered person. Passions run high, teams become tribal. Win or lose can feel like life or death.

Mal

That competitive spirit keeps our teams coming back week after week. Keen to improve their knowledge and their scores. It's a force for good, General, and that's why The Shadow Knights are so valued at The Case. We'd be honored if you made us your home quiz.

The General

Would you be open to some suggestions from us?

Mal

Absolutely! Fire away, General.

The General

If the two away fixtures we've attended recently are anything to go by, then your fellow publicans sorely need a lesson or two in how to conduct a robust, fair, and fulsome quiz. Would you invite them to The Case one Monday? You can show them how it's done.

Mal

I don't know. It's a good idea, but they've all got busy pubs to run. Much busier than ours.

The General

Monday will be their quietest day and it would be a one-off.

Mal

True. There are seven of them, but I'm sure they wouldn't all come. Sue and I joke that Peter Bond would crumble to dust if he stepped outside The Lusty Lass!

The General

The Lusty Lass? Their quiz is on Tuesdays.

Mal

I often wonder what Peter is like as a quizmaster. He never gives much away in his curt text messages.

The General
We'll see.

Mal
If The Shadow Knights were to attend Peter's quiz, then I'd be happy to learn from any good techniques he might be keeping under his hat.

The General
Good techniques? As you and I both know, the secret to a good quiz is all in the question.

Mal
It is. See you tonight, General.

Text messages between PCSO Arthur McCoy and Mal Eastwood, November 11, 2019:

Arthur
Scarifier.

Mal
Everything OK, Arthur?

Arthur
It comes from an antique scarifier—the spike they used to pin the body down. Probably one of the long traces that once hitched a horse to the main section.

Mal
A scarifier?

Arthur
A row of spikes turn the soil as it's dragged along. I notice you've got wheels and other bits of it nicely arranged in concrete for your bike rack.

Mal
So that's what it was! A scarifier. That rusty old thing in the shed. Well, you've given me an idea for a quiz question there, Arthur.

Arthur

Funny thing is, it's been sharpened. It was made into a spike. A weapon. Perhaps deliberately tooled as a device to hold the body down.

Mal

That's a thought.

Arthur

Anyone done work in your garden?

Mal

A couple of chaps on a community work scheme, Manny and Mark, came to help us with the bike racks. They were long gone by the time the murder happened.

Mal

But they would've seen the machine, known it was there.

Arthur

Funnily enough, the body had been in the water too long to carry any useful DNA evidence, but they did manage to find some trace DNA on the bit of spike above water. Not much to go on, mind, except it belonged to a female.

Arthur

In short, it could've been a woman who killed Mr. Goode, or at least pinned his body down in the water.

Mal

Well, that's unnerving. Scarifying even . . .

Arthur

As an ex-copper yourself, I don't need to tell you to look out for any suspicious activity—by persons male or female.

Mal

Eyes are peeled, Arthur. Eyes are peeled.

Arthur

Quick question. Fellow by the name of Harrison Walker. At your quiz the night of the murder. Anything to say about him?

Mal

Very personable, polite young man. Just asked Sue. She says the same.
Top drawer.

Arthur

He seems theatrical.

Mal

No idea what he does for a living.

Mal

Oh, sorry, do you mean gay?

Arthur

Something in his statement doesn't quite tally with the rest. I'm sure it's
nothing. Respect your opinion, Mal. You never lose your copper's nose.

Mal

Out of interest, who told you we used to be police? It's not something we
bandy about. Some folk get funny.

Arthur

Looked you up to see where you came from before you arrived here.
Don't worry, your secret's safe with me. See you soon.

**Extract from a witness statement made by PCSO Arthur McCoy,
November 12, 2019:**

On the evening of November 11, 2019, at 19:30, I waited near the bus
stop at the top of Bell End to have an informal chat with a witness
in the Luke Goode murder case. While collating witness statements, I
discovered that Mr. Walker was seen turning right as he left the pub at
the end of the evening, a route that would take him toward the river,
not toward his bus stop. He did not mention this in his statement made
on October 11, 2019. I wanted to speak with him discreetly.

Transcript of a conversation with Harrison Walker recorded by PCSO
Arthur McCoy's body-worn camera, November 11, 2019:

AM: Sorry to lie in wait for you, Mr. Walker, but may I have a quick
    chat? It's further to the statement you gave me a few weeks ago.

HW: Er, OK.

AM: Where did you go that night when you left the pub at closing
    time?

HW: Home.

AM: Straight home?

HW: More or less.

AM: You were seen walking toward the river.

HW: I hung around for a smoke. Can't smoke in the pub or on the bus.

AM: You stood outside the pub?

HW: No, I went down the lane to the river.

AM: Bit dark down there, isn't it?

HW: I had my phone light.

AM: How long were you there for?

HW: Can't really remember. I stayed for a bit.

AM: Only you weren't on the next bus. Or the one after that. You
    didn't use your Travelcard until 23:40.

HW: That would be right, yep.

AM: Is there anything you want to tell me? I won't put it in your
    statement. But I need to clear up the discrepancy. Go on. I've
    seen and heard it all, believe me.

HW: I went to meet someone.

AM: Who?

HW: Someone from Grindr.

AM: Ah. Right. A hookup, was it?

HW: In the end, no.

AM: This is off the record . . .

HW: I'd arranged to meet him by the old pier at 10:30 p.m. But the
    quiz was late starting because of the trouble. Didn't finish till ten
    to eleven but phones have to be off during the quiz so I couldn't
    let him know. I hurried down there as soon as the girls left, but it
    was deserted. When I switched my phone on, I saw the guy had

canceled two hours earlier, just after I turned my phone off. Here, look. Those are the messages.

AM: I see ... yep. OK.

HW: It's not a part of my life I share with other people. Not even the girls and they're my best friends. I'd be grateful if you didn't say anything to anyone.

AM: I understand. Why did you stay down there in the dark for so long, after you knew your date wasn't going to show?

HW: I don't know. It was creepy and peaceful all at the same time.

AM: Did you see anyone else at all? Spot anything unusual on your way back?

HW: No one. Just a dog that belongs to a woman at the pub. He must've slipped his lead. Jumped up at me a few times, then ran back up the lane.

AM: Just one other question. Have you ever worked in the theater, acting, entertainment?

HW: No. I work in admin for an insurance company and write short stories as a hobby. Horror stories.

Extract from a witness statement made by PCSO Arthur McCoy, November 12, 2019 (continued):

Mr. Walker confirmed that he had indeed wandered down to the water's edge to smoke. He saw a dog owned by a fellow quiz participant but no other people. I have no reason to disbelieve Mr. Walker. For context, publicans Sue and Mal Eastwood, both former police officers with exemplary records, consider him an honest young man, and I know them well enough to respect their opinions.

To: Dominic Eastwood
From: Polly Baker
Date: October 25, 2024
Subject: Re: Documentary idea

Hey Dom,

Are you still at The Case is Altered right now? I'd love to visit. Done a couple of quizzes myself. There's something addictive about finding out just how much you know.

Sue and Mal seem far more conscientious in their second career than they were ever given credit for when they were with the police. Were they really such second-rate officers? As you can tell, I'm getting quite indignant on their behalf. Do send through the rest. We're at a point where the viewer will think they know the characters and are probably trying to guess how it all ends. If we can hit them with a new hook now, then fire away!

Pol xxx

To: Polly Baker
From: Dominic Eastwood
Date: October 25, 2024
Subject: Re: Documentary idea

Hi Polly,

Yes, I'm still here, in the silent bar. I've learned a lot about my aunt and uncle through reading these documents, more than I bargained for when I began, that's for sure. The quiz nights must have been buzzing. It can't have been easy but, like you say, they were well-respected landlords. Parry dismissed them, but perhaps he didn't understand how they worked . . .

These documents reveal that Sergeant Sue and Constable Mal were curious about Operation Honeyguide and seemed to have an agenda that played out behind the backs of not only their superior officers but also Sue's friend and colleague Dee.

As for the "episode four" hook: mission accepted! I can now bring in another thread to keep viewers guessing. As you'll see, there *is* a further mystery woven into this story.

Best wishes,
Dom

Hulme Police
Operation Honeyguide

In association with the National Crime Agency
Anti-Kidnap and Extortion Unit (AKEU)
Senior Investigating Officer: Detective Chief Inspector Lewis Parry

The Beat Goes On WhatsApp group, May 7, 2014:

Monty
There's a charity quiz over in Winterby, 7 p.m. on the 28th, St. James's bell-tower fund. Little church hall, so good chance of a win. £12 pp, plus raffle.

Glen
Food?

Monty
Yes, but bring your own drinks. Must confirm numbers by Friday.

Sue
Wish we could, but work's tricky right now.

Jilly
You missed an outstanding quiz last night. Pacy, original, interesting connection rounds, and cheesy biscuits on each table. Lots of fun!

Monty
We needed our Eastwood contingent for music and sport. Only came third.

Sue
Gutted to miss it, but we're in the middle of a big op and the guv says we can't clock off.

Glen
Excrement colliding with the air-conditioning again?

Sue

Not yet! But there aren't many in the know, someone had to do a house visit, and the guv didn't think the league place was important.

Monty

Not a quizzer then.

Jilly

What operation's that?

Mal

Sue shouldn't have mentioned it. It's not important. We'll say yes to the Winterby quiz, but it's work permitting.

Jilly

Op Lockstep? I've heard that's a biggie.

Mal

Put us down for two tickets and cross fingers the guv's in a good mood.

Conversation between Sergeant Suzanne Eastwood and Constable Malcolm Eastwood, recorded in Unmarked Car 3, May 7, 2014:

SE: Hate this gearshift.

ME: It's a lemon. Always left in the yard. That's how I got hold of it.

SE: Won't break down, will it? Oh, go on, yer arsehole!

ME: Language, Sue.

SE: He was fucking about! You could get a bus through there. [*Silence*] Hate letting the team down.

ME: Hate missing quizzes, but hate being on Parry's watchlist even more.

SE: What if Dee finds out we've been going off message?

ME: If she gets upset, tell her we didn't want to jeopardize her promotion.

SE: She won't get upset. Never does. Very easygoing, is Dee, keeps everyone happy.

ME: And for crying out loud, do not blow open Hulme Police's top-secret maneuvers on the bloody quiz team WhatsApp!

SE: They're all other officers.

ME: It's restricted! Remember the first two rules of *Fight Club*. Do not talk about *Fight Club*.

SE: I know!

ME: We don't want to be taken off Honeyguide, do we?

SE: Here we are. Devil's Croke Woods, where Chloe met her abductor. This is old industrial land, isn't it? The Cunninghams must be hoping to build another posh estate on the edge of a beauty spot.

ME: Beauty spot? [*Silence*] Looks boggy to me.

SE: And me, but we aren't property developers. Like Parry says, not a single camera. [*Silence*]

SE: What're you thinking?

ME: Same as you, probably. That whoever abducted Chloe Cunningham had to have a forensic knowledge of local security-camera coverage.

SE: You might say an insider's knowledge . . .

ME: And you might also say there's more to Operation Honeyguide than anyone's letting on.

[*Phone rings*]

ME: It's the guvnor. Hello, guv. Yep . . . OK. We're coming in. [*Car engine starts*] Emergency meeting.

SE: Honeyguide?

ME: Yep.

Confidential Briefing Notes, May 7, 2014:

Thank you for coming in, everyone. Especially you, Rhys, I know you've had to leave Chloe's parents alone to be here. I won't keep you long.

Sadly, this is to let you all know the news I wish I wasn't delivering. We've found a body, dumped in the doorway of the derelict department store on the junction of High Street and Roman Way. It's not been formally identified yet, but off the record, there's no doubt it's Beata Novak. Too early to say how she was killed—autopsy pending.

I know it's not the outcome we wanted. We're working with the

Polish police to find relatives, but it seems that she never knew her father, mother left her as a baby, and she was brought up by her grandmother, who died a few years ago. Press blackout in place until the case is over.

Her death is a strong message from the Maddox Brothers to Darren Chester. Anyone who's worked this area for a few years will know that department store. It was called Chesters.

The word from AKEU is to keep our nerve. They are working flat out to make sure Chloe Cunningham doesn't become victim number two. She was kidnapped forty-eight hours after Beata. We hope that means we still have a day or two to find Darren.

We need to keep the parents calm. Reassure them, stop them going to the press, but at the same time prepare them for the worst.

That's all for now. Sue and Mal, can I have a word?

Conversation between DCI Lewis Parry, Sergeant Suzanne Eastwood, and Constable Malcolm Eastwood, recorded by DCI Parry's body-worn camera, May 7, 2014:

LP:　Where were you two? Took your time getting here—

SE:　Over by Devil's Croke.

LP:　Who told you to go up there?

SE:　No one . . .

ME:　We were checking for illegal dumping.

LP:　Checking for *illegal dumping*? Precisely where our second victim was abducted?

SE:　We've spent so much time with Chloe's parents . . . you get to thinking, don't you? We wanted to see where she'd gone missing for ourselves and, er, check for dumping at the same time.

LP:　Well, in future be where you *ought* to be, not where you *want* to be? It's called *work*. Now you're needed in Pinfield later. Rhys will let me know when he has to leave. In the meantime, both of you get over to The Glade shopping center for hi-vis public policing.

SE:　Oh, guv . . .

LP:　What?

SE: Just want to say thank you. For rostering us together, like we asked. When we were on separate shifts, it was a nightmare.

ME: Couldn't both quiz on the same evenings.

SE: And we know it's a headache for scheduling, so thank you.

LP: Uh-huh. Be ready to jump over to Pinfield as soon as you get the word.

Conversation between Sergeants Dee Obasi and Suzanne Eastwood and Constable Malcolm Eastwood, recorded in Unmarked Car 1, May 7, 2014:

DO: What did Parry want with you two?

SE: Asked where we were when he put the call out.

ME: We were last in the room, weren't we.

SE: Well, how were we to know it was gonna be such bad news?

DO: Where *had* you been?

ME: Don't *you* start, Dee!

SE: Went to the woods where they abducted Chloe. It was dead quiet and calm. You'd never know anything so violent had happened.

DO: Why'd you go *there*?

SE: Honeyguide . . . it's a strange case, don't you think?

ME: It's a puzzle.

DO: Small-time drug dealer comes from nothing, but he's a charmer, a good-looking risk-taker with limited empathy—and he's ambitious. He's always after more. With two girls on the go, he gets confident, wants a bigger piece of his bosses' pie than he'll ever earn being loyal to them. He mugs them off to the sound of a big tune and goes to ground, making plans for his future. When—if—he hears his bosses have kidnapped both girls, he moves on without a second thought. He'll soon get two more; ten more if he wants, once he's set up in his new area. [*Silence*] Honeyguide isn't a puzzle, Mal. It's tragically simple.

SE: Do you think there's things we aren't being told?

DO: It's a restricted op, of course there are. [*Pause*] Like what?

SE: There's no tape up in Devil's Croke.

DO: The area's been searched and not much there—tape taken down to protect the integrity of the operation.

ME: All the briefings are by Parry, not AKEU or NCA.

DO: They brief Parry, he briefs us. At this level it's need-to-know.

SE: Whoever abducted Chloe had a knowledge of camera coverage that bordered on the forensic. [*Silence*] *Insider* knowledge.

ME: Reminds us of another kidnap case we worked on years ago. Dead Rummy.

DO: Dead Rummy! Is that youth slang or what?

SE: You are funny, Dee! Dead Rummy was a racehorse. Handsome fellow.

ME: It looked for all the world as if a great big hulking animal had been spirited away in the middle of the night, when really the kidnappers just knew where the cameras were and avoided 'em. [*Pause*]

DO: Was the poor horse OK? On second thoughts, don't tell me if he wasn't.

SE: He was fine!

ME: They found him caked in mud, grazing under the overpass with a herd of Travellers' ponies, happy as a clam.

DO: Thank God!
    [*They laugh*]

DO: Ever wondered why, when something big happens, crucial camera footage can't be found or, if it is, then it's mysteriously deleted before it can be useful? Why that *one* camera that would've caught everything stops working on the very day trouble goes down? See, this is where my experience of city policing comes in. [*Pause*] All the big drug firms in Stopton had moles in the CCTV control room. I'll be very surprised if Axeford isn't the same.

ME: Moles?

DO: As soon as one's weeded out, another gets hired. Now you two'd best get to The Glade and I'd best get home, before I end up doing a double shift by accident and for no pay. And good luck with the Cunninghams. It's gonna be a tough day for everyone.
    [*Sergeant Dee Obasi leaves the car*]

SE: Little Miss Perfect.

ME: Apart from one thing.

SE: Oh yeah? What's that then?

ME: How does she know Parry sent us to The Glade?

Downview visit 3, May 7, 2014:

*Subjects: Caroline Cunningham, 47, and Piers Cunningham, 49,
Downview, Moorcroft Lane, Pinfield Village
Visiting officers: Sergeant Suzanne Eastwood and Constable Malcolm
Eastwood
Present initially: Family Liaison Officer Sergeant Rhys Davies*

SE: Hi, Rhys. How are they?

RD: As you might expect, they've taken the news about Beata very
      hard.

SE: Aw, bless.

RD: You're OK to stay late tonight?

ME: Well, we were going to meet up with our quiz team to . . .

SE: Of course we are, Rhys. No problem.

*[The following recordings were made during a seven-hour period on
May 7, 2014, when Sue and Mal Eastwood were with Caroline and Piers
Cunningham, edited for brevity]*

SE: Hi, Caroline, Piers.

CC: [*Barely audible*] Come in.

SE: You've got us for the rest of today. Rhys has to be elsewhere.
      [*Silence*]

CC: [*Barely audible*] Piers is . . . is upset. He's barely spoken.

SE: Bless, of course he is. It's the shock. You don't have to talk, Piers,
      not if you don't want to. All this is the gang's attempt to force
      Darren into cutting his losses and contacting them again.

CC: [*Whispered*] But it's *our* loss—it would be *our* loss . . .

SE: Remember we said . . . the transaction is all these people know.

ME: I'll make us some tea, eh.

[*Constable Eastwood leaves the room*]

[*Later, a whispered conversation, aside*]

ME: I'm not cut out for this, Sue. Might call in and go sick.

SE: You will not! Just sit there and *talk* to him.

ME: But what shall I talk about? He's staring into space.

SE: He's in shock. It's a coping mechanism. He'll come out of it. Talk about anything—ordinary, trivial things; tell him about the quiz league, go on. I'll help Caroline with supper in the kitchen. She wants to do something routine and ordinary, I can tell. If she says anything interesting, I'll let you know.

ME: OK, I'll go back in, but don't be surprised if the silence deafens you. I've got literally nothing to say.

[*A short time later*]

ME: ... but what makes a *good* quiz? That's the question, Piers. You see, people who don't quiz wouldn't be able to tell you. They might say "easy questions," but that is 100 percent *not* what everyone wants when they sit down and write their team names at the tops of their papers. When you're a quizzer, you're looking for questions that challenge you, that exercise the mind. Questions that get you thinking, stretch your memory, your powers of deduction, your whole life experience—and that of your entire team; it's all pooled together for every answer.

[*A short time later*]

ME: ... every member of The Beat Goes On brings something different to the table. That's why putting a good team together is crucial. We've got a better chance *now* of getting to the top of the national league than ever, and you wanna know the reason? Two members left the team—that's two members out of six. We had two seats to fill, but we didn't simply ask around to see who could make the next quiz night; no, we *auditioned* for new team members by making 'em do a short quiz to see where their strengths and weaknesses might lie. See, we've got music experts, we've got readers who know about books, a chap who's heavily into politics, and another who does his very best with sports stats, but we had no history or geography expert and *that* was what we were looking for ...

[*A short time later*]

ME: The quizmaster is king. I shit you not, Piers, in the room the quizmaster could tell you that Pope John the twenty-third was succeeded by Pope Pius the twelfth and you'd have to suck it up. No one's allowed to google while the quiz is going on. Afterward you might want to complain, especially if that question meant you lost by one point—which, by the way, is the most gutting experience you can have at the quiz table. That and when you know what the answer is, but the rest of your team swear blind it's something else and you have to watch that wrong answer being written down and handed in . . .

[*A short time later*]

ME: When Sue and I retire from the force, we're gonna set ourselves up in a little pub in the country. There'll be a homely fireplace, wood panels, oak tables, and a weekly quiz to bring the community together and drum up business on quiet nights. Monday, Tuesday, and Wednesday are *stone dead* in the pub game, Piers, especially these days. You need little carrots to drive footfall through the door. I'm reading this, look: "How to run a successful pub." First we'll get some frontline bar-work experience, then train in hospitality-specific business management and go the brewery route—can be limiting, but offers the most support for newbies. Oh, either way, we'll do it, Piers! We'll do it! And one thing I won't have to learn from scratch is how to set up a bloody decent quiz.

[*Later*]

SE: How are you, Piers?

PC: Uh-huh.

ME: He's back in the room, if you know what I mean. Aren't you, Piers?

PC: [*Shouts*] NO! [*Pause*] NO!

ME: You're OK—it's only us, Mal and Sue.

SE: Caroline has made us a lovely soup. She's just cutting some bread. [*Whispers*] Don't eat it, Mal, it's stale.

PC: No. No.

CC: It's all right. It's not our Chloe, it's the other girl. Our Chloe is still OK . . . she's still OK, isn't she?

ME: As far as we know.

SE: Yes, she is, yep.

    [*Much later*]

ME: There we go. And there. I found some biscuits eventually.

PC: This can't go on. It has to stop.

SE: We know—you feel powerless . . .

PC: Listen, you two. I want to cut a deal with the Maddox Brothers. Hear me out. Last time you were here, you said these people understand business. Well, so do I. Chester stole their money and drugs, and they want him to pay for it. They're all about the transaction. Well, I've got a deal for them. You go back to your inside man and tell him to tell his bosses I'll pay back whatever this Chester took from them.

CC: He was talking about this last night, before we heard about . . . the news this morning.

ME: It's certainly an idea.

SE: Piers, I understand you're frustrated, but paying off the Maddox Brothers—it goes against all the rules—

PC: I haven't got where I am today by sticking to the rules.

ME: There are protocols around kidnap: the experts negotiate, they play mind games with the gang—you'd be effectively paying a ransom, and that's not done.

SE: It only encourages criminals to kidnap people in future.

PC: That's just it. You lot care about future kidnaps, but I care about this one, about my Chloe. We want her back and we can afford to throw money at the problem. In our position, you'd do the same. Now how much did Darren take?

ME: We don't know—

PC: Then find out. We'll do the rest.

SE: It's not only the money. They kidnapped the girls because they want Darren. They want to punish *him*. Warn others in the gang not to try the same trick. They'll need a *huge* incentive to let go of a grudge that size.

ME: Six figures at least.

SE: Right.

PC: Then here's what you do. Go back to your contact. Find out what they're owed. However much they say they've lost, *double* it.

[*Silence*]

CC: Piers?

PC: *Double* it, to let Chloe go and forget about Darren. If they're the businessmen you say they are, they'll know a good deal when they see it.

SE: I don't know . . .

ME: I think that's a lot of money, even for the brothers. It may well work, but if anything goes wrong, you won't get that money back—

SE: Mal's right. It's a big risk. Are you certain you want to take it?

CC: They've killed the other girl. This could be our last chance.

PC: Tell them what our offer is.

SE: Could we, Mal?

ME: We could lose our jobs, but more than that, we're supposed to be looking after them. We can't let Piers go running around with a suitcase full of cash!

SE: We could do the drop-off, I suppose. But you're right, if our DCI found out, we'd be in serious trouble.

[*Silence*]

PC: Put it this way. If you two *don't* help us buy Chloe's safe return, we'll tell Rhys what Sue told Caroline yesterday. That you two covered up an unlawful killing, lied in a coroner's court, and let a murderer walk free.

[*Silence*]

In short: you have two balls and can set either one rolling. The one that stands a chance of getting Chloe back, or the one that puts you two behind bars. And we all know how popular ex-police are in prison.

CC: [*Barely audible*] Find out how much Darren Chester owes the Maddox Brothers. Tell your confidential informant that you two'll facilitate the transaction. We'll get Chloe back and everyone'll be happy.

[*Silence*]

Text messages between Thor's Hammer and Sue & Mal, The Case is Altered, November 11, 2019:

Thor's Hammer
Make sure he starts on time today, Sue.

Sue & Mal, The Case is Altered
Thanks, Chris, love, but Mal's wearing a watch, he has the time on his phone, and can see the clock from his chair.

Thor's Hammer
Just four minutes to go. Four minutes for The Shadow Knights to make an appearance.

Sue & Mal, The Case is Altered
Well, they've lost their usual table if they do.

Thor's Hammer
It's OUR table. We sat here long before they showed up.

Thor's Hammer
Is there a rule that once the quiz starts, no one else can join? If a team arrives late, then that's it?

Sue & Mal, The Case is Altered
I don't know why Mal would have that rule, because it wouldn't give anyone an advantage. If anything, they'd be at a disadvantage surely?

Thor's Hammer
Three minutes.

Thor's Hammer
Two minutes.

Thor's Hammer
Less than a minute.

Thor's Hammer
What? They did that deliberately to taunt us!

Sue & Mal, The Case is Altered
Phones away now, Chris. You know the rule.

THE CASE IS ALTERED PUB QUIZ

November 11, 2019

Rounds	Max points
1. Today's News	10
2. On this day in 1997	10
3. Sporting stars	
(Bonus point: say whether each is dead or alive)	20
4. Pantomime special: which panto is this character from?	10
5. Film & TV	10
6. Music: name the artist and song title	
(Clue: one or the other will include a reference to space)	20
7. Spelling bee	10
8. Money & Finances	10

Marathon round: Books

Name the author and title of these 50 book covers   50

Quiz teams and where they sat

The Shadow Knights
General Knowledge, Brigitte
Pamela, Lynette
Edward, Wilfred

Spokespersons
Erik, Jemma
Tam, Dilip

Let's Get Quizzical
Sid & Nancy Topliss
Bunny & George Tyme
Margaret & Ted Dawson

The Sturdy Challengers
Chris & Lorraine
Ajay, Keith
Andrew

Linda & Joe & Friends
Linda & Joe
Rita & Bailey
Cloud & Wind

Ami's Manic Carrots
Jojo, Evie
Harrison, Bianca
Fliss, Fiona

Final scores out of 150

The Shadow Knights	149
The Sturdy Challengers	138
Ami's Manic Carrots	99
Let's Get Quizzical	84
Spokespersons	79
Linda & Joe & Friends	78

Spokespersons Cycling Team WhatsApp group, November 11, 2019:

Tam
Well, that was embarrassing.

Jemma
Only one point ahead of the old folk.

Erik
Complete 'mare, start to finish. What went wrong?

Dilip
Disaster, mate. The Sturdy Challengers are closing the gap between them and The Shadow Knights. And that's after they lost the barmaid to the Manic Carrots. I swear Ajay is upping his game somehow.

Tam
He hardly speaks to us now. Not even on the rides there and back.

Dilip
Playing his cards close to his chest.

Jemma
Do we know someone who could take his place? We only have four people—most of the other teams have six. No wonder we're falling behind.

Tam
Any new team member would have to cycle and know lots of trivia to be any use.

Erik
Everyone, rack your brains and ask around. Think of this as a race, but not one you can train for. Getting across the line first is all about what you know.

The Sturdy Challengers Quiz Team WhatsApp group, November 11, 2019:

Thor's Hammer
Good work, team! Only eleven points in it and a small triumph on the road to success.

Lorraine

Andrew deserves a special mention for getting the periodic-table question right. What was it again?

Andrew

"Name the heaviest element by atomic weight." I knew the answer was oganesson because it's on my noble-gases mug, and that's where there's a slight fault in the varnish. When work is at its worst, I plummet into a frozen, fugue state. My mind retreats to the shadows, while the world turns under my feet and the chatter fades into silence. It doesn't really, but my hearing just goes. Anyway, I focus on that glitch in the varnish over the element "Oganesson—heaviest by atomic weight." I swear I've stared at it for an hour straight, several times. That's how I knew.

Ajay

Bravo, Andy! My old team were pissed off with their score. Bit of an awkward ride home.

Lorraine

Such a shame we lost Fiona. I notice the Carrots did much better than usual.

Andrew

I spotted that too.

Keith

Have a word, Andy. You're her friend.

Andrew

I'm her housing officer. She's decided to switch teams. There's nothing I can do about it.

Thor's Hammer

Whether she's the reason the Carrots scored better or not, we need the youth perspective to give us the edge.

Keith

Reckon she got a glimpse of Mal's question sheet?

Thor's Hammer

After last time, when "car tunes" became "cartoons," I doubt very much there was a security breach. Anyway Mal is a quizmaster of integrity.

Team, we're on the right course and, if we can get Fiona back, then that would be a bonus. We'll leave it with Andy.

Andrew

She barely replies when I text, but I'll try. There is something I want to speak to her about.

Lorraine

Thank you, Andy, you're a star!

To: Let's Get Quizzical [group]
From: Bunny Tyme
Date: November 12, 2019
Subject: We beat the cyclists!

Morning, all!

Well, we came fourth, but hey-ho, we were five points ahead of the cyclists, so can't complain. Now who's up for making next week's quiz a bit more interesting while raising some cash for charity at the same time?

I suggest we pledge to pay a pound for every correct answer. As you know, George and I help out at St. Mark's Hospice and it would be nice to donate the cash to them. I can ask Sue if she'll pop a collection box on the bar for the night too.

What does everyone say?

Bunny

To: Let's Get Quizzical [group]
From: Sid Topliss
Date: November 12, 2019
Subject: Re: We beat the cyclists!

Wonderful idea! I say a big yes to that and pledge to pay a pound for every correct answer. It's what pub quizzing is all about—enjoying ourselves, having a laugh and a drink, and helping the local community. Thanks for the suggestion, Bunny.

St. Mark's Hospice is a very serene place. It's where I've visited many friends and family in their final days. You'd think it would be depressing, but no. Have you ever wondered how you'll end your time on this earth? Easy to talk about when it isn't looming large on the horizon, eh! I can't decide between a peaceful but slow fading away and an unexpected but fast death. Am I the only one? It's swings and roundabouts. Is there such a thing as a moderately quick death, where you get to say goodbye to everyone and leave instructions for your funeral, but also avoid the lingering anticipation? If anyone has found a happy medium, please let me know.

Also find myself wondering if there's any good I can do after I'm dead and gone. Nancy and I are on the organ-donor register and there's the option of leaving your remains to medical science, but then your family don't have a grave to visit and that may help with their grieving. Would medical science even want me? Looking at it another way, is that whole thing just a vain hope that you'll still have an impact on the world after you've departed? Fame at last, eh? Well, these are questions that no one can answer, so let's get on with our lives and enjoy ourselves—while we still can.

Sid

Text messages between Andrew and Fiona, November 12, 2019:

Andrew
Hi, Fiona. Well done on coming third in the quiz. How are things?

Fiona
k

Andrew
I finally spoke to Ammia, your social worker, and told her what I know about Sue and Mal: that they're former police officers who drive you to college and pay you for a part-time, live-in job at their pub.

Andrew
Now, Ammia doesn't know me and has never laid eyes on The Case is Altered. She has no idea if a word of what I told her is true. I could be party to a people-trafficking scam. I could've been lied to myself. But far

from being concerned, she was thrilled. Closed your case folder like she was never going to open it again.

Fiona
time

Andrew
Which might be OK, so long as everything really is fine.

Andrew
Fiona, I haven't mentioned this to anyone else, but I noticed you disappeared for at least two rounds of the quiz last night. Is everything OK?

Andrew
I appreciate you're a bit isolated out there at The Case, and even the Manic Carrots are that much older, but if there's something on your mind, please don't let it eat away at you—speak to someone.

Fiona
k

Andrew
Is there someone you trust? Could be Sue or Mal, one of the Manic Carrots, someone at college—you don't need to tell me who it is, so long as there's someone.

Fiona
aw, bless u

Andrew
Is this a boyfriend? Should I be worried?

Fiona
😂💜

Andrew
Please tell me he's roughly your age, his prior convictions are all spent, and none of his tattoos are on his face.

Fiona
she

Andrew

Ah! No problem at all

Fiona

 just a frnd

Andrew

Also, while I've got you texting words again, how about coming back to The Sturdy Challengers next Monday?

Fiona

😂

Ami's Manic Carrots WhatsApp group, November 12, 2019:

Harrison

Yes! Third place.

Fliss

By 39 points and a full 50 points behind the winners. We only came third because the Spokespersons were worse than us.

Harrison

Still third place. Evie killed the marathon round.

Rosie

What was it?

Harrison

Name fifty books by their covers (which had title and author blanked out).

Rosie

Which books?

Evie

Lots of series. All the Harry Potters, His Dark Materials, Twilights, Hunger Games, Game of Thrones.

Rosie

I'd have got the Game of Thrones covers.

Jojo

Fiona was pointless. Literally.

Jojo

She missed the sports round and the arts round. Where did she go?

Fliss

Wherever it was, she can't have been googling. She didn't have any answers when she came back.

Harrison

Anyone think she was a bit off? Worried? Distracted?

Evie

She said last week her mom's in hospital. Maybe it's not good news.

Harrison

Her mom's in prison. Doing three years for drugs offenses. Don't tell Fiona I told you—she thinks Sue and Mal will throw her out if they know.

Jojo

Would they?

Fliss

When she left the table, she picked up her phone and I saw the end of a text she'd just got. It said "do it now." Didn't see the sender's name.

Evie

What? Massive red flag. Controlling partner doesn't like her "ignoring" his texts. Gets her to "obey" him. She MUST end it. We should tell her.

Harrison

I'm not telling anyone what to do.

Evie

Because you're a guy! I've been in a controlling relationship. I've had the "do it now" texts. This is how it starts.

Fliss

The text might have been Sue or Mal asking her to sort something out behind the bar.

Jojo

Or it could've been from Ed.

Harrison

He's just not into you, Jojo. Let it go.

Jojo

I'm only saying. He gave her his number.

Fliss

Ed can't have been texting Fiona last night during the quiz. Mal would've seen and disqualified him.

Harrison

This 👆

Fliss

We need more evidence before we go behind her back.

Text messages between Evie and Sue & Mal, The Case is Altered, November 12, 2019:

Evie

Hi, Sue. I got your number from the pub website. I'm on the Ami's Manic Carrots quiz team with Fiona. We noticed last night she seemed distracted and missed two rounds. She might have gone up to her room. We wondered if perhaps she's got a new boyfriend?

Sue & Mal, The Case is Altered

Aw, Fiona could do with a nice boyfriend, bless her! I noticed she disappeared, but I couldn't leave the bar. I checked with her later and she said she's just working hard at college and needed a nap.

Evie

OK. Well, please keep an eye on her. If she gets text after text from him. If he gets her to stop what she's doing to do something for him. That's how controlling relationships start.

Sue & Mal, The Case is Altered

Of course, Evie dear. I'll keep an eye on Fiona.

Text messages between Jojo and Sue & Mal, The Case is Altered, November 12, 2019:

Jojo
Did you know Fiona's mom is in prison?

Sue & Mal, The Case is Altered
Where did you hear that, love?

Jojo
Someone mentioned it. Thought you'd like to know, as she's living under your roof, where there's money and booze, etc.

Sue & Mal, The Case is Altered
Thank you, Jojo dear. That's nice of you, but if we judged everyone on what their family members did, we'd all be in prison with Fiona's mom.

Text messages between Sue and Mal Eastwood, November 12, 2019:

Sue
Fiona was upstairs for half an hour last night.

Mal
The Manic Carrots didn't score any higher than usual, so she can't have been cheating.

Sue
If she has a boyfriend, then she sees him at college. No one comes here to visit her.

Mal
Not seen her with anyone.

Sue
That first quiz she came to, she told me her mom's in hospital, but word on the street is that she's inside.

Mal
If we'd given it a second's thought, we'd have guessed that.

Sue
I know. Does it worry you she hasn't been honest with us?

Mal

She's her own person. She doesn't owe us information about her life. Now don't mention what you know about her mom, it'll only upset her.

Sue

I won't. Thought we should discuss it, that's all. If she's got a boyfriend, I hope he's nice and that things work out for her.

Text messages between Mal Eastwood and The General, November 12, 2019:

Mal

Congratulations, General! Another triumphant win for The Shadow Knights!

The General

A challenging and entertaining quiz, Malcolm. Thank you.

Mal

Are you going to The Lusty Lass tonight, as you were thinking last week?

The General

Why do you want to know?

Mal

Peter Bond, the landlord there, he's a man of few words, let's say. I'm more than a little curious about his quiz and what the atmosphere is like, etc.

The General

I see.

Mal

Being a quizmaster is a public-facing role that requires charisma, stage presence, confidence, an aptitude for performance, and that *je ne sais quoi* that enables one to command the room.

The General

And you feel Peter Bond lacks those qualities?

Mal

I'm curious, that's all. By the way, I haven't forgotten your suggestion of a landlords' quiz. Will mention it to the others next time we chat.

The General

The Lusty Lass is the oldest pub in the county, with records of an inn standing on that site as far back as 1484. Mr. Peter Bond appears briefly in an episode of Most Haunted, first aired in May 2004. You can watch it on YouTube.

Mal

I've seen the episode. Peter's interview with Yvette Fielding was almost animated. I hate to think that years of being a landlord have taken their toll, but he seems quite dour now.

The General

Later in that episode, spirit medium Derek Acorah discovered the ghost of a barmaid whose fiancé was involved in a duel to settle a debt. Apparently she jumped in front of her true love to prevent him being run through with a sword, yet in doing so was killed herself.

Mal

Tragic.

The General

It's a common story structure, versions of which surface in folklore tales, hauntings, and legends all over the country, if not the world.

Mal

Hah! They can't all be true, can they?

The General

And yet such perfect tragedies do occur and it's reasonable to imagine that, when they do, a ghost is formed to haunt the place where it happened.

Mal

Sue and I don't believe in ghosts.

The General

The Shadow Knights don't believe in coincidence.

The General

But to answer your question: yes, we'll be at The Lusty Lass tonight.

Text messages between Mal Eastwood and Peter Bond, The Lusty Lass, November 12, 2019:

Mal

Heads up: The Shadow Knights are coming to a quiz table near you. Forewarned is forearmed.

Peter Bond, The Lusty Lass

Planks doing a recce.

Mal

Peter, you're an intelligent man of the world. The Shadow Knights are either a brilliant quiz team or they're cheating. One or the other.

Peter Bond, The Lusty Lass

Mission accepted.

The Lusty Lass

Wheeg77
wrote a review yesterday
St. Albans, United Kingdom
6 contributions, 4 helpful votes

Date visited   **November 9, 2019**
Visit type   **alone**

Not haunted

Only thing haunted about this boozer is the look on the face of the dude behind the bar. Bet no one even died here. Gutted.

Response from The Lusty Lass
Responded on November 13, 2019

We're all searching for something, my friend. For you, it's the dead. Ghosts. Spirits. Bone-chilling echoes of unspeakably evil deeds the depravity of which the mind could never conjure lest the eyes had seen it for themselves. We are the evil we look for in this dark, twisted world.

Remember, I'm searching for something too.

Think these reviews are anonymous, Daniel Wheeler? Think again, while you still can.

Ye Olde Goat Ltd. WhatsApp group, Hertfordshire, November 12, 2019:

Peter Bond, The Lusty Lass
Entering the one-star party.

Sue & Mal, The Case is Altered
That's some entrance, Peter.

Mimi & Flo, Tom's Bar

Sean & Adrian, The Rainbow
Wheeg77 is no longer registered on the site! He removed his account as soon as you replied. It's hilarious!

Diddy & Con, The Brace of Pheasants
How did you find out his name?

Peter Bond, The Lusty Lass
Friends in dark places.

Sue & Mal, The Case is Altered
Speaking of dark places, I'd like to invite you all to our quiz at The Case is Altered on the evening of the AGM next week. Let's see if a team of quizmasters can beat The Shadow Knights!

Diddy & Con, The Brace of Pheasants
We're terrible at quizzes. Any team we're on will come last, that's guaranteed! But count us in. We'd love to see what you've done with The Case, Mal.

Mimi & Flo, Tom's Bar
We'll have to get cover for the evening, but in principle, yes.

Sean & Adrian, The Rainbow
They hold the AGM during the day, so we don't have to miss an evening in the pub. It's a tentative yes, but if we can't get the shifts covered . . .

Sue & Mal, The Case is Altered
Well, the invitation is there for everyone, and if you can brush up on your general knowledge in advance, then please do. Ye Olde Goat Brewery's reputation is at stake.

Peter Bond, The Lusty Lass

It is best to remain silent and seem guilty than speak and remove all doubt.

Sue & Mal, The Case is Altered

Attributed, probably incorrectly, to Mark Twain. Only it's "foolish," Peter. "Seem foolish," not guilty. Anyway, good luck for your quiz tonight.

Text messages between Linda and Wind, November 13, 2019:

Linda

Are you and Cloud still here for Monday's quiz?

Wind

I'll be reading my cards on Friday, that's when I'll know what the next moon has in store.

Linda

Tell the cards it's a special quiz. Bunny, from Let's Get Quizzical, has spoken to Sue and Mal about making the evening a little fundraiser for the hospice. Apparently there's a team of pub landlords coming, and Sue says that'll be a good fit with a charity night. It would be so nice to have you and Cloud there. Rita and Bailey are lovely, but she falls asleep after two doubles and he has that horrible habit of licking my ankles under the table.

Wind

I'll whisper it to the cards and see what they say.

Linda

Oooh, just had a thought! Would you be able (and willing) to give charity tarot readings in the intermission? That would be a nice way to entertain the quiz crowd, get the atmosphere buzzing, and we can raise even more for the hospice!

Wind

I don't know, Linda dear. Sometimes the cards reveal things people want hidden and, believe me, some secrets can kill the atmosphere stone dead.

Linda

Think of the good karma! I'll mention it to Sue tonight.

Ye Olde Goat Ltd. WhatsApp group, Hertfordshire, November 13, 2019:

Sue & Mal, The Case is Altered
Morning, all! Just to let you know, next week's quiz is turning into a bigger event by the second. One of our regular teams is pledging a pound to the local hospice for each correct question they answer (they usually come last with very low scores), which has led another team to offer tarot readings for charity in the intermission.

Sean & Adrian, The Rainbow
Tarot! I love tarot! Sounds like a lively night.

Diddy & Con, The Brace of Pheasants
You know what I hate about fortune tellers? THEY CAN SEE YOU COMING. Boom-boom!

Mimi & Flo, Tom's Bar
We couldn't have a tarot reader here. Our customers expect an air of cool refinement to match the cuisine. Perfect for The Case, though.

Peter Bond, The Lusty Lass
Mystery solved.

Sean & Adrian, The Rainbow
Tarot doesn't solve mysteries, Peter. It's guidance for the future.

Sue & Mal, The Case is Altered
What mystery?

Peter Bond, The Lusty Lass
The mystery of The Shadow Knights. Solved!

Sean & Adrian, The Rainbow
Hello? They turned up at yours, Peter? What's the gossip?

Mimi & Flo, Tom's Bar
How much did they win by?

Diddy & Con, The Brace of Pheasants
Your regulars get pissed?

Peter Bond, The Lusty Lass

They came third.

Sue & Mal, The Case is Altered

What?! Well, Sue and I are stunned. I've never known the Knights to take part in a regular quiz they didn't win!

Sean & Adrian, The Rainbow

You must have the toughest questions on the circuit, Peter.

Peter Bond, The Lusty Lass

I simply guessed their method of cheating and disabled it.

Sue & Mal, The Case is Altered

What was it? I've been studying The Shadow Knights for months and haven't spotted anything untoward.

Sue & Mal, The Case is Altered

What did they say? Did they deny it?

Peter Bond, The Lusty Lass

Their method was disabled quickly, quietly, and, most of all, without them (or anyone else) even realizing I'd discovered their secret.

Sue & Mal, The Case is Altered

This is huge. Peter, you have got to tell me what they're doing.

Peter Bond, The Lusty Lass

Better. I'll show you. Next Monday at The Case.

To: Dominic Eastwood
From: Polly Baker
Date: October 25, 2024
Subject: Re: Documentary idea

Hey Dom,

I'm trying my best to work out the connection between The Shadow Knights and Operation Honeyguide! I'm assuming there is one? Definitely something in the air at The Case is Altered. It's as if Sue and Mal are being watched or maneuvered into place or something. If so, is it because of Honeyguide or events before that?

Their last convo with Piers and Caroline is very sinister. The Eastwoods go from being two competent police officers just doing their job to being blackmailed into negotiating with a drug gang. And did they really cover up a murder?

Pol x

To: Polly Baker
From: Dominic Eastwood
Date: October 25, 2024
Subject: Re: Documentary idea

Hi Polly,

My aunt and uncle spent twenty years in law enforcement; it's inevitable they'd have dealt with some things not quite by the book. Police officers are allowed to exercise discretion—to decide for themselves whether a suspect should be arrested or simply given a verbal warning and sent on their way. However, in the case of an unlawful killing, it's tricky to see how discretion could have come into it.

Sue and Mal were being controlled by the frantic parents of a kidnapped woman. But there's a bigger question here: if they were prepared to blackmail two police officers to get their daughter back, how innocent are the Cunninghams?

Here's some more reading for you!

Best wishes, Dominic

Hulme Police
Operation Honeyguide

In association with the National Crime Agency
Anti-Kidnap and Extortion Unit (AKEU)
Senior Investigating Officer: Detective Chief Inspector Lewis Parry

Downview visit 3, May 7, 2014 (continued):

Subjects: Caroline Cunningham, 47, and Piers Cunningham, 49, Downview, Moorcroft Lane, Pinfield Village
Visiting officers: Sergeant Suzanne Eastwood and Constable Malcolm Eastwood

ME: I don't know what Sue told you, Caroline—

SE: [*Whispers*] Sorry—

ME: [*Whispers*] Jeez—

SE: I told you in confidence, Caroline. I wanted you to feel better. You were so upset . . .

CC: Not so upset I didn't realize that you two are just like us. You make up your own minds about what's right and wrong.

ME: What we did back then was in good faith. This . . .

SE: Paying the Maddox Brothers to let Chloe go . . .

PC: They understand business. That's what you said. They're all about the transaction. Those are your words. The gang has a code of honor—

ME: They do, but not everyone in the chain of command will live by it.

SE: The suitcase full of your cash might end up in the hands of a minor player who could see it as his route out of the gang. It might end up funding his escape, not Chloe's release.

CC: Then it's up to *you* to make sure it doesn't.

PC: I'll start getting the cash together. You two find out what the Maddoxes are owed and we'll double it for Chloe's return. Safe and sound, mind. Safe and sound.

**Conversation between Constable Malcolm Eastwood and Sergeant
Suzanne Eastwood, recorded in Unmarked Car 1, May 7, 2014:**

ME: What were you thinking? Why tell her about the Ramseys? How
did the subject even come up?

SE: I'm stupid! Stupid! We were in the garden yesterday. She was
upset, babbling, saying things she couldn't say in front of Piers,
obsessed with death. Proper morbid stuff. I wanted to reassure
her . . .

ME: Reassure her? By telling her about the time we covered up a
mercy killing, only to realize too late it was actually a murder?

SE: I didn't intend to tell her any of that. But it's the only time I've
ever seen someone pass away, and I wanted to reassure her it
was peaceful . . . Only she kept asking questions, about the
family, the circumstances, and in the end she worked out what
happened—she talked me into a corner; it was like being in a
bloody interview room on the wrong side of the desk!

ME: What else did you tell her?

SE: Nothing.

ME: Are you sure? You didn't say what happened next? Why it never
came to light?

SE: No! What're we gonna do? We can't tell Parry the Cunninghams
are trying to blackmail us, because that would mean telling him
why they're trying to blackmail us.

ME: They're not *trying*, Sue, they actually *are*. We can't afford to lose our
pensions. If we do, we can kiss goodbye to that pub in the country.

SE: So, what *do* we do?
    [*Silence*]

ME: We don't have a choice. They may be blackmailers, but they're
also desperate parents—people will understand why they're
doing it. But us: we're accessories to murder. We'll have to do
what the Cunninghams want.

SE: Take a suitcase of cash and pay a ransom to the Maddoxes, with
no guarantee it'll get their daughter back alive?
    [*Silence*]

ME: You know the answer to that, Sue.

Conversation between Sergeants Dee Obasi and Suzanne Eastwood, recorded in Patrol Car UA889, May 8, 2014:

DO: You seem a bit quiet.

SE: Do I? Honeyguide must be getting to me.

DO: Know what you mean. Wonder how AKEU are getting on . . .
     [*Pause*]

SE: Been wondering something myself, Dee.

DO: Go on.

SE: What if the Cunningham money *doesn't* come from property, and what you found online were just their laundering businesses.

DO: Sue!

SE: What if they have something to hide?

DO: What makes you say that?

SE: Oh, I don't know . . .

DO: No, go on. You've spent longer with them than I have—what's off about them?

SE: Nothing. They're simply parents desperate to get their little girl back . . . How was the night shift?

DO: Quiet. Only had two calls. An alarm going off at a farm and an old lady fallen over in her flat. Still beat, though.

SE: You best get some shut-eye while you can.

DO: I will, see you tomorrow morning. Have a nice day.

SE: Will do.
     [*Sergeant Obasi leaves the car*]

SE: [*Whispers*] If only you knew.

Conversation between Sergeant Suzanne Eastwood and Constable Malcolm Eastwood, recorded in Unmarked Car 3, May 8, 2014:

SE: I'm just saying, the more I think about them, the more suspicious I get. If the whole family is in bed with the Maddox firm, we could find ourselves . . .

ME: Dead.

SE: Wish I hadn't binged *The Sopranos* now. Ignorance is bliss.

ME: *The Sopranos* TV series screened 1999 to 2007. Starring James Gandolfini and Lorraine Bracco. Filmed in New Jersey.

SE: Won twenty-one Emmys and five Golden Globes.
     [*Silence*]

ME: If the Cunninghams were running laundering businesses they'd never call police in, even for this.
     [*Silence*]

SE: But there's another thought I can't get out of my mind, Mal. That this whole thing—this entire operation—is an inside job. The Maddox Brothers want Chester's head on a plate, so they force Parry, and whoever else is under their control, to set up a secret operation—to keep the parents quiet and the whole thing out of the public eye.

ME: So Honeyguide protects the brothers while they do what they have to do to get their man.

SE: And if that's true, then I don't think anyone—the Maddoxes or the police—were counting on the Cunninghams taking matters into their own hands.

ME: Their own hands, my ass! They've shoved matters into *our* hands.

SE: No CCTV footage. No police activity at Devil's Croke. [*Pause*] I had a little ring around all the morgues this morning.

ME: Why?

SE: To see where Beata Novak is. Curiosity.

ME: And?

SE: No body by that name anywhere.

ME: Come off it, Sue! [*Pause*] Why would they hide her body?

SE: Because they intend to pass her death off as accidental or natural causes. If the brothers are ever hauled in, there's no murder charge to answer. [*Pause*] Don't look at me like that.

ME: You gonna tell Dee?

SE: Dee? Dee who turned her own fella in for nicking lipstick? [*Ding. Ding.*]

ME: Wait, hold on.

SE: Bloody quiz WhatsApp! We've got to answer as normal.

The Beat Goes On WhatsApp group, May 8, 2014:

Glen
Anyone see The Chase last night?

Mal
No.

Sue
No.

Jilly
Watch the rerun! Forty grand between two!

Monty
One went minus, didn't answer ANYTHING in the final chase, and walked off with twenty grand!

Jilly
Minus offer jerk!

Mal
It's just a strategy. The Chase tests knowledge and attitude to risk. If I got on there, I'd be tempted to go low and maximize my chances of beating the Chaser.

Glen
There was a question about the Mayans and one about the Aztecs. We've never studied ancient civilizations of South America, and I think we should add that to our list.

Mal

Mayans and Aztecs are Mesoamerican, or Central American. The Incas are South American.

Jilly

We don't need to study—we've got Mal! Who's coming on Saturday?

Sue

He's googling. We can't make Saturday.

Monty

Can you find out what food they're giving us, Glen?

Glen

I'll ask, but they don't reply quickly, this lot.

Conversation between Sergeant Suzanne Eastwood and Constable Malcolm Eastwood, recorded in Unmarked Car 3, May 8, 2014 (continued):

SE: Set it to silent!

ME: Why'd you say I was googling? I knew they weren't South American, but had to check.

SE: We need to concentrate on *this*! Not whether we'd go high or low on *The Chase*. [*Pause*]

ME: Team'll think I google everything now. I'll lose my reputation. [*Silence*]

SE: Can't tell Dee we're conspiring with the victims of crime to pay a ransom, but when all's said and done, I hate lying to a mate. Worst thing about all this. Come on . . . we need to get it over with.

Downview visit 4, May 8, 2014:

Subjects: Caroline Cunningham, 47, and Piers Cunningham, 49,
Downview, Moorcroft Lane, Pinfield Village
Visiting officers: Sergeant Suzanne Eastwood and Constable Malcolm
Eastwood

SE: So we met up with our inside man. He's a slippery character, is Kyle. They live a very stressful life, these CIs. I heard a story once—

PC: I don't *care*! Tell us what happened—what did he say?

SE: OK, well, this chap's my colleague's contact really, so . . .

ME: Get to the point, Sue.

SE: I am! The long and the short of it is: Darren Chester hopped off with a shipment of drugs belonging to Frank Maddox and half a million in cash that Jerry Maddox was in the middle of doing some big international deal with.

ME: So Darren can disappear for a long time without sticking his head above the trench.

PC: How much is the shipment worth?

SE: According to Kyle, close on 1.2 million. Street value. That's what the drugs are worth when they're sold to actual users, not other dealers.

PC: I know what street value means! I've got close to seven hundred and fifty thousand in cash. Another four hundred thousand to come. So we're talking 1.7 to repay the debt . . . I'm rounding that up to two million. Two million in cash for Chloe's safe return.

CC: We'll put this house on the market. We can borrow against the proceeds of the sale. Our bank manager is usually very understanding.

ME: You can't tell him why you want the money—

CC: Of course not. I'll say it's for a medical procedure and residential care.

PC: We can have it all in twenty-four hours.

SE: Two million? That'll be huge bagfuls, won't it? How'll we get that to them? We've only got a Corsa!

ME: I bet it'll be in fifty-pound notes. They're red, with Alan Turing on 'em.

CC: What?

ME: Remember that marathon round at the Legion's quiz, Sue? Who's on which note . . . Alan Turing is on the fifty.

PC: It'll be in fifties and packaged in one large case or possibly two medium cases.

CC: You'll easily transport it.

PC: Go back to this Kyle and say two million cash, clean notes. You two will deliver it.

CC: We're depending on you both—and so is Chloe. Don't let us down.

Conversation between Sergeants Suzanne Eastwood and Dee Obasi, recorded in Patrol Car UA889, May 8, 2014:

SE: Now it's me who's beat.

DO: Busy day?

SE: You could say that.

DO: Sure you're all right? Only you got that look in your eye . . .

SE: What look?

DO: Psychic Sue. Like you know something bad's gonna happen. Remember that time we were sat under the bypass eating Nando's and you said, "I got a feeling, Dee, as if there's gonna be an accident." Then, not two minutes later, didn't a Range Rover rear-end a Kia right in front of our eyes.

SE: That was just watching the traffic. It was going too fast for that ramp.

DO: Psychic Sooooo. Go on, how will Honeyguide end? Tap into your powers and let's see if you're right.

SE: Oh, no idea. There's too much we're not being told. We don't even know how Beata Novak died, do we? And the secrecy. As if . . . as if it was some sort of inside job.
[*Silence*]

DO: You think? What, an undercover operation gone wrong?

SE: Whatever it is, those poor parents are caught right up in it. You can practically feel their desperation, Dee. Their fear that Chloe will end up on a slab, like Beata.

[*Silence*]

And do you know the strange thing? There's no record of Beata's body in any of the local morgues.

DO: You went looking for it?

SE: Phoned around. Caroline, Chloe's mom, was desperate to find out how Beata had died. Thought I'd be helpful and see, so I could reassure her that if the same thing was to happen to Chloe, it'd be quick.

DO: You did *what*? Sue, that's awful.

SE: They're in an awful place. How would anyone feel, eh? [*Silence*] Maybe she's in some other morgue, but . . . seems strange.

DO: You think there's something about the body we're not supposed to know?

SE: It's a thought, that's all.

DO: [*Pause*] Well, I can look into *that* at least.

SE: Don't jeopardize your promotion, Dee. I'd never forgive myself . . .

DO: Oh, I won't. Leave it with me.

Text messages between Mal Eastwood and The General, November 13, 2019:

Mal

Greetings, sir! How did your team fare at The Lusty Lass last night?

Mal

Was Mr. Bond an impeccable host?

The General

Good morning, Mal. In the episode of Most Haunted in which The Lusty Lass is swept for spirits in the name of entertainment, Mr. Bond reveals that he used to be in the army. Yvette Fielding, Blue Peter's youngest-ever presenter when she joined the iconic show aged eighteen in 1987, asks him about various decorative items on the walls and he explains that they are from when he served in the Middle East.

Mal

Yes, I recall that now. Most of us landlords tread a meandering path to the pumps. Were The Shadow Knights the victors last night?

The General

We conceded victory, I'm afraid.

Mal

Dearie me! Well, at least I have some good news. I've extended the invitation to our fellow landlords for our quiz next Monday. Luckily the brewery AGM is during the day, so they can wander over here for the evening quiz. It's a very good idea of yours. I hope you'll be able to come.

The General

I hope so too.

Text messages between Andrew and Sue & Mal, The Case is Altered, November 15, 2019:

Andrew
This is Andrew again. We've messaged before, but you probably don't remember. I'm a regular at your Monday quiz on Chris and Lorraine's team. I'm well, thank you.

Andrew
Not sure why I said that when you didn't ask how I was. Sorry. I'm at work even though it's 9:15 p.m., because this is the only time I get peace enough to think. It's constant phone calls, emails, texts, and site visits during the day. Makes my head spin.

Andrew
Never thought I'd end up in a job I hated this much. Not after committing three years, and so much money, to get qualified for something I found inspiring and purposeful. Thought this job would be a stepping stone until I found something better. Never did. Now I've been here so long I can't leave. There's rent to pay, and whenever I read the job ads I second-guess all the problems I'd have in that role and think about starting all over again and that fills me with terror. I don't have the energy. What if I hate the new job even more and regret leaving this one? I'm a hostage to the devil I know.

Andrew
Anyway, that's by the by. I'm messaging you about Fiona. She says she has a new friend. She's nineteen and it's only natural, but she's had a rocky start in life, as you know, and in my—sadly extensive—experience housing young people, she may not be in the best place to judge whether someone is good for her or not.

Andrew
I can't see her social worker for the cloud of dust in her wake, so I feel it's my responsibility to inform you about this development in her life. As former police officers, you'll have a good sense about people, I'm sure, so perhaps invite this friend around? Check them out. I don't want Fiona to cause you any trouble.

Sue & Mal, The Case is Altered

Thanks, Andrew. We may do just that. Oh and please don't tell people about our former careers. When they know you used to be police, some people overreact.

Text messages between Mal Eastwood and Peter Bond, The Lusty Lass, November 15, 2019:

Mal

Think you should know something in advance of Monday. General Knowledge of The Shadow Knights made a point of telling me you used to be in the army.

Peter Bond, The Lusty Lass

He may suspect I stopped them cheating, but he could never be sure how.

Mal

Will they cheat at Monday's quiz when they know you're there?

Peter Bond, The Lusty Lass

Cunning is as cunning does.

Mal

Does that mean yes?

Peter Bond, The Lusty Lass

We'll see. Either way, our operation will respect the seven Ps.

Mal

Prior planning and preparation prevents piss-poor performance.

Peter Bond, The Lusty Lass

Well done.

Mal

Full disclosure: I googled.

Text messages between Wind and Linda, November 15, 2019:

Wind
Sorry, Linda, but Cloud and I won't be at the quiz on Monday night.

Linda
Oh no! Has Lizzie put her foot down?

Wind
No, she's been quiet on the matter. So I asked the cards and drew the Devil, Death, the Tower, and the Fool, so Cloud and I are at home that night.

Linda
Oh dear. It's not as if we'd have any chance of winning, so if the cards are worried we'll lose, just tell them we're used to it and it's not the reason we quiz anyway. Tell them we enjoy the company and the atmosphere, and perhaps learning a thing or two we didn't know when we walked in.

Wind
It's not a two-way conversation. The cards never say exactly what will happen; they only offer gentle advice and guidance.

Linda
What was their gentle advice and guidance about the quiz then?

Wind
The Devil represents a negative side—the lower, darker side of someone or something will become apparent. Death foreshadows an ending. The Tower means an old structure will fall, perhaps to the ground, but more than that, it heralds a sudden change, which the Fool also indicates, only with the Fool that change is often a complete about-face, a total shift in direction.

Linda
The Case is Altered. The pub is named after a court case that changes direction. How can you be sure the cards aren't encouraging you to go to the pub?

Wind
These four together are signs that whatever is about to befall The Case is Altered, it's best we aren't there.

Ye Olde Goat Ltd. WhatsApp group, Hertfordshire, November 18, 2019:

Diddy & Con, The Brace of Pheasants
Where's everyone parking?

Mimi & Flo, Tom's Bar
The NCP.

Sean & Adrian, The Rainbow
In an Uber now.

Sue & Mal, The Case is Altered
Hoping to find a space in the hotel parking lot. Who's in costume then?

Sean & Adrian, The Rainbow
Thought we'd keep it low-key this year. I'm in my retro fifties-style dark wool suit, and Adrian is rocking black chinos and matching turtleneck. We look like Don Draper and Steve Jobs.

Sean & Adrian, The Rainbow
Only kidding! Of course we're in costume. I've borrowed a rainbow suit and dug out my headdress of rainbow feathers and glitter pods from last year's Pride. Adrian has a flared rainbow jumpsuit and has dyed his hair pink.

Diddy & Con, The Brace of Pheasants
No chance we'll miss you two then! Con has a boutonniere of pheasant feathers and I've got a little pillbox hat with a feather in it.

Sean & Adrian, The Rainbow
Careful, Diddy. Don't overdo it now.

Diddy & Con, The Brace of Pheasants
And did I mention the matching leprechaun suits? Mr. Roper insisted.

Mimi & Flo, Tom's Bar
Just chefs' hats for us. We hate all that. It's so tacky.

Sue & Mal, The Case is Altered
I couldn't get T-shirts made in time, so we've got our legal wigs and gowns on, same as last year. Hope Mr. Roper doesn't mind.

Mimi & Flo, Tom's Bar
Costumes aren't essential, Mal.

Sue & Mal, The Case is Altered
It's Sue. While I remember, if anyone needs their pub sign revamped, I found a marvelous sign writer who took ours down and gave it a thorough clean and varnish. He removed some stray paint and it looks like new. We didn't want you all to see our sign looking drab.

Diddy & Con, The Brace of Pheasants
That's good to know, Sue. What's the parking like at The Case now? We're going straight there after the AGM.

Sue & Mal, The Case is Altered
Do you all know where we are? It's a little road off the A416, just after St. Luke's Church and before the Morrisons turnoff. If our little parking lot is full, drive up to Turrington's Wood Yard and park in their driveway, they don't mind.

Peter Bond, The Lusty Lass
Bell End.

Sue & Mal, The Case is Altered
That's right, Peter. The road is called Bell End. Thanks for reminding everyone.

Sean & Adrian, The Rainbow
We're Ubering there after the AGM. It's a business expense after all.

Diddy & Con, The Brace of Pheasants
You must have a lot of bags if you're changing for the quiz?

Sean & Adrian, The Rainbow
OMG. We're sat here in traffic, looking at each other like a couple of Christmas fairies at Easter. We've forgotten our change of clothes. Will you mind if we show up in our outfits, Sue?

Sue & Mal, The Case is Altered
No, love! That'll bring some color to the landlords' quiz table!

Diddy & Con, The Brace of Pheasants
We'll all keep our costumes on for the quiz. Then you won't look out of place.

Sean & Adrian, The Rainbow
Aw, thanks, Diddy! Appreciate that, and I bet you two make a lovely pair of leprechauns!

Mimi & Flo, Tom's Bar
Are we all on the same team for the quiz, Sue?

Sue & Mal, The Case is Altered
It's Mal now. This is the plan. After the AGM you're all welcome to come back to ours for a drink and catch-up. After the big lunch today, I doubt anyone will want much to eat, but if you do, bar snacks are on the house for Olde Goat landlords. As I am the quizmaster, you have my dispensation to make up a table of seven.

Sean & Adrian, The Rainbow
Let's hope The Shadow Knights are there!

Diddy & Con, The Brace of Pheasants
We're leaving now. See you all at the AGM, folks!

Text messages between Warwick Roper, General Manager of Ye Olde Goat Brewery Ltd., and Sue & Mal at The Case is Altered, November 18, 2019:

Warwick Roper, GM
This quiz.

Sue & Mal, The Case is Altered
Hello, Mr. Roper. The AGM is a wonderful annual occasion! You're treating us with all this free tea and coffee. Thank you. Our compliments to the team behind such a well-organized event.

Warwick Roper, GM
8 p.m. tonight at The Case. Sean mentioned it.

Sue & Mal, The Case is Altered
Did he? Yes, we extended a casual invitation to our regional colleagues to make up a table at our quiz.

Sue & Mal, The Case is Altered
We're all keeping our costumes on. Mostly because Sean and Adrian forgot their change of clothes, but also because we can't get enough of Peter Bond in high heels, blond wig, and latex décolletage.

Warwick Roper, GM
Room for another?

Sue & Mal, The Case is Altered
Well, I imagine we could squeeze you in, if you don't want to go home straight after the AGM.

Warwick Roper, GM
Drinks on the house?

Sue & Mal, The Case is Altered
For you, Mr. Roper, of course.

Warwick Roper, GM
Excellent! I'll get a team of managers together.

Sue & Mal, The Case is Altered
A whole team? No problem! We look forward to seeing you all.

Hulme Police
Operation Honeyguide

In association with the National Crime Agency
Anti-Kidnap and Extortion Unit (AKEU)
Senior Investigating Officer: Detective Chief Inspector Lewis Parry

Conversation between Constable Malcolm Eastwood and Sergeants Dee Obasi and Suzanne Eastwood, recorded by Sergeant Obasi's body-worn camera, May 8, 2014:

ME: How'd you know Beata's body's here, Dee? Coleport, of all places.

DO: Made a couple of calls on the off chance. One chap I used to work with at Stopton West End and another in Central.

SE: If her body was found at the old Chesters department store, why's she being kept so far out of the area?

DO: This is a long-stay morgue. Bodies come here that need to be shipped overseas. Who knew?
[*Silence*]

SE: Not done much of this, you?

DO: Yeah, in Stopton. All the time. Or perhaps it just felt that way.

ME: You'd be mad if you enjoyed this side of things.

DO: Oh, I don't know. If there's no emotional connection to the person on the slab, well, you see a side of life most people never do.

SE: Yeah, lucky bastards.

DO: We don't want to think about it, do we? Yet we all die—it's one of life's few certainties.

ME: Said the great philosopher Melody Obasi.

DO: Get away! Mind you, they don't make these places pleasant, do they?

SE: All this stainless steel and tile . . . reminds me of that abattoir we went to, Dee, remember? They'd had a break-in, lost a few dead animals.

DO: Now *that* were worse than this by a long shot.

SE: No sooner had we left and ordered coffee and fries at the Wimpy, when we heard a couple of blokes were going around the estates selling cheap meat.

DO: They'd piled two dead cows and one dead pig into a transit van and driven 'em to their garage, cut them into bits with a Black and Decker jigsaw, divvied it up, and were hawking the bags for twenty quid each!

SE: Only they weren't trained butchers, so didn't remove the skin or bones, and one bag had two great big bloody hooves sticking out!

ME: I remember you telling me this.

SE: Dee and I had to go around the estate asking if anyone had bought a bag of dead animal and, if they had, not to eat it, due to the insanitary conditions it had been prepared in.

DO: To be fair, when the abattoir found out, they offered to wash and prepare the meat properly for anyone who'd bought a bag in good faith. These people weren't well-off and that were nice of them.

SE: There was one old boy who'd bought a pig's head and was boiling it up on his stove when we knocked on the door. Said he didn't effing care how it had been prepared because it all added to the effing flavor of his effing stock.

DO: That pig gave us a look too.

[*A mortuary attendant arrives*]

MA: Can I see your warrants, please. Thank you. Did the pathologist invite you?

DO: No, DCI Lewis Parry did.

MA: Hmm. I'll prepare the room.

[*The mortuary attendant leaves*]

SE: Careful, Dee. You don't want to get in the shit this close to your panel interview.

DO: Don't worry. She'll call Parry's office and discover he's on leave today. No one else will know anything—that we can guarantee.

SE: First time you've ever overstepped the mark. Is that our influence?

ME: You're breaking bad, Dee. TV series screened 2008 to 2013. Set and filmed in Albuquerque, New Mexico. Starring Bryan Cranston as Walter White. Seventy-two episodes.

[*Silence*]

DO: You got me thinking, Sue. What if Honeyguide is really Hulme Police covering for the Maddox Brothers? What if we're helping 'em find Darren by keeping the kidnaps quiet?

[*A tense pause of surprise*]

ME: You think that too?

DO: I can't lie. It's crossed my mind.

MA: OK, come through, please.

[*The party moves to another room*]

MA: These are the remains.

[*The mortuary attendant leaves*]

SE: Thank you.

[*Long pause*]

SE: Well, hammers it home, doesn't it? What it all boils down to. A zipped-up bag.

ME: You all right, Dee?

DO: I've gone cold. I'll sit over here. You two go ahead.

[*As Sergeant Obasi is farther away, the following is fainter*]

SE: It's chilly in here. Doesn't help, does it? I'm all shivery too.

ME: Take a moment . . .

SE: Don't know why; it's not like I haven't seen a dead body before. Seen loads. Accidents, overdoses, old folk who pass away in the night.

ME: Shall I unzip it?

SE: I'll be fine. It's just the buildup to this one. Feel like I know her. Dee?

DO: You do it, Sue. I'll stay over here.

[*Sergeant Eastwood and Constable Eastwood unzip the body bag and examine the contents. There is a long period of silence*]

SE: You can tell it's her. Poor mite.

ME: No head injuries, no? [*Barely audible whisper*] Oh.

SE: I don't feel right unzipping it all the way. Out of respect.

ME: I'll turn around. She won't mind another woman.

[*Long pause*]

ME: Anything?

SE: Here.

ME: Nasty puncture wounds. Both hands . . .

SE: She was a drug user?

ME: Or was kept drugged while she was held.

SE: Maybe. You wanna come and look, Dee?

DO: OK, I'll . . . [*Pause*] Can't see how she died, though. Phew! Don't know why I'm feeling so . . . all hot and sweaty—must be going soft!

SE: That'll be your friend, Dee. You're more sensitive after a bereavement. Remember you were sick at the scene of that car crash, Mal? This was just weeks after his dad passed and the fellow in the car was an old man . . .

ME: Thanks for the memories, Sue. Let's zip her up and get back.

Conversation between Sergeants Dee Obasi and Suzanne Eastwood and Constable Malcolm Eastwood, recorded in Patrol Car UA889, May 8, 2014:

DO: Feel a prat!

SE: You underestimate how well you get to know a victim. Even when you never so much as glimpsed them when they were alive.

DO: Maybe you're right and it's something to do with poor Nat.

ME: So, that solves the mystery of where Beata Novak's body is and how she died.

SE: Does it?

ME: Puncture wounds on both hands. She was a drug addict. It's not out of the question she overdosed. She was being held by the Maddox Brothers, and one thing they aren't short of is heroin. Wouldn't be the first time.

DO: It's a thought. Anything else that might shed some light? Bruises, cuts, or tattoos? What about piercings or jewelry?

SE: Didn't see any tattoos and no jewelry or metalwork. They take all personal effects away—or they're meant to.

ME: What a sad end, eh?

DO: Shame no one's come over to claim her. She's stuck here waiting for paperwork.

SE: While Caroline and Piers are waiting at home, terrified Chloe will be next.

ME: Best not think too much about it. If we do, we'll be no good to the Cunninghams. They need us upbeat. Come on. Thanks, Dee, you cleared something up for us there.

DO: You're welcome, Mal. If you need anything else, give me a ring.

SE: You go ahead.
  [*Pause while Constable Eastwood leaves*]
  Dee, just want to say thank you.

DO: What for?

SE: Being a mate, you know. Covering when I leave early, chatting about everything under the sun. Getting the brews in. Being you.

DO: Don't be daft! That's what mates do. You're a solid-gold one yourself.

SE: I know, but . . . when you see what we've just seen. You want to make sure everything's said, don't you? Because you never know when it's too late. When you'll never see people again.

Conversation between Sergeant Suzanne Eastwood and Constable Malcolm Eastwood, recorded in Unmarked Car 3, May 8, 2014:

SE: I want to see her autopsy.

ME: You can't, not now. We need to keep our heads down. Stay out of Parry's sight line.

SE: If Beata died accidentally and wasn't killed, there's a shred of hope for Caroline and Piers.

ME: Don't go telling 'em that. Let's get this over with.

SE: Then we best get to Pinfield.

ME: This is it. The big one. Good luck.

SE: You too, you too.

Text messages between Thor's Hammer and Sue & Mal, The Case is Altered, November 18, 2019:

Thor's Hammer
What's happening tonight?

Sue & Mal, The Case is Altered
The quiz is 7:30 for 8 as usual, Chris.

Thor's Hammer
Where are you two?

Sue & Mal, The Case is Altered
At a chain hotel in the middle of a roundabout at the junction of four A roads.

Thor's Hammer
Is that a cryptic clue?

Sue & Mal, The Case is Altered
Mal drove, so I don't know exactly where we are.

Thor's Hammer
Why aren't you at The Case?

Sue & Mal, The Case is Altered
The brewery's AGM. Landlords from around the country.

Thor's Hammer
Is the quiz still on?

Sue & Mal, The Case is Altered
Yes. CEO speech. Switching phone off.

Sue & Mal, The Case is Altered
There's hours to go yet, Chris. We'll be back for the quiz.

The Sturdy Challengers Quiz Team WhatsApp group, November 18, 2019:

Thor's Hammer
False alarm. Saw Fiona alone behind the bar at lunchtime and thought something must be wrong with Sue and Mal. But the quiz is still on.

Fiona

k

Andrew

Fiona means, "Yes, that's right."

Keith

Popped into The Case on Sunday. Mal said they have an AGM and some of the other landlords will be coming tonight. They could be competition for us, Chris.

Andrew

Perhaps the marathon round will be "Guess the pub name from the sign."

Ajay

It would be just like Mal to organize a themed quiz if his fellow landlords are there!

Keith

Guess the alcohol brand from the logo?

Lorraine

Well, Rita's team may even beat The Shadow Knights on that one. She's usually hammered before the quiz starts!

Andrew

Speaking of "hammered," there's something I've been meaning to ask you, Chris. Why does your name come up as Thor's Hammer?

Ajay

Everyone start looking up pub facts and figures. History, legislation, events.

Keith

Notorious pubs, like The Star Tavern, where the Great Train Robbery was planned, or The Plumbers Arms, where Lady Lucan reported her husband's murder of their nanny.

Lorraine

The Blind Beggar, where Ronnie Kray murdered George Cornell.

Andrew

Obviously I know what Thor's hammer is, but why have it as your ID?

Keith

The Magdala, where Ruth Ellis lived, the last woman to hang.

Ajay

Who can forget The Ten Bells, where some of Jack the Ripper's victims drank?

Keith

And fictional pubs! The Rovers Return, The Queen Vic, The Woolpack, The Bull Inn.

Lorraine

The Three Broomsticks from Harry Potter.

Keith

The Three Cripples from Oliver Twist.

Lorraine

Mal wouldn't have that as an answer, it's offensive.

Keith

Alcohol brands that young people might drink. Fiona, that's your department. Us elderly folk should remind ourselves of the old ones. Everyone clear on what to look up before tonight?

Andrew

Is it because you like Nordic mythology? Or has anyone mistaken you for Chris Hemsworth recently?

Ajay

It's not important, Andy, mate.

Andrew

I know it's not life or death, but I've wondered for ages, that's all. If it's a big bad secret, well, sure, keep it.

Lorraine

It's not a secret. Go on, Chris, explain to Andy.

Lorraine

It's something our son did when he was in hospital for the last time. We watched the film together in the ward. Our surname being Thorogood, Logan said his dad was Thor. Well, Chris hated the film; and Logan, being cheeky, changed the name on his phone to Thor's Hammer. Chris pretended he was annoyed, but he wasn't really.

Lorraine
Whenever he gets a new phone he calls it Thor's Hammer.

Thor's Hammer
It's been six years, but I don't want to change it.

Text messages between Andrew and Fiona, November 18, 2019:

Andrew
Not one single thing I do is right. Why can't I just enjoy some simple banter with friends from the quiz team? No. I go and put my great big fucking foot in it yet again.

Fiona
aw

Andrew
I don't know what that means—whether you're laughing at me or don't care, or are sympathetic. No idea.

Fiona
lor sad its ok

Andrew
Why couldn't someone have taken me aside before now and explained they had a son who died? I wouldn't have mentioned Thor's Hammer. But I had to go and do it, didn't I? Now I feel terrible, and I've got a full day of work with this extra weight on my chest before I have to sit and look everyone in the eye at the quiz.

Andrew
Did you know about Chris and Lorraine's son?

Fiona
ys

Andrew
How? Who told you?

Fiona
Sue as losing a kid b worst thing ever

Andrew
And that's precisely why I feel like a great big disgusting turd, for going on and on about the Thor's Hammer thing. Why did I even do that? It's not like I care what his phone thinks his name is. I assumed it would be a funny story.

Fiona
time

Andrew
Well, I'm glad my misery is your amusement, I really am.

Ye Olde Goat Ltd. WhatsApp group, Hertfordshire, November 18, 2019:

Sean & Adrian, The Rainbow
Are you lot still behind us? Sue and Mal's car is silver and has a stream of feathers trailing out of the back window.

Mimi & Flo, Tom's Bar
You fit in then?

Sean & Adrian, The Rainbow
No. Mr. Roper has half my headdress in his car.

Diddy & Con, The Brace of Pheasants
We lost you at the first lights, so the satnav is on.

Mimi & Flo, Tom's Bar
We're behind you, but there's a Prius and a VW in the way.

Sean & Adrian, The Rainbow
Are you still with us, Peter?

Diddy & Con, The Brace of Pheasants
He's on his own in the car, so if he replies he's a naughty boy.

Peter Bond, The Lusty Lass
Yes.

Peter Bond, The Lusty Lass
Hands-free.

Text messages between Sue Eastwood and Fiona, November 18, 2019:

Sue
Fiona, love, we've got another extra table for the quiz. That's two more than usual. Everyone will have to squish up.

Fiona
k

Sue
It's free drinks for the landlords and Olde Goats tables ONLY. At least half are driving, so we're counting on soft drinks.

Fiona
k

Sue
We're almost there.

THE CASE IS ALTERED PUB QUIZ

November 18, 2019

Rounds	Max points
1. Today's News	10
2. On this day in 1964	10
3. Sporting sponsors	10
4. Art & Literature of Scotland	10
5. Film & TV: doctors on-screen	10
6. Music: name the artist and song title (Clue: one or the other will include a reference to drinking)	20
7. Aviation: history and present day	10
8. Global disasters	10
Marathon round: Name these 20 pubs from their signs	20

Text messages between Peter Bond, The Lusty Lass, and Mal Eastwood, November 18, 2019:

Peter Bond, The Lusty Lass
There are whispers on the floor. Too many landlords. Too few goats.

Mal
Diddy and Con claim to be poor quizzers. They say they count as one person, and I am the quizmaster. My decision is final. And I don't know why anyone would object to the Olde Goat team only having four members.

Peter Bond, The Lusty Lass
No Shadow Knights.

Mal
The General said they were coming. I've saved their table, but there's only five minutes to go. It would be just my luck that they never show again, precisely when we know how they're cheating!

Mal
HERE THEY ARE! All six. The game is on.

Peter Bond, The Lusty Lass
Let the veil be slowly drawn away.

Text messages between Mal and Sue Eastwood, November 18, 2019:

Mal
Peter keeps winking at me and tapping his nose. In the costume he's wearing, it's confusing.

Sue
So he thinks he knows how The Shadow Knights cheat and can stop them?

Mal
Yes.

Sue
Just like that?

Mal

Apparently.

Sue

And what then?

Mal

Chris and Lorraine will win, I expect. That's what I'd like to see anyway, after they've been robbed of the top spot for weeks. Of course, you can never discount our two new teams.

Sue

Does Peter know that's what you want?

Mal

We haven't discussed it, why?

Sue

He's not planning on causing trouble, is he?

Mal

Peter Bond? Cause trouble in front of the brewery big shots? No!

* * *

Sue

It's gone!

Mal

What has?

Sue

What we thought was in the safe—it's gone.

Mal

It's hidden under a pile of papers.

Sue

I looked under the pile of papers and it's NOT there! When did you last see it?

Mal

Can't remember.

Sue

Then we don't know when it was taken.

Mal
I don't check it daily!

Sue
Whoever took it would have to know it was there AND the combination for the safe.

Mal
There's nothing I can do now, the quiz is about to start.

Sue
Fucking Fiona!

Text messages between Linda and Sue & Mal, The Case is Altered, November 18, 2019:

Linda
Who's the table of funeral directors, Mal?

Sue & Mal, The Case is Altered
It's Sue. They're our bosses from the brewery. Bless them, they're not a colorful bunch.

Linda
I don't know, one is wearing a very sparkly suit.

Sue & Mal, The Case is Altered
That's Mr. Roper and it's not a sparkly suit. He stuffed Sean's headdress into his car, but a glitter pod burst when he shut the door.

Linda
That's made me chuckle!

Sue & Mal, The Case is Altered
From his face, we can safely say it's too soon for HIM to see the funny side. I'd love to chat more, Linda, love, but Mal and I are quite busy this evening.

Linda
I understand! By the way, you can tell that's a wig.

Sue & Mal, The Case is Altered
We're in costume.

Linda
I'm joking!

Sue & Mal, The Case is Altered
This is Mal. Put your phone away, Linda. It's time to quiz.

Text messages between Thor's Hammer and Sue & Mal, The Case is Altered, November 18, 2019:

Thor's Hammer
Not happy.

Sue & Mal, The Case is Altered
Why not? Quickly, Chris, I'm about to start.

Thor's Hammer
These two new teams. They upset the playing field. I'm telling you now THIS QUIZ DOESN'T COUNT.

Sue & Mal, The Case is Altered
Doesn't count? These are pub quizzes. In the grand scheme of things, none of them "count."

Thor's Hammer
Gutted. Been looking forward to it all week.

Sue & Mal, The Case is Altered
Sorry, Chris. I'm flattered our quiz means so much to you—it means a lot to me, as you know—but perhaps enjoy it for what it is, an entertaining evening out with friends, rather than focus on winning?

Thor's Hammer
Winning is everything, Mal. Why take part if not to win? What else is there? I'll tell you what, for Lor and I that's nothing. We have nothing. Let us have our quiz.

Sue & Mal, The Case is Altered
You've lost more than most, Chris, and our hearts go out to you. But you have each other. You have a good job in aviation. I understand it's a top-secret role that you can't talk about, and pretty much everyone in this pub would love to know what it is—except me. All I know is that it's important, that people depend on you, and the work you do has great significance now and in the future. Tonight we have an aviation round in your honor—how about that?

Thor's Hammer
I work on a production line packing airplane food.

Thor's Hammer
Minimum wage. Minimum everything. Nothing I do is important. Nothing except the quiz.

Thor's Hammer
You hear me talk about "dangerous operations." Well, you try keeping bang bang chicken crisp if it's not packed at exactly the right stage of cooling.

Thor's Hammer
Those mysterious machines I hint at? The collider mixes gravy and vegetables with meat.

Thor's Hammer
Can't have a "leak" in this game—it can stop production for half a day.

Thor's Hammer
Didn't know all that, did you?

Sue & Mal, The Case is Altered
Chris, if I were sitting on a long flight with no grub, or was served a meal that was badly packed, it would ruin my trip.

Sue & Mal, The Case is Altered
Think of all the thousands of people who've enjoyed those dinners. Who discovered a new food when they had it on a flight.

Sue & Mal, The Case is Altered
What you do is no less important than any other part of the aviation industry.

Sue & Mal, The Case is Altered

Now Sue is giving me the evil eye, because it's nearly ten past eight.

Thor's Hammer

A whole aviation round? Bring it on.

Sue & Mal, The Case is Altered

Phones away!

Text messages between Sue Eastwood and Fiona, November 18, 2019:

Sue

Come up to the bar. I want a word.

Sue

So for once you've put your phone away. We'll speak after the quiz.

Quiz teams and where they sat

The Shadow Knights
General Knowledge, Brigitte
Pamela, Lynette
Edward, Wilfred

Spokespersons
Erik, Jemma
Tam, Dilip

Let's Get Quizzical
Sid & Nancy Topliss
Bunny & George Tyme
Margaret & Ted Dawson

The Landlords
Peter
Sean & Adrian
Mimi & Flo
Diddy & Con

The Sturdy Challengers
Chris & Lorraine
Ajay, Keith
Andrew, Fiona

Linda & Joe & Friends
Linda & Joe
Rita & Bailey

Ami's Manic Carrots
Jojo, Evie
Rosie, Bianca
Fliss, Harrison

The Olde Goats
Warwick, Denise
Tony, Trevor

Found in my Uncle Mal's notes:

Good evening, everyone, and welcome to this very special edition of The Case is Altered quiz. I'd like to extend a warm welcome to not one but two guest teams. The first is The Landlords, each dressed in a costume that represents their pub—each and every one an exceptional drinking destination in the ceremonial county of Hertfordshire. Ditto, Sue and I are begarbed in black gowns and white wigs, in homage to The Case is Altered. And to my right are The Olde Goats, the senior management team at Ye Olde Goat Brewery Ltd. They aren't in fancy dress, except that I believe some accident befell an ornamental headdress in Mr. Roper's car and it's nice to see him being such a good sport about it. I believe Wind has finally been persuaded to "blow in" during the intermission to give tarot readings, with all proceeds going to the hospice, so . . . maybe ask her what questions will come up in the second half! With no further ado, let's quiz.

Text messages between margaret and Sue & Mal, The Case is Altered, November 18, 2019:

margaret
this is margaret where's the taro

Sue & Mal, The Case is Altered
What a surprise. You've never texted us before, Margaret, and you do it for the first time on the frantic night of a very important quiz. Now, taro is an exotic root vegetable, the like of which I doubt The Case is Altered has ever seen.

Sue & Mal, The Case is Altered
If you mean "Where is Wind with her charity TAROT readings," then I'm pleased to say she's just maneuvered her little table through the door and is setting up in the corner.

margaret
oooo good sorry I hate these buttons they're so small prefer email

Sue & Mal, The Case is Altered
The marathon round is still out, put your phone away, please.

margaret
that's awful

Sue & Mal, The Case is Altered
It's the rules. You may only be checking the news headlines, but equally you could be looking up the marathon answers. The rules apply to all.

margaret
sue drew justice wheel of fortune judgment and death

Sue & Mal, The Case is Altered
Sue just wants to support Wind and donate to the hospice. Neither of us have any time for that hokerypokery.

margaret
winds packing up because her lizzie doesn't like the cards

Sue & Mal, The Case is Altered
Wind is packing her things away because the intermission is over and, Margaret, if Let's Get Quizzical weren't currently last on the board and wouldn't even place top three if they scored full marks in the marathon and every round from now on, I'd consider disqualifying you. Phone away, please, the second half is about to begin.

Text messages between Sue Eastwood and Sue & Mal, The Case is Altered, November 18, 2019:

Sue
I'm having second thoughts.

Sue & Mal, The Case is Altered
Not you as well! Is it not obvious how busy I am?

Sue & Mal, The Case is Altered
Second thoughts about what?

Sue

Exposing The Shadow Knights in front of Mr. Roper. We don't want to start something. Not when it's missing from the safe.

Sue & Mal, The Case is Altered

No one's going to start.

Sue

Can you tell me what the plan is at least?

Sue & Mal, The Case is Altered

Peter will stop The Shadow Knights winning, that's all. They don't realize he knows their secret, so there's no reason for them to complain. In the unlikely event there's a tie for first place, I've got a very special killer question to ask.

Sue

Keep it light, FFS!

Sue & Mal, The Case is Altered

This is Mr. Entertainment you're talking to! The Shadow Knights will see the funny side, I know it.

Ami's Manic Carrots WhatsApp group, November 18, 2019:

Rosie

What's happening?

Fliss

Don't use phones! We'll be disqualified.

Jojo

These folks have some crazy prior beef, don't they?

Harrison

OMG.

Evie

Is this part of the quiz?

Rosie

The vibe is yikes.

Evie

Shall we go?

Bianca

I vote to go.

Harrison

Weird shit going down here.

Fliss

Mal and Sue look like they're taking control again. It'll settle in a minute.

Evie

The atmos is toxic. I feel unsafe.

Bianca

We're out of here.

Fliss

We can't just leave.

Jojo

Mal and Sue aren't taking control—The Shadow Knights are.

Bianca

That Shadow Knights guy, The General. He's super-menacing all of a sudden.

Evie

Let's go.

Fliss

WE CAN'T LEAVE.

Evie

Why not?

Jojo

The quiz is over.

Fliss

Two of The Shadow Knights are guarding the doors. NO ONE can leave.

Provisional scores out of 110

The Shadow Knights	96
The Sturdy Challengers	96
Spokespersons	89
The Landlords	81
The Olde Goats	79
Ami's Manic Carrots	73
Let's Get Quizzical	62
Linda & Joe & Friends	49

Extract from a police statement made by Harrison Walker from Ami's Manic Carrots, November 22, 2019:

You want to know about that last quiz at The Case is Altered. There was a *lot* of baggage being unpacked. And when we finally managed to escape, the doors closed behind us and The Case is Altered never opened again. It was that much worse because Sue and Mal had been so nice to us the whole time we knew them.

You might wonder why we went to the quiz at all. It's not really a young person's thing, right? And yeah, the first time we went was a complete accident. Someone heard drinks at The Case were cheaper, and even though the pub was a bit crusty and remote, we turned up one Monday just to try it out. We didn't realize that was their quiz night. We said we'd do it as a joke. An ironic statement. But we joined in and something happened.

What does our team name mean? Oh, it's a long story. Really? OK, well, here goes. We'd all been to a wedding the weekend before that first quiz and were still hungover. I went to pull out a pen to fill in the quiz paper—and pulled out a cold, slimy heritage carrot. I'd dropped it at the reception dinner, quickly slipped it into my pocket so no one noticed, and then forgot all about it. I stared at it and said, "Man, that's manic."

Meanwhile, a couple of weeks earlier, we'd been to karaoke for our friend's bachelorette party and I'd sung "This Is the Life" by Amy Macdonald. The girls were still calling me Amy. We had to write our team name at the top of the page but were all too hungover to think of one, so Evie wrote, "Ami's Manic Carrots"—because she can't spell ... Yeah, most people wish they hadn't asked.

Anyway, that evening was the first time we'd put our phones away for a whole three hours—since we were kids, probably. Even when you're in a meeting, or at the cinema, you always sneak a look now and then, don't you? Well, during a quiz you can't. No distractions. No interruptions. You're present with your team and all the other people in the room. Not many moments like that.

The next week we went back and, from then on, Monday night was when we all put our screens down, stopped texting, scrolling, and googling. A weekly digital detox.

Most of the quizzers were boomers and Gen X, so the questions were usually about things that happened before we were born. We were always close to the bottom of the table, which didn't bother us at first—we weren't there to win. But then a few weeks before that final quiz, Mal switched things up. He asked a one-hundred-year-old lady to answer the questions and we had to guess not the correct answer but the answer she'd given. Amazingly, we came first and it was the most incredible feeling ever! Suddenly we understood why people want to win so badly. I was walking on air at work the next day, telling anyone who'd listen over the coffee machine that we'd won! Seriously, it was mad.

The following week we were back at the bottom, but we'd had a taste of victory. Every quiz after that was more and more frustrating, because we had no chance of getting that fix again.

It was much busier in the pub on the night of that final quiz. Lots of strangers. There was a different vibe in the room. After his usual introduction, when he tells us about the rounds and reminds everyone that if we're caught cheating we'll be disqualified, Mal introduced a team of landlords from other local pubs. They'd been at a convention or something, and most were in fancy dress. Sue and Mal were wearing robes and wigs like barristers and I realized what "The Case is Altered" actually refers to: a piece of evidence so explosive that an entire court case changes direction. There was also a team from high up in the brewery. They looked serious and out of place.

The quiz itself was fine. The first half was normal, with The Shadow

Knights in the lead, but in the second half they dropped behind. Instead of nines and tens, they were getting sixes and sevens. There's an unusual round almost every quiz and this time it was "aviation." We only scored five out of ten there, but Chris and Lorraine's team, The Sturdy Challengers, got full marks because he works in the industry. I think it's something classified. Apparently he's not allowed to talk about it anyway.

It all started when the quiz was over and we were waiting for Sue and Mal to give us the final scores and announce the winner. Not everyone would notice this, but I did. The landlord of The Lusty Lass, who was dressed as a drag queen, clicked across to Mal in high heels and showed him something in his hand. The pair of them whispered together for a bit, then the drag queen went back to her seat.

Mal stood up, knocked three times on the table to kill the chatter, and said, "We have an unprecedented situation tonight. Two teams have scored the exact same points and that calls for a tiebreaker."

That was the start of a toxic atmosphere that grew and grew. By the end of it all, the Manic Carrots were texting madly under the table— well, we couldn't speak out loud. The girls wanted to go, but we couldn't because a couple of The Shadow Knights had moved to the doors and blocked our exit. They were like court ushers and no one could get past them. It was as if the whole thing had been planned, although if it had, our team wasn't in on it.

Hulme Police
Operation Honeyguide

In association with the National Crime Agency
Anti-Kidnap and Extortion Unit (AKEU)
Senior Investigating Officer: Detective Chief Inspector Lewis Parry

Downview visit 5, May 9, 2014:

Subjects: Caroline Cunningham, 47, and Piers Cunningham, 49,
Downview, Moorcroft Lane, Pinfield Village
Visiting officers: Sergeant Suzanne Eastwood and Constable Malcolm
Eastwood

SE: That's two million pounds? They look like ordinary suitcases.

ME: Feel the weight of that? You'd never get it through customs.

PC: It's in fifties, like I said.

SE: Can't wait to see what so much money looks like! [*Pause*] Oh! The clasp is stuck . . .

PC: It's a secure case with a tamper-proof closure system, only accessible with an electronic code.

SE: How will we open it?

PC: You won't need to open it.

ME: We'll have to show our contact the money. These people weren't born yesterday and they're paranoid.

PC: Here's how it works. You deliver the cases to your man, then come back here. He takes them to his bosses. When the Maddox Brothers have them, they call you and I speak to them. I arrange to collect Chloe and give them a code. They open the first case and see the cash. Once Chloe is safely back home, they call again and I give them a code for the second case.

SE: I don't know if they'll like that, Piers . . .

ME: These people hate being told what to do. They need to feel in control.

PC: They *are* in control! They have our daughter, for God's sake! [*Violent sobbing*]

CC: Come here, Piers. Ssssh. It's OK, it's OK, we'll get her back. Sssh.
      [*A period of silence while the Cunninghams recover*]

SE: It's heartbreaking to see you two like this. [*Pause*] Isn't it, Mal.

ME: Yep, uh-huh.

SE: But we'll do our best. We'll take these to our man and hope to
      God he's understanding.

ME: Are you sure you can't give me the codes—or the code to one
      case even—just so I can show him there's real money in there?
      Believe me, the sight of it will oil the wheels . . .

PC: No. They have my word and if they are the commercial operation
      you say they are, then they will honor the payment and deliver
      the goods. I don't have faith in many things, Mal, but I have
      faith in the sanctity of a financial transaction between men of
      business. It hasn't let me down yet.

ME: OK, well, you take that one, Sue, I'll take this, and we'll pop them
      in the Corsa.

SE: We'll have to take out our cooler and hiking sticks . . .

ME: They'll fit on the rear seat, come on.

SE: We'll be back for the codes as soon as we can.

CC: Break a leg. Remember, that's what Chloe always says before she
      does anything risky.

PC: Break a leg, you two. Break a leg.

**Conversation between Sergeant Suzanne Eastwood and Constable
Malcolm Eastwood, recorded by a Ring doorbell at the rear entrance
to Downview, May 9, 2014:**

SE: Look! Look at that over the fence. It's in the front garden. A For
      Sale sign.

ME: Caroline said it was on the market. Still, with all their money, they
      won't be living on the breadline, will they? Bound to have a million
      or two left. They'll be OK. Come on, let's go tell them it's done.

SE: We need that first code. Fuck!

ME: Sue!
      [*The following is all in furtive whispers*]

SE: There's a patrol car parked in the drive. We're meant to park out the back. What if the Maddoxes see?

ME: The guv. Parry! He's marched out of the front door with a cardboard box. Putting it in the trunk of the patrol car.

SE: Have they had word the Maddoxes aren't watching the house now?

ME: Pull your head back in! Don't let him see us. [*Pause*] The guv's never visited the Cunninghams, has he? Trust our luck he's here on the very day we're paying a bloody ransom for them.
[*A long silence*]

SE: D'yer reckon Piers and Caroline have told him what we were doing?

ME: Don't say that.
[*Stunned gasps*]

SE: Rhys is in uniform. Have they found Chloe's body?

ME: Don't say that either.
[*Silence*]

SE: Curiosity is getting the better of me. Let's go.

ME: What shall we say if they ask why we're here?

SE: We keep our cool, say we wanted to check on Caroline and Piers, like the concerned officers we are. We'll think of something. Around here, look, gate's open.

Footage recorded at the side of Downview by Sergeant Rhys Davies's body-worn camera, May 9, 2014:

[*The following is spoken in harsh whispers*]

SE: Sorry to make you jump, Rhys. Anyone would think you were up to no good. What's Parry doing here?

RD: What are *you* doing here?

SE: Checking on Caroline and Piers. Pastoral care of victims. That's why we were brought in on Honeyguide. Parry made it quite clear it wasn't our policing skills anyway.

RD: Guv! Guv, out here . . .
[*DCI Lewis Parry steps out of the house*]

LP: Sue, Mal. [*Pause*] You two should be at the ramp to the A90 with a speed camera, if my memory of today's roster serves me correctly.

SE: Piers was poorly when we last visited . . .

ME: We thought we'd pop over, see how they were . . .

SE: Has anything happened we should know about, guv?
[*Sergeant Obasi steps out of the house*]

DO: Sue and Mal! What a surprise!

SE: Could say the same about you, Dee. [*Silence*] Are we in the dark about something? We pop by on the off chance and you three are already here, uniforms and marked cars, bold as brass. What happened to "no police presence"?

DO: Well . . .

SE: That couple's daughter has been kidnapped; they don't need bent coppers lying to them, sweeping her abduction under the carpet cos all *three* are in the pay of the local gang.
[*Silence*]

SE: Well, go on—deny it! Tell us we're barking up the wrong tree!
[*Silence*]

SE: There we go. You're all helping a drugs firm smoke Darren Chester out of the woodwork!

ME: That's why Operation Honeyguide was set up, wasn't it! Bet no one counted on one of his girlfriends having wealthy parents who were smart enough to demand answers and need round-the-clock monitoring to keep them fucking quiet.

SE: You're all looking at each other like a gang of naughty schoolboys, while the Cunninghams sit in there, heartbroken. I thought you were ambitious, Dee. Did it all by the book—

DO: I do, Sue—
[*Ian Frost steps out of the house*]

IF: I've packed everything of ours . . . Oh.

SE: Piers! [*Silence*] It *is* Piers, isn't it?

ME: What's going on?
[*Tanya Frost steps out of the house*]

TF: I'm ready too . . .

SE: And Caroline! But . . . you're not. What's going on?

ME: They look different.

SE: What the fuck, Dee?

ME: [*Whispers*] Language.

DO: You thought I was ambitious, Sue, well, I am. Not only for myself; I'm ambitious for *us*. The force. And that's why I've spent the best part of a year joined at the hip with you—with you *both*, as it turned out. Day in, day out, listening to your stories, laughing at your jokes, making you think you knew me. Psychic Sue! And there were times when I thought you might have worked out that little Sergeant Obasi wasn't all she seemed. Well, I've been Detective Inspector Obasi for three years and all of them spent investigating bent coppers. If you're wondering what was in those suitcases you've just dropped off at *your* storage unit in Axeford, it's old newspaper. Two million quid? You must've been planning to hop on the next flight out. Suzanne Eastwood, Malcolm Eastwood, you're both under arrest on suspicion of two counts of deception for financial gain and one count of stealing a horse and concealing its whereabouts from its rightful owners. All over a period of sixteen years. Oh, and the more recent theft of a fake diamond ring from the morgue. Sue, we've yet to investigate your claim that you both covered up a murder, although I suspect money was involved there too, somewhere. You do not have to say anything, but it may harm your defense if you do not mention when questioned something that you later rely on in court. Anything you do say may be given in evidence. Do you have anything to say?

[*Silence*]

ME: No comment.

SE: No comment, except who the fuck are *they*?

DO: Two very talented and courageous actors. They were brilliant, weren't they?

RD: Fantastic job, guys.

SE: But Kyle . . .

DO: Undercover officer.

ME: What was true, what wasn't . . . ?

LP: Operation Honeyguide? All of it made up.

SE: This house?

DO: Rented.

SE: You were *lying*. You manipulated us. Every time we voiced our doubts you dismissed them. Thought you were a friend, Dee.

DO: So did everyone you two conned over the years. Lovely couple of coppers who only want to help the victims of crime—so long as those victims have a few shillings to pay.

SE: Come off it!

ME: They could all afford a few pounds!

RD: You only robbed from the rich, eh? Conveniently forgot to give it to the poor.

DO: So if someone has something you want, you're entitled to take it? That's like saying a woman walking down the street at night, dressed however she wants, is asking for—

LP: A couple whose only child is being held hostage by a gang, and all you can see is what *they* have and you haven't? There's some serious karma waiting to bite you two in the arse, and that's after we're done throwing the book at you.

DO: Come on, let's get the cuffs on.

SE: We were friends, Dee. I'd have done anything for you.

DO: I know. Operation Honeyguide—named after a bird that leads humans to beehives so it can steal the honey. And you two repulsive, disgusting excuses for police officers are thoroughly fucking *nicked*.

[*Ding*]

The Beat Goes On WhatsApp group, May 9, 2014:

Glen
Toad-in-the-hole. Veggie option available, but if you want booze, bring your own.

To: Polly Baker
From: Dominic Eastwood
Date: October 25, 2024
Subject: Re: Documentary idea

WTF!!! What happened? If you've got any more, please send it. I'll read the rest at home. Pol xxxx

---

To: Polly Baker
From: Dominic Eastwood
Date: October 25, 2024
Subject: Re: Documentary idea

Hi Pol,

At this point I should mention the reason my family lost contact with Sue and Mal when I was a child.

My father is Mal's younger brother, but with ten years between them, they were never close. When I was born my parents had an ambition to buy a flat rather than rent, and spent years living very frugally to save for a deposit. Just as they were starting to gather their finances together, Uncle Malcolm turned up with a proposition.

He and Sue had bought their little council house in the early 90s, but now wanted a flat nearer their work. The house had two bedrooms and would be the perfect starter home for Mom and Dad. They couldn't believe their luck: an actual house they could afford. So Dad agreed to buy it from his brother at a very competitive price, because Uncle Mal would save on estate agent's and legal fees, seeing as it was a private sale.

Now, Mom and Dad had grown up in rented homes. They weren't familiar with the process of buying property, didn't know what to check or what to be wary of. In any case, Uncle Malcolm was family—Dad's big brother—and he would only have his best interests at heart, wouldn't he? So they didn't consult a lawyer or a surveyor, just paid the deposit to Uncle Mal's account, supposedly to secure the sale. Only *then* did they approach the bank for a mortgage. There was no hurry, Uncle Mal would wait as long as it took for them to arrange one.

I can't recall now quite how they discovered what had really happened, but suddenly Uncle Mal and Auntie Sue weren't in when Dad called. Their phone was never answered. When the mortgage lenders did their due diligence, they were sorry to confirm what Mom and Dad had begun to suspect. The house they'd paid a deposit on still belonged to the council. They'd handed over five years' worth of hard savings to secure a house that wasn't the Eastwoods' to sell—Uncle Mal and Auntie Sue disappeared with the money.

Quite understandably, they never spoke again.

I'm sure this sort of thing happens within other families, but that was no consolation to Mom and Dad, who had lost their chance of moving to their dream house and didn't feel they could go to the police, because it would mean informing on family—in any case, Uncle Mal *was* the police. They chalked it up to bitter experience and spent the next five years saving hard again. We moved into my childhood home the day before my tenth birthday.

Sue and Mal were ruthless when it came to conning money from people. They felt entitled to whatever other people had that they didn't. I'm sorry my parents didn't feel able to report them all those years ago, because if they were caught then, they'd have been sacked years earlier. As it is, they only grew in confidence.

I'm so pleased you're enjoying the story, and I can assure you there are more twists to come! I wonder if this particular series of events would make a good cliffhanger at the end of episode five? If so, then episode six could look at the night of that final quiz. But before then, it's time I sent you some correspondence from earlier in this story. I'm sure it will take up half an episode all by itself!

Best wishes,
Dom

Hulme Police
Operation Honeyguide

Senior Investigating Officer: Detective Inspector Melody Obasi

Confidential Briefing Notes, May 5, 2014:

Hello, everyone, and thank you for coming in today. You've all been personally selected for your expertise working undercover and, most importantly, your discretion. This operation must not be discussed inside or outside the force, nor must its existence be acknowledged. If we are to catch these two bent coppers red-handed, they must believe—without doubt—in the kidnap plot we're about to set up. We've called it Honeyguide, and it certainly isn't a kidnap.

Suzanne and Malcolm Eastwood appear for all the world like a nice middle-aged couple who work to live. Drives out of town, walks in the country, amateur quizzing, and meals out. But don't let that fool you. The Eastwoods are insidious predators who are thought to have conducted multiple confidence frauds in the course of their twenty-year careers. But they are very difficult to catch because they pick their targets so well. They have a knack for spotting people who will keep quiet about the ruse they've fallen for. And we suspect there are other victims who don't even realize they were conned. Even now there are only two other cases we're confident of nailing down.

Another reason we haven't caught them is that the Eastwoods are prepared to wait for the right mark. They aren't compulsive, they aren't complacent, and so far they haven't made mistakes. Well, my colleague and I spent a couple of years observing them from afar, trying to catch them at it, and now I've decided to force their hand and put temptation in their way.

As all of you know, I arrived in Hulme almost a year ago, officially on a compassionate transfer from Stopton. When and if Sue asks me, I'll tell them about a dodgy partner I had to kick out, followed by the tragic loss of my friend—both true, as it happens. In reality that transfer was the first stage of Operation Honeyguide.

The second and most tricky part is where you all come in. We've rented a big house on the new executive estate in Pinfield. We're setting up a well-to-do couple there, whose daughter has been kidnapped by a drugs gang, thanks to dodgy dealings by her secret boyfriend. I'm going to show the Eastwoods the opulent lifestyle this vulnerable couple enjoys—let's see if they bite.

Ordinarily the Eastwoods wouldn't expect to be involved in a case like this, but as we all know, staffing levels in Axeford and Pinfield are lower than they've ever been. They will be asked to sit with the anxious parents when the FLO can't be there. Meanwhile I'll be pulling strings from afar and allaying any doubts Sue and Mal may have about the case. I'm already close to Sue and we are rostering the Eastwoods together whenever we can.

You might be wondering about the undercover officers with the acting chops to play the parents. In this case we're going off book, bringing in civilians. I went to a nasty case last year, Stopton North, a violent burglary in sheltered dementia accommodations. In the course of that I got to know the son and daughter of a resident who was beaten up and robbed. They're both trained actors, do extras work and some theater. I went to see the son in a play, *The Glass Menagerie*—dead tense. Anyway, Tanya and Ian Frost are hoping to get back into the profession now their mom has sadly passed. Meanwhile we need a couple who can pretend to be frantic parents facing the imminent murder of their only child. They need to convince two officers who, for all their lack of ambition in the force, are excellent people-readers. Lucky for us, Tanya and Ian look nothing like each other—different dads, apparently—and I have no doubt they can pull it off.

I know it's unusual to involve outsiders in an undercover case, but this is different. We need that couple to be spot-on for this operation to work. The Frosts can improvise and stay in character. There's chemistry between them. What's more, after their experience with their mom last year, they're highly motivated to catch anyone who preys on the vulnerable.

To: Tanya Frost
From: DI Melody Obasi
Date: May 5, 2014
Subject: Honeyguide

Hi Tan,

Hope you and Ian are settling in at Downview. What a place, eh! Wish my inspector's salary could stretch that far . . . I'd apologize for asking you to live there for the course of this operation if it weren't so utterly bloody glorious!

We've set up the "first" Honeyguide briefing for tomorrow morning. Myself and Suzanne Eastwood will come around after that. Please note: the Eastwoods do not move quickly and usually stop for a chat and a brew before doing anything. While I'm with them I work at their pace. You'll meet Mal soon, but I'd like to settle into the scenario first and can do that best if I'm there, at least for this first meeting. So it'll be just Sue and me.

Sergeant Rhys Davies will arrive first. Sue and Mal know him as an FLO—that's family liaison officer—who would be posted with a household going through this sort of ordeal. He will then leave us, and Sue and I will get to know "you."

We've installed listening equipment in most of the rooms they're likely to go into. However, if they suggest moving out of earshot, we'd rather you kept your characters and went with the flow than worry too much about being recorded—at this stage anyway.

We'll debrief after every meeting, so try to remember the gist of any convos that take place out of range.

Remember: you are Caroline and Piers Cunningham, whose twenty-two-year-old daughter, Chloe, has been kidnapped by the drugs gang her secret boyfriend worked for. He's robbed them and they want his head. They have a history of carrying out their threats and have already kidnapped the boyfriend's other girl. This is part of the strategy we talked about in our second briefing meeting.

Not that you'll need it, but I'll say it anyway: break a leg!

Dee

To: DI Melody Obasi
From: Tanya Frost
Date: May 6, 2014
Subject: Re: Honeyguide

Hi Dee,

I need to tell you what Sue said to me in the garden. Obviously no microphones, so this is as close as I can remember. It's very disturbing and nothing to do with Honeyguide. I felt Caroline would take the opportunity to speak freely when Piers wasn't in the room. Like all us women, she holds it together for the men in her life. So, when I was alone with Sue, I allowed Caroline to be freer with her fears for her daughter's safety. Her thoughts have been morbid and she's focused on Chloe's potential death—obsessed with how the gang might kill her, how quick it would be.

Sue told Caroline about a call she and Mal went to years ago. I assume she wanted to reassure her that dying can be peaceful even in cases of murder. Only I think she revealed more than she realized. She said she and Mal were called to an unexpected death at home. When they got there—to a bungalow where a woman had reportedly passed away—the husband wouldn't let them in.

At first she said that when they finally found a way in, through a side door, they got to the woman's bedside and found she was still alive, just—she said it's not always easy for a stressed family member to determine exactly when a person dies—however, the woman passed away, peacefully, shortly afterward, with Sue, Mal, and her husband there in the room. Caroline asked Sue what that had to do with Chloe, who was surely facing a far more violent death. And that's when Sue had to fill in some details.

When the Eastwoods walked down the side of the bungalow, they peered through a window and saw the man in a blind panic trying to suffocate his wife by holding a pillow over her face. They burst in and caught him red-handed. He told them she'd looked dead, so he'd made the call . . . then she'd started breathing again. He broke down and explained she was terminally ill and had begged him to end her life. He thought he'd got it right by dosing her up on her sleeping medicine, but in an effort to suffocate her without leaving any bruises he'd not done the job properly, so he had to do it again. Sue and Mal then stood there and let him continue suffocating her until she really was dead and reported back that they'd arrived and found life extinct in a terminally ill cancer patient.

Sue must've thought that would reassure Caroline—that even victims of unlawful killing can have a peaceful death, but Caroline is no fool. She had more questions—and they got her to the real story. A few weeks after their callout to the bungalow, Sue and Mal saw a picture in the local paper: the man, on the steps of a little church, marrying a much younger woman. The caption said he'd inherited land worth millions on his wife's death, and that the wife had just started divorce proceedings when she unexpectedly passed away from complications after her *first dose* of chemo.

Of course at that moment Sue realized she'd said too much, but Caroline was too wrapped up in her own anxiety to give away what she'd heard between the lines.

I wanted you to know, that's all.

Tanya

Text messages between DI Dee Obasi and Tanya Frost, May 6, 2014:

Dee
I know we said not to text, but holy shit! Did they mention any names—where or when this happened?

Tanya
No.

Dee
Not sure what I can do with the info right now. Don't want it to distract from Honeyguide.

Tanya
Thought you should know what Sue told Caroline, that's all.

Dee

It's dead funny to hear you talk about Caroline as if she's a different person!

Tanya

She is. She's a character I inhabit. I'm sure it's the same for you when you play the role of Sergeant Obasi for Honeyguide.

Dee

No, not really. I'll see if I can think of it in that way, though.

Tanya

When are you or the Eastwoods likely to come back to Downview?

Dee

I'll keep you posted. We've got an undercover officer playing an informer called Kyle and I'm taking Sue to meet him.

Tanya

Break a leg! We're listening to music that a woman of Chloe's age might like. Beyoncé, Katy Perry, Lily Allen. We've been reading about parental bereavement and anxiety, and this is something parents do to try and manifest their lost child.

Dee

Righto. The Eastwoods will be sent to sit with you, and one of our officers will push a ransom note through the door. I'd bet my own money on neither of the Eastwoods being motivated enough to chase after the postman.

Dee

The note will give Darren twelve hours or a girl dies, making you even more desperate than you are already. I know you'll pull off that performance!

Dee

And Lewis Parry will be listening in then, not me.

Tanya

Oh no. Why not?

Text messages between DCI Lewis Parry and DCI Dee Obasi, May 6, 2014:

Lewis
Shit, forgot they go to quizzes. Had to get hard on them or they'd wriggle out, and we want them to be there when the note arrives.

Dee
Thanks, Lewis.

Lewis
Did they wonder why I reacted like that?

Dee
Yep, but I reassured them you're up against it from NCA and AKEU.

Lewis
Cheers, matey!

Dee
Just doin' my job!

To: DI Melody Obasi
From: Tanya Frost
Date: May 7, 2014
Subject: Re: Honeyguide

Hi Dee,

I hope your friend's children enjoyed their play. Theater is perfect for building confidence and providing an escape for shy or traumatized youngsters.

Caroline and Piers met Mal last night. He made a few inappropriate observations, but nothing too offensive. The Eastwoods didn't chase the "postman," as you predicted! But they were genuinely shaken up by the note.

Caroline and Piers are in the grip of such darkness and fear they haven't noticed anything amiss in the Eastwoods' behavior yet, but of course Ian and I have. Before the note arrived they were talking about drug gangs being all about money and business transactions. This is the start of their grooming process.

Let us know when they're next coming.

Tan

To: Tanya Frost
From: DI Melody Obasi
Date: May 7, 2014
Subject: Re: Honeyguide

Hi Tan,

It's still funny to hear you talk about the Cunninghams like it isn't you two!

Well done last night, but a bit of feedback for you, as I've spent some time with the Eastwoods this morning. They're starting to question the integrity of the operation. We can't raise their suspicions in any way. Even if they don't guess what Honeyguide really is, if they suspect *anything* is fake, they won't take the bait.

They've picked up on how composed and "quiet" you two are. They think parents facing the kidnap and potential death of their beloved only child would be more vocal or expressive or angry—anything. Perhaps you could have a couple of outbursts during your next meeting with them? Tears, wailing, sobbing, that sort of thing.

Thanks!

Dee

To: DI Melody Obasi
From: Tanya Frost
Date: May 7, 2014
Subject: Re: Honeyguide

Hi Dee,

We beg to differ. You see, crying tears is all about the release of long pent-up tension. There's no release for Caroline and Piers yet, not even the resolution of knowing their daughter is dead. They are trapped in the first moment of trauma and their emotions are in suspended animation, held deeper even than the fight-or-flight response.

That's why they're so quiet, reserved even. Weeping, wailing, and chewing the furniture is very *EastEnders*. Caroline and Piers are more Juliette Binoche in *Three Colours: Blue*.

Tan

Text messages between DI Dee Obasi and Tanya Frost, May 7, 2014:

Dee
Haven't got time to send another email, but it's not about how the Cunninghams—or how anyone—might typically react, it's about how Sue and Mal expect two people in that situation to behave.

Dee
They've flagged the Cunninghams' behavior as different. Suspicious.

Tanya
Then tell them they're wrong. Meisner, Adler, and Alexander agree with us.

Dee

I MADE IT CRYSTAL CLEAR YOU MUST NOT DISCUSS THIS CASE WITH ANYONE!

Tanya

They are the acting methods we use.

Dee

OK, I've had to sit down and breathe. Tanya, I don't want to come this far only to have the op not work.

Tanya

It'll work. Ian and I are fully immersed in the characters and will expose Sue and Mal Eastwood for the predators they are.

Dee

Thank you, now please give the next meeting your all.

Tanya

Trust us, Dee, we're classically trained.

Text messages between DI Dee Obasi and DCI Lewis Parry, May 7, 2014:

Dee

They've only bloody gone to Devil's Croke! Call them back. Say it's urgent.

Lewis

Just called them. They're coming in.

Dee

I spend AGES putting together social-media profiles for the entire Cunningham family—have they so much as GLANCED at them? No. I assume Hulme Police's laziest officers are not gonna trek up to the Croke, so I don't leave any trace of an investigation there and it's the first place they go!

Lewis

You'll style it out. You're a Capricorn.

Dee

They're focused on why there's no camera footage of Chloe's car before or after the abduction. They suspect an inside job.

Lewis

I was right, we should've recorded a grainy blur, to screen at the briefings.

Dee

If we focus Sue and Mal on the Cunninghams, we won't need to spend valuable working hours setting something up that invites scrutiny. I'm gonna tell them the Maddox Brothers have moles in the security hub, like they did in Stopton.

Lewis

Careful what you wish for, Dee!

Dee

Lewis

But won't their suspicions around Honeyguide make them less likely to act?

Dee

Not once we deliver briefing three.

Lewis

OK. The big one. Today? Now?

Dee

Yep. It'll take them ages to get back from the Croke. I'll get the team together for a Honeyguide briefing and we can all give them a cold stare when they shuffle in last. A body will distract them from the camera thing, from the secrecy of this op, and will force their hand—they'll have to close in on their mark now, or never.

Lewis

Right. I'll get my notes.

Dee

Be angry, then send them to The Glade for the morning—keep them busy before they're due at the Pinfield house this afternoon. Rhys will brief Tanya and Ian.

Lewis

Are they ready?

Dee

Ready? They've practically become the Cunninghams. This will be the performance of their lives!

Text messages between Sergeant Rhys Davies and DI Dee Obasi, May 7, 2014:

Rhys

Ma'am, I've briefed Tanya and Ian that they should act as if I just told them Beata has been found dead. I've suggested their natural assumption is that their daughter will be next and that they haven't got long to save her.

Dee

👍 Leave the Eastwoods with them. Give them an opportunity to bring up the subject of money again.

Dee

They're at the peak of their desperation and most vulnerable to reckless suggestion. If Sue and Mal don't take advantage of that, they're not the Sue and Mal I've got to know.

Rhys

Sorry, ma'am, but is there something strange about Tanya and Ian? They're speaking and acting as if Caroline and Piers are separate people from them.

Rhys

This morning I said, "Would you like tea or coffee?" They said, "Caroline would drink a weak coffee at this stage, and Piers would more likely drink a strong tea."

Dee

Yep, they're proper actors. Like Robert De Niro and Daniel Day-Lewis. Whatever Sue and Mal think about the secrecy around Honeyguide, they MUST believe in the raw desperation of the wealthy parents.

Rhys

They're still acting when it's just me here. Bit weird, ma'am.

Dee

All going to plan! Thanks, Rhys. The Eastwoods should be with you around 1 p.m., although knowing their timekeeping, perhaps 2.

Text messages between DCI Lewis Parry and DI Dee Obasi, May 7, 2014:

Lewis

How's it going?

Dee

Like a dream.

Lewis

Rhys says Tanya and Ian are very . . . immersed in their roles.

Dee

Yep. They're playing desperate parents quietly, like in an arty French film, not with screaming tears, like in a soap.

Lewis

If this works you'll be the hero of the hour.

Dee

Not just embezzlement. Sue let slip that years ago she and Mal saw a man kill his wife, but didn't report it because the perp said it was a mercy killing. They never came clean when they realized otherwise. I reckon they took cash off the husband to keep quiet.

Lewis

I've seen it time and again. You're working on a case and something you never even thought of comes to light and gets solved at the same time. As if it was waiting for you. As if it was meant to be.

Dee

They want to retire and open a pub. Run quizzes to bring the locals together on weeknights. I reckon that's where some of this money is going. What they haven't spent on a hot tub, steam room, and eating out—tucked away for the future. Well, the Proceeds of Crime Act will have something to say about that!

* * *

Lewis

Any news? Have they suggested paying the Maddoxes for Chloe's return?

Lewis

The best fraudsters make a victim believe it was their idea, when in reality they've been subliminally suggesting it all along.

* * *

Lewis

All OK? You've gone quiet.

Dee

FUCKING NO! NO WAY!

Dee

I can't believe what those two chumps have done!

Lewis

What's happened?

Dee
They've screwed the whole thing!

Lewis
WHO? HOW?

Dee
Everything was running like pure fucking molten gold—Sue and Mal pulled a CLASSIC move. "We don't think it'll work, it's a risk for us, but we'll do it for you."

Dee
WE HAD THEM IN THE PALMS OF OUR HANDS!

Dee
Then Ian jumps in with "If you don't help us, we'll report that you two saw a murder and covered it up"!

Lewis
SHIT! Why did he say that?

Dee
FUCK KNOWS—I DON'T!

Lewis
Center yourself. Breathe. This is only a misstep on the right path.

Dee
Why did I ever think two actors could handle an undercover op?

Lewis
We'll study the recordings, work something out. It might not be the end of the world and, if our stars align, this won't even be the end of Honeyguide.

DI Dee Obasi visits Downview, Moorcroft Lane, Pinfield Village, where Tanya and Ian Frost are playing Caroline and Piers Cunningham. Recorded on DI Obasi's body-worn camera, May 7, 2014:

DO: What the fuck did you two just do?

TF: Caroline and Piers got Sue and Mal Eastwood to organize a cash drop in exchange for their daughter.

IF: That's what you want, isn't it?

TF: I don't know about you, Ian, but I felt it went like clockwork.

DO: You *threatened* them!

TF: An illustration of Caroline and Piers's naked desperation.

DO: *Blackmail?*

TF: In as far as we had a script, we went off it, but it *felt* right. Do you agree, Ian? People in the throes of desperation will do *anything*— issue threats, ultimatums. The Cunninghams are at that stage now. I feel that very strongly.

IF: They'll *kill* to remove whatever's standing in their way . . .

TF: And of course parents will do *anything* for their children.

DO: Not twenty-four hours ago you were in an arty French film. Today you're forcing police officers to pay a ransom to a drugs gang. How fucking *EastEnders* is that? I practically heard the theme tune kick in when you said it!

IF: When *Piers* said it.

DO: Oh, for crying out loud!

TF: Hardly *EastEnders*—more Volumnia pleading with Coriolanus to stand as consul—

IF: Caroline and Piers don't care whether they break the law, so long as they get Chloe back.

TF: Piers's line "You lot care about future kidnaps, but I care about this one" was genius.

IF: Thank you.

TF: No, really. It's the perfect dramatization of the personal versus the political.

DO: You don't *understand*, Tanya—

TF: Caroline—

DO: *Tanya!* The second you made their participation in a ransom payment conditional on you *not* reporting something that did—or, let's face it, perhaps *didn't*—happen years ago, the Eastwoods went from being bent coppers about to get caught to the *victims* of threats and blackmail. Their lawyer will argue they were acting under duress!
[*Silence*]

TF: Oh.

IF: Ah.

DO: And more than that, it's behavior that smacks of underworld connections. The Cunninghams are sitting here in a big house with access to millions in cash, their daughter is dating a drug dealer and now kidnapped by his bosses—even police officers as shit as the Eastwoods are going to suspect them of money laundering.

TF: What difference does that make?

DO: If we run them in, they'll just say they were fearful for their *lives*, let alone their livelihoods and liberty.

IF: Right...

DO: It makes you look suspicious—I mean the Cunninghams; fuck, you've got me talking like that now—and if Sue and Mal suspect they're getting involved with the Maddox Brothers, they won't dare take the money.

DO: Look, I'm gonna speak to Lewis Parry—he's the DCI who briefs the Honeyguide team—and see if we can salvage something from this. But chances are we won't be able to take this all the way now.

TF: Is that it? Is Honeyguide over?

DO: Over? [*Pause*] I promised Nat. We planned this operation together. There were days when I lay with her on her hospital bed and we went through it, accounted for every scenario... I swear it kept her going those last few months. [*Pause*] No, this isn't the end of Honeyguide. I've still got a card left to play. If I have to.

Text messages between DI Dee Obasi and DCI Lewis Parry, May 8, 2014:

Dee

Sue thinks Hulme Police are collaborating with the Maddoxes, helping them smoke Darren out.

Lewis

Then we have to call it off. The Eastwoods won't risk crossing the brothers. We won't catch them red-handed now.

Dee

Sue rang around the morgues. Couldn't find Beata.

Lewis

Then it's over. Finished. We need to close down Honeyguide. If it's meant to be, then the universe will present you with another opportunity when the time is right.

Dee

No. I can bring it back. Leave it with me.

Text messages between DI Dee Obasi and Constable Kyle Reeves, May 8, 2014:

Dee

Have Sue and Mal spoken to you on the phone that we gave you for Honeyguide?

Kyle

No. Why?

Dee

They're at the Pinfield house right now, telling Chloe's parents a long story about how they met up with you and chatted about what Darren owes the Maddoxes.

Kyle

Nope. Phone's been silent since we met on Tuesday.

Dee

Thanks, Kyle. That's interesting. They're planning something. Don't know what yet, but so long as it involves robbing those parents, we've got 'em.

Text messages between DI Dee Obasi and DCI Lewis Parry, May 8, 2014:

Dee

Two million! They're telling the Cunninghams the figure they want is two million, cash. Spun a long story about how they got the info out of Kyle. He hasn't heard from them.

Dee

They suspect we're covering for the Maddoxes, and they're still going ahead with their plan.

Dee

They're going for it! The shits! The little shits. I love them!

Lewis

Then this is the big one. The second they get their hands on that cash, they'll be out of here. We'll never see them again.

Dee

Except it'll be a suitcase of newspaper . . .

Lewis

Let's run them right in!

Dee

No. No, there's something I want to do. This is important, Lewis.

Conversation between DI Dee Obasi and Marion Marshall, attendant at Coleport Mortuary, May 8, 2014:

DO: I'll bring them both in here and you show us the body, as if I'd made a regular police appointment. Act as if this visit is nothing special. Leave us alone as soon as you can. Oh, and could you take this ring and put it on her finger? Make sure it's prominent, so when they unzip the bag it's instantly visible. Don't come back—we'll tidy up and show ourselves out.
[*Silence*]

MM: How will I get the ring back to you?

DO: Don't worry. One of us will take the ring.
[*Silence*]

MM: I see those particular remains are due to be shipped overseas. The family are awaiting some paperwork, that's all . . .

DO: Yes, yes, I understand that too. I need to . . . Only she's the right age, gender, height, everything. This is part of an ongoing operation. I need these people to believe it's real.
[*Prolonged silence*]

MM: Why?

DO: So an operation we've been working on for *years* doesn't fall apart simply because two actors can't stick to their script.
[*Silence*]

MM: If I'm to "play along" with your . . . operation, I'll need to know a bit more. A person's remains are precious. They aren't props to be used in—

DO: Look, believe me. I know what I'm talking about, and . . . those remains, they would be proud to know they'd helped catch two criminals. [*Pause*] It's what they would've wanted.

Text messages between DCI Lewis Parry and DI Dee Obasi, May 8, 2014:

Lewis
Where are you?

Dee
Just got back from Coleport morgue. Fucked off with myself for having a panic attack as we viewed the body. What a prat!

Lewis
Why were you out there? What body?

Dee
Beata. Took Sue and Mal to see her. They were wondering why her body was being kept so far away. Turns out human remains wait for customs clearance at Coleport.

Lewis
Beata's body? Beata doesn't exist.

Dee
Shit, yeah, sorry. I've caught this thing off the Frosts—talking about the story as if it's actually real.

Lewis
WTF? You didn't. You didn't just do what I think you've done?

Dee
If all else fails—if Honeyguide goes to shit—then we've got them on one thing: stealing a fake diamond ring from a body bag. This operation will not be in vain, Lewis.

Text messages between Tanya Frost and DI Dee Obasi, May 9, 2014:

Tanya
We've texted them to let them know the money is ready.

Dee
Rhys delivered the cases, good.

Tanya
Yes, and they look exactly as you'd imagine. It makes such a difference when props are authentic.

Dee
Remember the process re the codes. We need Sue and Mal to take the cases away, then return for the codes. They'll try every trick in the book to get the second code out of you, don't be swayed. We JUST need them to stash the cases on their own property, then come back to the house.

* * *

Tanya
Did you hear it? Ian was phenomenal! It was the best performance I'd ever seen him give. He took all of Piers's repressed emotion and threw it at the wall. So moving.

Dee
Bravo! Hope he's chilling out after that.

Tanya
Chilling? No! Caroline and Piers are both pacing, lost in thought while their daughter's life hangs in the balance.

Tanya
Annoyed I said "Break a leg" as the Eastwoods were leaving. Stupid! Luckily I covered, and then Piers jumped in to help.

Dee
Teamwork makes the dream work, Tan! I'll keep you updated.

* * *

Lewis
The Eastwoods have arrived at a self-storage unit under the Axeford bypass.

Lewis

They've stored the cases in the cheapest locker and are drinking tea in their car. Passing an expensive flask between them and watching the world go by.

Dee

I wish we'd been able to bug the Corsa. I'd love to know what they're talking about right now.

Lewis

OK, the Corsa's starting up. See you back at the house.

Dee

Gonna enjoy this so much! The For Sale sign is up. Just wait till those two see us all here!

To: Dominic Eastwood
From: Polly Baker
Date: October 25, 2024
Subject: Re: Documentary idea

Hi Dom,

Right, so Operation Honeyguide was Detective Inspector Obasi's pet project—hers and her friend who died. Clearly Dee totally underestimated how committed her actors would be to their roles, but couldn't face the thought of failing to catch the Eastwoods.

I'm guessing she used only police officers for undercover work after that! Can I ask: Are you in touch with Dee and is she open to being interviewed on camera?

Pol x

To: Polly Baker
From: Dominic Eastwood
Date: October 25, 2024
Subject: Re: Documentary idea

Hi Polly,

Yes, Dee and I have struck up a correspondence over the months and I'm sure she'll agree to be interviewed. But the revelation about Operation Honeyguide isn't the final twist.

I expect you're wondering why I've included so much detail about the second life that my aunt and uncle led at The Case is Altered: the small-town disputes over the quiz, the body in the river, the local landlords who formed a community all their own, and the brewery officials who ventured out to the isolated country pub for the first time the night of that final quiz.

Well, a lot happened that night. It's sure to be the crescendo of our series: the sixth and final episode. I'll send it through now.

Dom

Extract from a police statement made by Bunny Tyme from Let's Get Quizzical, November 22, 2019:

I saw everything! Well, everything visible from my seat anyway. Let's Get Quizzical had no chance of winning, so I could enjoy watching the other teams battle it out. But more than that, we had a little sting going. Sid had set up me and my husband, George, by getting us to buy the team drinks, so we were getting him back!

He'd agreed to donate a pound for every correct answer to the local hospice. Well, we hardly score anything, so he was on to a safe bet there. We'd printed out his email pledge and, when Mal held up the final scoreboard, we had a surprise planned.

Only before we could hit Sid with it, in front of the entire pub, events overtook us. You see, The Shadow Knights scored ten out of ten for every round up to the intermission; after that, they went downhill and only scored average for a regular quiz team. Their faces were as long as the odds of Let's Get Quizzical actually winning! There was nothing different about those questions, either, except perhaps the round on airplanes. Meanwhile The Sturdy Challengers got a couple of tens and nines and pulled into the lead.

There was something in the air. Tension, expectation. Beating The Shadow Knights would be big for any team, but the quiz means so much to Chris and Lorraine, everyone was willing *them* to win and not The Shadow Knights.

I should mention that their boy died—a few years ago now. An only child. Not sure everyone at the quiz knows, but it explains how they are.

So, we get to the final round and there's fewer than ten points separating the Spokespersons—that's the cycling team—The Sturdy Challengers, and The Shadow Knights, but after an unusually sticky sports round for the Spokespersons, they dropped behind, while The Sturdy Challengers and The Shadow Knights ended up on equal points. A draw. There's a ripple of excitement. No one remembers a draw at The Case is Altered quiz. What happens now? Do they split the winnings? Will Mal take their marathon scores and decide the winner that way? Perhaps you had to be there, but believe me, it was tense.

Mal knocked on the table to get silence and pulled a sealed envelope from under his papers.

"This," he says, "is what we do in the event of two or more teams tying for first place. To decide the winner, we'll conduct a tiebreaker. Here in this envelope—which was sealed before the quiz started—is a question. Each tying team selects one member to answer it. The winner is decided on a sudden-death basis, so each representative may give answer after answer until one is correct. The first correct answer wins, unless the other team decides they cannot answer."

Hah, a killer question and a sudden-death round! Well, our little revelation to Sid about the trick we'd played on him could wait. Sturdy Challenger versus Shadow Knight? This was going to be quite the spectacle.

Everyone pushed their chairs back to clear a space in the center of the room. General Knowledge from The Shadow Knights and Chris from The Sturdy Challengers stood facing each other in the center, and Mal, still wearing his barrister's robe and wig, showed them both the sealed envelope. He waited for a hush to descend over the room before—very theatrically, I must say—he tore open the envelope with a flourish and pulled out a piece of paper with a question written on it. I'm going to tell you what he said next, as best as I can recall.

"Remember: the first to answer *correctly* is the winning team. Here we go: The Shadow Knights scored perfect tens in every round before the intermission and, from then on, their scores plummeted. The killer question is this: Exactly *how* have The Shadow Knights been cheating their way to victory for the last ten weeks?"

Extract from a police statement made by Ajay Choudhury from The Sturdy Challengers, November 22, 2019:

Now, that really was a killer question, because The Shadow Knights knew exactly how they'd been cheating. The General could deny it, but if Mal had evidence then that would be the wrong answer. But if he revealed the team's secret, the entire team would be disqualified—for cheating. It's a Catch-22 situation, based on the book by Joseph Heller, published in 1961. Do you know it? It's a book that comes up a lot in quizzes, so I try to remember facts about it.

Chris stood in the center of the room, determined to win for The Sturdy Challengers, and even *he* was stunned into silence—admittedly not for long.

"Hiding phones up their sleeves! Googling on a smartwatch!"

We all laughed along with Chris, but The General stood there, his face as white as a sheet, staring at Mal. He glanced back at his team, who all shifted uncomfortably, solemn looks between them. I felt like I was watching a game—one I didn't know the rules to. The rest of us, we were all spectators.

"They each have a section of the periodic table tucked under their waistband! They watch Mal set the quiz through hidden cameras! They've bribed Sue to tell them the questions in advance—sorry, Sue!"

More laughter, while The General stared at his team, at his feet, and finally at Mal. Chris had that win in his sights.

"One of them has an invisible screen behind their glasses that's plugged into Siri."

"I take it, from your silence, that you have no answer to the tiebreak question, General?" Mal said quietly, and held up his hand to stop Chris spouting any more wild answers.

"I hereby declare The Sturdy Challengers the winners, on the de facto withdrawal of The Shadow Knights from tonight's quiz."

You should've seen Chris! He punched the air, hugged Lorraine, the whole Sturdy Challengers team; we were ecstatic, while The Shadow Knights sat impassively in their seats.

But before we could celebrate properly, one of the visiting landlords stood up. He was wearing a long blond wig and pink dress, with a pair of false boobs. Have you seen the film *Oliver!*? Released in 1968, based on the musical by Lionel Bart—also a popular subject for quizmasters. Well, this guy was dressed like Nancy, Bill Sikes's girlfriend. She was played by Shani Wallis. Sorry, Inspector, you get like this when you quiz a lot. Telling people the trivia you've memorized is a good way to retain facts, and I'm sure they enjoy hearing it.

Anyway this landlord gets up and says, "The Shadow Knights have fooled everyone. They've claimed prize money that wasn't theirs, but more than that, they've cheated honest quiz teams out of the joy of winning. When they came to my establishment, The Lusty Lass, I worked out how they did it, and I'm going to show you all now. Please know that—far from being bad quizzers—you're simply honest quizzers. I intend to expose The Shadow Knights for what they really are."

It was strange because Sue and Mal were dressed as lawyers. The Lusty landlord in his wig and dress, he was the judge. The two new teams, the landlords and the brewery bosses, together looked like they might be a jury, and the rest of us made up the public gallery. Before our eyes The Case is Altered morphed into a court of law and The Shadow Knights were on trial.

Hulme Police
Operation Honeyguide

Senior Investigating Officer: Detective Inspector Melody Obasi

Confidential Briefing Notes, May 10, 2014:

Hello, everyone, and firstly may I offer my congratulations on the success of Operation Honeyguide. As you all know, it had nothing to do with investigating the kidnapping of two young women, and everything to do with catching two bent coppers in the act of defrauding innocent victims of crime. Having studied the Eastwoods for so long, we knew how clever they are at picking the right victims. With your help we were able to create a honeytrap that lured them in and triggered their instincts for financially motivated deception.

You were all chosen by Detective Chief Inspector Parry here for your exemplary records when it comes to fairness and honesty. He also knew which officers could keep a secret!

Finally, to DCI Parry, just a few months short of retirement, thank you for working with me to coordinate the operation and for monitoring the Eastwoods so closely these last few weeks.

Now the actors have gone, the keys to the rented house have been returned to the estate agent, and Operation Honeyguide is officially over. Thank you.

Police interview with Suzanne Eastwood, May 9, 2014:

Interviewing officers: Detective Inspector Dee Obasi and Detective Chief Inspector Lewis Parry
Lawyer to the Eastwoods: Amy Wright

DO: How are you feeling, Sue?
SE: OK.
DO: Good. Now, as you know, Operation Honeyguide was set up to catch you and your husband, Malcolm Eastwood, in the act of

defrauding apparently wealthy victims of crime. Do you have anything to say?

SE: No comment.

AW: I understand Operation Honeyguide was entirely fictitious. A situation of entrapment?

DO: It was.

AW: And, in the course of that operation, my clients were threatened with exposure for an alleged historical misdemeanor?

DO: What we would like to do is present some of the evidence we have pertaining to two previous *genuine* cases—one that began as a case of theft at a hotel called the Tudor Lodge, and another involving the kidnap of a racehorse and subsequent ransom demand.

AW: Can you make clear, please, what my client is under arrest for?

DO: Theft and kidnap of a racehorse in 2001, two counts of conspiracy to obtain money by deception, failure to report an unlawful death, and the theft of a ring. For the moment.

AW: Thank you.

DO: So, Sue, on January 9, 2001, a man by the name of Anthony Magibbon called Axeford police station to complain that he was owed a significant amount of money by a creditor who was defaulting, leaving one of his businesses perilously short of cash. You and Malcolm visited the desperate Mr. Magibbon to explain there was little you could do about his client, as debts are a civil matter, but you had some advice. What was that advice?

SE: No comment.

DO: He says, "They were sympathetic, but not helpful, until I mentioned that I owned a share in a racehorse. They grilled me about this, asking how much he was worth and where he was stabled. Then the officers said they knew someone who often stepped in with cash where the bank had refused. They talked about how he'd saved failing businesses in the past, until I *had* to ask if he might do the same for me. They ummed and ahhed, said their contact owed them a favor and they'd ask him if he'd loan me money against Dead Rummy. Once I was paid, I would pay him back and the other owners wouldn't need to know. I said yes and gave them the door code to the stable, so their contact could go in at night and look over the horse. But instead the horse was stolen. That's when the Eastwoods told me their man was a violent criminal who wouldn't think twice about killing me if I didn't pay him, let alone killing Rummy. I hadn't received a penny, but he had the horse and I had to tell his other three owners what had happened. The Eastwoods said we would get the horse back if we paid their man fifty thousand pounds. Over a couple of weeks we all got the money together and got Rummy back, although he was out of shape as he'd been in a field the whole time. We were all terrified of the gang."

Now it turns out you and Mal were paying Travellers to keep Dead Rummy with their horses. There was no underworld contact—it was you two who'd orchestrated the entire scam. You even went to the stables in the dead of night and led a Thoroughbred horse two miles down country lanes to the bypass, avoiding every security camera on the way. You saw a pot of money, and a group of friends who had the wherewithal and the passion for something that would mean they'd pay to get it back.

SE: No comment.

DO: Then there's the Tudor Lodge case. In July 2009 a hotel owner called the police to report suspicious activity on the hotel's bank account. Small regular amounts had been draining away for months and every action they'd taken to stop it had failed. It had to be a member of staff, but more than thirty people worked there and they had no clue who it could be. Sue, you and Mr. Eastwood assured them you'd trace where the money was going. Sure enough, you got back with the news that whoever was behind the theft was using the money to buy drugs from a notorious underworld distributor, one you two happened to know well. The Tudor Lodge owners were told that nothing could be done unless this distributor informed on the thief, and he wouldn't do that without a substantial cash payment. Luckily this underworld character owed Sue and Mal a favor. Sound familiar, Sue?

SE: No comment.

DO: He'd only require twenty thousand pounds to expose the thief...

which they paid. They then magically received the information that, even back then, I know would have been provided within days, and for free, by our forensic accountants.

SE: No comment.

DO: Then we have the revelation you made to the woman who was working undercover as Caroline Cunningham for Operation Honeyguide—

AW: This fictitious case?

DO: Yes. Sue, you told the actor posing as Caroline that you and Mal discovered a man in the act of killing his wife. He told you it was a mercy killing, only later you learned that might not be the case. In many ways that revelation was the final piece of the puzzle. We found a record of the visit, a couple by the name of Ramsey. It was in 1998 and predates *all* the other instances—and potential instances—of fraud that we've compiled so far. The man has since passed away, but he was wealthy and at one point during Operation Honeyguide Mal says to you, Sue: "You didn't say what happened next? Why it never came to light?" and you say: "No." That, we believe, is a reference to a deal you two made with Mr. Ramsey—if he paid you, you'd keep quiet about what you saw. After that, you got a taste for victims' money. We'll never know exactly how many people you targeted or the extent of what you stole.

AW: Do you have actual proof of my clients' roles in any of these cases, because as far as I can see, we have circumstantial evidence, one person's word against another's, entrapment, and—in the Ramsey case—pure conjecture.

DO: I'm getting to it.

AW: Please.

DO: After your arrest, we searched the storage unit where you stashed the suitcases you believed contained two million pounds. You couldn't open those cases without involving someone else, someone with specialist equipment, so you intended to continue the charade, get the codes from the Cunninghams, take the money, and run. Fly overseas. Start a new life.

SE: No comment.

AW: The Cunninghams aren't actual witnesses. They are characters played by actors, is that correct?

DO: Yes and, you know something, your clients play their roles exactly like actors do. They immerse themselves to the point they almost believe what they're saying. They'll even speak to each other as if the situation is real. Been listening back to the recordings in the unmarked car—it's dead unnerving when you know what they're planning.

AW: Can we get to the evidence, please?

DO: I'd like you to look at these two photographs. In the unit were two big suitcases and two small bags containing what we might describe as overnight essentials. One suitcase contained pretty much everything you two'd need to start a new life. Passports in different names, documents, air tickets to Cuba, medications. The other suitcase was empty. So when you had both codes, you'd just transfer the cash, pick everything up, and go. You'd be abroad before anyone realized you were missing. Is that right?

SE: No comment.

DO: I almost wish we could've given you the codes and then watched your faces when you saw the newspaper. That would've been gloating, though.

SE: No comment.

DO: Finally, Sue. That last time we spoke, outside Coleport morgue, you spouted all that shit about us being friends and that you never know when it's too late to say what's important. You were saying goodbye, weren't you?

SE: There's one thing I want to know, Dee. If Honeyguide is fake, if Chloe and Beata never existed . . . then whose fucking body was that?

Extract from a police statement made by Sean Coley from The Landlords team, November 22, 2019:

Peter Bond, landlord of The Lusty Lass, stood in front of the whole room. Teeth, tits, and tan that would win our drag contest even on a Saturday night—and his face was as serious as if he was about to announce a death: "You might not think it, to see me now," he boomed, and he left a long pause after each sentence . . . "but I used to be an army man." Literally his words hung in the air above us. "Did my time with the troops and ended up in intelligence gathering. I've kept my hand in, shall we say, but don't ask me how."

Now even though Adrian and I had been guzzling the booze up to that point—well, we weren't driving—I had sobered up, so he'll tell you what I'm about to say is quite accurate:

"There are no second chances out in the field," Peter said, "you need every tool at your disposal. One piece of kit I was never without was the NanoComm. As tiny as a match head. As light as a bead in a child's bracelet. It's dropped into the ear canal, where it sits, completely invisible. The agent wears a hidden microphone concealed in their clothing and, wherever they are, whatever they're doing, they can receive instructions directly from the ops room.

"Mal confided in us landlords that he thought The Shadow Knights were cheating, but he'd tested them and couldn't prove it. So when the team arrived at The Lusty Lass last week I decided to try something out. If any of them were wearing a NanoComm or anything similar, I'd never see or hear it, however close I managed to get. But I'd kept something from my time in the service. An electromagnetic signal jammer."

He held up a little box with six bizarre probes sticking out of it.

"This," he boomed, "*this* is so effective, it's technically illegal." And I swear you could hear the earth turn, the place was so quiet.

"For the second half of the quiz, I switched this on and watched as the team was thrown into confusion. My jammer killed their connection stone dead. They had no way of knowing it was me behind the breakdown in communications and probably blamed the weather or their equipment. No one else in the room realized what I was doing, because phones must be off for the duration of the quiz. Either way,

The Shadow Knights were forced to answer the questions based on their own knowledge, and it seems they are no better at quizzes than your average decent team.

"The question that had been puzzling us landlords was finally answered. All that was left to do was confront them with our evidence. But why not have some fun first? We did the same tonight. We let The Shadow Knights cheat as usual for the first half of the quiz, and then in the intermission we blocked their signal. The rest is history. Quite how this quiz team are in possession of such unusual professional devices, only they can tell us. And there's another question too. Who, exactly, is on the other end of those earpieces? I've just switched the jammer off, so I'm sure we'll soon find out."

Hulme Police
Operation Honeyguide

Senior Investigating Officer: Detective Inspector Melody Obasi

Debriefing of Tanya and Ian Frost, May 15, 2014:

DO: Thanks for coming back for this debrief, very much appreciated. And for bringing in all the clothes, though feel free to keep them. We'll just be taking them back to the charity shop where we bought them anyway. I want to say thanks to you both for your roles—literally—in this successful operation. You played your parts absolutely to a T. It was very moving listening to the recordings and watching the CCTV.

TF: Now it's over, I feel like I always do after the final performance in a run.

IF: Deflated. Anticlimax. Always the way.

TF: You're a good actor yourself, Dee. Very convincing.

DO: But you two are professionals. We were watching and listening to everything that happened in that house and you didn't break character once.

TF: Thanks. As you know, we lost our mother last year, a few months after she was terrorized by those burglars . . . Well, the tears were never far away, were they, Ian?

IF: No. And violence isn't necessarily physical. Those cold-blooded predators sat with us, hiding behind their uniforms, all understanding and sympathetic, trying to con people they believed had lost their daughter—made my blood boil.

DO: The Eastwoods chose victims who could afford to lose a bit of money, and mostly asked for amounts that wouldn't break the bank. Probably because that would mean their marks would be less likely to pursue the case if and when they were rumbled. Doesn't make what they did any better, but it made Operation Honeyguide very tricky.

TF: We're proud to have been a part of it.

DO: You were both stars. Was it weird playing husband and wife?

IF: A bit, I suppose. We made the Cunninghams a very hands-off couple, thank God!

DO: You're a talented family.

TF: Wish casting directors felt the same. Couple of years ago we had to start a cleaning company to make ends meet.

IF: Everything had to fit around caring for Mom; we can't blame the industry for everything, Tan.

TF: I know, but—

IF: At our ages, we're too young to play old people, and too old to play most decent roles. We're wondering what else we can do, especially now we don't need to—

TF: Especially now Mom's ... passed away. It's something when your last parent dies, you reevaluate your whole life.

DO: I'm sure.

IF: It's a horrible turning point.

DO: Have you thought about joining the police?

IF: Good God, no! We're pushing fifty!

DO: In a civilian capacity, perhaps? I can keep my ears open for vacancies, if you like. It's never too late to make a change.

TF: I don't think it's for us, somehow ...

DO: Our commanding officer, Lewis Parry, who you met at the end: he's retiring next month, got a new girlfriend and is going traveling with her. Having a gap year later in life. Good luck to him.

TF: All right for some. We're back to crowd scenes and walk-on parts. When will the court case come up, and will you need us to testify in person?

DO: Court case?

TF: The case against the Eastwoods. Corrupt police officers have to be tried, don't they?

DO: Ah ... that's where we've hit a problem, and we always knew we'd be lucky if the charges stuck. The Cunninghams' case is fictional, so they haven't committed a crime there. For the earlier two cases—the racehorse theft and the hotel fraud—the prosecutor wouldn't give us the go-ahead to prosecute, due to insufficient evidence: too many witnesses died or suffered mental incapacity before we could speak to them. We cited your report of Sue's confession that they witnessed a murder, and we found the case, but everyone involved in it has passed away. The Eastwoods' lawyer argued successfully that nothing from Operation Honey-guide, including my attempt to collar them on the theft of a ring, can be submitted in any case against them. She said it was entrapment and should be erased from the record.

IF: Sorry, Dee, but you said this case was a success. How can it be, if the Eastwoods aren't going to prison?

DO: They've been sacked, they've lost their pensions and won't work as police officers ever again.

TF: But they must have been close to retirement anyway!

IF: Will they have to pay back the money they stole?

DO: They don't appear to have it anymore. We got warrants for all their bank accounts and there were no savings. What they stole they spent—on luxuries for their flat, on vacations and eating out.

IF: Then they've got away with it!

DO: The main thing is we've weeded out two bent coppers and cleaned up our station. You two have been instrumental in that. Thank you.

To: DI Melody Obasi
From: Tanya Frost
Date: May 30, 2014
Subject: Sue and Mal Eastwood

Dear Dee,

Ian and I have been trying—and failing—to forget something you said at our last meeting. We feel we must write and air our thoughts. Sue and Mal Eastwood are con artists who preyed on vulnerable people. Now they won't face any justice apart from losing their jobs. Surely, having got away with theft and deception for so many years, and having spent all the money they stole, that's simply not punishment enough. Shouldn't their faces be plastered across every newspaper?

Can we really not make them pay for what they did?

Yours sincerely,

Tanya and Ian Frost

To: Tanya Frost
From: DI Melody Obasi
Date: June 2, 2014
Subject: Re: Sue and Mal Eastwood

Dear Tanya and Ian,

I understand how you both feel. However, as I explained during our debrief, the prosecutor felt the evidence available from the historical cases wasn't sufficient. Regarding Operation Honeyguide, the Eastwoods were acting under duress when they agreed to take the "money." That, and the fact the setup was technically entrapment, meant the prosecutor ruled it's not in the public interest to pursue a case against them. We simply wouldn't win.

They are no longer serving police officers and have lost their police pensions. It's true the case hasn't been reported in the media. We're committed to seeking out and removing corrupt officers, but the public needs to trust the majority of us, who are honest and dedicated.

The Eastwoods didn't benefit long-term from the crimes they committed. They have no savings and I'm sure they'll struggle for money themselves in old age, especially as I understand they're estranged from their family. Whenever I have to settle for an outcome that I disagree with, I remember something our old boss Lewis Parry said before he retired—that karma is very creative in how she pays back a criminal.

Two predators can no longer abuse their positions of power, and that can only be good for the community. Many thanks again for all your hard work and commitment to Operation Honeyguide.

Very best wishes,
DI Melody Obasi

To: DI Melody Obasi
From: Tanya Frost
Date: August 20, 2017
Subject: Sue and Mal Eastwood

Dear Dee,

You may not remember us, as it's been three years since we worked together, but we've just discovered something very worrying and feel we need to share it with you.

Ian and I have been watching Suzanne and Malcolm Eastwood. They still live at the same address and drive the same car so it's quite easy to keep an eye on them. Don't worry! We use costumes and wigs to disguise ourselves and haven't been spotted yet.

We can tell you that since being sacked by Hulme Police, both Eastwoods have been working in pubs. Sue is assistant manager at The True Lovers' Knot while Mal started as barman at The Coach House and is now the manager. We drop in every week or so, but last Thursday they were missing from their posts. Both bar teams said they'd taken the week off (which they've never done before) but didn't know, or wouldn't tell us, why. So, on Friday, we waited outside their address and watched as they left the flat together at 6:30 a.m.

We followed them to the Whyteleaf Express Hotel in Corley and, to cut a long story short, we discovered they're in training to become pub landlords. They've signed up to a course run by Ye Olde Goat Brewery, which owns scores of pubs and bars around the UK. They attended the introductory course last week. If they pass a series of smaller courses, interviews, and placements, then they could be running a pub anywhere in the country within months. A pair of experienced con artists are aiming to place themselves at the heart of a community, where vulnerable people may confide in them or look to them for support.

We contacted the brewery to tell them exactly the sort of people the Eastwoods really are, but they were extremely curt with us. They said the Eastwoods left the force with exemplary records and that ex-police make ideal landlords. They also claimed it "isn't the first time criminals have tried to sabotage applicants' chances of running a pub"!

I find it impossible to believe you'd have allowed the Eastwoods to leave the force with "exemplary records," so we're certain they've forged whatever documents the brewery has seen. I can give you all the contact details for relevant personnel at Ye Olde Goat and hope you'll be able to confirm with them that what we said is true.

I look forward to hearing from you,

Tanya

To: Tanya Frost
From: DI Melody Obasi
Date: August 20, 2017
Subject: Re: Sue and Mal Eastwood

Dear Tanya,

Thank you for contacting me. I hope you and Ian are well, but I must warn you that shadowing the Eastwoods as you describe amounts to stalking and is illegal. If they make a complaint you'll find yourselves in very serious trouble.

Like I said at the time, none of the charges stuck. The Eastwoods were acting under threats and blackmail, thanks to Ian going off script. It wasn't the only reason the case ended as it did, but it didn't help.

As Sue and Mal lost the employer contributions to their pensions when they were dismissed, they will have to support themselves some-how and perhaps running a pub will be the making of them.

I strongly advise you both to move on. Forget Operation Honeyguide. You don't want to be in trouble with the law yourselves.

Very best wishes,

Dee

To: DI Melody Obasi
From: Tanya Frost
Date: August 21, 2017
Subject: Re: Sue and Mal Eastwood

Dear Dee,

Thank you for your email. You're right, we're going to put the whole matter behind us. As you know, we were carers for our mother for so many years, it was a big readjustment when she passed away. Operation Honeyguide gave us something to focus on precisely when we needed it. We want to apologize for our role in its failure to bring the Eastwoods to justice. If we could right that wrong, we would.

But we intend to move on and plan to go traveling. If you email us at this address you may have to wait for a reply, given the time differences. And if you need us for any further acting work, I'm afraid we're unavailable.

Best wishes,
Tanya and Ian

Final scores out of 110 + tiebreak 1 point

The Sturdy Challengers	97
Spokespersons	89
The Landlords	81
The Olde Goats	79
Ami's Manic Carrots	73
Let's Get Quizzical	62
Linda & Joe & Friends	49
The Shadow Knights	Disqualified

Extract from a police statement made by Lorraine Thorogood from The Sturdy Challengers, November 22, 2019:

We were *thrilled* we'd won! Chris was ecstatic. I don't know what gave him more of a kick, knowing The Shadow Knights had been exposed as cheats, or winning against them when they'd been cheating for half the quiz. Our whole team was hugging each other, even Andy, who is usually very reserved. Only while we were celebrating, the rest of the pub were staring at the landlord in the blond wig and low-cut frilly dress.

"What I'd like to know is," Mal said, "who exactly is on the other end of those earpieces? The Eggheads? The Chasers? Or someone with a steaming laptop and a fast finger on Shazam?"

"That's not important," The General muttered. "What's important is *why* we cheated, not how."

And this is where he dropped a bombshell.

"We didn't come here to win," he said, "not at first. We came to watch."

"Watch what?" That was Sue, and it was strange, but she seemed different somehow. Not as homely and ditzy as usual.

"To watch two dodgy coppers," The General whispered. "A gentle, bumbling middle-aged couple, apparently unambitious for themselves, but prepared to put their jobs on the line to help the victims of legal loopholes and bureaucracy. Only they were really a pair of vultures who conned victims out of whatever cash they could—"

"And were they found guilty of those crimes in a court of law?" That was Mal.

"You know very well they weren't. They'd spent the money and never faced trial. In every sense of the phrase, they got away with it. When we found out they'd reinvented themselves as landlords of a shabby country pub, we decided to pay them a visit.

"And let me tell you, that reinvention was complete. I barely recognized the police officers I quizzed with back then. Well, five years is a long time."

"So you intended to take the law into your own hands? To be as bad as you thought they were?" Sue's voice wobbled, but in her wig and gown she looked every inch a litigator!

"We wanted them to know what it felt like to be cheated. How do con artists act when conned themselves? Would they fall for it or spot the ruse immediately? I'm happy to report we drove Mal to distraction. He did his best to try and catch us out, using every trick in the book. In the end it was the simplest explanation—we had someone looking up the answers for us and feeding them to us through earpieces. How does it feel to be conned, Mal?"

By now Sue and Mal were as white as their legal wigs were yellowed. The table of brewery people were muttering. I heard one saying he'd received an anonymous letter, but checked their record with the police and it was clean. The table of landlords looked very upset. One of the men in rainbow outfits said, "Is this true? Did you cheat people out of money?"

The Eastwoods looked at each other again, before turning to everyone and saying...

"Yes, it's true."

Well, even *our* table quietly took our seats again. Our Sue and Mal! None of us regulars knew what to do with that. But no one was more upset than the landlords' table.

"Well, that's that then." The taller rainbow man shrugged off his feathery cape. "We'll have no more to do with you."

"Wait!" Mal said. "Let us explain ourselves at least."

Sue walked to the center of the room and swung her robes very dramatically.

"There was a time when we took advantage of people," she said. "We didn't seek them out, but when an opportunity came our way, we'd seize it."

"Then your luck's run out," said one of the leprechauns.

"When we lost our jobs and our pensions, we learned the hard way what it's like to be vulnerable. We worked long hours in bars and pubs until the opportunity arose to become landlords ourselves. We decided to draw a line under our past. In short, we've changed.

"Ask anyone who has had anything to do with us these last two years, from Mark and Manny who helped us renovate the alehouse garden, to Shirley Thompson at Bayview Care Home, to Fiona over there, who has spent the last six weeks living and working here while she gets back on her feet. Yes, we did some terrible things, but when we came to Fernley with our entire world packed into our old Corsa, we vowed to leave the past behind and do only good. I invite anyone here to have their say if they believe otherwise."

There was silence. No one could think of anything bad they'd done. I couldn't.

"The thing is," Mal added, "does knowing what you know about our past change how you feel about us? Or do you judge us on how we are *now*? That choice is yours."

"Luke Goode isn't here, or he might have something to add," The General said. "I'll remind everyone that Mr. Goode was the man who left The Case is Altered on September 2 and was found a month later under the old jetty at the end of the lane. One might assume his murder had something to do with his lifestyle, but it didn't, did it, Mal?"

At that, Mal squared up to The General.

"In answer to that," he said, "I'd like to call upon our fellow landlords. All of them can attest to the reign of 'The Cheats'; they caused trouble in practically every pub in Hertfordshire. There's no telling how many enemies Luke Goode had made."

The two chefs stood up and one said, "It's true they won our quiz unfairly and were disruptive the whole night."

The other landlords nodded in agreement.

"That's Mimi and Flo from Tom's Bar on the high street. Thank you, Mimi. You see? Mr. Goode was a troublemaker who terrorized the local pubs, cheating honest quizzers out of their winnings, just like The Shadow Knights. So I'd suggest *you*, of all people, leave Mr. Goode out of this."

"Oh, it's not me," The General says, "it's the person talking in my ear. They're parked in Morrisons' parking lot, where they've been almost every Monday night for the past ten weeks. Listening to the quiz. Looking up the answers. Even to the picture rounds, thanks to these camera glasses. There's the odd question that can't be found, and anagrams were always tricky. But the voice in my ear knows a lot about you two."

That was when there was a loud banging on the doors. The Shadow Knight who'd been guarding it stood aside and in stepped Cloud.

"Peace," he whispered. "I'd like to give a witness testimony that will make you rethink this entire story . . . In fact, you could say, 'The case is altered.'"

Hulme Police
Operation Honeyguide

Senior Investigating Officer: Detective Inspector Melody Obasi

Police interview with Malcolm Eastwood, May 9, 2014:

Interviewing officer: Detective Inspector Dee Obasi
Lawyer to the Eastwoods: Amy Wright

DO: So, Malcolm, feeling OK?

ME: Not really.

DO: Good. Now you know what Operation Honeyguide really was, do you have anything to say?

ME: No comment.

DO: Which of you was the mastermind behind these activities? If I had to guess, I'd say Sue was the sharper tool, but appearances can be deceptive.

AW: You need to charge my client with something. This setup case isn't admissible—

ME: I've got one question for you, Dee. Who the fuck did we see at the morgue?

DO: Funny, Sue asked the same question. But isn't it obvious? You both met the late DS Natalie Chase. We trained together and worked together until after her second son was born, when she was diagnosed with cancer. Never came back to work.

ME: You go showing us your dead friend's body, after passing her picture around, telling everyone she's a Polish nail technician— yet you have the cheek to say Sue and I are corrupt?

DO: I'd say it's what she would've wanted, only that'd be wrong. It's what she *demanded*. All the time she was having treatment, stuck in bed at home or in hospital, I'd keep her up to date on plans for Honeyguide. It gave her a focus. She was gagging to be a part of it, and I always hoped she would, but Nat was fading fast, talking about . . . after the inevitable. It started when I asked if she'd write letters to the boys, for them to open when they're older. Offered to help if she needed it. But she shook her head. "The kids are two and four," she said, "Callum will remarry and they'll have a new mom. A wonderful new mom too. I know, because Callum has such fabulous taste. They won't remember me and that's the way I want it, Dee. My dad died when I was young, so I know I won't make the mark on their lives I thought I would when they were born, but plans change, eh? I can make my mark on the world in other ways." Then she pulled me close and whispered, "I *can* be a part of Honeyguide. Use my picture for the first kidnapped girl. Then if you need a body, you've got one!" Her eyes shone with tears *and* excitement. "I haven't lost my hair, so they won't know I had cancer, but they'll see these injection sites and assume I'm on heroin or been drugged by the kidnappers. Make those bastards fall for it, hook, line, and sinker."

What could I say? I didn't know how ethical it was. But Nat was my best friend and that was her wish. At the same time, my God, how brilliant would it be to have a real body? If you doubted the Cunninghams' story or needed to be distracted from something we didn't want you to see, nothing would beat a corpse. I'm sorry I can't say any more without—

AW: That's amazing.

DO: I know. I'm really sorry, I can't . . .

AW: Do you want some tissues. Here . . .

ME: Eh? Are you representing me or counseling her?

AW: But Natalie Chase died months before you showed the Eastwoods that body. Did her family not want a funeral?

DO: Nat had no truck with funerals. She was traumatized by having to attend her dad's as a kid and was determined hers wouldn't have to. Same time, she was disappointed not to get further in her career, or do the good she'd hoped to do. When she made that suggestion about Operation Honeyguide, she was already making plans to keep fighting crime *long* after her death . . .

AW: Donating her remains to medical science? That's nice. Oh, look, I'm off myself now.

ME: Hello? I'm still here.

DO: Have a tissue, there you go. No, not medical science—forensic science.

Story from HertsNews, November 29, 2014:

Tragic police officer to "continue fight against crime" in the US

Detective Sergeant Natalie Chase, who died of cancer at the age of 32, is to continue the fight against crime after her tragically early death. According to the officer's wishes, her body will be sent to a so-called body farm at Texas State University, where it will be utilized for world-leading research into the forensics of decomposition. Ms. Chase's friend and former colleague Detective Inspector Melody Obasi said, "Nat's final wish was to help people for as long as possible and make an impact on the world long after her death."

May 16, 2014

Dear Mrs. Eastwood,

I am writing on behalf of Hulme Police to terminate your contract of employment with immediate effect.

As discussed at your final disciplinary hearing, all pension contributions made by Hulme Police have been withdrawn and your personal contributions transferred into a civilian pension fund. As you are aware, this represents a £101,493.07 reduction in funds.

In light of your many years of service, and legal restrictions on such disclosures negatively impacting an individual's ability to earn a living, no mention of the reasons for your contract termination will be made on your official record or testimonial.

It is with regret that I am writing this letter and a similar one to Mr. Eastwood. If you require any further information, please instruct your legal representative to contact HR on the numbers below.

Yours sincerely,
Ailsa Duncan
Director of Human Resources
Hulme Police

Ye Olde Goat Brewery
[extract from] Application Form for Prospective Landlords

Name(s): Suzanne and Malcolm Eastwood
Date: July 3, 2017

*Why do you want to work with Ye Olde Goat Brewery in its
tenant-landlord partnership program?*

Between us, we clocked up almost forty years working on the front line of law enforcement with Hulme Police, and now we've retired, we are looking for a new challenge. We've spent three years working in a variety of pubs and bars in the North of England, both of us rising to management positions. Being landlords of our own pub will enable us to build on that experience, utilizing the passion we have for bringing people together and building a community. We both have sophisticated and well-practiced conflict-resolution skills and can get along with people from all walks of life. It's our dream to work at the heart of our community again, nurturing isolated groups, like the elderly or those who live alone, and giving them a chance to meet others. We firmly believe the pub is a force for good within the community and we hope to generate interest and business with quiz nights, competitions, and other activities that will bring people together. Most of all, we love a challenge and are happy to work long hours over many months and years to achieve our aims.

Extract from a police statement made by Andrew Moore from The Sturdy Challengers, November 22, 2019:

If I'm honest, what happened that night took the shine off our win. One minute we were celebrating Chris beating The General, the next everything turned serious. Sue and Mal having to leave the police because they conned people out of their life savings. And there was Fiona, a vulnerable teenager living with them. Not that she had any money I knew about, but it was yet another thing I'd have to action at work the next day.

It was like being hit by a bolt of lightning. Nothing will ever go right. I try to do something good for someone and it turns to shit. We win and yet it's still not enough. I decided I'd had it—I was handing in my notice. I'd retrain in something more rewarding. Anything to get away from my office, my flat, this pub, and the tiny shitty little world they represent.

Sorry, Officer, where was I? Yep, Cloud, the vegan from the barge, walked in.

"Peace," he said, "I'd like to give a witness testimony that will make you rethink this entire story . . . In fact, you could say, 'The case is altered.'"

You shouldn't judge a book by its cover, that's the saying, but I'm sure everyone in that room was judging Cloud. He's late fifties at least. He's white, but his hair was in dreadlocks, long matted beard—and he was wearing what looked like every stitch of clothes he could find in the charity bin. Still, as he spoke, he started to look more commanding. Like he was reverting back to someone he used to be.

"I spent ten years as a detective inspector at Hulme Police, where I had the misfortune to work with a pair of married police officers called Suzanne and Malcolm Eastwood.

"I can confirm that what The General says is true. In thirty years of service, the Eastwoods had an average record on the surface, but they hid a dark side and pulled one too many scams. It came to light when two of our young officers stumbled on an old case the Eastwoods had been involved in—it could only have been them who stole the racehorse at the center of it. Then they found another case that didn't add up. As these sergeants rose up the ranks themselves, they made it their business to catch the Eastwoods at it, even when one of them was diagnosed with cancer. After she passed away, her colleague went undercover to put their plans into action.

"In short, we set up a sting, they fell for it, and we sacked them. But we couldn't prosecute; there was too little evidence from the historical cases, and the sting was inadmissible. Still, we'd weeded them out. The Eastwoods couldn't do any more harm. Or so we thought. Then we heard they were looking to open a pub well away from anyone who'd know about their past."

For the first time that night, Sue and Mal seemed completely blindsided. Up to now, they'd stood their ground. They didn't deny what they'd done back then, and were more than convincing when they said they'd gone straight. So who was this guy Cloud?

"I went by another name back then," he said, "and looked very different from how I look now. You have to conform when you're in an organization like that. But I wasn't happy. In the months before I was due to take early retirement, I went to a talk about karmic renewal and the universe spoke: I met Wind there. We moved into *The Whittling Vegan*, and after a full-moon renaming ceremony, I could finally be myself. Now it turns out I'm not the only one who's had a personal reinvention.

"There's a much bigger crime here, as The General knows. He was on Sue and Mal's old quiz team The Beat Goes On. With his permission, I'll reveal the final piece of evidence."

The General nodded, very respectfully, to Cloud, giving him the floor.

"Now, I worked with those police officers, day in and day out, for ten years. I knew them as well as I knew my own family—better even, given the hours we worked. And I can categorically state that this pair here are NOT Suzanne and Malcolm Eastwood."

To: Mal Eastwood
From: Warwick Roper
Date: October 23, 2017
Subject: The Case

Dear Eastwoods,

Well done on completing your final placement. As your previous manager, Edwin Laing, has left, it's down to me to confirm in writing that you have passed whatever they need you to pass these days and that you are now eligible for a partnership tenancy with us.

I suggest you visit The Case is Altered. Situated down a country lane and adjacent to the Colne River, "The Case" has a long history with us, but in recent years has seen a nosedive in business, thanks to a new bypass and the turnoff to a supermarket that diverted a B road. The previous landlords retired and we've been forced to close its doors. The empty premises are currently on the market, but if you were interested then we would withdraw it from sale.

New blood could breathe life into this place, and your reported enthusiasm for building a community at whichever establishment you take on will be required.

You're welcome to visit. The keys are held by a local estate agent, but if the interim manager is available, he'll show you around.

Yours,

Warwick Roper, General Manager

To: Warwick Roper
From: Mal Eastwood
Date: November 7, 2017
Subject: Re: The Case

Dear Mr. Roper,

We were disappointed not to meet you, and to hear that the interim manager has now left the company.

How soon can we start at The Case is Altered? Our flat is sold and we're staying in an Airbnb, so the sooner the better. In fact we can move in right now, while the tenancy is still going through, and begin doing the place up. We could aim for an opening date in early spring next year, if not sooner. The longer it's left empty, the more work (and money) it'll take to open again.

Best,

Sue and Mal

To: Mal Eastwood
From: Tee F
Date: December 4, 2017
Subject: Free quote

Dear Sue and Mal,

I saw your card on the Morrisons' community bulletin board this afternoon and would like to introduce myself and my family-run commercial cleaning business.

It says you're moving into The Case is Altered on Bell End. We live nearby and know the establishment very well. Our company specializes in bringing such properties back up to snuff and we'd like to quote for an initial deep clean and then daily services. You'll know its previous cleaners were laid off when the pub closed and, to be honest, the premises were not being maintained to our high standards.

My brother and I are fast, efficient cleaners, well used to high-footfall commercial properties. I look forward to meeting with you as soon as possible. Please feel free to call or text on the number below.

Tee

Text messages between Mal Eastwood and Tee F, December 4, 2017:

Mal

Thanks for your email. We're moving into The Case tomorrow, and looking through the window now, we'd like to take you up on the offer of a quote for a deep clean! It certainly needs it. We can discuss an ongoing contract after that.

Tee

You're there now, but moving in tomorrow?

Mal

Someone from the estate agent will bring the keys in the morning, so it's a couple of sleeping bags in the car for us tonight.

Tee

You poor things!

Mal

This move has been every bit as mad as it sounds. Everything done through third parties or over the phone. One night in the car is a small price to pay. We want the pub open and people through the door again as soon as possible.

Tee

How can we help?

Mal

The bar area needs the deepest clean you can manage. We visited a few weeks ago and upstairs wants sandblasting, from what I remember. Pop around when you like and we'll talk about getting this place half decent again. We'll be in the Corsa outside.

Tee

See you tomorrow morning.

Extract from a police statement made by Chris Thorogood from The Sturdy Challengers, November 22, 2019:

We won! We beat The Shadow Knights. Nothing could wipe the smile off my face that night. Not even the palaver that followed. Happy to fill you in on what happened, as far as I recall.

"Of course we're Sue and Mal," Sue said. "We worked as police officers at Hulme for more than twenty years. We're ashamed of a few things we did there, but we've never been anything but honest at The Case."

"OK," said Cloud, the scruffy fellow from the barge, "in that case, who am I? If you're Sue and Mal Eastwood, then you worked with me for ten years. I've grown my hair and I'm more sunburned than I was, but if you knew me then, you'd know me now. I've been moored at the old jetty for six weeks and coming to your weekly quiz for just as long, with not a flicker of recognition from either of you. And even if you don't remember my face, you'd remember the name of your old guv from Axeford police station. Go on, tell everyone the name of your DI when you were sacked for misconduct."

"I'm telling you!" Sue shouted, but her voice was wobbling. "We *are* Sue and Mal. We moved here to start a new life and run a country pub, like we always dreamed. Mr. Roper knows that! He'll tell you!"

Since then I've thought back to how clueless they were in those first few weeks at The Case. Didn't know how to put a barrel on, flush the taps, or manage the inventory. I'd worked in a bar before so offered to help. Checked out the kitchen and almost had a fit when I saw the fridge: cooked ham stored next to raw prawns! They passed it all off as first-week jitters, but thinking about it, they didn't have the first idea about running a pub, however many books they'd read.

One of the suits on the brewery table, with a face like thunder, muttered, "Sue and Mal met the interim manager, not me. This place is nothing but trouble. First a murder, then all this—and don't think I haven't spotted those vegan protein shakes behind the bar. I know for a fact they haven't been going through the books. The sooner we close this place, the better." The other suits nodded, disgruntled.

That was when the door opened and in walked a woman I'd never seen before, but Sue and Mal obviously recognized her because one of them—I can't remember which—said, "Dee! What are you doing all the way down here?"

The woman sighed and said, "Tanya Frost, Ian Frost, you're both under arrest on suspicion of murder. Three murders. First, Suzanne and Malcolm Eastwood on or around December 4, 2017, and then Luke Goode on September 2 this year."

The couple we thought were Sue and Mal looked at each other, like they knew the game was up.

"And who are *you*?" The Lusty Lass asked the new woman.

"Sorry, should've introduced myself. I'm Detective Inspector Melody Obasi, in plain clothes right now because it's brass monkeys in the Morrisons parking lot. The Shadow Knights are my team of under-cover officers, who also happen to be Hulme Police's most successful quiz team."

"Sue and Mal killed the cheat?" That was one of the landlords—I think it was a leprechaun.

"Mr. Goode was once an actor, but he fell on hard times and was living in a hostel, trying to kick the booze. He recognized them as soon as he saw them that night. You'd all been in a play together—can't for the life of me remember what it was—"

"*The Magic Garden of Stanley Sweetheart.*" Mal couldn't stop himself, even though he was under caution. If there's something he knows that you don't, he has to say it!

Anyway, the inspector carried on. "Luke didn't realize how signifi-cant his arrival was, but you panicked. If a heavy drinker given to loud behavior started telling your regulars who you really were, and that you used to tread the boards with him, anyone in the room could start looking closely at your story. You'd already killed twice. A third time was just . . . administrative."

That's when I spoke. Don't know why. I'm not the sort of person who gets involved usually. But I said, "Is that true, Sue? Did you and Mal kill the real Sue and Mal?"

They looked at each other again, then back to the room.

"No comment." And they said it in perfect unison.

The Shadow Knights leaped into action. They handcuffed Sue and

Mal and marched them out. The young lad was one of them. Couldn't help but notice he winked at young Fiona on the way out.

Finally, The Lusty Lass stood up and boomed, "Our quizmaster is indisposed, so I declare this quiz over!"

Now I have something to declare here, in this statement: The Shadow Knights may well have been police officers on an operation, but they stole our table and cheated in the quiz for months on end, and I'd like that on the record!

Text messages between DI Dee Obasi and Fiona Hammond, November 11, 2019:

Dee
Thanks for speaking with me, Fiona, and sorry to approach you in the college canteen. I had to make sure neither Sue nor Mal overheard us.

Fiona
k

Dee
I couldn't be sure you'd even call Ed, the young Shadow Knight, from that number on the coaster. Thanks for being understanding when you realized the number was mine.

Fiona
k

Dee
Good! Now I'm very pleased you've settled in so well with the Eastwoods, but we talked about how I'm concerned for their safety and that I'd like you to get me a picture of that firearm you say you saw in their safe.

Fiona
got it

Dee
It's best they don't know we're in touch with each other. I don't want to worry them. That's very important.

Dee
Thing is, the Eastwoods were never issued police firearms, so I'm not sure where this has come from.

Fiona
got it

Dee
You understand the assignment or you've got a picture?

Fiona
time got the gun

Dee

You've got the gun? OMG, Fiona, PUT IT BACK!

Dee

NO! Don't put it back—DON'T TOUCH IT!

Dee

Just stay calm, take a picture and send it to me.

Fiona

quiz?

Dee

I know, but you could zip upstairs to have a rest or something.

Dee

Do it now!

Fiona

[Picture file]

Dee

What the heck is that? It looks like an old Remington 1858. Surely it doesn't work!

Fiona

just clicks no bullets got an ingrave inn on silver plack

Dee

What does it say?

Fiona

[Picture file]

Dee

"Presented to Ian Frost. You've got your gun."

Dee

"Annie Get Your Gun at Chichester Festival Theatre. May 1990."

Dee

OMG, Thank GOD! It's a stage prop.

Fiona

time

Dee

Fiona, now remember what I said: it's very important you don't tell Sue or Mal or ANYONE that I'm here. It's for their own good. I'll explain everything once this is all over.

Dee

But for now, please don't worry. Ed will keep you updated and you've got his number as well, in case you see anything you feel we should know about.

Fiona

k

Extract from a police interview with Fiona Hammond, November 22, 2019:

Interviewing officer: Detective Inspector Dee Obasi

DO: So now you know why I was watching the Frosts, or the Eastwoods as you knew them. Sorry I couldn't tell you the truth sooner, but sometimes the less you know, the better. In any case, there's only so much you can say over a text message, don't you find?

FH: Yeah, I'm dyslexic. I hate texting.

DO: I guessed that from your replies!

FH: Yeah. Sorry.

DO: I'm curious, Fiona, what was life like with the Frosts? Did they ever talk about their lives before they came here?

FH: Not really, but they had loads of stuff in the safe. Bank things, passports, paperwork from Hulme Police. When I saw it, Sue told me they don't mention their past life in case anyone they arrested shows up here with a beef. She said they kept their police gun—I thought it looked too old for one a Fed would have, but didn't want to push it. Then she said I should forget I saw it, because if you act in the heat of the moment you have to live with the consequences.

DO: I bet. You never saw old photos of them in costume? Things from their real lives?

FH: No. They never talked about acting or the theater. That gun must've been the only thing they kept. But Mal . . . sorry, Ian, always included questions about, you know, Shakespeare and stuff, in the quiz.

DO: When I knew them, they threw themselves into their roles— became the people they pretended to be. Seems they did it completely when they arrived here. They "became" the Eastwoods to cover up the double murder, but got trapped. I suppose if you pretend to be someone you're not, there comes a point when you're not pretending anymore. That's just who you are.

[*Silence*]

Sorry. Thinking out loud. Is there anything you'd like to ask me?

FH: Why'd you wait five years to look for Sue and Mal again?

DO: Operation Honeyguide was . . . tough. So I put it behind me. I started a new relationship and he had two young boys, so I was learning to be a stepmom to two lads who'd lost their mom. But once they were both at school and I had more time to think, I found my mind wandering back to it—I had unfinished business. The Frosts had told me the Eastwoods had gone into the pub trade, so I looked them up. The Case is Altered ran a quiz night— something I always remembered Mal talking about. Felt I should look in on their new life, check they weren't pulling any scams. But at the same time I didn't want to walk through the door and have a conversation with them ever again. The thought made my skin crawl—but more than that, if they *were* running a racket, I didn't want them to know I was watching.

I talked about it with a colleague, Glen Knight, who'd quizzed with the Eastwoods' team The Beat Goes On, back in the day. He's got his own police quiz team now called The Shadow Knights, mostly undercover officers—no one Sue and Mal would know. He said the Eastwoods wouldn't be suspicious if he turned up, as it wasn't unusual to quiz further afield now and again. I said to just let them recognize him, see how they reacted when they saw someone who knew what they did.

I could've stayed home that night, but something told me I had to be there.

To: Polly Baker
From: Dominic Eastwood
Date: October 25, 2024
Subject: Re: Documentary idea

Hi Pol,

A quick note about the following documents. You'll notice some are not chronological. I wanted to time the reveals as they may occur in a documentary, rather than in the order they actually happened. Perhaps this could be illustrated with some special effects on-screen, either whizzing the "action" back in "rewind" mode or animations of a timeline that we slide up and down. I'm full of ideas!

Dom

Text messages between DI Dee Obasi and Glen Knight, September 9, 2019:

Dee

Morrisons is only around the corner. I'll sit in the parking lot. If there's anything off about their setup in that pub, text me—I'm marching straight in there.

Glen

I know you are!

* * *

Dee

Hope you're warmer than I am. Thanks for introducing me to the team. What did that fella call you? Glenral?

Glen

General! General Knowledge. It's an in-joke after I got 20 out of 20 in a GK tiebreaker a couple of years ago.

Dee

Like it! You have that military look. I'm changing your name in my contacts.

* * *

Dee

Who's the young lad? Don't look old enough to be a copper.

The General

Feeling your age? Happens to the best of us. Ed's just started at Axeford. Our secret weapon for questions about recent music and computer games.

Dee

Good luck. If you're stuck on a question, text me and I'll look the answer up for you.

The General

You will not!

Dee

I have no problem cheating a cheat.

The General

Fair's fair. We don't know they're still at it. Anyone can turn over a new leaf.

* * *

The General

It isn't Sue and Mal.

Dee

What?

The General

Not them. They're another couple called Sue and Mal Eastwood.

Dee

No way.

Dee

That pub is an Olde Goat pub. I heard Sue and Mal went to work for that brewery. Same names AND same brewery? I don't believe in coincidence.

The General

Here, check them out. It's not the Sue and Mal I quizzed with.

[Picture file]

Dee

HOLY FUCKING SHIT!

The General

Unless they've both had a very expensive makeover, it's not them.

The General

The quiz is starting and we have to put our phones away.

Dee

This is big, Glen. Potentially REALLY big. I'll explain later. In the meantime, all of you, be calm and inscrutable, don't give ANYTHING away— especially not that you're police.

Dee
If anyone asks, say young Ed is the son of one of you—explains why he's with a bunch of oldies. Are you all OK with that?

The General
We're shadows, Dee, of course we're OK with it.

Dee
Break a leg, General.

Text messages between Glen Knight (The General) and DI Dee Obasi, September 16, 2019:

The General
I'll sign some NanoComms and mics out of the stores. These glasses are new, we don't know how well they work in the field.

Dee
It'll be a good test of the tech. I've got my laptop open on the Google home page, phone on Shazam—I'm ready.

The General
Let's go get 'em!

Dee
Whatever the Frosts have done, we'll find out!

Transcript recorded by the NanoComm, September 16, 2019:

DO: My God, yes, I recognize Tanya's voice. And Ian's. They're using their regular Sheffield accents, like when they played the Cunninghams. They're not impersonating the Eastwoods' voices at all. No one down here knew the real Sue and Mal, so they can create two new characters with the same names and backgrounds. But they have to keep up the pretense, because everything hinges on their contract with Ye Olde Goat and their license to operate the premises—which were signed by the real Eastwoods.

* * *

Dee: Done it! Full marks! Well done, all. Let's see what the Frosts make of that. I want to rile them into making a wrong move and, till then, let's fuck with their minds. Secret Shadow Knight signing off.

Transcript recorded by the NanoComm, September 23, 2019:

Dee: These are much trickier. The little shit is trying to break The Shadow Knights. But we will not be broken.

* * *

Dee: It's a FAKE track from a short piece of music uploaded TODAY by a new account. We can't get this one right. Write down: "Got to Do Better Than That" by the Dualers. Repeat: "Got to Do Better Than That" by the Dualers.

Transcript recorded by the NanoComm, September 30, 2019:

Dee: I've got the whole periodic table in front of me. Top row, left to right, here goes . . .

Text messages between DI Dee Obasi and Glen Knight (The General), October 8, 2019:

Dee

Tanya just texted The General—invited him to drop by "for a chat."

The General

She was giving me the eye on Monday.

Dee

She must know she can't start a relationship with anyone. Ian won't want her upsetting their little scenario. Whatever they've done with the real Sue and Mal, it's trapped them both in the lie.

The General
Should I shut her down? Could mention I'm married, family man,
expecting a baby, etc.

Dee
No. Keep that air of mystery. I'll send you screenshots of the messages
so you know what "you" said to her. Ignore the flirting. If she asks you
outright on a date, then say you're unavailable. Give as little away as
possible.

Dee
Heads up: I asked them about Chris and Lorraine, so the Frosts think it's
them The Shadow Knights are interested in. A little preemptive deflection
never hurts.

The General
Got it.

Transcript recorded by the NanoComm, October 28, 2019:

Dee: He's set us up with this one. What sort of quiz is this?

Dee: I think it's time we went to some other pub quizzes. After a
     disaster like tonight, The Shadow Knights would go elsewhere.
     Only Olde Goat pubs, so it gets back to the Frosts.

Text messages between DI Dee Obasi and Glen Knight (The General),
November 5, 2019:

Dee
Hey, Glen, sending you more message screenshots before tonight's quiz:
I told them The Shadow Knights saw an ex-offender who'd conned the
elderly when they quizzed at The Brace. I then used a few bits of trivia to
talk about revenge.

The General
Reason?

Dee

To see if they'd give anything away.

The General

Did they?

Dee

Hmm.

The General

Careful, Dee, if they think they've been recognized as the Frosts, they'll run. We'll have to go in fast and hard to catch them.

Dee

I'm going to suggest a special quiz, with all their landlord friends. Lewis will listen in with me and let you know when to go in. We'll play it by ear—literally!

Transcript recorded by the NanoComm, November 12, 2019:

Dee: Glen. Glen, can you hear me? Cough if you can hear me. Shit— connection gone. First time the tech has let us down. Must be the weather. Shit! Well, you're on your own, so I hope The Lusty Lass quiz isn't as tough as The Case is Altered.

Transcript recorded by the NanoComm, November 18, 2019:

Dee: Not again. Fuck! Bloody tech.

* * *

Dee: You're back! OK, where are we? Glen, Lewis said he'd listen at the window and intervene if anything went down, but the tech's working again now.

Dee: I heard that. OK. Don't mention the Frosts. Talk as if we were watching the Eastwoods—here we go: "a gentle, bumbling middle-aged couple, apparently unambitious for themselves, but prepared to put their jobs on the line to help the victims of legal loopholes and bureaucracy. Only they were really a pair of vultures who preyed on the vulnerable and conned them of whatever cash they could—"

* * *

Dee: What are they playing at? They're trying to convince everyone they're the Eastwoods—asking forgiveness for stealing. I bet they are. They'd rather be scammers than murderers. I'm coming over there; it'll take me a few minutes. If Lewis comes in, let him do the talking.

Extract from a police interview with Fiona Hammond on November 22, 2019 (continued):

Interviewing officer: Detective Inspector Dee Obasi

FH: Andrew asked me to the quiz because they wanted to beat The Shadow Knights.

DO: We stirred up the whole community, but it was Tanya and Ian Frost we wanted.

FH: Why didn't you walk in and ask them what they were doing?

DO: You get a sense for things. I felt there was something bigger there, and I didn't want them to do a runner before I could get to the bottom of what happened to the Sue and Mal I knew.

FH: Cloud was a legend! He slayed it . . .

DO: After he retired I stayed in touch with Lewis—Cloud Parry—and knew how much he'd changed. My colleague Rhys moved to Spain with his partner, so there weren't many coppers left who knew the Eastwoods *and* the Frosts. And Cloud was the only one who'd changed enough to go into the pub and see "Sue and Mal" at first hand. The Frosts only met him the once, and not for long. He said he'd do me a favor and moor his barge up there. Only intended to stay overnight. Then he found the body.

FH: You drove down from up north every Monday?

DO: And back again afterward. We all did. I messaged the pub phone as The General, and every Monday I listened in and provided any answers the team didn't know. There's something compelling about a quiz, about testing your own knowledge. We knew Ian in particular was fascinated by The Shadow Knights, and Tanya had taken a shine to The General, so to keep up the pretense they were just a quiz team, we also quizzed at a few other pubs in the county.

FH: You're a bunch of Feds and you were cheating—oh, my days!

DO: I wouldn't say cheating, more manipulating the outcome—it might take a cheat to catch a cheat, but this Sue and Mal aren't cheats, they're murderers. It's no wonder they tried to convince everyone they were the real Eastwoods. Did you ever suspect they weren't husband and wife, but brother and sister?

FH: Ew, gross! Sue always said Mal snored, so that's why they had separate bedrooms.
[*Pause*]

DO: Was there anywhere in the grounds or buildings that were out of bounds? Anywhere they seemed protective of? Nervous if you went near it, that kind of thing?

FH: No.

DO: OK. Well, that's all for the mo. Where are you living now, Fiona?

FH: Andy got me a room in a youth block with a warden.

DO: And you can still go to college?

FH: He gives me a lift in and back.

DO: Oh. I got the impression he was tied to his desk.

FH: He's left the council. Going to college himself in January. Training to be a teacher.

DO: Well, that's nice. I won't keep you, Fiona, but before you go, have you got any questions for me?

FH: Yeah. Who painted over the pub sign? Sue went extra over that!

DO: Full disclosure. It was me. I got a ladder out of the shed. Did it the first time we came here, before I was listening in. Stupid.

FH: Amazing. But why?

DO: [*Pause*] Why. Isn't that the killer question? It was nothing to do with the Frosts, I can tell you that much. It was the sign and what it represented. The law. Justice. It all boils down to those two fat lawyers arguing across a room. If Sue and Mal had been punished for their crimes, the Frosts wouldn't have done what they did.

FH: What were the real Sue and Mal like?

DO: An ordinary couple who did their jobs, then enjoyed a quiz of an evening. Who liked their food and their little luxuries. Went for country drives or walks when they had time off. Who were suspicious of the internet and preferred to write things down. Who had no social-media footprint at all. Who lost all their friends along with their jobs, but still had each other and were making a go of new careers. We'll never know if they intended to go straight in the pub game or not. When the Frosts killed them, they not only assumed their identities but gained access to their entire lives. Mal wrote down every password, security code, and account number they had. Tanya and Ian created new characters for themselves, but some things they picked up from the real Eastwoods seemed to stick—Ian would spout facts and figures exactly like Mal used to. Tanya gave herself an air of homely niceness that the real Sue had. The Frosts lived law-abiding lives in Fernley, helped several people in the community—yourself included—but they killed to maintain that normality.

FH: How do you know the originals are dead and that our Sue and Mal killed them? You haven't found their bodies . . .

DO: We know Sue and Mal were preparing to spend a night in their car while they waited for the keys. Tanya and Ian Frost came here that night to confront them—whether they intended to kill them or not, we may never know—but when the estate agent arrived next morning it was the Frosts who took the keys. They had their own commercial cleaning company, so they could remove any evidence, and the fact the murder took place outside meant the interior of the pub was of little forensic value. Rest assured, after I'm finished with The Case is Altered, we'll know if anyone is buried anywhere in the vicinity.

To: Let's Get Quizzical [group]
From: Sid Topliss
Date: November 19, 2019
Subject: What the heck?

Dear all,

Have we ever had such a night at The Case? Well done, Bunny, on catching me like a fish with my promise to pay a pound to the hospice for every correct answer! Turns out I'd agreed to pay a pound for every correct answer given by every team in the whole quiz! She's even included the 96 points The Shadow Knights scored before they were disqualified. I shall be writing a check for £626 later today and hope they keep a bed warm for me there when my time comes!

So our Sue and Mal weren't the real Sue and Mal. The real ones were just bent coppers, whereas our two were triple murderers and are now prisoners on remand. They were brother and sister too, not even a married couple! Who'd have thought The Case could hide criminals of that caliber? Shame it's closed now. Nancy says we could take a trip into town for The Rainbow's quiz, as those two gents who were dressed up like Mardi Gras seemed so nice. Then there's The Brace of Pheasants run by the leprechauns. Who knows, perhaps The Case will open again when they find another couple to run it.

Funny how you get couples who commit crime together. Is it that they reinforce each other's strengths and compensate for each other's weaknesses? Or is it the reluctance to be alone that bonds them? It doesn't apply only to romantic couples, either, but to friends, relatives, colleagues. How many good things, and how many crimes, have been the work of a bonded pair?

Speaking of bonded pairs, I saw Peter Bond, the army man in drag who knew how The Shadow Knights were cheating, talking very intently to Rita. He's got a dog exactly like Bailey and they're going on a walk together, all four of them. I don't want to start a rumor, but she might be drinking in The Lusty Lass now and, who knows, maybe in future that pub'll have a couple running it too! That's another quiz we can try—how about it? Now The Case is closed, the world is our oyster.

Well, think I might park up by the wood yard and watch the excavations. That policewoman is determined to find two bodies. Arthur says the river will be searched as well as the lane and the woods. If they're there, she'll find them!

So, who's up for the Rainbow quiz next week?

Sid

Story from HertsNews, November 28, 2019:

Bike rack hides gruesome find

Human remains from two bodies have been found in the cement foundations of a pub bicycle rack. Police searching for the whereabouts of Suzanne and Malcolm Eastwood, both formerly of Hulme Police, are currently at the scene. The Eastwoods are thought to have been murdered almost two years ago, in December 2017, the night before they were due to take over The Case is Altered pub in Fernley. Detective Inspector Melody Obasi says that "Initial indications are that the pair were battered to death in a spontaneous, frenzied attack." Former actors Tanya and Ian Frost are currently on remand, awaiting trial.

Story from HertsNews, March 18, 2021:

Life sentences for actor siblings who killed three and ran pub for two years under stolen identities

Tanya (53) and Ian Frost (55) have been jailed for a minimum of twenty years each for the murders of two former police officers, pub landlords Suzanne and Malcolm Eastwood, in 2017 and their customer, former actor Luke Goode, in 2019.

The Crown Prosecution Service's case stated that the Frosts stole the Eastwoods' identities and ran a pub using their names for two years. When Mr. Goode recognized them from their previous lives, he too was murdered. Judge Teresa McKee today called them "a pair of method actors whose professional experience set them in good stead when they assumed the identities of the couple they killed."

The Eastwoods' bodies were found buried under a bike rack in the garden of the pub they had been hired to run, The Case is Altered, in Fernley. Cause of death was given as blunt-force trauma. Trace DNA from Tanya Frost was found on an antique garden implement that had been used to conceal Mr. Goode's body in the River Colne.

Detective Inspector Melody Obasi said, "Neither Tanya nor Ian Frost has spoken about either crime, but, in sentencing, the judge described them as chameleons who morphed into the characters they'd killed, not hesitating to kill again when threatened with exposure. The world is safer now they are no longer at large."

To: Polly Baker
From: Dominic Eastwood
Date: October 25, 2024
Subject: Re: Documentary idea

Dear Pol,

So I left the final twist for the final episode! The Sue and Mal Eastwood who opened up The Case is Altered on the first morning of their tenure were not the same people who arrived the night before. They were killed by the Frosts, who, in exacting retribution for the Eastwoods' crimes, committed a far worse one.

Eventually I received a crate of my aunt and uncle's personal effects from the police. It was only what could be identified as *definitely* belonging to them before the Frosts assumed their identities. At the bottom I found several folders of quiz questions, books about the hospitality industry, and two big files of coursework from the Eastwoods' time on the brewery's business scheme for prospective landlords. It was all the information Tanya and Ian had about how to run a pub. It's no wonder they struggled with the basics at first.

Well used to researching for their acting roles, they had made notes in the margins: "Sue is intuitive, personable, but inside does she simmer with resentment?" "Mal is socially awkward, unless talking about quizzing, where answers are either right or wrong and nothing in between. He is the rock and Sue is the wave, washing over it." These were the roles of their lives.

I'm hoping that now you've read everything, you and your boss will think it's suitable to develop. It's a complex, multilayered case with lots of twists and turns, perfect for a documentary. It's shocking without being too controversial—most of the main players are dead or in prison—and there are plenty of details that never came out during the Frosts' trial that will appeal to true-crime fans.

You will have a wide choice of colorful "characters" to interview from the local quiz community and, as I said, I'm sure Detective Inspector Dee Obasi will agree to speak. All the landlords in Ye Olde Goat's Hertfordshire region are still in situ, so will be keen to promote their pubs. These days landlords can't rely on just local custom, they need to attract business from further afield and make theirs a destination venue.

I'm still sitting in The Case is Altered now, watching the sun go down over the trees outside. It'll soon be too dark to find my car, so I had better leave soon. The estate agent told me, quietly, that the brewery will accept a *much* lower offer than advertised. But still, it will cost a great deal of money to get this place up and running, so its future is far from certain.

Well, that's the case of Sue and Mal Eastwood in not so much a nutshell as a lot of emails and documents. I'd like to thank you for reading them, and so quickly too.

Best wishes,
Dom

To: Dominic Eastwood
From: Polly Baker
Date: October 25, 2024
Subject: Re: Documentary idea

Hi Dom,

It's been awesome! This is TV gold. My boss is back on Monday. I'll put all this together and suggest she make it a priority. It would be great to get you in for a chat and, if she's as enthusiastic as I am, we can get the ball rolling asap.

Pol xxx

To: Polly Baker
From: Dominic Eastwood
Date: October 25, 2024
Subject: Re: Documentary idea

Dear Pol,

That's wonderful news! Meanwhile, I'll send through any other documents

I come across that may help. I hope TV viewers find this case as compelling as we do!

Many thanks again and best wishes,
Dom

Text messages between DI Dee Obasi and Cloud Parry, October 1, 2019:

Dee
Thanks for doing this, guv, much appreciated. I'm properly intrigued as to why the Frosts are calling themselves the Eastwoods, but even more so because the Eastwoods have disappeared off the face of the earth.

Cloud
Me too. Let's see what they're up to. We're mooring early—I'll wander along the lane to the pub, have a look around the garden before anyone's up.

Dee
If there's an innocent, harebrained reason for all this, then I apologize and hope it's a nice place for you to drop anchor for a few days.

Dee
Sorry to ask this, guv, but can you NOT mention to your partner the real reason you're in Fernley? That's a big ask and I apologize.

Cloud
Dee, we're each of us traveling alone through time and space. Wind and I, we choose to be alone together, whatever shape our journeys may take.

Dee
Is that OK, then?

Cloud
Wind understands there are forces at play in each and every one of life's turns. Whatever leads us to Bell End—even if it's a reason I know and she doesn't—is all part of a far greater plan than anything you or I could ever dream of.

* * *

Cloud
It's overgrown. Derelict. Jetty looks rotten. Wind says the atmos is leaden.

Cloud
Lizzie is urging us on, helping us find the mooring point. We have business here, she says.

Dee

Who's Lizzie? Thought there was just the two of you.

Cloud

She's a Victorian servant girl. Wind's spirit guide. We need all the help we can get—The Whittling Vegan is stuck.

Dee

Be careful, guv, Lizzie might not know how to steer a barge.

* * *

Dee

Going OK?

Dee

If it's too dangerous, just move on.

Cloud

A body! A fucking body floated up. Whole jetty collapsed. I nearly went in!

* * *

Dee

I know you're busy, guv, but keep me up to date.

Cloud

The local PCSO's arrived and he's calling The Case is Altered now. Knows "Sue and Mal" very well.

Dee

I'm stunned, Lewis. I don't know what to say.

Dee

CLOUD! Sorry, guv, I meant to type Cloud.

Cloud

He's marching down the lane. I can see him plain as day. Bloody Ian Frost—the actor from Honeyguide.

Dee

Don't want to jump the gun, but that body . . . is it Sue or Mal Eastwood?

Cloud

No. Special Investigating Officer says he's been in the water "about a week." Well I've seen more bodies than she has—this one's been under a month at least.

Dee

Don't let on you're ex-police. Not even to the PCSO.

* * *

Cloud

He's scoffing Wind's scrambled tofu like a starving man. Not a flicker of recognition.

Dee

He only met you once five years ago and no offense, guv, but you didn't have dreadlocks, a long beard, beads, and a crocheted cap back then.

Cloud

Peace.

* * *

Cloud

He's gone. Invited us to the quiz next Monday.

Dee

Guv, have I got yours, Wind's, and Lizzie's permission to put your retirement on hold for a bit?

Cloud

You do. Lizzie says we're needed here.

To: Dominic Eastwood
From: DI Melody Obasi
Date: November 5, 2024
Subject: Re: Sue and Mal Eastwood

Dear Dominic,

Thanks for your email. Yes, I stayed in contact with Lewis Parry—still speak to him, but struggle to call him Cloud and just say "guv" like the old days. I've attached my text convo with him on the day he arrived at The Case. Wind still claims it was Lizzie who wanted them to moor at the old jetty, although it was my phone chat with the guv that decided it. You'll get conflicting accounts—always the way. If you're looking for a spooky angle for the TV show, then I'm sure Wind will give you an interview! Maybe Lewis believes all that, or maybe he's simply in love with Wind.

It's strange to think the Eastwoods' case will be made into a true-crime documentary, but well done for getting it off the ground. Must be cathartic to tell your aunt and uncle's story. As for being interviewed on-screen, I don't know about that yet, but I'm happy to answer your other questions as follows:

We know Tanya and Ian Frost met the real Sue and Mal outside The Case is Altered the night before they were due to move in. Did they go there with the intention to kill them? Or simply to confront them? Was it suppressed grief for their mother, expressed in one fatal moment? Neither sibling has revealed exactly what happened that night, so it's something we may never know.

I heard Ian Frost runs acting classes in prison. Apparently he's teaching other inmates how to walk away from trouble without losing face and present the best of themselves at job interviews, that sort of thing. I wouldn't be surprised if Tanya was doing the same. I can't think of two people better qualified, can you?

Yours sincerely,
Detective Inspector Dee Obasi

To: Polly Baker
From: Dominic Eastwood
Date: August 1, 2025
Subject: New development

Hi Polly,

You won't believe this, but I've got hold of some new evidence!

A former prison officer emailed me. She's called Maria D'Agostino and worked at HMP Larkford—where Tanya Frost is serving her sentence. She'd read about *The Killer Question* documentary going into production and said she had something we'd be interested in.

Apparently Tanya runs playwriting workshops and directs other prisoners in their own plays. This former officer said she'd clashed with her over something. Reading between the lines, I can't rule out the possibility that she's in possession of this purely because she realized how valuable it might be.

I don't want to be accused of withholding evidence from the police, so I've sent it to Dee Obasi as well—but you should read it asap.

We're still in the edit, so can we cut in an interview with her? I know it's eleventh-hour, but possible? Extract from Maria's email below:

Performing stories helped some inmates work through their issues, which is why we didn't often censor what they came out with—for, you know, adult themes, because after all, that's partly what the classes were for. That and building confidence. A lot of the women lack confidence, so they fall in with bad crowds or under the influence of men. Tanya would say, "Act confident, then people will treat you with respect and your actual confidence will grow." Basically: fake it till you make it. She called it a "safe space" and, say what you like about her, she runs a good drama class.

One day I was overseeing, which is basically just watching. Tanya had written her own play and was going to stage it during the class. This wasn't a new thing, because learning how to act in a little play would help the girls control their behavior outside— basically good discipline, right?

This play was one of those modern ones, with no words or music, only movement. Is it a mime or a dance? I don't know. Anyway, that sort of play was popular because the girls didn't need to put things into words, it was all feelings and exercise too.

As overseer, I had to read through the script in advance. It's usually a cursory glance, but immediately I could see exactly what this was. So I took Tanya aside and said, "Look, you can't put this on, Tan, it's too much." She got pissed off, said she needed to see it, but I said, "Well, these girls don't need to see it."

Anyway we had a row, I confiscated the script, and she directed another little play in the end. But I kept it and didn't show anyone. Thought it might be interesting to someone one day.

Anyway, Maria wanted £5,000 for the script, which is in Tanya Frost's handwriting. I knocked her down to £1,000. Scan attached.

Dom

The Face is Altered by Tanya Frost

A silent, interpretive play for two couples: A and B, Y and Z. Told through movement and expression; we never hear them speak.

NB: Y and Z never touch each other, but perform with a synergy of movement that reflects their bond.

A and B wear baseball caps. Y and Z have bare heads.

A and B wait in the center of the stage, happy and excited. They are confined to a small space, but are happy together. They look out from this space with great anticipation, at the world, at the future. What they see energizes them.

Y and Z creep onstage left. Furtive, hesitant, they cross upstage behind A and B, dodging out of their sight lines.

A and B finally settle down to sleep.

Y and Z leap out of hiding and swirl around the stage, a living, breathing turmoil of emotions. In perfect harmony, but never touching.

Y makes a noise near the "space"—she and Z stand back to watch A and B wake up in surprise at the sight of Y and Z.

A and B, wary, scared, step out of their "space" to face Y and Z on equal ground. Y and Z dance—small, "quiet" movements. They invite A and B to participate, but they refuse. There is something desperate about Y and Z—they want to talk. Still A and B will not engage, until finally A and B laugh. They laugh so hard they can hardly stay standing . . .

Y and Z are confused at first. Then upset, then angry. Nothing seems to stop A and B laughing. Y hits A. Z hits B.

Slowly, but building to a climax, the actors use improvised movement and dance to show the two couples engaging in a raw fight.

A and B are better and stronger fighters. After the balance of power has shifted to and fro, finally Y and Z are overpowered and lie helpless on the ground. Almost.

As A and B re-bond after the fight, Z struggles to his feet and pulls out a weapon—it's a GUN, but we will mime—and aims it at A and B.

Y should react with shocked surprise, as A and B cower and beg.

At gunpoint A and B lie on the stage, heads toward the audience. Z passes the gun to Y, who is uncomfortable holding it, but doesn't want to let Z down.

Z searches the stage, soon returns with another weapon—a large chunk of rubble, but we will mime. A and B jump up and try to escape, but Z smashes the rock first on A's head, then B's.

We hear nothing, yet we know they are both screaming and writhing. Y cannot put her hands over her ears because she has to hold the gun. But she turns to face the audience, because she cannot face the sight in front of her—it is her face we see.

Neither is dead, so Z must leap from A to B until they lie motionless onstage, their fingers intertwined, hands gripped together across the stage in a heartbreaking effort to maintain their bond.

Eventually Y and Z perform a dance all around the stage, around the bodies of A and B, but this is a frantic, horrified dance, out of step, out of synergy, until finally they reel back together, center stage, to regard the bodies. Y's problem is Z's problem too. It is one they must solve together.

Tentatively, as if an idea is only just forming in their minds, they pluck the baseball caps from A and B's heads.

The caps are inexplicably heavy and tricky to lift, but both Y and Z put them on. They struggle with the weight at first, but soon get used to it. They reassure each other, silently, that they fit and look good.

Still the bodies of A and B are center stage. Y and Z have grown in confidence. They work together to drag the bodies offstage right.

In a final energetic, synergistic dance, Y and Z whirl around the stage and end up in the small space once occupied by A and B. When day dawns, both look out at the world, exactly as A and B did—with excited anticipation—yet they each must wear a heavy hat on their head.

To: Dominic Eastwood
From: DI Melody Obasi
Date: August 25, 2025
Subject: Re: New development

Dear Dominic,

Well, what can I say? If this is true and it was Ian who actually killed the Eastwoods, then it doesn't surprise me. In one of the texts you'll have read from the files, Tanya says to Ian, "You dealing with things 'in the moment' is what got us here."

But in the spirit of joint enterprise, you don't have to wield the weapon to be guilty of murder. They both belong firmly behind bars, as far as I'm concerned.

Tanya might have called her drama class a "safe space," but it wasn't for her—not if the prison officer assigned to oversee the class only saw an opportunity to make a few shillings out of it and even denied her the catharsis of directing it, all because she didn't want anyone else to have that valuable document. She's not the only one either. This case is full of people taking advantage one way or another. I've been reading all the news items about *The Killer Question* and a couple of interviews with you in the media.

There's something you didn't tell me in all the months we were corresponding. Was that because you wanted me to agree to an interview? You didn't want me to know *you* had an ulterior motive. Well, you got what you wanted.

There's no need to contact me again.

Dee

NEW ON NETFLIX FOR SEPTEMBER 2025

The Killer Question
2025
Certificate 15
Limited series
True-crime documentary

When Sue and Mal Eastwood take over as landlords of an isolated pub, they hope a weekly quiz night will turn its fortunes around. Their plan works, until a body is found and a mysterious new team arrives. Has a deadly grudge followed them from their previous life? Find out in this explosive documentary.

Story from HertsNews, September 3, 2025:

A "Case" to be solved!

The Case is Altered on Bell End by the River Colne at the outskirts of Fernley is set to reopen this Friday (September 5), the same night a new documentary about the pub will be broadcast on Netflix.

New landlord Dominic Eastwood—along with catering manager Chris Thorogood and assistant Fiona Hammond—has revamped the venue, giving it a cheeky new theme of True Crime. Patrons can enjoy drinking where three notorious murders took place and listen to weekly talks by law-enforcement and crime experts. Dominic is looking forward to launching a range of cocktails and bar sliders named after famous serial killers and to hosting a weekly quiz with a creepy true-crime theme.

Dominic has a very personal reason for revamping the fortunes of the old pub. His aunt and uncle were killed there in 2017. In answer to accusations that he is simply making money from his family members' deaths, he said, "It feels right to be honoring my family in this way. Auntie Sue and Uncle Mal deserve to be remembered as a couple who took every opportunity they saw, and I think they'd approve of me doing the same."

The Killer Question is available to view on Netflix from this Friday.

How much do you know?

**Test your criminal knowledge
with our deviously twisted killer questions**

Every Monday night
at
The Case is Altered
Bell End, Fernley, Hertfordshire

Teams of up to six
£1 per person

All welcome

As seen on the Netflix documentary *The Killer Question*

Acknowledgments

Writing began on *The Killer Question* at the end of 2023 and continued throughout 2024 when the most heated debate in publishing was the role of artificial intelligence in the creative arts. Like anyone who hopes their finger is firmly on the pulse of current debate, I downloaded ChatGPT to explore its possibilities and limitations.

This story required many place-names, so I asked it to list "sinister-sounding fictional towns in the North of England." Its suggestions included Dreadwich, Gloomstead, and Bleakhaven. Meanwhile "sinister-sounding fictional place-names in the Southeast of England" led to Grimshire, Deadmere, and Daggerford. It seems that to generate the most effective results, the software must be fed the most effective questions—which chimes with the themes of this book on an eerily esoteric level. While some place-names here have been inspired by the results of those searches, I have no plans to use AI in the future and do not consent to my books being stolen to train it.

No fewer than three human editors lent their talent and expertise to the development of *The Killer Question*: Miranda Jewess at Viper, Kaitlin Olson at Atria in the US, and Charlotte Greenwood, also at Viper. The experience was, as ever, a joy, and the result is a story I am very fond of and close to; one that explores the impulse some of us have to exercise our knowledge. But quizzing is about much more than simply parading what you know. It's about escaping the world for a few hours, spending time with old friends and making new ones, learning about the world, and being reminded of what you once knew. It's also, increasingly, about freedom from the compulsive tyranny of the phone screen.

This book is dedicated to quizzers and quizmasters everywhere, but in particular my quiz team Friends & Family and their evolving membership of Gary Stringer, Sharon and Keith Exelby, Kim Hobson and Lynne Vass, Keith and Ruth Liles and sometimes Neill and Sarah Fowler, and Graham Bartram, among other occasional teammates and, of course, me. Our home quiz is the Legion in Ruislip, where I'd also like to say a big hello and thank you to all our rival teams and awesome quizmasters, who fulfill such a skilled and difficult role. Kim Hobson sets and runs many fantastic quizzes. Her knowledge, expertise, and creativity were a big inspiration for the quizzes and questions here. I hope this novel is as much a tribute to the question setters as it is to those who answer them.

Despite disbanding in 2013, the Raglan Players are never far away—we occasionally quiz with former Raglan Players Keith and Felicity Baker, Ann and Brian Saffery, Darrell Van der Zyl and Hilary Seaberg, Vince and Helen Alderman, and honorary Old Rags Lisa and Dave Turner.

A key theme that emerged as I wrote *The Killer Question* was the power of two. There seems to be a superhuman strength generated by two people, compared to one, three, four, or any other number. Whether the pair are spouses, friends, colleagues, siblings, or partners, two people are always more than the sum of their parts, able to achieve the impossible, and when it comes to crime, history is littered with couples who committed the most appalling acts, largely because they shared such a strong and exclusive bond.

Two people who are very much more than the sum of their parts—and partners in crime of a different sort—are my lovely UK agents at Sheil Land Associates, Gaia Banks (books) and Lucy Fawcett (screenwriting). They are, without question, always on my team to answer any dilemma I present them with. Thanks, too, to Natalie Barracliffe, Lauren Coleman, and Rebecca Lyon, also members of the Sheil Land family.

Meanwhile, Markus Hoffmann at Regal Hoffmann & Associates and Will Watkins at CAA represent my work stateside with similar team spirit.

At Viper in the UK I am indebted to the amazing head of publicity Drew Jerrison, marketing director Dahmicca Wright, marketing executive Emily Jarman, and freelance marketing consultant Rachel

Quin, who together make sure everyone who needs to know about this book will get to hear of it. And on the managing editorial and production side, to Georgina Difford, Jack Murphy, Ali Nadal, and Anna Howarth. Without copyeditor Mandy Greenfield this book would be a tribute to my hasty typing and poor math skills. Meanwhile the cover, like my others, is designed by the wonderful and talented Steve Coventry-Panton.

The hugely talented US team at Atria consists of Kaitlin Olson, editorial assistant Ife Anyoku, senior production editor Sonja Singleton, managing editor Paige Lytle, managing editorial coordinator Lacee Burr, and managing editorial assistant Sofia Echeverry. Publicist Megan Rudloff and marketer Maudee Genao bring this book to its widest possible audience and are always super-efficient and a joy to work with.

I had to conduct a little more research into police procedure for *The Killer Question* and would like to thank my police informer, Laura Flowers, for her insight and advice. Sometimes I chose not to take it, for dramatic and poetic reasons, so all errors are mine—but the author's decision is final, even when she is subsequently proven to be wrong.

My friends remain a great source of inspiration and support. Former Rags and current witches Sharon Exelby, Carol Livingstone, and Wendy Mulhall, old school friends Alison Horn and Samantha Thomson, my leading lady Ann Saffery, and last but not least, my leading man, without whom the Friends & Family team would stand no chance of scoring full marks in a music round: the wonderful, supportive, and gorgeous Gary Stringer.

About the Author

Janice Hallett studied English at University College London and spent several years as a magazine editor, winning two awards for journalism. She then worked in government communications for the Cabinet Office, Home Office, and Department for International Development. After gaining an MA in Screenwriting at Royal Holloway, she cowrote the feature film *Retreat* and went on to write the Shakespearean stage comedy *NetherBard*, as well as a number of other plays for London's new-writing theaters. She is the author of five *Sunday Times* bestselling novels. Her debut novel, *The Appeal*, was a Waterstones Thriller of the Month and won the John Creasey New Blood Dagger award. *The Twyford Code* was a *Daily Mail* Book Club pick and was named Crime and Thriller Book of the Year at the British Book Awards, and *The Mysterious Case of the Alperton Angels* was a Richard & Judy Book Club pick. When not indulging her passion for global travel, she is based in West London.